FORGE®

P9-AOB-649

$4.99
($5.99 CAN)

THE SEVEN SINS

Jon Land

978-0-7653-1534-2 / 0-7653-1534-3

A high-stakes game of wealth, power,
and international intrigue

"The Godfather reinvented
for a new generation."
—Vince Flynn

"Impossible to put down."
—Lee Child

"A high-octane thriller!"
—Sandra Brown

"You'll be spellbound."
—David Morrell

In hardcover June 2008

9 780765 361110

ISBN-13: 978-0-7653-6111-0
ISBN-10: 0-7653-6111-6

50499

JON LAND

THE BLUE WIDOWS

PRAISE FOR THE NOVELS OF JON LAND

The Blue Widows

"It is simply eerie reading Jon Land's latest thriller, *The Blue Widows*. With the reality of war occupying our minds, Land spins an absolutely plausible tale of terrorism based in religious fanaticism and the diabolical mind of an Arab billionaire plotting to destroy the United States. . . . *The Blue Widows* moves at a lightning pace, adding to the excitement of this fascinating and mysterious story. . . . Land's storytelling is superb . . . Filled with the intrigue and mystery that makes Land's thrillers a joy to read."

—*The Providence Sunday Journal*

"The journey is swift and sure, fast and furious, a page-turner that never sags, strays, or disappoints. . . . *The Blue Widows* will keep your heart and pulse racing and your mind alert to try and figure out what's going on. And you won't."   —*Prime Time Magazine*

"*The Blue Widows* is an action-packed provocative tale that has more curves than a twisted pretzel."

—*The Midwest Book Review*

"A high-voltage thriller. Mr. Land is a literary contortionist, twisting a tale of intrigue and suspense, passion and power."   —*East Bay Life*

"If there is one book that is this season's must read, this is it. *The Blue Widows* is red hot and promises to be a summer scorcher."   —*BookCrossing*

"Just when you think you may have figured out a piece of the plot, Land throws a curve and derails you. Amazingly it all fits together impeccably well at book's end and makes total sense, but during this whirling dervish of a yarn, you think you've found a strand of narrative you can finally understand and fathom, only to find out that Land has expertly deceived and thwarted us again."

—*East Side Monthly* (Providence, RI)

"In our ever-shrinking world, it seems that religion, politics, and even relationships are becoming intertwined. But *The Blue Widows* makes one consider that perhaps they always were inextricably connected."

—*Romantic Times*

Blood Diamonds

"Digs deeply into Arab/Israeli horrors—resolvable perhaps only by the 'miscegenation' that Ben and Danielle stand for." —*Kirkus Reviews*

"Publishers like to say that books with topical themes have been 'ripped from the headlines.' Here's one that's practically torn from a whole newspaper."

—*The San Francisco Chronicle*

"The action scenes are as plentiful and professionally rendered as ever, ranging this time from Israel's West Bank and a doomed Russian town to a bloody Sierra Leone landscape where the rebel leader (known as the Dragon) trades her country's uncut diamonds for weapons of supreme terror." —*Publishers Weekly*

"Land, like other great genre talents, is the kind of guilty pleasure you never really have to be ashamed of reading. Like Clancy, Cussler, Leonard and Le Carre, he has defined a turn of his own." —*Boston Book Review*

"A solid entry in a series that consistently uses setting as an integral part of the story." —*Booklist*

"A brilliant tale of the intrigue that is a true page-turner. . . . If a perfect diamond is flawless and rare, then *Blood Diamonds* is the literary equivalent of the perfect stone with just the right cut, color, clarity and carat. As with all of Land's novels, *Blood Diamonds* will leave you yearning for the next one."

—*The Jewish Voice and Herald*

"Land's split-second timing keeps you on the edge of your seat. . . . The dizzying dynamics of the fast-forward, breathless plotting keep the book in midair, careening from incident to incident, revelation to revelation, and horror to horror. . . . Keeps the heart pumping, the pulse racing, the mind alert and the sense of adventure and intrigue that grabs you right up until the final gut-clutching finale."

—*East Side Monthly* (Providence, RI)

"A wild, no-holds-barred thrill ride with nothing less than the fate of the United States hanging in the balance. . . . Land's latest doesn't so much redefine the genre as re-assess it. Indeed, *Blood Diamonds* might well be the first great thriller spawned by the post-9/11 age. A jewel of a book that sparkles enough to read without the lights on."

—*BookCrossing*

"Mr. Land is a master at creating many subplots and intrigues, all of which are occurring simultaneously. . . . Action addicts should be in heaven."

—*The Mystery Reader*

Keepers of the Gate
"A strongly plotted, impressively solid new entry."

—*Kirkus Reviews*

"This is a big, complex mystery propelled by a genuinely compelling plot and its likable lead characters. We enjoy watching these smart, efficient detectives sort out what's what and we enjoy watching the author have fun with his bigger-than-life plot, carefully calculating how far he can go without turning his story into a cartoon. . . . A lively and well-told yarn, sure to please fans of high-concept thrillers."

—*Booklist*

"A labyrinthine tale of conspiracy and deception. . . . Land is adept at gauging the unique effects the Mideastern culture and history will have on the emotions and motivations of his protagonists."

—*Publishers Weekly*

"International intrigue and double feints are par for the course in this thrilling tale. Be advised, when you think you've figured it out, Land has more surprises in store. . . . A white-knuckled read. Land has packed eight days of action into his tersely written, well-plotted work which races towards its surprising conclusion."   —*BookSense*

"*Keepers of the Gate* will keep you turning pages until the Gatekeepers are finally uncovered at the risk of Ben, Danielle, and their child's life. Land is one of a few authors who seem to have beaten the mid-story slump that plagues many writers in the mystery/adventure genre. The action stops only long enough for the reader to catch a breath, and the plot twists faster than a mid-summer tornado."   —*The Cape Coral Daily Breeze*

"Whoever thinks that elements of a suspenseful murder mystery, a dramatic love story, and an insightful political thriller can't be intertwined into a novel has yet to read Jon Land's latest page-turner, *Keepers of the Gate*. . . . The dynamics of this novel excel to an extraordinary level. Mr. Land knows how to make you keep the pages turning and he uses suspense to its utmost degree."
    —*The East Bay Window*

"A brilliantly conceived, ingenious tour-de-force. The best book yet from a writer at the absolute top of his game."   —*Bookviews*

"*Keepers of the Gate* is even tighter than its predecessors with more twists than a Six Flags roller coaster and immensely more enjoyable. It was far more exciting than the latest from Ludlum, Clancy, or any of the other writers in this genre. This book stands out in a sea of mediocre offerings, and is definitely this spring's must read."
    —*The Jewish Herald*

BOOKS BY JON LAND

*Published by Forge Books

JON LAND

THE BLUE WIDOWS

A TOM DOHERTY ASSOCIATES BOOK
NEW YORK

This is a work of fiction. All the characters and events portrayed in this book are either products of the author's imagination or are used fictitiously.

THE BLUE WIDOWS

Copyright © 2003 by Jon Land

A Forge Book
Published by Tom Doherty Associates, LLC
175 Fifth Avenue
New York, NY 10010

www.tor-forge.com

Forge® is a registered trademark of Tom Doherty Associates, LLC.

ISBN-13: 978-0-7653-6111-0
ISBN-10: 0-7653-6111-6

First Edition: March 2003
First Mass Market Edition: July 2004
Second Mass Market Edition: May 2008

Printed in the United States of America

0 9 8 7 6 5 4 3 2 1

For the men and women of the 120th Evacuation
Hospital,
U.S. Army, World War II:
The lessons they remember
make it impossible for the rest of us to forget.

ACKNOWLEDGMENTS

Odds are if you're reading this page, you've been with me before. So I hope this finds you in all respects as well as or better than the last time we met. If *The Blue Widows* marks your first trip down this road, welcome and be assured the drive will be a fun one.

That's due in large part to the fact that I'm surrounded by great people who share a relentless desire to keep me improving. The list starts with Toni Mendez and Ann Maurer, agent and editor extraordinaire, respectively, who form a terrific literary family (going on twenty-two years) I'm proud to be a part of. That goes for my Forge editor, Natalia Aponte, as well, whose influence and genius lie on every page of *The Blue Widows,* making our many lunches at Bolo a great investment for the company.

The Tor/Forge family is to be commended for proving the sum of the parts can indeed exceed the whole. That starts with the passion and leadership provided by Tom Doherty and Linda Quinton and extends to department heads Irene Gallo, who gave this book another award-winning cover; Fiorella de Lima, who made the inside look just as good; and Jennifer Marcus, who helped make sure you knew about it. I promised not to terrorize my terrific publicist, Jodi Rosoff, this time, but, of course, I lied.

The Blue Widows also found me blessed with an even larger stable of readers and advisors, starting with Emery Pineo, Rabbi James Rosenberg, Nancy and Moshe Aroche, molecular biologist Dr. Leonard Shapiro, the Dearborn, Michigan, Chamber of Commerce, Dr. Kevin Vigilante, and my old friend Rob Lewis.

As for me, I'm still trying to break into the film business. But don't worry; so long as you're out there scouring the shelves, I'm not about to quit my day job. You can still reach me at jonlandauthor@netscape.net to give me your feedback. If you don't hear from me right away, it just means I'm busy working on the next one. For now, turn the page, climb in, and let's go for a ride.

The end of all things
is at hand.

1 Peter 4:7

PROLOGUE

"*So, we are certain there will be no mistakes this time.*"

Hanna Frank tried to push the earphone deeper into her ear, hoping it would make the voices coming from her husband's office seem less muffled. The identity of the speaker was a mystery to her; it could be one of any number of men with whom Abdullah Aziz Rahani did business. But her husband's own voice replying was unmistakable.

"*The government would not have agreed to sanction funding if proper assurances were not provided. The key element, this time, is utter surprise.*"

"*Attacking on the highest of their holy days . . .*"

"*Precisely.*"

On her lap, Hanna's three-year-old daughter began to sob again, and she covered the girl's mouth with her hand, afraid to miss any part of the conversation two floors above the nursery. She glanced at the door, realizing she hadn't locked it. One of the servants could walk in at any time and catch her holding the earphone. Hanna prepared a lie, ready to pretend she was listening to one of the two radio stations broadcasting from nearby Riyadh instead of the transmitting device she had planted in her husband's office.

The device was voice activated, state of the art. Normally conversations were recorded by a tiny machine

Hanna kept hidden in the false bottom of her jewelry case. But today she had seen her husband greet the unidentified man warmly in their palace lobby before ushering him upstairs, and decided to listen to their conversation as it transpired.

"Once the war is won," came the stranger's voice again amid the static, *"the resources of the Bank of Rahani will be vital."*

"We have supported the buildup," said Abdullah Aziz Rahani, *"transferred all funds as requested. We are ready to assist in any way we can, once the enemy is vanquished. Inshallah."*

"Allah will be willing, my friend. Israel, this time, will not survive."

Hanna removed her hand from three-year-old Kavi's mouth and the toddler's sobbing replaced the sounds of the conversation in her ear. Hanna had gone cold. Her hands trembled. Her mind raced, contemplating her next move. She had to get word out, use the procedure she had followed religiously to file her usual reports for the past six years. But there was nothing usual about this discovery, and she prayed her report would be taken seriously and acted upon.

Hanna would phone a number in Riyadh, be told she had the wrong number. Her contact would then wait at a drop point in the central bazaar every day at noon until she was able to appear. She checked her watch: eleven A.M. Too late to manage the task today. Tomorrow, then. *She had to get there by tomorrow,* Hanna thought as she hugged the sobbing Kavi tighter to her.

"Is she sick?"

The question startled Hanna and she turned to the doorway to find her five-year-old daughter, Layla, standing there.

"No," Hanna replied, as the earphone fell to her lap.

"Then why is she crying? Is something wrong with her?"

"Of course not," Hanna told Layla, tucking the earphone into her pocket with her free hand. "Nothing's wrong at all."

DAY ONE

CHAPTER 1

Danielle Barnea felt the submachine guns clacking against her as she ran through the woods. Brambles scraped at her face. Exposed roots and fallen logs tried to trip her up, but she rushed on through trees wet with the residue of a quick-moving storm.

She had no firm plan of action set in her mind. She had earlier committed to memory the plans of the People's Brigade compound in the central-Idaho community of Pine Valley on Heydan Lake. The best way of getting inside without being detected, she had noted, was through a culvert, a long drainage pipe that bypassed the security sensors, trip wires, and booby traps that otherwise dotted the woods surrounding the compound. The culvert originated within the barbed-wire security fence, so that once inside Danielle would have only perimeter guards to contend with.

"America's lost her fucking spine," came a voice through her headset, which she recognized as that of Hollis Buchert, leader of the People's Brigade. *"You think the government would have learned from 9/11, but it hasn't learned a goddamn thing. So you know what, son? If Washington can't do the job, then we will. Gonna teach this country a lesson she'll never forget. That why the FBI sent you to snoop around here?"*

"I told you," she heard Ben Kamal's voice insist. It sounded raspy and nasal, as if his nose had suffered the first brunt of Hollis Buchert's ire. *"I'm not working for—"*

A heavy *whapping* sound ended Ben's words.

"We don't like Arabs and we don't like liars and you're an Arab liar, son. Means we'll have to kill you twice. Or make the first time last twice as long. You from the F, B, I?" the man repeated, drawing out the letters.

"No."

"Because word is they've been trying to set us up. Why, I've even heard it told they got somebody on the inside. Maybe trying to learn something, you ask me. Shit, can you believe that?"

"I—"

The *whap!* that followed sounded like a strap striking flesh.

Danielle shuddered and quickly checked her watch. The interrogation was eleven minutes old. She wondered how much time she had left before Hollis Buchert tired of the process and simply used his gun.

Hold on, Ben, she willed, picturing the man she had known for seven years and wondered if she could live without. *Just hold on. . . .*

The assignment undertaken on behalf of their company, Security Concepts, had gone horribly wrong. Ben and Danielle had been retained by one of Detroit's most influential Arab businessmen, Victor Rantisi, to surveil the compound and provide proof that his kidnapped son was inside. Rantisi had sought out their private security agency after being repeatedly rebuffed by the FBI, settling upon Security Concepts specifically because an ex-Palestinian-American detective, Ben Kamal, was in the company's employ.

Danielle had been against the job from the start. Her missions for the elite Sayaret, the commando teams forming the Israeli Special Forces, had invariably been accompanied by firm intelligence on the positioning of targets. Not so this time. She loathed the notion of undertaking even a simple reconnaissance mission without intelligence on where the People's Brigade's guards were posted, or how many she and Ben would have to confront.

The plan was for her to infiltrate the lake side of the compound, while Ben entered from the land side to the north. She had just begun her sweep along the shoreline when Ben's jaw-mounted microphone broadcast the sounds of his capture. Fearful there would be too much open ground to cover from that point of entry, Danielle had looped around to the eastern side of the compound and located the culvert from memory, a bit distressed to find it was smaller than the scale map had indicated. She had no other choice but to shimmy inside on her stomach and pull herself along through the rank-smelling muck that had accumulated inside the pipe.

The culvert was no longer functional, just a leftover relic from a time when the People's Brigade's twenty-acre compound had been a farm. Danielle shifted her submachine guns so they rode atop her back, stilled now. But her pistol dug into her side and she tried to reposition it as well, to no avail. Fortunately she had clipped her knife sheath far enough back on her hip to keep it out of her way.

Reaching the other end of the culvert, she peered out and found herself just inside the tree line on the compound's eastern perimeter. She guessed the barbed-wire fence would be a hundred to a hundred and fifty feet back. Beyond her, trails sliced through the thick woods hiding the open stretch of land that led to the complex of buildings noted on her schematic.

No guard stood in her line of vision. Danielle pulled herself from the culvert and dropped in snakelike fashion to the moist ground, pushing forward until she heard the booted footsteps of the first guard patrolling. She stayed prone, camouflaged by a thick patch of brush adjoining the trail down that he was striding. An M-16 dangled from the guard's shoulder, too far from his grasp to cause Danielle much concern. His combat boots crunched the twigs and underbrush scattered along the path, and she waited for him to pass her position before lurching to her feet, knife in hand.

Danielle swept the blade forward at the same time she wrapped a hand around the guard's head, closing her palm over his mouth as she jerked the killing knife through his ribs into his heart. The man thrashed briefly, then stilled. Danielle lowered him softly to the trail and dragged him into a thick patch of underbrush, where his body was likely to remain hidden.

Her hand was soaked with the guard's blood and she wiped it off on her pants. The coppery stench hung with her as she dashed along the line of the trail, drawing deeper into the compound. The barbed-wire fence ran inward at an odd angle here, and Danielle found herself pressed against it briefly before the woods widened again and she heard a branch snap ahead.

A second perimeter guard stood facing away from her. A plume of smoke lifted over his head as he shook a match free and began puffing away on a cigarette. Drawing closer, Danielle could see he wore headphones over his ears, the muffled din of rock music wafting up lightly when she closed.

This guard's frame was slighter than that of the first, his fatigues a bad fit, as if he had not yet grown into them. She knew as she made her final lunge he was young, barely out of his teens. But the gun on his back and walkie-talkie clipped to his belt concerned her more. She had killed for the first time herself when she was not much older than he. Still she blocked his youth from her mind, focusing instead on Ben, whose plight denied her the luxury of conscience. Danielle used her hands this time, breaking the guard's neck. But she avoided looking at his face when she dragged him into the damp overgrowth that rimmed the fence line.

Danielle drew the first of her Heckler and Koch submachine guns around in front of her and made sure the silencer was screwed in properly. After so many years using an Uzi, the heft and added length of this gun discomforted her. But it was well balanced and carried a reputation of shooting truer at moderate distances than any other gun in its class.

She smelled wood smoke burning on the wind and angled toward it. She clung to the trees as much as possible, knowing she would have to take the next guards from a less comfortable distance.

The first one saw her an instant before Danielle saw him, M-16 leveled straight and ready instead of slung. But he hesitated for a second, and that was all the time she needed to fire a silenced burst into his chest. A mist of blood sprayed into the air, settling atop his body.

Danielle ran on, took the next two guards as they walked side by side. Her heart felt strangely quiet in her chest after the initial thundering against her rib cage. Her brain had settled in, found the zone she recalled so well from her tenure with the Sayaret.

As the woods dipped, Danielle found herself nearing a slight hill beyond which she could now see clouds of wood smoke floating into the sky. She heard voices, laughter, multiple footsteps slashing through the brush. Five men, maybe six or even more, lumbered unsuspectingly across the compound. Too many and too far away to rely on any submachine gun's limited range of accuracy. And she was out in the open, no viable cover to rely on before they crossed the ridge.

Danielle tossed her nearly spent Heckler and Koch to the ground and tore open her shirt to expose her sports bra. She staggered forward, moaning, muttering, clinging to branches to pull herself along when the men reached the crest of the hill.

"What the fuck," she heard one of them say.

Six, Danielle counted as she collapsed to her knees, making sure her second submachine gun was hidden behind her. The men above froze briefly before starting down the hill en masse. She whipped the second Heckler and Koch around the moment they drew within her killing range and emptied its clip into them.

Danielle slammed a fresh clip into the submachine gun and charged upward, the men's bodies tumbling past her to the foot of the hill. It dipped slightly at the top, offering a clear view of the buildings comprising the center of the People's Brigade's sprawling compound.

The farmhouse and barn were covered in weathered silvery shingles, standing out amid the dull brown bunkerlike buildings, barracks, and storage depots that were products of more recent construction. Danielle clung to the cover provided by the last of the trees, watching a few men in military uniforms traipsing about between buildings. She knew the bodies she'd left in the woods wouldn't go undiscovered for long, meaning she had to act fast. So she studied the activity coming to and from the various buildings, ultimately focusing on the barn, where three men stood before the heavy door as if to guard it.

THE STRAP had left Ben's jaw swollen, the teeth on the right side of his mouth loose, and one eye puffy and closing. Ben coughed and spit out blood. He closed his eyes and thought he might have passed out briefly. When he opened his eyes, Hollis Buchert was still standing before him. Buchert was short and stocky. He had a thick neck, straw-colored hair oiled to his scalp, and a face like worn shoe leather crisscrossed with prune-deep wrinkles. He was wearing jeans, boots, and an army fatigue jacket.

Buchert took a step forward and stooped down close enough for Ben to catch the stench of dried sweat rising off him. He grabbed a chair that was a twin of the one Ben was laced to, spun it around, and sat down leisurely. "See, here's the thing. You're gonna tell me what I want to know. Everybody I bring into this barn does. I'm making it my mission to send anybody the government sends after me back to them in pieces. Whether I do it while you're alive or dead, well, that's totally up to you."

Buchert dragged his chair a little closer.

"So what do ya say, son? How we gonna play this?"

Ben remained silent.

The wrinkles on Buchert's face seemed to stretch a little. "Ain't nobody coming to your rescue, son. You best put the possibility outta your mind. Only one thing you gotta concern yourself with now and that's how much you wanna take. You thirsty?"

Ben wet his lips.

"Yeah, you're thirsty all right."

Buchert drew a nine-inch hunting knife from a sheath on his belt and cut Ben free of the chair, though his arms remained bound. The man had an iron grip, his body hard and densely packed with muscle. Buchert effortlessly dragged Ben to the water trough and shoved his face down so it rode just over the ripples on the surface.

"Here, son, have a drink."

Buchert pushed his head under the water, Ben straining his neck to fight him, to no avail. His chest heaved and his lungs begged for air. His brain clouded up, felt as if it were going to explode, when Buchert jerked him back out. Ben gasped for breath, managed to catch it an instant before Buchert plunged him under again. He waited a little longer this time before yanking Ben back out and letting him catch his breath again. Rancid water pasted Ben's hair to his scalp. His stomach quaked. He retched and coughed up a stream of greenish trough water. Then he smelled Buchert's stench looming over him once more.

"Man," Buchert said, jerking Ben back into his chair, "you're a fucking mess. Washington oughtta be able to do better."

He launched a boot into Ben's chair and it tipped over backward. Ben's head smacked against the hard barn floor. A series of flashes exploded before his eyes. He was upside down, half in the chair and half out, arms still bound behind him.

The People's Brigade soldiers surrounding him laughed hard and kept laughing, until the gunshots sounded outside and suddenly the barn went dead quiet.

A MAN had emerged from the barn. Another had gone in. Danielle estimated there was a hundred feet of open ground to cover between the tree line and the barn. She waited until there were three men standing in view before she charged.

Danielle began her charge across the ground and opened fire the moment they spotted her. Her bullets punched them backward, and the barn door opened a crack from the force of one of them crashing into it. Danielle kept firing until the submachine gun clicked empty. Then she drew her nine-millimeter pistol and kicked the barn door open all the way, crouching as she entered and measuring her shots at shapes partially lost to the dim light of the barn.

A soaked figure stirred on the dusty brown floor near a trough of water.

Ben! she thought, as a shape near him lunged for a shotgun leaning up against a beam.

A fissure of dirt and wood burst up at her feet before she managed a shot, and Danielle spun to find a man steadying a hunting rifle on her from a raised perch in the loft above her. She fired at him fast, her first bullet missing, but her second taking the man in the leg and pitching him over the side.

She heard but never saw him land, swinging back just in time to see Ben, hands tied behind his back, slam into a man she recognized as Hollis Buchert an instant before Buchert managed to steady his shotgun.

Ben kicked his leg out and landed atop him. His wrists ached as he pummeled Buchert, his laced hands smashing into the leathery face now even with his.

"Ben!" he heard Danielle scream just before a fresh hail of fire from the doorway forced him to spin off the People's Brigade leader and roll for cover.

Across the barn, Danielle clacked off single rounds toward the new gunmen as she rushed toward Ben.

"Let's get out of here," she told him.

"Buchert," Ben gasped between labored breaths. "Where's Buchert?"

Danielle grabbed Ben by the sopping shirt and lifted him to his feet, pistol poised in her free hand. "I don't know. We can't worry about him now."

She sliced the rope binding Ben's wrists with her knife and led him through a side door. Behind them they could hear a commotion as more People's Brigade soldiers rushed the barn. Danielle tried to plot the best route back to the culvert, but any route in that direction would mean confronting the converging force head on. That left the Heydan Lake side of the compound, to the west, as their best option for escape, despite the stretches of open space with which they would have to contend.

Danielle had started to lead Ben in that direction when the first of the helicopters appeared overhead.

"Federal agents!" a voice hailed over an amplifier. *"Drop your weapons!"*

Some of the People's Brigade members began shooting up at the choppers, bullets dinging off their steel skin. The choppers fluttered into a rise while gunmen perched in the open cabin doorways returned fire. Danielle drew Ben away from the lingering sounds of the battle into the woods, which quickly gave way to thinner brush. She could hear the sound of water lapping at the lake's edge, mixed oddly with the heavy whir of helicopters flitting over the compound.

They stumbled over a rise and rushed toward the barbed-wire fence. Beyond that lay Heydan Lake, dotted with skiffs and small outboards to aid their flight. They reached the fence, and Danielle used the rest of her torn shirt to cushion their climb over the barbed wire.

She had just dropped down after Ben when a burst of automatic fire stitched across a tree just over their heads. Danielle spun and saw the figure of Hollis Buchert a hundred yards back, firing an M-16 from the other side of the fence. An exposed root caught his foot and tripped him. He went flying, hit the ground hard, and struggled to find his feet again.

His fall gave Ben and Danielle the time they needed to plunge into the frigid lake waters, swimming toward a small dock twenty-five yards north where a pair of small boats had been moored.

Buchert's fire chased the two of them as they struggled in the water toward the dock. When the firing stopped, Danielle looked back and saw a heavily armed troop of FBI agents converge on his position in the woods. She waited for the expected exchange of fire, but it still hadn't come when she and Ben reached the dock and climbed into the nearest skiff.

"Stay low!" Danielle told him, as she started the skiff's engine and sped off across the lake.

Day Two

Ten Months
Later

CHAPTER 2

The shrill alarm echoed in Colonel Walter Mc-Clendon's ears as personnel around him hurried to evacuate the USAMRIID building. He had switched his watch into stop mode at the alarm's first sounding, satisfied with the progress of the evacuation thus far.

"All personnel, we have a Red Flag contamination. Repeat, we have a Red Flag contamination. All personnel, evacuate. All personnel, evacuate."

The warning was repeated at thirty-second intervals, temporarily interrupting the deafening blare of the alarm. It was triggered automatically once the sensors picked up something amiss, and, along with the alarm, was designed to eliminate any possibility of human error or misjudgment.

With good reason, McClendon thought.

The U.S. Army Medical Research Institute of Infectious Diseases (USAMRIID), housed on the sprawling 1,200-acre grounds of Maryland's Fort Detrick, contained the largest stores of biological weapons in the United States military arsenal. Of course, they were no longer considered by most to be offensive weapons, the possibility that they would ever be utilized so remote as to be unthinkable. Instead, the reserves of anthrax, smallpox, botulism, plague, and other toxins were maintained as a hedge against the possibility they might be needed for future research.

McClendon conducted drills like today's to prepare the facility's personnel for the unlikely scenario of a contamination event from either the 50,000-square-foot Biosafety Level 3 area or the 10,000 square feet taken up by the much more dangerous contagions stored in Level 4. Both these areas were located underground, accessible by only select personnel and easily sealed in the event of an accidental release.

Colonel McClendon had been in charge of USAMRIID for almost fifteen years now, going back to the facility's most shining moment, when its personnel rode to the rescue in nearby Reston, Virginia, and prevented a potential Ebola outbreak. Since security had been considerably increased since the September 11, 2001, attacks, McClendon's own assessment had identified two threats to the facility and two threats only: an invading force from without and a contamination from within. Either scenario was compounded by the fact that Fort Detrick, which housed a number of nonmilitary departments employing civilian workers, was an open base.

But USAMRIID had been cordoned off from the rest of the base and maintained its own light-armored force, a marine reserve unit, for security in the event of an attack from without. An attack from within called for rapid evacuation by all personnel and the immediate insertion of a specially trained Hazardous Materials team permanently outfitted three miles away. Three miles because McClendon had determined that distance to be the safe zone in the event the facility's deadly contents were somehow unleashed.

"All personnel, we have a Red Flag contamination. Repeat, we have a Red Flag contamination. All personnel, evacuate. All personnel, evacuate."

McClendon had tried both male and female warning

voices, ultimately settling on the male when repeated drills showed it led to a faster response. The colonel slipped through a fire door amid the rush of personnel following procedure. As a precaution against unwarranted entry in the wake of such a drill, all facility personnel would have to show their identification badges before being granted access to the building again. That included McClendon.

At USAMRIID, nothing was left to chance.

McClendon emerged into the crisp air of Frederick, Maryland, and surveyed the tight clusters of people gathered outside the various buildings. Decontamination vehicles—converted motor homes, essentially, with specially built showers and containment shells—would already be en route, just minutes behind the HazMat crew.

McClendon checked his watch again when the stainless-steel truck rolled onto the grounds. It had barely come to a halt before the holding line a hundred feet from the facility, when a half-dozen men wearing oxygenated isolation suits that shut out all air from the outside world burst from the rear. Their motions were mechanical, virtually robotic, they had been practiced so often. They hit the ground running, every movement synchronized, each man with a position and a role to play. McClendon watched them stream into the building and then reseal the doors behind them.

Two minutes, fifty-five seconds . . .

An all-time USAMRIID record, the colonel noted proudly. If this weren't in fact a drill, at this moment the HazMat team would be isolating the area of contamination toward determining the source and precise location. Since there were enough biotoxins stored inside to kill the world's population many times over, the precautions and procedures were mandatory. In all its years of operation since 1972, though, USAMRIID had avoided any outside contamination. And during McClendon's tenure the HazMat crew had been activated on merely three occasions and strictly as a precautionary measure.

McClendon checked his watch again, prepared to give the all-clear signal to end the drill as soon as the HazMat team emerged from the building. Five minutes had passed since their entry now. The drill continued to run right on schedule. The colonel nodded to himself, satisfied.

"Colonel McClendon, come in!" came the slightly harried voice of the base dispatcher, breaking radio silence over an unsecured band. "Colonel Mc—"

"I hear you, son," McClendon broke in. "This communication is not authorized. Please sign off."

"I'm sorry, sir, but I've just had an emergency call from the State Police responding to a call at Station One," the dispatcher said, referring to the offsite locale where the HazMat team was headquartered, just off Route 70 in Frederick. "They're dead, sir. All of them."

"That's impossible. They're inside the building."

"I'm sorry, sir. They're confirmed dead. I have the state police commander on the other line."

"Oh my God," McClendon muttered, realizing at once what had happened, walkie-talkie at his lips in the next moment. "Seal the building! Repeat, seal the building! We have a breach. Repeat, we have a breach!"

McClendon charged back inside with the first wave of marines, their mission changed from simply securing the perimeter to retaking the building from the invading force.

"Seal all grounds!" he continued into his walkie-talkie. "Seal all grounds! No personnel in or out of Fort Detrick, civilian or military."

McClendon accompanied a specially selected commando team in the elevator down to Level 4, yanking his arms and legs awkwardly through an isolation suit grabbed from a closet on the way. He had barely gotten his helmet secured when the elevator hissed open, revealing a series of three airtight doors.

All of them were still open.

The six members of the commando team unshouldered their weapons and moved out into the hall, ventilators making their breathing sound wheezy and loud.

"Hold your fire unless absolutely necessary," McClendon ordered. The words resonated in his helmet as he struggled to hold a sidearm in his gloved hand.

They passed a series of sealed laboratories, approaching the vaultlike entrance to USAMRIID's primary Level 4 storage area.

It, too, was still open, the red light aligned over the titanium steel flashing in bursts of blinding light to signal a breach. But the sensor lights below it still glowed green, indicating there had been no release of the deadly toxins stored within a chamber few even knew existed.

"Clear!" the captain of the commando team shouted into the headset built into his helmet, after twisting into the vault.

McClendon was the next one inside, his eyes darting instantly to the open storage holds that had been emptied of their contents. Trembling slightly, he backed into the hall and lifted the receiver from a digitless phone mounted on the wall. Then he yanked off his helmet and pressed the receiver against his ear.

A brief ring was followed by a mechanical whine. The colonel cleared his throat.

"McClendon. USAMRIID," he said as calmly as he could manage. "I'm reporting a Code Seventeen. Condition Red."

DAY THREE

CHAPTER 3

Ben Kamal slid the leather identification wallet across his desk and watched the tall man rise slightly, bending forward to reach for it.

"Now, Mr. Lewanthall," he said when the man before him was again seated, "what exactly can Security Concepts do for the State Department?"

Alan Lewenthall forced a smile, enough of one for Ben to see his teeth were brown along the edges. The smile of a man stealing away for as many cigarette puffs as he could manage between meetings in a nonsmoking world. "It's not Security Concepts we're interested in, Mr. Kamal," the man from the State Department explained. "It's you."

"My employer, Mr. Najarian, neglected to mention that."

"We both thought it best if he saved that task for me." Lewanthall pried a paper clip free of his wallet and then returned the impressive ID to his jacket pocket. But he held on to the paper clip, working it between his thumbs. "Mr. Najarian has agreed to let us retain your services."

"The U.S. State Department wants to hire me?"

"You're an American citizen, aren't you?"

"You wouldn't be here if you didn't already know the answer to that."

"Well, that's the only real requirement these days. This kind of thing happens more frequently than people realize," Lewanthall explained. "Budget cuts had slashed departmental pools of nonessential personnel long before

9/11. We often find ourselves in need of well-paid consultants. Contracting outside vendors has been standard procedure for five years now."

"I was out of the country for almost eight," Ben said, but of course a man like Lewanthall would know that.

"Serving as a detective with the Palestinian police in the West Bank, headquartered in Jericho." The man from the State Department nodded, holding his paper clip briefly still. "I've read all about your many exploits in that part of the world. A most impressive résumé, though no more impressive than your performance as a Detroit detective previous to your departure." Lewanthall gazed about Ben's twentieth-floor office in Boston's International Trade Building, the East Coast headquarters of Security Concepts. Through his window the view was of an inlet that opened into the ocean, with the far ends of the Logan Airport runways clearly visible to the left. Planes coming and going to and from places he had no desire to see anymore. "I envy you the private sector."

"I think we're still hiring," Ben told him.

"So are we," Lewanthall said, and started to bend his paper clip apart in a futile effort to straighten it.

"To do what exactly?"

"Your brother is Sayeed Kamal, a professor at the University of Michigan."

Ben felt a rise of heat behind his cheeks. "If you've come here about—"

"Please," continued Lewanthall, "let me finish. I'm not here about your brother, although, I suppose, I could be."

"He was cleared of any wrongdoing eighteen months ago."

"That hasn't stopped him from continuing to sponsor Palestinian immigrants in this country."

"Palestinian *students,*" Ben corrected. "And he hasn't sponsored any new ones; he's just fulfilling his obligation to those who are completing their undergraduate work at his university. He also finds homes in Dearborn for Palestinians orphaned by Israeli overreaction."

"It's not an orphan we're interested in, Mr. Kamal; it's one of those your brother sponsored: Mohammed Latif."

"I'm sorry, I don't know the name."

"I wouldn't expect you necessarily would. He's on our watch list. And he's disappeared."

"Then, I guess, you weren't doing a very good job of watching him."

"Our assets are limited, especially in the Dearborn area, where Latif resided."

"And where I grew up."

"Latif has known ties to Akram Khalil, whom I'm sure you have heard of, a ranking member of Hamas."

"*The* ranking member now that Israel has eliminated all those above him."

"You know Khalil?" Lewanthall queried.

"We met once. I investigated the murder of his daughter," Ben said, not bothering to elaborate.

"The Israelis believe Khalil is holed up in Gaza. The last batch of intelligence they sent us indicated he recruited Mohammed Latif personally for a cell here in the United States."

"Probably for fund-raising purposes."

"We have reason to believe that Latif is involved in far more than that."

"Does this reason include any evidence?"

Lewanthall got his paper clip as straight as he could and then set about twisting it back to its original form. "These days we don't need either for an arrest."

"The Israelis call that administrative detention."

"And, apparently, they were right all along."

"If you believe that, you've come to the wrong man."

"I've come to a man who is the brother of Sayeed

Kamal and who, I suspect, is very likely to want his brother kept out of this. His family too."

"My wife and kids have been dead a long time. Or did someone forget to update that part of my file at State, the part about the serial killer who targeted me when I got too close ten years ago?"

"Of course we know. It was the reason you moved to the West Bank."

"Moved back. I was born there."

"Your niece and nephew weren't," Lewanthall reminded. "And your brother's actions have placed them all under scrutiny, along with your mother. It would be a shame if any of their lives should be needlessly disrupted by being called in for questioning."

Ben did his best to ignore Lewanthall's thinly veiled threat, and responded evenly, "America still had a Constitution last time I checked, unlike Israel."

"You're right, of course. How silly of me. It's just that, well, the indications we've accumulated about Latif are rather frightening. Cell phone calls traced to known Hamas drop points gaining frequency in recent weeks. Meetings with known al-Qaeda operatives who managed to slip off our radar. Now his disappearance." Lewanthall paused, hoping for effect. "We believe he's up to something that has Akram Khalil's blessing."

"In the U.S. . . ."

"To be launched *against* the U.S."

"And you want me to find him."

"The alternative is seizing all his known associates . . . and sponsors. Am I making myself clear?

"Quite. How much of this did you tell Najarian?"

"Nothing. I informed him I needed you for some surveillance work on a suspected terrorist cell in the Dearborn area. I didn't mention anything about your family's direct connection."

"My brother's. And we're not sure it's direct."

Lewanthall twisted his paper clip tight enough around his own index finger to shut off the blood to the tip, the flesh going deep red. "I was trying to be discreet. These are difficult times for people of Arab heritage in this country, and I sympathize with that. Word of a relative's involvement with Hamas could derail a career, even render a man unwelcome in his adopted country."

"I'm an American citizen, Mr. Lewanthall. So is my brother."

"I was speaking in generalities, Mr. Kamal. But look at it this way," he added, leaning forward in his chair enough to deposit the mangled paper clip on the edge of Ben's desk. "At least you have another country to go back to."

CHAPTER 4

The six women made their way down Teryet Street, the main thoroughfare in Deir al Balah. Located on the Gaza Strip mere miles from a host of Jewish settlements, Deir al Balah headquartered an office of Yasir Arafat's Fatah group and remained home to a number of militants wanted by Israel.

The women carried straw baskets of bread and supplies. Four wore the baskets slung from their backs while the remaining two toted them with both hands wrapped tight around the handles, exercising the same caution they would had the baskets contained babies instead of supplies.

Head scarves obscured the lower portions of the women's faces. Shapeless robes, called *abaiyas,* hid their bodies. It would have been easier to take the supplies by car. But moving vehicles made too inviting a target for the Israeli helicopter gunships that often cruised the skies high overhead. Furthermore, they required gasoline, an expensive commodity these days. So the women, along with most of the inhabitants of Deir al Balah, walked down the dirty streets pitted by disrepair and stray shrapnel, the residue of past attacks.

The women ambled past the edge of a refugee camp and continued on to a nest of shops that stayed open despite little merchandise and few patrons. The barter system was used almost exclusively, no one having the money to trade or exchange for the goods. The women avoided the gazes of a pair of old Palestinian men sucking tobacco smoke up the long flexible tubes of water pipes and lugged their straw baskets down a narrow alley wet with mud and waste water. A fence lay before them, with a gate that opened to the inside.

The gate was unguarded, the latch unhooked.

"Wait for my signal to move," Danielle Barnea said into the tiny microphone hidden by her head scarf. She tried to ignore the discomfort she felt at the absence of the guard her intelligence had indicated was always posted here.

Almost to the open gate now, watching it sway slightly in the breeze . . .

"Now!" Danielle ordered.

In the next instant all six baskets were dropped, hidden weapons torn from the still-warm bread and other supplies. The women rushed the gate in single file, Danielle Barnea at their lead. She slowed only slightly at the gate, smashing it inward with a sandaled foot, twisting her Uzi round the compound's courtyard in search of Akram Khalil's guards.

Intelligence indicated the Hamas leader would have six of them, including two here in the courtyard. Khalil's men had staged a daring raid a few days before at the isolated Israeli settlement of Netzarim. Daring because they drove straight through the gate disguised as Israeli soldiers, their Jeep painted a slightly off-color shade of green, which should have alerted the posted guards but didn't. The terrorists had killed eight and wounded twice that many before being cut down themselves.

Danielle, now commander of Israel's National Police, thought her plan of disguise and entry to be especially fitting, under the circumstances.

The gate had barely banged up against the stone wall when she almost tripped on the downed body of one of the compound's guards, blood running beneath his white robes from a half-dozen bullet holes. The body of a second guard lay facedown amid the courtyard's overgrown brush, halfway between the main building and entrance. An assault rifle lay just out of his grasp, lost when a spray of bullets felled him.

The five female commandos lunged into the courtyard behind her and fanned out as planned, as Danielle stooped enough to touch the blood pooling beneath the nearest guard's body.

Still warm.

She felt the prick of the unexpected unnerve her and rose swiftly.

Fifty feet ahead, her commandos had reached the entrance to Akram Khalil's refuge. She drew up even with them, steadied her Uzi, and gave the signal to breach the doorway.

The commandos on the immediate left and right of the heavy wood door shot their way through, kicking the door in ahead of them. Danielle could feel the muffled spits in her stomach, an echo of vibration rather than sound. The stench of cordite and sulfur burned her nostrils as she surged through into the murky, half-lit haze.

The bodies of three more dead Palestinian guards lay

before her. A fourth had slumped against a doorjamb across the floor, assault rifle bracketed and standing straight up between his legs. He had tried to retreat, perhaps to warn or protect Khalil, before the invaders' bullets had caught him.

Very professional. Handled just the way her team would have handled it. Neat and clean.

Someone had gotten here ahead of her. The army, perhaps, or Mossad. Unlikely but not unheard of in the annals of jurisdictional overlaps in Israel. Her intelligence, though, had been secure and exclusive. Of that much, she was certain.

Who, then, had done this?

Danielle smelled the smoke when she was halfway to a door that had been splintered by bullets. Flames crackled, their glow illuminating the interior of the room beyond.

Danielle found the body of the terrorist leader inside. Akram Khalil had collapsed near a spilled trash can still coughing flames. Perhaps he had knocked it over when he was shot down, spewing its smoldering contents across the scratched tile floor. The remains were a charred, smoking mess, yet salvageable. Danielle stamped out the remnants of the flames with her boots, hoping to preserve as much of the pages as possible.

"Commander," came the voice of one of the commandos posted in the compound's front through her earpiece, "we have movement at the head of the alley."

"Pull back for evac," Danielle ordered.

"You better have a look at this first, Commander."

Danielle moved to an area of the floor where another of her commandos was inspecting one of the pages spared when the contents of the spilled trash can had been extinguished. Danielle hovered over her, submachine gun at the ready.

"Can you read Arabic, *Samal sheni*?" she asked, addressing the woman by her rank of corporal.

"Not this dialect," the woman replied.

Danielle took the scorched page from her, noting it was covered with Arabic letters, when the three commandos she had posted beyond this room rushed inside in a blur.

"Enemy approaching, Commander," one blurted, nearly out of breath.

"We take all this with us," Danielle said, gathering a handful of charred pages from the floor. "Bag everything you can."

The commandos looked at each other. The sound of voices echoed not far away.

"Do it!" Danielle ordered. "Now!"

CHAPTER 5

"I got the feeling there was something our friend Mr. Lewanthall wasn't telling me," John Najarian, head of Security Concepts, said to Ben after the man from the State Department had left.

"There was: He suspects my brother is involved in some plot. He held that over my head to convince me to take the job."

"You should have told the bastard to go fuck himself."

"I will . . . after I prove him wrong about my brother."

Najarian folded his forearms. They were covered in dark, coarse hair, as were his chest and legs. That had been the first thing Ben noticed when they'd first met at the Jericho Resort Village in the West Bank. Najarian had been among the resort's only guests when he came to recruit Ben three years before, and he would be among its last. The resort had closed its doors for good a few months later, a victim first of Israeli blockades and a crumbling Palestinian economy, and later of punitive Israeli shelling when it was mistaken for the police academy.

Najarian's office was three or four times the size of Ben's, complete with a sitting area and wet bar that was more for show than use. The angle of the windows hid all of Logan Airport from view while showcasing the water from all sides.

"You understand why I agreed to this, of course," Najarian said.

"Business."

"We could do worse than government contracts. I asked Lewanthall if he wanted to discuss the fee for your services." Najarian smiled broadly. "He just told me where to send the bill."

"So how much am I worth?"

The head of Security Concepts started to smile again, then stopped. "There's something else you should know, Ben. He asked about Danielle Barnea."

Ben felt the skin prickle along his spine as he did every time Danielle's name came up. "And what did you tell him?"

"That she was employed here for two months prior to her return to Israel to take over as commissioner of National Police."

"Commander," Ben corrected.

"Pardon me?"

"Commander, or *nitzav*. The job of commissioner is still open."

"But that job was promised to her after a year's time, wasn't it?"

"Under certain conditions."

Najarian sighed. "Politics."

Ben closed his hands into fists atop each thigh. "That's what Lewanthall asked you about?"

Najarian stretched his arms out over his desk. "Actually, he was more interested in whether or not the two of you had lived together over here."

"Briefly."

"I told him that."

"He must already have known the answer."

"I know," Najarian said with a grin. "That's why I told him."

"Did Pine Valley come up in the conversation?" Ben wondered.

"Lewanthall didn't ask about it, and I saw no reason to tell him."

"Good."

Najarian's face squared off in concern, his jaw seeming to protrude forward. "You've got to stop blaming yourself for what happened there."

"Men died at Pine Valley, John. One of them was an FBI agent. You could have been ruined."

"But I wasn't, you and Danielle got out safely, and there were no repercussions."

"There were for the Rantisi family; their son was later found buried on the property."

"The two of you had nothing to do with that. And the offer for her to become the first female head of Israel's National Police was on the table before Pine Valley." Najarian cleared his throat, shifted his thick shoulders. "What now?" he asked Ben.

"I fly to Detroit this afternoon and see how cooperative my brother wants to be in helping me find Mohammed Latif."

The phone on Najarian's desk buzzed, and he snatched up the receiver in a beefy hand. "Yes?" He found Ben's gaze from across the desk. "No, just tell her to hold for a moment."

Najarian switched the receiver from his left hand to his right. "You should take this in your office, Ben."

"Who is it?"

"Danielle Barnea."

CHAPTER 6

Danielle Barnea had stopped in the doorway of the commissioner's office on the fourth floor of National Police headquarters in Jerusalem as she always did on her way back to her own. The spacious office reserved for the *rav nitzav* had been vacant since the interim replacement for the slain Moshe Baruch had been summarily reassigned upon Danielle's appointment to serve as *nitzav,* or commander, ten months before. She had painstakingly refurbished the office to look exactly as it had in the years it had been occupied by her mentor, Hershel Giott; she had even found Giott's old desk down in the basement. Someday soon she would sit at that desk, though she'd never be able to fill it as he had.

"Is that you, Commander?"

The voice coming from the darkened rear of the office startled her, and Danielle turned to see Deputy Minister of Justice David Vordi standing by the window.

"Good evening, Minister."

Vordi smiled slightly at her. "We're alone. It's permissible to address me by my first name, Danielle."

At forty, Vordi was a few years older than Danielle, young to have achieved such a high position in the government. His hair was still full and thick, though slightly graying at the temples. His intense eyes retained the same piercing brown Danielle recalled from fifteen years earlier, when Vordi had served as one of her trainers in the elite commando force of the Sayaret. He had kept close tabs on her career ever since, ultimately leading him to offer her the job of commissioner of National Police upon attaining his current position nearly a year before.

"I was hoping we could talk," Vordi said quietly. He had a boyish look to him and was undeniably handsome. "When I didn't find you across the hall, I couldn't resist coming in to see what you've done with Commissioner Giott's office. I hope you don't mind."

"Not at all," Danielle told him, still in the doorway.

Vordi gazed about the office, then slid a hand almost reverently across a lamp table Danielle had recovered from the trash room in the basement upon her return. "Did I tell you he brought me into the Ministry of Defense?"

"No, Minister."

Vordi seemed perturbed by Danielle's formal address. "I had just completed my last active mission with the Sayaret when I received a call from Commissioner Giott. He said the Ministry of Defense was looking for someone like me to serve as a liaison with the police agencies. That was what, five years ago?"

"Six," Danielle corrected.

Vordi looked at Giott's desk again. "It doesn't seem like he's been gone that long. I learned a lot from him, Danielle. The first thing he did when I came to the ministry was warn me not to take unnecessary risks. My reputation had obviously preceded me." Vordi's eyes flashed warmly toward Danielle. "As yours did, I assume."

"And then some."

"I didn't always listen at first, of course." Vordi

sighed. To Danielle, the gesture seemed forced, meant to make him seem warmer, more a man and less a superior. "Commissioner Giott called me into this office each time. A few times he just stared across his desk, didn't say a word. Sound familiar?"

"Quite."

Vordi moved from the desk closer to Danielle. "How do you think he would feel about your actions this morning, Danielle?"

"He would trust my judgment. He wouldn't have believed my actions this morning constituted an unnecessary risk."

"But I, unfortunately, don't have the luxury of his experience. We are all prisoners to the perceptions of others, Danielle, and some of my colleagues in the Ministry of Justice don't know you as well as I. They fought against me when I chose you to take over as *rav nitzav,* concocted this absurd proving period to show you were up to the job. Against my wishes, of course."

"I'm sorry if I've made your position difficult, Minister."

"David, please. It would help things greatly, if I could offer my colleagues some explanation as to the necessity of your actions."

"My intelligence was hot. There was no time to seek authorization through another channel."

"If I could tell them the source of this hot intelligence, we might be able to put this matter to rest."

"Anonymous. You know how these things work."

"All too well." Vordi nodded, fighting to keep displeasure from creeping into his voice. "And you must do everything you can to protect his identify or risk losing his trust. There's also been some concerns raised about the composition of your team. All women, I believe."

"There are, as you know, actually far more men assigned to Rapid Response than women. I chose women this morning because of the logistics."

Vordi smiled slightly and took another step closer to Danielle. "Rapid Response. I like that term."

"I was merely responding to the results of the investigation into the recent terrorist action in Netzarim, Minister."

"Oh I'm sure my colleagues will have no problem there. But they might question why you didn't pass the results of your investigation on so the response could be handled by more appropriate entities."

"Apparently more appropriate entities handled it, after all. As my report indicated, all inhabitants of the compound were already dead when my team arrived."

Vordi shrugged his muscular shoulders. "I'm afraid neither Mossad nor the military was involved in the strike at Khalil's compound."

Danielle tried not to look as surprised as she felt. The strike had been carried out with quick and deadly precision. Who else could have done it? Who else could have had reason to do it?

"You can see why the identity of your source would be important to my colleagues," Vordi continued. "Clearly, he must have shared the same information with another interested party outside of this government."

"He didn't."

"You sound very certain."

"Because he's reliable."

"Could it be that he was trying to get you killed, Danielle, that you were walking into a trap?" Vordi asked, trying very hard to sound concerned.

"No, that's not possible."

Vordi looked down, then up again. "You could have called me personally. I thought we trusted each other."

"I told you—"

"I know what you told me. But I'm in a difficult position here, and actions like this make it more difficult."

Danielle swallowed some breath. "I apologize."

"No need. We're friends, aren't we?" He eased himself a bit closer to her. "Well, aren't we?"

Danielle shrugged.

"I would like to be able to assure my superiors we can avoid incidents like this in the future."

"I can't predict the future, Minister."

Vordi frowned. "I want this to work, Danielle. For both of us."

"So do I."

"Then you can't afford to make any more enemies. You already have more than your share in the Ministry of Justice. Don't give them the ammunition they need to hurt you, hold you back."

"Tell them I was doing my job, Minister."

"Your job, they would say, does not include matters of state security, only local. That means raids on the hideouts of suspected terrorists are forbidden jurisdictionally. That means the commando force you've developed is forbidden." Vordi started to reach out to touch Danielle, then changed his mind. "I'm sorry. I know you're right. But being right is not all a position like commissioner of National Police is about. I thought you knew that."

"I guess I'm still learning."

Vordi forced an uneasy smile. "You always were a tough student."

He started to reach for her again, and Danielle took a step back out of his range. "Have you analyzed the pages we recovered from Khalil's hideout?" she asked him.

"The pages," Vordi repeated, flustered. "I haven't checked yet. Why don't we go get something for dinner? We can check on the results afterward."

"Sorry, I have plans already," Danielle told him.

"Another time, then," Vordi said stiffly. He moved

forward, brushing against her on the way to the door. "Think about what I said, Commander."

"I will."

Danielle waited until the elevator doors had closed behind him before heading into her own office. She moved to her desk and lifted the blotter to reveal the copies she had made of the pages salvaged from terrorist leader Akram Khalil's compound. Then she picked up the phone and dialed Ben Kamal's number in the United States.

CHAPTER 7

"I need to fax you some pages," Ben heard Danielle say as soon as he picked up the line in his office. "Not even a hello first?"

No matter how seldom they spoke, or how long the duration between calls, her voice still had the same effect on Ben. His stomach fluttered, turned queasy and hollow. For an instant he could feel her softness against him, the scent of jasmine rising from her hair. Hearing her voice made him realize how much he missed her, brought back the memories. All of them, the happy ones as well as the unpleasant. The truth was that most of what her voice brought back to him was agonizing. There had been so many difficulties and setbacks in their relationship, so much struggle to maintain what culture, and fate, deemed impossible.

Some of the happiest times had been the two months they had spent here in America, first in Detroit and then in Boston when John Narjarian had relocated his cor-

porate headquarters in the face of an unprecedented
boom in the personal security business. The World
Trade Center bombing, September 11, 2001, had turned
Najarian into a wealthy man overnight, even as it made
life for Ben newly impossible.

Strange. He thought he had gotten to know bigotry
well upon his return to the West Bank to help train the
fledgling Palestinian detective force ten years ago. Never
quite trusted, even though *he* was Palestinian. Always
held in suspicion, an American first, and often only, in
the eyes of his people.

His people. Americans were more his people. He had
grown up among them in Dearborn, been raised as one,
and seldom considered himself anything else. After
9/11 his decision to live again as an American seemed
not as wise. People looked at him hatefully, scornfully—
the gazes similar to the ones cast at him in Palestine,
except they lacked the fear and trepidation. In the West
Bank his problem was often that he didn't look Palestinian enough; in the United States, suddenly his problem was that he looked too Arab.

The hate had eroded slowly as the months dragged on,
but the suspicion did not abate. Even his conversation
with Lewanthall from the State Department had been
more or less typical. They needed Ben for only one reason: He was an Arab and only an Arab could penetrate the
world of Mohammed Latif.

Just as he had been hired to help bring down the People's Brigade by an Arab father who had lost his son to
the twisted vision of Hollis Buchert. If Ben had simply
said no, recommended against the assignment as Danielle had urged, he believed she might still be with him
today.

And yet the whole point of going after the People's Brigade in Pine Valley had been to make her stay. He knew
she'd never leave if her work became more interesting

and challenging, and he didn't want to let go of her again. The two months they had shared together were not easy or blissful so much as promising in terms of what that period held for the future.

Then the offer had come for her to return to Israel and National Police. Ben had almost insisted that she take the job, because he knew how much it meant to her, knew it from the look on her face when she told him about the phone call and from the dreams she'd shared with him over the years. The chance to become the first female head of Israel's National Police was too much to pass up. A career milestone as well as a vindication. Ben could have lived the rest of his life working for Security Concepts, but he could tell Danielle quickly tired of the tedium and daily minutia. He hoped going after the People's Brigade would offer her the opportunity for the kind of action she had thrived on in the past.

But it hadn't worked out that way. Quite the opposite, in fact.

"Is the fax private?" Danielle asked him now, ten months to the day since she had saved his life at Pine Valley.

"Direct to my office. Why?"

"Because I don't want anyone else to know I sent these pages to you. They're in Arabic. I need you to translate them for me," Danielle continued, as her fax machine sucked the first page down to be stored for transmission, quickly followed by the second.

Ben pictured her on the other end of the line. It was hours later in Israel, the end of what must have been a long day. But her skin would still be flushed with color, the waves of her hair tumbling naturally just past her shoulders. He imagined her smiling in the way that could make everything seem all right for him, no matter what.

"Is there a sudden shortage of translators over there?" Ben asked her.

"No, just of trust."

"Nothing sudden about that. Care to tell me where these pages came from?"

"A raid."

"On behalf of National Police?"

"Yes."

"Was it successful?"

"No thanks to me."

"What do you mean?"

"The target was already dead when we arrived."

"Anyone I know?"

"Akram Khalil."

"You're kidding," Ben said, after a brief pause.

"Why?"

"Never mind."

"Ben—"

"I'll explain later," he interrupted, thinking of Mohammed Latif's connection to Akram Khalil and Hamas, along with his brother Sayeed. He didn't feel like saying more right now.

"How quickly can you finish the translation?" Danielle asked him.

"I'll work on it tonight on the plane."

"Where to?"

"Detroit."

"Visiting your family?"

"Something like that," Ben told her.

CHAPTER 8

Colonel Nabril al-Asi, head of the Palestinian Protective Security Service, was sitting at the corner table in the exclusive restaurant off the lobby of Jerusalem's King David Hotel when Danielle entered. She watched him sipping red wine from an elegant crystal goblet, balancing it lightly by the stem. He saw her approaching and rose, laying his napkin down on his chair before he moved to pull hers out for her.

"I'm so glad you were able to join me, Chief Inspector," he greeted, smiling fully. "I trust things went well today."

Danielle sat down and pulled her chair up to the table. "There were some complications we need to discuss."

"Of course. As soon as we order. You've eaten here before?"

"Actually, I haven't. The menu's not exactly in keeping with a chief inspector's salary."

Al-Asi held his glass out in the semblance of a toast. "What about a commissioner's?"

"I'm still commander for another two months yet."

"Yes. You must forgive me for continuing to address you as 'Chief Inspector.' It brings back memories of happier times."

"I spoke to Ben today."

"He's well?"

"Sounds it."

"But you have your doubts."

Danielle took her menu in hand but didn't open it. "You haven't spoken to him yourself?"

Al-Asi sighed, the shine fading from the bright eyes framed by his perfectly coiffed salt-and-pepper hair. "Any correspondence I might have with Inspector Kamal in this political climate could prove most inconvenient and uncomfortable for him. It's difficult, yes, but . . ." The colonel's face brightened slightly. ". . . at least I have you." He sipped his wine again, gazed about at the tables of people enjoying their meals. "You know, for the first time I think I know what Inspector Kamal felt like in his years over here."

Danielle leaned forward, curious. Officially, contact between the head of National Police and a Palestinian official of al-Asi's rank and stature was strictly forbidden. Although he was still head of the powerful Protective Security Service, the Israeli crackdown of the past several years had destroyed his organization and negated much of his influence. His headquarters had been leveled, and most of his personnel had either been arrested or gone into hiding.

Though his power was diminished, al-Asi found himself in the uncomfortable position of acting as liaison between the Palestinian Authority's ruling cadre and Israeli officials charged with keeping the peace. Since Palestinian officials lacked the power to control the worst of the militants, the latest intelligence on them was supplied from time to time by al-Asi to the appropriate parties in Israel, who would then take appropriate action. That was how Danielle had learned the location of the elusive Akram Khalil.

"What do you mean?" she asked the colonel.

"Inspector Kamal never felt comfortable among his own people. He felt isolated, shunned. It is that way for me now. Before, at least, I could rely on fear and intimidation. Not anymore. So I spend more and more of my time away from my home, my family. Here, inside Israel, I am protected because I provide a service. A few miles away I would be targeted for providing that same service. Hamas and the Islamic Jihad have a price out on my head."

"It's a dangerous game you're playing, Colonel."

"Fully supported by those above me, I assure you, Chief Inspector."

"Those who don't have the guts to turn in the butchers themselves."

"They fear for their lives."

"And you don't?"

"I fear for my world, for Palestine, if these radicals are not dealt with. We know where they are but can't do anything about it. You can do what must be done, but you don't know where they are."

"Someone else must have known where Khalil was; they got to him ahead of me."

Al-Asi set his wineglass down. "That is disturbing news."

"The deputy minister of justice assures me it wasn't Israeli Specials Ops."

"That would be David Vordi?"

"You know him?"

"Not personally. I understand he was instrumental in securing your current position for you."

"Vordi was one of my trainers in the Sayaret."

"You should know he has pictures of you in his apartment. Surveillance photos, I believe."

Danielle squeezed her lips together. "Recent?"

"Minister Vordi seems to have taken a keen interest in you, Chief Inspector, and I doubt his motivation is as unselfish as mine."

Danielle started to look around the room.

"Don't worry," said al-Asi. "I already checked. Apparently the minister is leaving you on your own tonight."

"He was married once. His wife divorced him."

"Pity." Al-Asi looked down at his wine, thinking. "The assault on Khalil's hideout was professional?"

"Very. Almost no bullet holes in the walls."

"So the gunmen didn't miss."

"Or waste any effort," Danielle added. "They knew what they were doing as well as I do."

A waiter came and took their orders: seared duck breast for Danielle, a veal tenderloin for al-Asi, who ordered a second bottle of wine.

"I'm glad you were able to join me in spite of these unexpected complications." Something in the colonel's gaze had changed. No longer was it distant and dreamy, but focused and sure. "I thought giving you Khalil might be of benefit to your current situation, a favor I was hoping I could exchange for another."

"You only had to ask."

"I prefer not feeling that I am in your debt."

"I haven't forgotten all you've done for me—and Ben—over the years."

"But it's just the two of us now."

Danielle sipped the wine the waiter had poured for her. "How can I help you, Colonel?"

Al-Asi looked instantly more relaxed. "If it isn't too much trouble, I'd like you to look into the murder of an Israeli-Arab woman living in the village of Umm al Fahm. Her name was Zanah Fahury. Lived alone. In her sixties, I believe."

"She was murdered in Umm al Fahm?"

"Her body was found in Jerusalem two days ago. It's being called a robbery gone bad."

"And you have reason to believe it wasn't."

"I have no reason to believe anything at all, since the police have dropped the investigation."

"Because the woman was Arab."

"I think you see my point."

"And there's nothing else special about this Zanah Fahury?" Danielle asked, keenly aware that many of al-Asi's pursuits over the years involved a larger purpose.

"Other than the fact that she apparently died for no reason and no one seems to care she was ever alive, no," he replied sharply.

"I'm sorry, Colonel."

"No, Chief Inspector, I'm the sorry one. So many senseless deaths, so many innocents left in unmarked graves. Nothing I can do about most of them. I was hoping you could help me do something about this one."

"I'd be happy to," Danielle said, and took another sip of her wine, settling back in her chair.

"What are you smiling about, Chief Inspector?"

"All the years we've known each other, Colonel, and this is the first time you've asked me for anything."

"I'm not used to asking anyone for anything."

Danielle shook her head slowly, sadly, amazed by the subtle power and dignity al-Asi had maintained through the latest period of strife. He had managed to redefine and remold himself, to blend with the times instead of fighting them. "All the things you've done for people over the years, all the favors they must owe you . . ."

"True power lies in leaving the paybacks out there to remain available. Of course, even if I wanted to I would have trouble collecting from the people in my debt."

"Why, Colonel?"

"Because, Chief Inspector, most of them are dead."

en Kamal walked down Warren Avenue in Dearborn, watching the last of the businesses still open closing up for the night. His flight had landed late, and he had driven his rental car straight here from the airport, bypassing the Hyatt Regency a few miles away for the time being.

He hadn't called ahead to tell his brother he was coming. The trick was to convince Sayeed to help him find Mohammed Latif, and alerting his brother to his coming would do more harm than good.

Sayeed Kamal was one of nearly 300,000 Arabs who now called the metropolitan-Detroit area home—the largest Arab community in the nation. Not far from where Ben stood on Warren Avenue, construction on the Islamic Center of North America, the largest mosque in the country, had recently been completed. And this street itself remained a commercial haven, lined with signs in Arabic advertising insurance, cosmetic dentistry, brokerage services, food goods, and bargain blue jeans. Since Ben had left for Palestine a decade before, nearly two hundred new businesses had opened, stretching for miles and gobbling up old houses and vacant lots he barely remembered.

He passed a pair of restaurants that were just closing for the night, and the New Yasmeen Bakery, where lights burned beyond the window in the kitchen. A clerk at an all-night market had a short line at his register, and the owner of an old-fashioned newsstand was boarding up his wares for the night, leaving leftover copies of *Al Bayat,* the Beirut daily newspaper, tied up by the curb to be collected by the city's recycling trucks.

Ben had come here to feel at home, he supposed, or at least a reasonable facsimile of it, but this was a different place from the one he had left following the murder of his family. He wanted to feel something, a sense of nationalism, perhaps. Instead he felt oddly sad, struck by the fact that Palestinians across the world could no longer walk down similar streets in the West Bank at night, or even travel to nearby towns, thanks to Israeli curfews, roadblocks, and patrolling troops. A Palestinian here could walk twenty miles in less time than it took a Palestinian over there to drive the same distance.

And yet if he closed his eyes, Ben could almost convince himself he was back in Palestine. Almost, because the pungent aroma of kabob and spicy grilled meat was not marred by the wafting scent of gun smoke or the residue of fires left to burn themselves out. Warren Avenue was not Palestine reborn or transplanted. Warren Avenue was an American street in an American city where people walked without fear and businesses operated without being subject to persecution. It was the world in which he had grown up but had lost track of in his years away, hoping against hope that someday the streets in Ramallah and Nablus would be the same.

Ben neared a cozy-looking restaurant called Al Madina and stopped, attracted by the scents of fresh grilled meats that drifted out into the cool spring air. He had forgotten how hungry he was and still didn't feel like going to the hotel just yet. Besides, a quick meal would give him an excuse to read the pages Danielle had faxed him. He had tried to manage that task on the plane but drifted off to sleep each time he started.

Inside the softly lit Al Madina, a hostess ushered him to a table for two set between the bar and an open grilling station and left him a menu. Ben made his selection, laid the pages on the table, and began to read, listening to the sizzling sounds of meat and fish cooking just a dozen feet away.

The condition of what was written on the pages had been further degraded by the fax. The poor quality of the transmission made it difficult to identify the precise damage done by the flames; gray or black patches of varying sizes blotched each sheet. Another inspection of them confirmed what a more cursory one on the plane had suggested: He would be able to translate the Arabic words into English, but stringing them into a cohesive context was another matter altogether. Ben thought the entire endeavor would likely prove fruitless.

He realized how wrong he was barely two pages in, the tone and rhythm of the writing clear even before he came to the substance. Not the location of ordnance and men. Not rambling communiqués written in some undecipherable code.

The writing rambled, all right, but there was sense and logic to it. Ben was rereading the pages in more detail when his food arrived, then reread them again as it cooled on the table before him.

His appetite was gone. The pages teased him, dared him to discern their meaning amid the garble due to fire and phone line.

Ben realized he was sweating, even though the restaurant felt cold. The door opened and a sudden wind flipped the pages across the table. He gathered up the sheets and summoned his waiter for a check. The man looked puzzled by his still-full plate, asked if Ben wanted the meal wrapped up. To avoid complications Ben said he did, then put his coat on and was halfway to the door by the time the waiter returned with a Styrofoam box.

Ben tucked it under his arm, the pages stuffed in his

pocket now, pages that held the portent of a plan excruciatingly lacking in detail but terrifying real in purpose.

Al-mawlidu n-nabawi . . .

The Last of Days.

CHAPTER 10

The plane trembled, buffeted by head winds and turbulence that tossed it about like a toy in the sky. Its steel weight seemed helpless against the power of the storm it confronted head on.

Layla Aziz Rahani, the plane's lone passenger, had fallen asleep hours before, as she always did on long flights, her repose bothered not by the pounding swells of air but by her own dreams, which clutched hard and wouldn't let go.

"PLEASE. PLEASE, don't do this."

The woman's voice was faint and pleading, her words broken up into grating, raspy utterances. Harsh sand swirled about in the air and stuck in her eyes and mouth. Buried in the ground up to her head, she was powerless to wipe them free.

"I'll do anything you want," she pleaded, straining to see the figure looming before her through the glare of the sun. "How many times can I say that?"

The man turned and stepped back until the sun streamed over his shoulder and burned into the woman's

eyes. The folds of his robe fluttered in the wind. His
keffiyeh *left the bulk of his bronze, angular face and
perfectly manicured beard exposed.*

*The man walked toward a thin grove of olive trees,
the woman following him with her eyes until sand kicked
up by his sandals sprayed into her face and mouth and
left her retching.*

"You can't do this," she gasped.

"You've left me no choice."

"You're my husband."

*The man's features flared briefly. "That didn't stop
you from having relations with another man. Did you
think I would not learn of it? But I looked the other way,
convinced myself it was a one-time indiscretion committed years ago. Then you tried to steal my daughters,
and that I could not overlook."*

"For the love of God . . ."

*"We have different gods," the man said, and walked
on until he reached the figure of a young girl, nearly
lost in the shapeless confines of her robe. She stood in
the narrow ribbon of shade among the others who had
accompanied them here.*

*The woman watched the man stretch his hand down,
watched the little girl take it.*

*"Please, take her away. Don't let her watch. It's the
least you can—"*

*Sand swirled into the woman's mouth and again made
her gag. She spat it out as best she could and struggled
mightily to move her hands, her legs, her feet—anything.
But the sand had been packed down too hard and any
hope had evaporated before the afternoon burned hot
and drained the last remnants of her strength. She had
prayed she might pass out, realizing now even that minor solace would be denied her.*

*The woman's eyes burned hot with tears, finally clear-
ing to the sight of the man standing a few yards before*

her still holding the little girl's hand. In their free hands, each of them clutched a rock pulled from the large pile halfway between her sand-packed tomb and the olive trees; the man's fist-sized, the girl's smaller but still seeming absurdly large in her tiny grasp.

"No," the woman muttered, the word muffled by the sand trapped in her mouth. She tried to speak again, but her voice quickly dissolved into a rasp that further scraped her raw throat.

The little girl watched the man approach the woman and kneel down so he could slip a dark hood over her face. He tied a pair of sashes together, taking up the hood's slack so the woman's breathing made it pucker in and out.

The man returned to the little girl's side and nodded. Then the little girl started to bring her free hand upward, her tiny fingers tightening around the rock she held in the last moment before she released it.

THE DREAM ended. Layla Aziz Rahani's eyes opened to the sight of the Manhattan skyline through the window, something having stirred her awake. She looked down at the armrest and realized the built-in satellite phone was ringing. She cleared her throat and brought it to her ear.

"Yes," she said groggily.

"Have you forgotten our own language, my sister?" a harsh, slightly slurred voice demanded.

"No more than you have forgotten the Muslim rules concerning alcohol, my brother," Layla returned.

"I know what you're doing," Saed Aziz Rahani continued. "Did you think I would not find out? Did you actually believe you could get away with this?"

"I am doing the business of our family, Saed, something you have never shown any interest in."

"That is not your place."

"It has always been *my* place."

"I speak to you from our father's palace in Riyadh, my sister. This charade will go no further."

So her brother had learned the truth of their father's condition. Layla tried not to feel overly concerned. It was inevitable he should find out, after all. She was lucky to have kept it a secret from Saed for this long.

"Are those his words, Saed? Do you speak with his voice?"

"No more than the signature on your visa is really his. Forgery is a serious crime in our country, my sister."

"So long as our father is still alive—"

"He will not be alive much longer, and at that point his final instructions will be carried out. For now your instructions are to return home."

Hot tears of rage burned Layla Aziz Rahani's eyes. "I'll do no such thing."

There was a pause, and Layla thought she heard the sound of ice cubes jangling about on the other end of the line.

"Yes, of course," Saed Aziz Rahani resumed, "you have an important business meeting to attend, a deal to close."

"How could you know—"

"They called Rahani Industry's Riyadh headquarters to confirm. I happened to take the call."

"It must have been between happy hours."

"You will not find them receptive to your proposals."

"You don't even know my proposals."

"All the same, I made sure to provide them a better alternative. They are meeting with you only as a courtesy. I look forward to watching you lose what little face you have left. But fear not: Your exile from the company once I take over will be gradual."

"Once *you* take over?"

"The line of succession is clear, and I am the oldest child."

"You are seven years younger than I."

"Oldest *son,* my sister."

Layla scratched at the phone's plastic with her fingernails. "Our father still lives."

"And if you turn your plane around, you can be here for his last breath without humiliating yourself."

"You don't want me as your enemy, Saed."

"I accepted that long ago. Neither of us can change the inevitable. You waste your life trying."

Layla Aziz Rahani switched the phone from one ear to the other. "We'll talk when I return."

"There is no return from what you are about to do, my sister. It is I who will step into our father's shoes. Complete his dreams, his vision."

Layla smiled ever so slightly. "You have no idea how wrong you are, my brother," she said, and returned the phone to the armrest.

CHAPTER 11

"What does it mean?" Danielle asked groggily, trying to chase the sleep from her head.

"It's a prophecy from the Koran, signifying the destruction of the world, the end of man."

"So these pages . . ."

"They appear to be a religious *fatwa* from a cleric

giving the holder permission to bring it about. In the United States."

Danielle found herself suddenly alert. "Armageddon."

"Not exactly. The New Testament calls a similar prophecy something else: the end of all things," Ben continued. "According to the Koran, the Last of Days would begin with the coming of al-Mahdi, a messianic prophet. Al-Mahdi would arise to restore justice to the world, return it to the hands of those pure enough to hold it. Or at least destroy the infidels who corrupted mankind."

"Americans."

"According to this *fatwa*."

"You're saying that's what Akram Khalil was involved in?" Danielle asked, wondering if Deputy Minister Vordi had deliberately held back the truth from her, or whether it had been held back from him as well.

"That's what these pages say."

"But they don't say how."

"The final section is missing."

Danielle rubbed her eyes with her free hand, picturing the final moments of Khalil's life. Under attack, he had retreated to the rear of the compound, where he began to destroy evidence of his work, his plans. Getting a fire going in the trash can would have taken a few precious moments. Then, in the moments before bullets cut him down, he must have lifted a clump of papers and dumped them into the flames.

"Who else might have had a reason to kill Khalil?" Ben asked her.

"That's what I'm trying to find out." She waited for him to respond and resumed speaking when he didn't. "What's wrong?"

"Why do you think something's wrong?"

"Because whenever you lapse into one of your uncomfortable silences, it's because there's something you're not telling me."

Ben smiled in spite of himself. "I'm calling from Detroit."

"Not to visit family."

"No. The U.S. State Department hired me to help them find a terrorist they believe is plotting a strike on America."

"And this terrorist is somehow linked to Akram Khalil and Hamas, isn't he?"

"Yes," Ben said, letting his answer hang in the air.

DAY FOUR

CHAPTER 12

"I wanted to hear from you first, before you report to the National Security Council," the president said from behind his desk in the Oval Office.

"I understand, sir."

Stephanie Bayliss, director of homeland security, was seated in a chair opposite the president. Bayliss came from a military family. Her father was a retired marine corps general, her three brothers all ranking officers. But she had surpassed them all, becoming the youngest female colonel ever commissioned by the army. She had volunteered for every combat mission available to her, been dispatched to all of them but, much to her regret, had never taken up a forward position where she could engage the enemy. Despite this, the army gave her a fat promotion and a transfer to intelligence, which she embraced publicly while seething inside.

Privately, those who had held back her combat career complained she was too pretty. Stephanie tried different hairstyles, stopped wearing makeup. It didn't help. The only offers she got were from someone putting a "Women in the Military" calender together and a men's magazine that offered her fifty thousand dollars to do a centerfold.

Her selection as the nation's latest director of homeland security came as much a surprise to her as to everyone else. Her background was military, not political, but the president had decided that's what was needed. Someone who took no shit and was comfortable behind a microphone. She had never given a press briefing before in her life, Stephanie told them. That was okay, they said, she wasn't being hired for her looks.

"So far we've been able to keep this whole mess out of the press," the president said. "I don't know how much longer that will remain the case. We'd better make sure our wagons are circled in the meantime."

"We're doing our best, sir."

"Give it to me from the top, from the moment USAM-RIID personnel realized they had admitted imposters onto the base and the commanding officer issued—what was it called?"

"A Code Seventeen."

"A Code Seventeen," the president repeated.

"We believe those imposters executed the real Hazardous Materials team moments after the contamination signal came in."

"They had that station under surveillance, then."

"That's the assumption at this point, yes, sir."

"When was the last drill conducted?"

Bayliss consulted her notes. "Twenty-six days ago, sir."

"So they must have been watching the Hazardous Materials station for at least twenty-five days."

"Not necessarily, sir."

"Not necessarily? I was under the impression that no one other than the base commander knew the timetable for Monday's drill."

"That's no longer the case, Mr. President. The last two unannounced drills both caused such chaos for others working on the grounds of Fort Detrick that base commander Walter McClendon agreed to furnish the date of the drill, though not the time, to local officials."

"Can we assume that's where the leak sprang from, Director?"

"Not entirely, Mr. President. Departments of Defense

and State were also informed as a matter of courtesy."

"Courtesy," the president repeated, as if it made no sense to him.

"After 9/11, communication among the various departments and agencies became the new watchword. Everybody sharing everybody else's business."

"No longer a need-to-know basis."

"Procedure, sir."

"So the imposters entered the base disguised as the HazMat team after learning the timetable," the president concluded.

"They were inside the building for six and a half minutes, enough time to raid the Level Four containment area and escape with the entire stores of Strain EF309."

"Smallpox." The president had learned that much from a previous briefing. "And just how did these imposters manage to get USAMRIID's entire stores of the virus off the grounds?"

Stephanie Bayliss took a deep breath. "We're still looking into that."

The president made no effort to disguise his displeasure. "What now, Director?"

Bayliss tried to sound as professional as she could. "We've increased security at all airports, but the vials that were stolen can be disguised so many ways I don't hold out much hope any increased security will produce very much."

"I don't like that attitude, Director."

"I'm just being realistic, sir. You've got a highly trained, highly mobile, highly efficient team here. They had everything planned to the exact second and clearly that must have included escape."

"And what are we doing about it?"

"I'm bringing in the country's foremost expert on biological warfare and terrorism, Mr. President. He was with USAMRIID during the Ebola scare of eighty-nine.

There are those who say he single-handedly saved the country. I expect him to be ready to brief you personally within twenty-four hours."

"Can you answer me one thing now, Colonel Bayliss?"

"I'll try, sir."

"I was under the impression we had destroyed the last reserves of smallpox years ago."

"No, sir. Pentagon personnel decided to retain a relatively small amount for future studies."

"And how much is this relatively small amount, Director?"

"Enough to infect half the world, sir."

The president spun in his chair and gazed out the window over the lawn, imagining the city and world beyond. "Too bad these Pentagon personnel didn't realize that half might be ours."

CHAPTER 13

"Khalil's been on our watch list for years," Harry Walls told Danielle the next morning, using the euphemism for what everyone knew meant targeted for possible execution. They had met in the shade of some young olive trees in a grassy, tree-lined park in Jerusalem, set between the Jewish and Moslem quarters, called the Forest of Peace. Brown splotches of earth, scattered in slivered, rectangular sections, formed a reminder of the days before all the benches had been removed to discourage loitering.

Walls was a Mossad agent who had been recruited for

the Sayaret, Israel's most elite commandos, at the same time as Danielle fifteen years before. They had gone through training together under David Vordi, two out of a hundred ultimately selected for membership, and remained friends to this day.

"I understand that until the settlement attack he'd been keeping quiet," Danielle said.

"Still have your sources?" Walls asked her.

"A few."

"We don't believe Khalil was responsible for the settlement attack at all."

Danielle tried not to look as shocked as she felt.

"We believe," Walls continued, "that he'd been focusing all his energies on a cell he was running in the United States."

"Al-Qaeda?"

"The links were there, yes."

"And the Americans knew this?"

Walls narrowed his gaze. "If you're thinking they were the ones who took out Khalil, forget it. The Americans don't work that way—at least not without informing us."

"I'd be more interested in learning who wanted us to believe Khalil was behind the attack on the settlement."

"The same force that wanted him killed. What's the difference now that the bastard's dead? Rogue operations are only called into question when they fail, Danielle."

Walls shifted his weight from his right leg to his left. He had retained his rugged good looks, even though his many years of service had brought a cold, steel glimmer to his eyes that washed the emotion straight out of them.

"But you're telling me you don't know whose operation it was."

"That's right."

"If Khalil was targeted, you must have been watching

him," Danielle insisted. "From time to time, when he surfaced. The watcher would provide location and intelligence in case a strike was mandated. For God's sake, Harry, I know how this stuff works."

"You want to speak to our watcher."

"That's right."

"You can't, because he's dead. We found what was left of his body a week ago. The only thing I'm sorry about is I didn't get to kill Khalil myself."

"There must be someone else I can go to, another contact."

Walls shook his head. "You're never going to learn, are you?"

"About what?"

"Politics. Restraint. You're two months from taking over as commissioner of National Police, and you're ready to throw it all away. For what? *Nothing*."

"I asked you to trust me."

Walls frowned, his face a mask of harsh indifference. "I do, and I care about you too. I'll tell you something else. When I first heard what happened in Idaho, at Pine Gulley or Valley or whatever you call it, I thought of you, because there aren't ten people in the world who could pull off what you did. And every time you call I come because I hope you've given up being one of those ten."

Danielle swallowed hard. "So you can't help me."

"Actually, I can. Be careful of David Vordi."

"Thanks for the warning."

"I'm serious, Danielle. He likes getting what he wants, behaves badly when he doesn't."

"Anything else, Harry?"

He smiled slightly at her and walked off.

Danielle was watching him go when her cell phone rang, startling her. She drew it quickly to her ear, expecting it might be Ben.

"I gather your friend wasn't very helpful, Chief Inspector."

"Colonel al-Asi?" Danielle swept her eyes about her. "Where are you?"

"It doesn't matter. I figured you would be following up the circumstances surrounding the strike on Akram Khalil's compound and thought I might be able to help. In return for your looking into the Arab woman's death."

"I told you that wasn't necessary."

"I know what you told me, Chief Inspector, but your help would leave me in your debt and I can't accept that."

"You gave me Khalil; that's enough."

"I gave you Khalil, and someone else ended up killing him. I find that as troublesome as you do. So I'm doing this as much for me as for you. The question is, do I do it alone or with you?"

"Do what?"

"Pay a visit to Gaza to see a man who survived the attack on Khalil's hideout."

CHAPTER 14

"Am I supposed to be happy to see you?"

Ben found his brother Sayeed in the detached garage of his Victorian home. The gray clapboard house was located on Coleman Street in north Dearborn near Patton Park. He ducked to slide beneath the half-open garage door where Sayeed was at work on the classic MG sports car he had painstakingly restored from scratch. But the car looked no different than it had in the wake of the death of Ben's nephew three years before, as if Sayeed just kept polishing the same paint over and over again.

"*Sabaha l-hayr,*" Ben greeted. "Good morning."

"What's good about it?" Sayeed asked and went back to his polishing.

Ben knew his brother had never managed to lift himself from the sullen gloom that had ensnared him after his son's murder. This in spite of the fact that he had two other children, a son and daughter both in high school, and an excellent job as a professor at the University of Michigan. None of that had cleansed the bitterness from his eyes. They were angry, raw, looking rubbed forever red. Sayeed had let his hair grow longer, but it was virtually all gray now. His shoulders had taken on a perpetual slump, and his belly stuck out over his belt, as if exercise too had become a thing of the distant past.

Normally when Ben came back home, he made it a point to drive by his old house in the Copper Canyon section of Detroit, where his own wife and children had been slain a decade before. He had finally gotten to the point where he didn't have to stop anymore, and this morning he actually took another route altogether. He drove straight to his brother's home, passing Fordson Park and Woodmere Cemetery, where his family was buried, on the way instead.

"You could at least pretend you're glad to see me," Ben said.

"And listen to you tell me how to straighten out my life again? Why should I?"

"A man from the State Department came to see me in Boston yesterday."

Sayeed Kamal didn't look up, kept polishing the fender. He was darker and taller than Ben, though his perpetual slouch made it impossible to tell.

"You promised me you had given up your participation in Palestinian interest groups."

"No, I told you I'd think about it."

"According to the State Department, you must not have thought about it very hard."

"So they sent you out here to make me a better citizen."

"Would you rather they had sent someone else?"

"Are you threatening me, my brother?" Sayeed asked, finally looking up. "Then again, it always seems to come down to that. You come here on the pretext of my interests when it's really your own you're pursuing. Save yourself the trouble this time. I'm not interested." And he went back to his polishing, then stopped again. "By the way, I have something to show you."

Sayeed left the rag on the fender and moved to a box tucked near the MG's front tires. He located a framed photo on the top, swiped the dirt off the glass, and handed it to Ben.

"I found it in the attic. I've been saving it for you."

Ben studied the framed eight-by-ten photograph of him and Sayeed as young boys standing on either side of their father. He remembered his mother taking the picture, remembered everything about the day, their first in the cabin their father had purchased on Saginaw Bay in central Michigan. Thinking back, Ben could never recall a time in his life when he'd been happier, not realizing that two months later his father would travel back to Palestine never to return again.

"I'll make you a copy," Ben offered, tucking the frame under his arm.

"Don't bother," Sayeed said and went back to the fender. "Our mother still owns the cabin, you know. Refuses to sell it, even though she hasn't been there in ten years."

"That's her decision." Ben drew a deep breath and

took a step closer to his brother. "The State Department believes you're still active in raising funds for Hamas."

"Raising funds, yes. For Hamas, no. I have raised and will continue to work toward raising money for the Palestinian Educational Fund."

"Which continues to sponsor Palestinian students."

"You have a problem with that?"

"The State Department does," Ben told him, "so long as they are students like Mohammed Latif."

"A fine young man."

"Who happens to be an associate of Akram Khalil. Hamas."

"I know who Khalil is."

"But not apparently who Latif is," Ben said and dropped the pages Danielle had faxed to him in Boston the previous night on the hood of the restored MG.

"What's this?"

"Khalil was killed in a raid yesterday. These were found burning in his Gaza headquarters."

Sayeed Kamal kept the polishing cloth in hand as he began to read, disinterestedly at first until he neared the end of the first page. Then the contents grabbed all of his attention, and he brought the pages up off the hood and held them close to his eyes in the garage's murky light, a sheen of sweat rising to his brow.

"The Last of Days," he said, squeezing the pages when he was finished. "Khalil's plan?"

Ben nodded. "And the State Department seems certain that Latif was involved with Khalil and that his presence in this country was part of some operation. A big one."

Sayeed looked uncertain for the first time. "I know this boy. That's ridiculous."

"The government knows him too. They don't agree."

"They got you to do this by threatening me."

"You were Latif's sponsor. That doesn't look good, under the circumstances."

"So what did they promise you? To let me off? Not charge me with treason?"

"They just want Latif. Apparently, he slipped off their radar."

Sayeed handed his brother back the now curled pages. "He had some problems and dropped out of school. That's all."

"You've been in touch with him, then."

"I have his new address," Sayeed said defensively.

"You checked Latif out before agreeing to sponsor him, of course."

"I knew his mother had died of dysentery in a refugee camp and his father died of an Israeli bullet. I didn't ask any other questions."

"That's your procedure?"

"He was a young Palestinian who required my help. First a victim of the Israeli government and now a victim of the American government."

Ben wanted to lash out at his brother, to scream at him, but he couldn't. Besides, he knew it would do no good. He saw too much of himself in the slightly older man before him trying to lose himself in a car that would never be finished. Both of them headstrong and stubborn, swayed by their emotions even in the face of the most rational of arguments.

"Why don't we go pay Latif a visit?" Ben suggested. "So I can see for myself."

CHAPTER 15

"You're certain he's *here*?" Danielle asked, as she and Colonel al-Asi approached the entrance to the refugee camp in Gaza.

"Certain, Chief Inspector? No. In my world certainty is a relative term. Am I certain a single witness survived the assault on Akram Khalil's stronghold? Yes. Am I certain he is now desperate for sanctuary? Absolutely. And am I certain he was in this camp, hiding out with relatives as of yesterday?" This time the colonel only nodded.

"How could you know all that?"

"Because he was my source." Al-Asi narrowed his gaze. "What's wrong, Chief Inspector?"

"Mossad doesn't believe Khalil was behind the settlement attack."

The colonel considered her words for a moment before responding. "Which would mean I was wrong."

"Or your source was."

"Same thing, Chief Inspector. And, worse, it could mean I was manipulated, used. I find that most disturbing."

"I'm sorry, Colonel. I didn't mean to . . ."

"I'm not mad at you, Chief Inspector. It's just that something like this would have been unthinkable two years ago, even one. It makes me realize how far I've slipped."

Danielle wished she could have said something to comfort the colonel. All of Ben's experience with him indicated that he was a shrewd, cunning, and immensely reliable operator. A man who had the best sources of any operative in the West Bank and Gaza, coupled with the capacity to employ them. But all that had changed with the dismantling of the Palestinian Authority's security infrastructure.

There was no formal entrance to the camp, no stretch of fencing surrounding it. This section was simply a mud-drenched, rank sprawl of tiny shanties, tents, tin huts, and concrete shells squeezed together without reason or discernible organization. Flat patches where the remains had been cleared, and strewn piles of rubble where they hadn't, provided grim testament to the Israeli bulldozing efforts some months back. Nearly every building Danielle and al-Asi passed showed the divot, pockmark, or hole left behind by a bullet.

This particular camp was in even greater disrepair than the ones in the West Bank, with which Danielle was more familiar. There was no running water, no facilities for washing or bathing. No ovens, stoves, or electricity. Al-Asi had taken the lead once they entered the camp and, walking beside him, Danielle watched children playing soccer in a cemetery. The children, all boys, trampled over freshly poured graves to chase a ball ricocheting off the remnants of gravestones. Not even half wore shoes. Beyond the cemetery, in a strip of tin and concrete shacks, women had fashioned makeshift ovens out of stone slabs. The smell of bread baking mingled with the stench of raw sewage, spoiled food, and unwashed bodies.

Colonel al-Asi seemed to know where he was going, and Danielle did not question him.

"You still have your sources, Colonel," she offered lamely, feeling the need to say something as they progressed deeper into the camp.

"Only temporarily, Chief Inspector. I have so many

because I have always taken care of them. Now my resources are drying up, and I will not be able to take care of them much longer."

"I'm sure my government would be willing to help."

"Perhaps make me a line item in your annual budget, eh, Chief Inspector?" al-Asi quipped, but Danielle had already realized the folly of her remark. The colonel could only function if he was autonomous. Instead, now he risked being trapped between two disparate and warring cultures, too dangerous to be accepted by either.

"It's a moot point anyway," he continued, "because eventually the worst of the terrorists, the ones who are known to me, will be gone and we will be left with only the new ones I have no intimate knowledge of. I fear that day for both of us."

Al-Asi swung left down a rut-filled dirt road wide enough to accommodate a single vehicle, then turned right down another. He had dressed casually for the journey, in khakis and a work shirt with the sleeves rolled up to the elbow. A bandanna already soaked through with sweat circled his neck. Strangely, though, the difference in wardrobe did nothing to diminish his regal demeanor. For al-Asi, Danielle knew, appearance was based on attitude; it was the lack of his legendary security entourage that made the colonel seem naked by comparison with years past.

The roads weren't marked by any signs Danielle could see; that would make it too easy to apprehend suspects taking refuge in the camps. But there must have been some kind of order to the place that the colonel understood. His sense of direction never wavered; he never gave a hint that he did not know exactly where he was going.

The homes grew slightly more presentable as Danielle and al-Asi drew closer to the center of the camp, the residents more settled but the stench much the same.

Though larger, these shacks seemed to have more people to squeeze inside them, no square footage left to waste.

"The unemployment rate is seventy percent in Gaza," al-Asi explained. "No money coming in and none going out. The worst kind of cycle. With peace, these places would have come down and luxury apartments would have gone up. I've seen the plans for this very land, to be built primarily with Israeli venture-capital money. I wonder what's become of those plans now."

The road banked up a modest incline, and Danielle followed the colonel up it toward a shanty with a tin roof and burlap windows. A woman was boiling water in a rusty pot atop an open flame. As they filed past her to a door fabricated of stray boards nailed haphazardly together, the woman peered inside a cracked stone oven to check on the progress of a loaf of bread baking there.

"My source's mother," the colonel said. "Hakim," he called through a break in the uneven slats. "Hakim?"

When there was no response, Al-Asi eased open the door and entered. Danielle followed without being told to, not realizing her mistake until the colonel swung round in the darkness after he heard the door rattle shut. She froze, reaching instinctively for her gun when she felt a knife pressed firmly against the flesh of her throat.

CHAPTER 16

The blade trembled against Danielle's flesh, the edge dull and jagged, the hand attached to it dry with cracked calluses.

Before her, Colonel al-Asi hadn't so much as flinched. "Let her go, Hakim. She's a friend."

"I wasn't expecting you to bring anyone else!" The words emerged in a rasp, the man's breath dry and rank.

"She can help you, Hakim, but not if you slit her throat. This woman is an Israeli official who has agreed to arrange safe passage for you and your family to Turkey, as you requested," al-Asi promised, even though he had never discussed the offer with Danielle.

Hakim pulled the knife away from Danielle's throat and released her, sliding sideways. She turned and saw he was short and stout, with a face that looked too narrow for his frame. Danielle figured he must have stretched up on his toes to reach her neck.

"My brother is in Turkey," he said.

"Now sit and tell us the tale that has you so scared. Give my Israeli friend a reason to secure passage for you to Turkey."

Al-Asi glanced at Danielle as Hakim retreated to a rear corner of the small shack and sat down with his legs crossed. The colonel gazed down at him, his eyes twinkling mischievously. She began to understand the subtle power and grace Ben had often described. How he got things done in a world that defied professionalism.

"What happened yesterday at Akram Khalil's hideout in Gaza?" the colonel prodded.

Hakim flapped his legs together nervously. "I made myself scarce in the late morning, as you suggested. There's an escape hatch hidden where the garden used to be that leads into a tunnel. I was halfway down it when I found the tunnel blocked." He tried to focus on al-Asi, but his eyes kept darting warily to Danielle. She could see he had stuck the knife back into his belt, the blade pitifully small and pitted. Probably used to slice potatoes or fruit. "So I came back and slipped back up through the hatch. I started to walk around the building, figuring I'd have to take my chances with the guards, tell them I was running an errand or something, when I heard the voices."

Danielle and al-Asi exchanged a glance. Hakim was getting more agitated, starting to tremble as he spoke.

"They were all strangers to me. I didn't recognize a single one, so I stayed hidden behind the building and peered out. Khalil knew them, but he kept his distance, especially from the biggest one." Hakim waved a hand in front of his right eye. "The big one's eye was covered in a patch, and he had a long, jagged scar down the same side of his face. And he was tall, very tall. He seemed to be someone important, high up in the movement. I could not see the rest of his face. But he carried a weapon and wore a gun belt. Those I could see."

"Khalil let the man keep his weapon?" al-Asi asked.

"All the men kept their weapons," Hakim said. "Four men, I counted four. Well, not men exactly . . ."

"What do you mean?" Danielle asked him.

"Keep her silent or I will speak no more," Hakim told al-Asi fearfully.

"Commander Barnea is the one who can get your family to safety, Hakim," the colonel advised. "It is not in your best interests for me to give her orders."

Hakim shot Danielle a disparaging glance, then returned to his story. "There was arguing, very heated. Khalil was shouting the loudest. Both sides drew their weapons, but then things seemed to calm down. Two of the strangers stayed with Khalil's two guards in the courtyard while the other two, including the giant, disappeared into the back with Khalil and the rest of the guards. The first gunshots came very quickly after that."

"Silenced?" Danielle posed.

Hakim nodded rapidly. "In short spurts, two or three shots at a time. Just a single rifle, the tall man's—I know it."

Professionals for sure, then, Danielle concluded, short,

controlled bursts being the trademark of seasoned killers with extensive training.

"As soon as the first shots sounded," Hakim was saying, "the strangers who had remained in the courtyard drew their weapons and cut down both guards."

"What had they been arguing about before?"

"I couldn't make out all the words. Something about a plan, an operation. I heard the United States mentioned several times."

Danielle exchanged a glance with al-Asi.

"They were disagreeing over something that had happened," Hakim continued, "something that had changed."

"What time was this?" Danielle asked Hakim.

"I do not know exactly. Morning prayers had just been completed."

"Around ten A.M.," she figured. Then, to al-Asi, "Barely a half hour before my team arrived. What happened next?" Danielle asked Hakim.

"There was no next," he answered and swung quickly back toward al-Asi. "I went back and hid in the tunnel until they were gone. Then I came here to the camp, only to learn there had been men asking about me, men no one had ever seen here before."

"How did you get in?"

Hakim looked toward al-Asi before responding.

"Tell her," the colonel instructed.

"There are secret routes used by our people to escape when the Israelis come."

"But these men who killed Khalil and his guards, they weren't Israeli."

Hakim shook his head demonstratively. "No. And one of them . . ."

"What?" Danielle prodded when he let his statement tail off.

"No." Hakim lifted his gaze back up unsteadily. "No.

You want to hear the rest, get me and my family away from here. Not until then do we speak again. Agreed?"

"Yes," Danielle said.

Hakim seemed to relax when al-Asi spoke suddenly. "You lied to me about the raid on the settlement in Gaza, didn't you?"

"No, Colonel, I would never—"

"This is me you are talking to, Hakim," al-Asi said amicably. "You can keep your family safe from Hamas, but . . ."

He let his comment drift off, his point made.

"I wasn't actually there," Hakim confessed, "at the settlement."

"Keep talking."

"One of Khalil's soldiers boasted about the attack to me."

"Was this soldier killed at the compound yesterday?"

Hakim looked down at the floor. "No."

"When was the last time you saw him?"

"Three days ago when he gave me the news."

"IT WOULD seem I was set up," al-Asi said, almost too softly to hear, after he and Danielle had emerged from Hakim's shack.

Danielle nearly collided with a tall man walking the narrow street, his head bent down and his eyes on the ground. "We both were, Colonel, by someone who wanted Khalil's execution to become a priority." Danielle thought of something else. "By the way, passage to Turkey for an entire family?"

"Most generous of you, Chief Inspector. You should know Hakim has four children."

"I was supposed to be the one who took Khalil out,"

Danielle said, trying to make sense of what she had learned.

"Obviously something changed."

"Including the timetable. Whoever sent this one-eyed man and the other assassins couldn't risk waiting for me to show up to do the job." Danielle reviewed Hakim's tale briefly in her mind. "Khalil knew his killers."

"And had been expecting them, by Hakim's account."

"Things didn't happen yesterday morning as I thought they did at all. Khalil couldn't have burned those pages in the midst of the shootout. It had to have been the killers who set them on fire."

"Because there was a message in the contents they didn't want getting out to the world."

"The end of all things. But let's assume Khalil and his killers were both involved in the plot. What could have happened to change them from allies to foes?"

They passed a trio of women carrying baskets heavily laden with clothes, having made a trip to what passed for a laundry in the camp: wooden barrels of boiled water, thick and dark with the soil of numerous loads. The women turned away from Danielle, their bare feet sloshing through the muddy ground.

"Oh, my God," she realized, stopping.

"Chief Inspector?"

"That man we passed back there in the street outside of Hakim's, the one who was hunched over, his shoes were *new*. . . ."

Danielle tore past al-Asi, heard him pounding to catch up as she retraced her path back through the camp. Her sense of direction betrayed her at an intersection and she started to veer left instead of right until the colonel clamped a hand on her shoulder and pulled her onward.

They reached the shack's mud-strewn yard to the stench of the bread burning in the outdoor stone oven. Coarse black smoke drifted from the opening. Danielle reached the shack just ahead of al-Asi and threw back the door.

Hakim lay on his back on the floor, his eyes blinking rapidly, blood oozing from both sides of his mouth. His mother lay nearby on her stomach, her bullet-riddled back drenched in blood.

"Stay with him!" Danielle ordered al-Asi, and burst out of the shack.

CHAPTER 17

Danielle had seen the killer mere moments before and hadn't realized it: a tall man walking with his head down, hunched to disguise his true height but unable to disguise the fresh pair of sandals that had given him away. She looked down at the mud, saw the imprints of large, heavy feet leading around the rear of the house to a connecting street.

Danielle ran swiftly, following the trail to the wider road laden with ancient, rusted hulks of trucks and cars, their tires sinking into the ground, they had been parked in place so long. She swung left, right, searching for a head rising above the clusters of people moving about one of the camp's main thoroughfares. Climbed atop the carcass of an old barrel to get a better view.

She spotted the tall man a hundred yards ahead, clinging to the side of the street where camp residents bartered goods from rickety pushcarts. He turned briefly, and she saw the patch that covered his right eye. Danielle climbed down from the barrel and hurried along the street, keeping her eyes fixed on him as she slipped between Palestinians lugging wares and possessions to exchange for more needed ones.

She picked up her pace, adrenaline surging through her veins. She could feel the familiar sense of her body tightening, preparing for battle. Heard a voice to her side, then another.

Danielle glanced about, suddenly aware of the stares being cast upon her, multiplying by the moment. She tried to refocus on the tall man, just ten yards from her now, but the crowd closed from the sides.

"Israil," she heard spoken. Then, *"Surtiyyah."*

Policewoman.

Suddenly she was being jostled, shoved from side to side.

"Out of my way!" she ordered in English, unable to form the phrase quickly enough in Arabic.

The command infuriated the crowd further, drew more attention to her. Danielle's eyes swept the street ahead, trying to keep the tall man in focus as he widened the gap between them.

"Qif!" she shouted in Arabic, raising her gun. "Stop!"

The crowd closed around her, stealing her line of vision. She tried to wrench herself free, but something heavy, a sack it felt like, struck her shoulders and pitched her sideways. She fought to resteady her gun on the tall man's shrinking shape, but a trio of boys kicking a torn and tattered soccer ball, perhaps the same ones she'd glimpsed in the cemetery earlier, lurched in her way.

The tall man turned back. Their stares met. She could see the scar dominating the right side of his face, the exposed parts of his arms lean and sinewy with muscle.

Someone slammed into Danielle and her pistol went flying. She ducked and groped for it, but a filthy shoe kicked it aside into a sea of churning feet. She felt herself being pummeled with fists and covered her face, the shouts and screams echoing in her ears, the vast rage of her attackers finding a vent at last. She tried to twist free of the mob, caught the glimmer of her pistol, but another hand swiped it off the ground before she could grab it.

Something hard struck the back of her head. A fist pounded her stomach, others flailing at her ribs. Then a man's hand closed on her arm, yanking her sideways and upright, shoving her behind him.

"Ila l-wara!" Colonel al-Asi shouted, shielding her with his body as he brandished her pistol. "Stop!"

Some of the crowd, enough, backed off, recognizing him. Al-Asi jammed Danielle's pistol into his belt, wheeled about to make sure his command was heeded.

Danielle heard a few of the refugees protest, taunting al-Asi as he led her away, testing him. A rock glanced off the side of his head, mussing his hair. The colonel turned and waved a reproaching finger at the stubborn crowd.

"I know your faces," he warned. "Leave now and I will forget them."

He swung back to find a crowd had formed before him as well, surrounding the colonel and Danielle in the midst of the all-encompassing squalor. Al-Asi didn't hesitate, just started walking forward again with Danielle pressed tightly against his side. They reached the edge of the crowd, which seemed on the verge of holding its ground, when suddenly it parted, providing a slim passage through the center.

The colonel led Danielle forward, meeting the hateful gazes of all he passed, freezing them with his stare. Before Danielle knew it they were back at Hakim's shack, guarded by a pair of camp elders al-Asi must have set in place before heading out after Danielle. The elders stood their ground firmly, preventing the further advance of the crowd that had followed Danielle and al-Asi there.

The colonel swung back toward the throng one last

time. *"Sa'ati marratan ubra,"* he announced icily.

"What does that mean?" Danielle asked him.

"That I will come another time."

ANOTHER OF the camp elders had placed a pillow beneath Hakim's head. His face was ghastly pale and his eyes darted fearfully toward death. Still he managed to latch on to Danielle's wrist with steellike strength when she knelt over him.

"My children," he rasped, "my wife . . ."

"I'll get them to Turkey. I promise," she said, wincing from the pain of her own wounds.

Hakim tried to nod, struggled for breath. "A woman . . ."

"What?"

"A woman came with those who killed Khalil." Hakim swallowed and the breath caught briefly in his throat. He gagged and more blood and spittle leaked from the sides of his mouth. "She was tall, looked like . . . When I first saw you, my knife," he continued, rambling. "Because I thought, I thought—"

"You thought what?"

"That it was you," Hakim rasped, just before his eyes locked open.

CHAPTER 18

"I am starting to wonder whose side you're on, my brother," Sayeed said, as they made their way down the third-floor hallway of a small, decrepit apartment building.

"This isn't about sides."

"The American government would like nothing better than to round all of us up. Put us behind some fence where they could watch us all the time like animals in a zoo."

"We are Americans too, Sayeed."

"All the more reason why we shouldn't stand for this, my brother." He stopped and checked a number painted in peeling paint over the door. "This is Latif's new apartment."

"Did you call?"

Sayeed Kamal raised his hand and knocked loudly on the door. "He's not answering his phone. Mohammed?" Sayeed called through the wood. "Mohammed, it's Sayeed Kamal." He stopped and rapped harder on the door. "Mohammed, I need to talk to you."

"Let me," Ben said, sliding in front of his brother as he removed a slim black case from his pocket.

"What's that?" Sayeed asked.

Ben zippered the case open. "Lock picks."

Inside a dozen picks fit into neatly tailored slots, none of them ever used. The kit had been a gift from John Najarian, given along with his tacit approval to use its contents.

"A police officer?" Sayeed raised, shaking his head.

"I'm not a police officer anymore," Ben reminded him, selecting the proper pick and going to work on the door.

He had learned how to pick locks during his last investigation as a Detroit detective. A serial killer called the Sandman had slain three entire families as they slept: No signs of forced entry were found at any of the murder sites. Ben concluded someone capable of picking locks was the killer and wanted to learn the process, see how difficult it was.

Much more than he had imagined, as it turned out, leading him to investigate the possibility that the killer was a locksmith. He was out canvassing names when the Sandman showed up at his home in Copper Canyon, picked the lock on the front door, and moved upstairs to where his wife and children were sleeping. Ben arrived just after the killer's work was done and the smell of blood was rising in the air.

The single lock sprang easily and the door to Mohammed Latif's apartment swung open.

"We shouldn't be doing this," Sayeed protested.

But Ben had already entered ahead of him, found the light switch and flipped it. A dull haze enveloped the room's dingy confines. A single couch, chair, and an old television accounted for all the furniture in the living room area. A bare mattress and box spring stood alone in the bedroom. No food remained in the refrigerator or the cupboards.

"He's gone," Sayeed Kamal said, swallowing hard.

"For some time," Ben said, kneeling down to inspect a layer of powdery dust that had collected in a gap between the tile of the small kitchen and faded, chipped wood of the living room. But the consistency was wrong for dust, and the color too. Ben touched his finger to his tongue, trying to identify the substance. "When was the last time you actually saw or spoke to Latif?"

"The students I sponsor are not required to keep me informed of all their movements," his brother said defensively.

"How long?" Ben persisted.

"Five or six weeks."

"Which?"

"Six."

Ben tasted some more of the powdery dust. "Did Latif have a job?"

"No, he was a full-time student. I arranged for the grants and scholarships, even a living allowance."

"From one of the Arab charities?"

"Where else?"

"Those charities are terrorist fronts. They used you."

"I give Palestinian youths a chance! I sponsor good kids!"

"Latif is connected to a known Hamas leader. And now he's disappeared."

"You should never have come back here," Sayeed said.

"To Dearborn or America, my brother?" Then, without waiting for a response, Ben ran some more of the powdery, sweet-tasting dust through his fingers. "Taste this," he said to Sayeed, smoothing some of the white dust upon his fingertip.

Sayeed Kamal touched the substance hesitantly to his tongue, swirled it around his mouth.

"Recognize it?" Ben asked, watching his brother's nose wrinkle.

Sayeed shook his head.

"Commercial flour. Did Latif ever work at a bakery?"

"I already told you, no."

"You're certain?"

"I'd know if he had."

"Just like you knew where he lived." Ben stood up.

"He was here in this apartment briefly, but long enough to leave plenty of residue behind."

"I'll find him," Sayeed said obstinately. "Just let me make a few calls."

"Don't bother. I've got a better idea."

CHAPTER 19

"Please understand, Ms. Rahani," the man named Shipley said, "these men were expecting to hear from your father."

"You did not receive his e-mail?"

Shipley, lead broker for the venture-capital group that was waiting in an adjacent boardroom, shrugged. "Only yesterday."

"And did it not explain how he had been summoned by the royal family and wished me to speak in his stead?"

Shipley shrugged again. "Then let us proceed, Ms. Rahani."

But Layla held her ground. "Is something else wrong, Mr. Shipley?"

He sighed. "Only that the group has been less than enthusiastic over the prospects of your father's proposal from the start. The fact that he is unable to address them personally . . ."

"Just let me worry about that."

"There is also the matter of your brother."

"My brother." Layla felt herself begin to seethe once more. That Saed had uncovered the truth of their father's condition shouldn't have come as any surprise. That he had moved so quickly to assert himself, though, left her taken aback.

She watched Shipley's face crease with concern. "He offered considerably better terms than you have proposed. Told me to disregard your proposals."

"My brother is not well versed on the intricacies of this deal, I'm afraid. He does not share my father's confidence."

"All the same . . . Well, they're waiting for us. We should get started, I suppose."

Layla followed Shipley into the conference room and knew instantly he hadn't been exaggerating. The men and women seated around the mahogany table were fidgeting nervously, clearly with designs on being somewhere else. Their polite glances cast her way made Layla's flesh crawl even more severely. She had not been back in the United States in fifteen years, since midway through her sophomore year in college. The horrible memories had been buried deep, not forgotten but kept distant. Returning here had brought them all back. The air had done it more than anything, Layla thought. The stench that claimed the city as soon as she had stepped off the plane.

Shipley completed his introduction and beckoned Layla to join him at the head of the table, where she took her place behind a lectern upon which rested a laptop computer to use for the Power Point presentation she had planned. Looking at the bored, disinterested gazes on the investors' faces made her rethink her strategy in midstream. There were eight men and three women, which gave her an idea.

"My apologies for the absence of my father, Abdullah Aziz, who could not be here with you today. It would have pleased him to see three women in the room, because women are the centerpiece of the opportunity he has sent me to present to you today."

Those around the table exchanged glances, unsure of where Layla Aziz Rahani was going. They consulted their notes, as if some clue might have been contained within them, then looked back up when they found none.

"I say that because in my country this kind of gathering, of men and women together, is prohibited. In Saudi Arabia you would need special permission from the ruling council to participate. And, of course, I would not be permitted to address you."

Layla Aziz Rahani moved slightly away from the lectern.

"You see me today dressed in a suit that can be bought at Macy's, or Saks, or Bloomingdale's. But I would not be allowed to wear it in my country, where the dress code is very strict."

She refocused her gaze on the nearest woman.

"In my country," she told her, "you would not have been able to drive the car that brought you here. You would not be able to walk in the street in the company of a man unless it was your husband."

Layla retrained her stare on a second woman at the table. "You would not be allowed to travel without written permission of a male relative. And if you dared have sex before marriage, a male relative could kill you without fear of punishment.

"It's called an honor killing," she said to the third woman. "But where is the honor in such a cruel and cowardly act? There is none, of course. There is only dishonor and repression in a society, a culture, that refuses to grow or change.

"Being alone with a male who is not an immediate relative," Layla Aziz Rahani continued, backpedaling toward the podium, "is called *khilwa* and is watched for diligently by *mutaw'een*, our religious police, who patrol the streets in SUVs built in your country. Get caught and you receive thirty days' confinement in jail and twenty lashes across your back."

A number of those gathered around the conference table, both men and women, winced.

"In lieu of driver's licenses we are permitted to carry identity cards. You must be at least twenty-two years old to obtain one and have the consent of a guardian and letter from an employer if you work. Two hundred fifty thousand women have joined the workforce in Saudi Arabia now, and six thousand of those operate their own businesses. Of course, in the latter case all financial transactions outside of the workplace must be conducted by men.

"Recently an all-male advisory board known as a *Shura* permitted a delegation of women to take part in a consultative council. We were segregated in a different hall and presented our list of suggestions for meaningful change behind closed doors with our veils on.

"Not a single one has been acted upon thus far," Layla Aziz Rahani finished.

"But what does all this have to do with you? Why do I raise these issues instead of simply presenting you with the facts and figures my accountants have assembled?" She waited, as if for a response. "Because it is very pertinent to the investment I am seeking. We are a closed society, but we are not going to remain that way for long. Oh, no. The high cost of dowries and marriage has left one and a half million women without husbands in my country. Our repressive social policies are destroying our economy, and drastic changes in the near future are inevitable. They have to come or, simply stated, Saudi society will cease to exist in any recognizable form. The answer is compromise. And, in this case, compromise means tourism."

Layla Aziz Rahani slid back behind the lectern and switched on the laptop computer. She heard a soft whir and almost instantly a three-dimensional artist's rendition of a massive theme park filled the screen. The computer-generated motion provided scale, and the investors around the conference table gasped at the scope.

"Tourism is the long-term answer to Saudi Arabia's long-term problems," Layla continued. "Not today, or tomorrow, but within the decade it takes for construction to begin on this and five other major resort projects I am proposing to this consortium. Tourism is my country's last hope, and those with the foresight to realize that will also realize profits beyond their wildest imaginations. Tourism is the answer to our employment problems, as well as our growing poverty. Tourism will be the means by which women will someday be accepted as equal partners in a society that currently rejects them."

Shipley moved in front of the screen as another vantage point of the massive theme park was projected. "Ms. Rahani, your brother provided a prospectus on your proposal, and the numbers simply don't add up."

Layla spoke facing the conference table. "That's because my brother gave you the wrong numbers." Again she moved out from behind the lectern. "You see, all funds you invest will be insured by shares in ten-year Saudi oil futures. So the numbers are these: You risk nothing with your investment. If my predictions and my plan fail, your negative costs are guaranteed."

Glances were exchanged around the table. A man Layla knew to be a media magnate named Carpenter leaned forward.

"Let me get this straight," he began. "You don't really need our money, so what is it you need?"

"Your names," Layla replied, "and the influence you carry with the royal family. The ideas of influential businessmen and foreign investors are greeted warmly in my country, especially when their projects will guarantee employment for up to one million Saudis in the construction phase alone. I'm talking about a historic partnership here of the kind that has not been seen since the early days of Aramco. I'm talking about projects where no expense will be spared and the threat of loss to you will be virtually nonexistent. I'm talking about turning Saudi Arabia into a mecca of entertainment."

She could see by their faces that she had them then, a triumph made all the greater by her brother's failed interference. Their money would help build a new Saudi Arabia, but they would never enjoy the profits. Because by that time their world would have begun an inevitable fall toward its own destruction. Money would be the last thing on their minds at that point.

Layla Aziz Rahani's expression changed ever so subtly as she studied their faces, thinking of a task much greater than building theme parks that had fallen to her with her father incapacitated. She believed in it as much as he, looked forward to the day when his vision, and now hers, would be realized.

"We'll need some time to study your proposal in depth," said the man named Carpenter. "Crunch the numbers.

"Take all you need," Layla told him. "I'm a patient woman."

CHAPTER 20

Ben had made a list of eighteen bakeries in the Dearborn area when he finally closed the phone book. Sayeed watched from across the hotel room as Ben called each and every one of them, thickening his accent, speaking Arabic. Making notes as the voices on the other end of the line provided answers to his questions.

"Hal ladaykum gurfa," he would ask first. "Do you have a room to rent?"

Sometimes he was referred to landlords. Other times the person who answered, or someone else in the bakery, was able to answer his questions simply and amicably. If he learned all available rooms above or attached to the bakery were rented, he crossed the establishment off his list. But if he was told there was, in fact, space available, he crossed that establishment off his list as well.

"Why?" his brother asked him.

"Because Latif would have moved somewhere no one would expect him, where no one would think to look. No trail left to follow. That's the way men like this do things."

"This is a kid we're talking about."

"He stopped being a kid when he signed on with Hamas, my brother."

"I still think you're wasting your time."

"I hope so," Ben said, thinking of Akram Khalil's execution the day before.

When he was finished, six bakeries remained on his

list, each claiming they had no rooms to rent. The next step was to check each of them out.

"You can go back to your students now," Ben told his brother, clipping on the holster holding his Sig-Sauer nine-millimeter pistol.

"You can't expect me to walk away," Sayeed protested.

"The rest is up to me."

"You could just call the State Department."

"But I haven't found Latif yet. That was the deal."

"And in return they leave me alone. Is that it?" Sayeed Kamal asked snidely.

"Close enough."

"I don't need your help, Bayan."

"Yes, you do, Sayeed. And for that I need leverage," Ben said. "That means I need to bring them Latif, a man you should never have allowed yourself to become linked to."

"I am a prisoner of my ideals, Bayan, just like you are. You went back to Palestine to fight your battle. I stayed here to fight mine." He paused, letting his point sink in. "It would appear both of us have lost."

"You belong in a classroom. You're in my world now."

"I've made it mine. I will go with you to find Latif, or I will go alone. Choose."

OF THE six bakeries remaining on Ben's list, three were located in strip malls that lacked any possible facilities for rented rooms. The others had rooms above them, although in the case of one it became quickly clear that the lone upstairs apartment was the home of the bakery's owner and his family.

That left two establishments, three miles apart from each other on opposite ends of Warren Avenue. Ben and Sayeed spent an hour parked across the street watching each. Ben made some notes, said almost nothing.

"This used to be your life," Sayeed said at one point, as if he were trying to understand.

"A good portion of it."

"You have your lock picks, your multiple identifications. Why don't we just check the rooms out?"

"Because we're not sure if the owners of the bakeries are connected somehow."

"Safe houses?"

"You help Latif get into the country. Somebody else takes things from there."

"So what do we do now?"

"We wait for Latif."

Sayeed looked across the seat, surprised. "You know the one where he's been hiding out?"

"Absolutely," Ben said, starting the engine. "I'll show you tonight."

CHAPTER 21

The helicopter hovered over the small clearing, kicking up dirt and tearing at the thick tree branches that formed a canopy over the scene. From higher up the clearing was barely visible, the cabin contained within it even less so.

The chopper pilot gnashed his teeth as he settled lower, the rotor blade's powerful sweep whipping the branches about wildly. Instruments were useless. He had to go on sight and instinct, aware all the time that the slightest miscalculation would send the rotor slashing into wood and the chopper careening out of control to its death.

"This must be very important, sir," he said to the army major seated next to him, after they landed.

The major was having trouble releasing the catch on his safety harness. "It is, Corporal, believe me."

"Well then, you better make it fast, sir," the pilot said somewhat irreverently, feeling he deserved the liberty. "There's a wind coming up in the mountains, and if we don't take off real soon, we don't take off at all."

"Just keep the meter running," the major said as he stepped out.

Finding the cabin deserted, he traipsed down a rough trail into the woods. After several minutes he heard a heavy thumping sound and followed it through some brush. He emerged in a slight clearing to find a man splitting wood with an ax. The man wore a terry-cloth bathrobe over his naked torso and jockey shorts. A pair of bedroom slippers covered his feet.

"Professor Paulsen?" he called, checking the photo ID one more time to make sure he had the right man.

The ID was dated a dozen years earlier, almost to the day, making it difficult to match faces. The man's graying hair was thick on the sides now, growing wild in stark contrast to his bald dome. He had a stubbly growth of beard and a boxer's nose that looked flattened at the top and bent outward at the bottom.

"Professor," the major called again, satisfied this was the same man.

The man hefted his ax again, his torso flexing with a band of taut muscles that had lengthened, fighting age to keep their shape. Albert Paulsen, the major calculated, would be in his midsixties now.

"Professor Paulsen," he said one more time.

"Never heard of him," the man in the bathrobe said without looking away from his toils.

"I'm Major Tory, Army Special Intelligence, sir," the major said, advancing farther into the clearing. "I'm here to advise you that we have a Code Seventeen."

"Never heard of that either."

Tory stopped out of range of the old man's ax. "Sir, my information indicates you developed the Code Seventeen procedure."

"Not me. Somebody else."

"Professor Paulsen—"

"He died. I buried him in the leaching field." The old man's gray-blue eyes finally looked Tory's way, shocking in their intensity. "You can arrest me if you want. But then you'd have dig through all that shit for the evidence." He dropped the ax to waist level, making sure Tory could see the blade. "Nothing new for you army types, shoveling the shit."

"Sir, we have a Code Seventeen alert."

"You said that already."

"I've been ordered to—"

"What? Take an old man somewhere against his will?"

"Sir, my orders are—"

"You're not carrying a gun, Major."

"Sir, I—"

"Real soldiers always carry guns. How do I know you're who you say you are? Could be from the Girl Scouts of America come to track me down for those mint wafers I never paid for. Little bitches come knocking on your door looking for you to sign your life away to them. It's a scam, you know."

"Honestly—"

"Oh sure. Think about it, Major. Every year same box, same cookies. You think they bake new ones? Hell, no.

They just keep shipping the old boxes until they run out. Win their merit badges for recycling."

"You were assigned to USAMRIID, sir," Tory said, trying to move the old man back on track.

"In point of fact, I helped modernize it." Paulsen started to hoist the ax again, then stopped. Sweat glimmered across his chest hair. His muscles looked as though lean bands of steel had been wedged beneath his skin. "You know the best thing about living out here? No junk mail. Army APO siphoned it all out. You like junk mail, Tory?"

"I . . . guess not, sir."

"Good thing. Here's a fact that might interest you. Every year, you know how much paper goes into junk mail?" Paulsen didn't wait for an answer. "The equivalent of ten thousand acres of trees, Tory, ten thousand goddamn acres. I come up here, chop some wood for my stove, and all the time I'm thinking of all the circulars, catalogs, and advertisements I'm denying the world. Wonder who's behind it all. Girl Scouts of America maybe, using all their cookie profits to poison us with paper. Think about it, Tory."

"We really should be going, sir."

Paulsen steadied another log on the block before him. "Don't let me keep you."

"Sir, I'm authorized to—"

"To what, shoot me? Take off your uniform, Tory, and prove to me you're not a goddamn Girl Scout come to extract revenge. That's why I came up here—they put a hit out on me. I'm bad for lard and artificial sweeteners. Here's a fact, Tory. An artificial sweetener you might have put in your coffee this morning is actually a poison. Deadly as hell in the right composition and environment. Capable of wiping out a whole city if the wind currents are favorable. Think about it."

"That's what I'm here about, sir."

"Sugar substitutes?"

"Code Seventeen, sir. USAMRIID. You're needed at the White House."

Paulsen's mouth wrinkled up into the semblance of a grin, deepening the creases and furrows that lined his face beneath the beard stubble. "Something get away from them, Tory?"

"I'm not at liberty to say, sir."

"Of course you're not. You wouldn't be. Tell them I'll be along shortly, in my own good time."

"I'm not authorized to wait, sir."

"Didn't expect you would be, Tory. Just be on your way. As for me, I've got wood to chop. Winter's coming."

"It's April, sir."

"Winter's always coming. Waiting around the corner, just like the Girl Scouts. Got to be ready for them. Got to be prepared, Tory." Here Paulsen held his gaze, the grin melting from his face. "Because you never know when things are going to get fucked up."

CHAPTER 22

"Commander Barnea?"

Danielle finally looked up at the young man standing in the doorway.

"I'm Sergeant Ehud Cohen, Commander. I was told you wanted to see me."

Danielle cleared her throat, waved the young man into her office. She recalled the phone call she made to the detective bureau in Jerusalem requesting to see him as soon as possible. But she had made that call before accompanying Colonel al-Asi to the refugee camp in Gaza. Now all she could think about was that visit, especially Hakim's last words.

A woman! A woman had been among those who had executed Akram Khalil the day before!

"Thank you for coming to see me, *Samal rishon*," she said, settling her thoughts. "Please, sit down."

Cohen nodded and approached the chair in front of her desk. He was the lead investigator on the murder of the old Arab-Israeli woman from Umm al Fahm, Zanah Fahury, a murder Danielle had promised Colonel al-Asi she would look into.

Ehud Cohen leaned forward a little. "Ma'am?" He had a thick shock of curly brown hair that made him appear younger than he was. Danielle had seen his file. In his early twenties, Cohen had served as a military policeman in the Israeli Defense Forces before joining the Jerusalem police as a detective.

"Do you know why you're here, Sergeant?" she asked him.

He smiled confidently, clearly used to having his way with women. "I assume it has to do with a case, Commander."

"And so it does. A murder investigation, actually." Danielle turned a manila folder toward him and eased it across her desk. "Here, take a look."

Cohen rose slightly out of his chair to grab the folder, then sat back down stiffly to open it. "It's empty," he noted, befuddled.

"Maybe because it's the file on the investigation into the murder of Zanah Fahury."

Cohen repeated the name under his breath, as if trying to remind himself where he had heard it before.

"Surely you know the woman," Danielle continued. "You're leading the investigation into her murder. Her body was found in a Jerusalem alleyway three days ago."

"The Arab," Cohen recalled, nodding.

"*Israeli* Arab. Or has your investigation not proceeded that far yet?"

Cohen remained silent. He had probably considered many explanations for why the acting head of National Police would want to see him, and this was certainly not one of them.

"Tell me, Sergeant Cohen, how did Zanah Fahury die?"

"It was a robbery, Ms. Barnea."

"That's *Commander* Barnea, Sergeant, and that wasn't what I asked you. How was the women killed? Shot? Stabbed? Beaten? Blunt force trauma to the head, perhaps?"

"She was beaten to death. I believe her head was caved in."

"You *believe*?"

"My investigation is still in the preliminary stages."

"After three days?"

"I've been backed up."

Danielle rose and came around the front of her desk so she could glare down at Cohen. "You're sure it was a simple robbery, Sergeant?"

Cohen squirmed in his chair. "All indications point to that, yes."

"And how was the victim dressed when she was found?"

"In shabby clothes."

"So a poor Arab woman wearing shabby clothes was the target of a robbery. Have I got that right?"

Cohen fidgeted nervously again. "Why am I here, Commander?"

"Because a murder was committed in your jurisdiction that has not been properly followed up. The reason for this must be either incompetence on your part or the fact that the victim was an Arab. I'm curious as to which, Sergeant."

"Neither, Commander," Cohen said, less defensively than Danielle expected. "Since the woman was a resident of Umm al Fahm—"

"I'll ask you again, what evidence do you have that this was a robbery?"

"The pockets in the victim's coat were turned inside out."

"Empty?"

"Except for her identification card, yes."

"What about in the vicinity of the body?"

"Just a bus ticket for Jerusalem. But we have no way of knowing whether or not it was hers."

"Did you check to see if it matched her fingerprints?"

"No."

"Then you do have a way, don't you? What about speaking with the victim's neighbors in Umm al Fahm, others who knew her?"

"We interviewed witnesses on the scene."

"Witnesses?"

"The couple who found her body."

"In an alley."

"That's right."

"How long had it been there?"

"I'm not sure."

"You called the medical examiner, yes?"

"We transported the body."

"And the crime scene?"

Silence.

"The crime scene, Sergeant Cohen, you secured it, of course."

"No, Commander, we didn't."

"Because the victim was Arab or was from outside Jerusalem? Both, I would imagine."

Cohen had no response.

"And her home, did you check out her home?"

Cohen remained silent.

"I would have thought in the matter of robbery, a check of the victim's personal possessions would be called for. So you've never seen her home, have you, Sergeant? You never bothered to go to Umm al Fahm."

"No, Commander," Cohen said in a muffled voice.

"But you have her address. Please tell me you at least know that much from the ID you found on her person."

Cohen nodded.

"Then let's take a ride to Umm al Fahm and see what we find, eh, Sergeant?"

CHAPTER 23

Ben settled back into the front seat of the car holding a pair of coffees he'd purchased at a convenience store down the street.

"Did you find what you were looking for?" his brother asked, accepting the cup Ben held out to him.

"There's a fire escape in the back of the building," Ben reported, "but no exterior door leading to the upstairs apartment. That means the only way in is a set of stairs inside the building off the kitchen."

"Which explains why Latif tracked flour into the other apartment he moved out of."

"Exactly. If I'm right, he must have a key to the building. Comes and goes as he pleases through the kitchen."

Sayeed gazed across the street at the bakery again. "I

have never gone into this place, know nothing of the owner."

"I'm betting he's part of Hamas's network here in the States. An underling who provides a safe house when requested. You can bet Latif isn't the first to have stayed here."

"So, if you're right, we'll see Latif when he returns."

"*You'll* see him. I won't because I have no idea what he looks like, which explains why you are still here, my brother."

Sayeed shifted uneasily. His gaze drifted across the street, to the second-floor windows of the building. "The blinds are still drawn. He must not be home."

"Hamas teaches their agents to keep the blinds closed at all times, so their possessions can not be seen or photographed from afar."

"That's how you knew he was hiding out in *this* bakery."

"It's how I narrowed down the list, yes. I won't know for sure if Latif is staying here until he comes back." Ben settled back in the driver's seat and sipped his coffee. "Which could take a while."

TWO HOURS past nightfall, Mohammed Latif had still not shown up. The bakery had closed an hour earlier, only a single light left burning. In the night, even through the drawn blinds, Ben could tell no lights were on inside the second-floor apartment. He was beginning to doubt the validity of his own conclusions. Perhaps he had rushed to judgment, wanting too badly to spare his brother and family the agony of a State Department investigation. In the past eighteen months, Arab men had been detained indefinitely for far less than Sayeed was already guilty of. If he failed to deliver Latif to Lewan-thall, Ben feared that that was the fate awaiting his brother.

He had already lost Danielle to Hollis Buchert and his thugs at Pine Valley. She had saved his life and been forced to flee as a result. In trying to keep her with him, he had effectively lost her forever.

Lights shone in the rearview mirror, snapping Ben alert again. He reached up and adjusted the mirror slightly to eyeball a car that had slowed behind him, a block back. The car idled for a long moment before pulling up into a no-parking zone. A match sparked inside the car, the lighting of a cigarette enough for Ben to clearly discern at least three shapes: two in the front and one, he thought, in the back.

Sayeed stirred restlessly, started to stretch his arms, when Ben lashed a hand across the seat to restrain him.

"What are you doing?"

"Stay low in the seat and don't move. A car with three men inside just parked on the block behind us."

Sayeed turned slowly to look out the rear window but saw nothing through the darkness. He turned back to Ben and saw him pressing a number into his cell phone.

"You're calling for help," Sayeed said hopefully.

"Not exactly."

"Yes," a voice greeted.

"It's Ben Kamal, Lewanthall."

"You have news concerning Latif? Already?"

"Go fuck yourself. I know what's going on."

"Pardon me?"

"You've been following me all along. I find Latif and you send your thugs to pick him up. That wasn't part of the deal."

"I don't know what you're talking about."

Ben hesitated. "If you're lying to me . . ."

"I'm not."

Ben checked the rearview mirror again, the three shapes barely discernible in the light cast by a flickering street lamp.

"Are they in a car, Mr. Kamal? Can you get me a license plate?"

"I'm too far away."

"What about help, backup?"

A man approached the bakery on a bicycle and slid to a halt at the front door. Sayeed reached over and grabbed Ben's forearm.

"It's too late," Ben told Lewanthall. "Latif's here."

CHAPTER 24

B en started the engine and pulled away from the curb.

"Why are we leaving?" Sayeed asked him.

"We're not."

"*Kamal!*" Lewanthall's voice blared over the cell phone. "*Kamal, can you hear me?*"

Ben hit END and slipped the phone back into his pocket. Then he swung the car into the street, driving carefully so as not to attract the attention of the men in the car parked behind him. He caught a glimpse of Mohammed Latif dragging his bike through the bakery door, thought he might have seen the flicker of a dome light in the dark sedan, one of its doors opening.

Sayeed twisted to look behind him. "Who the fuck are they?"

Ben pulled down a narrow side street and then squeezed his rental into a back alley that separated the bakery building from a cluster of tenements at its rear. His mind strayed to Danielle's tale of Akram Khalil, the terrorist for whom Latif was working, being gunned down by a similarly mysterious group.

"Stay here!" he ordered his brother, starting to climb out through the driver's door he had thrust open.

"The hell I will!"

"For your own good."

Sayeed tried to squeeze out the passenger side, but Ben had jammed the rental in too tightly to leave enough space, so he began to shimmy across the seat. "It's for *your* own good I'm coming: Latif doesn't know you. How do you suppose he'll react?"

Ben started to close the door behind him, then stopped, conceding his brother's point. "All right. Follow my lead and stay behind me."

Sayeed laid a single foot on the pavement and saw the drawn pistol in Ben's hand. Ben moved off toward the fire escape before he could react. He leaped to grab the bottom-most rung and used his arms to hoist himself upward. Almost to the second-story window, he gazed back to find Sayeed struggling to follow.

The window was locked, the blinds drawn. Ben jimmied the window, found it unlocked, and opened it enough to lower his right leg through. He contorted his frame to ease his left after it, had just felt it scrape wood when something slammed into his spine.

The brunt of the blow fell on his right hip, deadening that leg for the moment while likely saving his vertebrae from cracking. Ben tumbled to the floor, struck it hard with nothing to break his fall. Flashes exploded before his eyes, his breath sucked out of him. He thought he might have momentarily passed out; came to, first to the realization that he still held the pistol in his hand and, second, to Sayeed's pleading voice.

"It's me, Mohammed, it's me!"

Sayeed Kamal must have climbed in through the window after him, and now Ben watched his brother approach Mohammed Latif with hands held open before him. Latif grabbed hold of his shoulder and spun Sayeed around, holding Ben's brother around the neck with one hand, while the other pressed a pistol to his skull.

"Stay where you are! Don't move!" Latif screamed in Arabic when he saw Ben begin to stir on the floor. "The gun! Drop it!"

Ben did as he was told.

"Push it away from you."

Ben shoved the pistol across the pockmarked wood.

"Now, sit up. Slowly."

Ben arched his back and felt pain explode down his spine, grimacing. A baseball bat rolled back and forth on the floor between him and Latif, obviously the weapon that had done the damage.

"Who is he, Sayeed?" Latif demanded.

"My, my brother."

"Your *brother*?" The terrorist's piercing dark eyes found Ben again, then rotated back to Sayeed. "What did you tell him about me? *What did you tell him about me?*" Latif dragged Sayeed across the floor without waiting for an answer, jerking his neck back further. "Are there others? Are there more?"

"Three," Ben said, before Sayeed had a chance to answer. "Outside, but they're not with us."

Latif yanked Sayeed to the front window and pulled the drawn shade back just far enough to peer into the street. "I can't see them. . . ."

"Let us help you," Sayeed pleaded.

Latif smacked him in the temple with the gun barrel. Sayeed's knees buckled and he nearly collapsed. "Liar! You brought them here! You must have!"

"No," Sayeed said, still grimacing in pain. "You can still make this right. Let us help you."

"Help me? You can't. No one can. The others are all dead. We were deceived. Khalil realized this, but by the time he reached me, it was too late. I had already made the delivery."

"What delivery?" Sayeed asked, holding Ben back with his eyes. "Tell us what you're talking about. Let us help you!"

Latif's grip on Sayeed slackened. "It's too late. After the ones outside, others will come. Khalil warned me, and now he is dead too."

"He feared for his own life?"

"The last time I spoke with him he did. He said something about making an enemy he wasn't expecting."

Ben nodded, trying to recall exactly what Danielle had said about Akram Khalil's executioners. "Why?"

"A disagreement with a superior, maybe."

"Khalil answered to a superior?"

"Well, not a superior exactly. It's been so long, let me just collect my thoughts. He was obsessed by our latest project, getting what we needed to do more harm to America than anyone had ever done."

"You're saying *that's* what you delivered?" Ben demanded.

"We couldn't be blamed, you see," Latif said. "Khalil had figured it all out. Someone else to do the work of God for us. But now this. It makes *no sense*!"

"Let me go, Mohammed," Sayeed Kamal said quite calmly. "We can still get you out of this. I promise."

Latif sighed and had just released his grasp on Sayeed when the door to the apartment burst open, splintered wood flying in all directions. Latif spun around, retraining his pistol, just as a stitch of automatic fire tore into his midsection. Ben thought he could see the orange trails of bullets, actually *see* them draw flecks of smoke from Latif's clothes.

The force of the bullets slammed Latif backward into

Sayeed, knocking Sayeed over and sparing him from the next barrage, which tore into Latif's neck and face before shattering the windows over the bakery's facade.

A pair of dark figures spun into the room.

Ben dragged himself to the side, managed to recover his pistol as his numb leg betrayed him and gave out. He fired from the floor, before the killers had recorded his presence. Fired and kept firing.

He didn't aim consciously, just shot at the shapes twisting in the apartment's darkness. The echoes stung his ears, left them ringing. But Ben had enough hearing left to make out the *thwacks* of his bullets striking home and the sizzling of bullets fired by the killers in desperation before they fell.

"Sayeed!" he called, pushing himself painfully to his knees, his ears ringing from the percussion of the gunshots.

"Here," the weak, terrified voice of his brother replied.

"Are you all right? Are you hit?"

"No. I mean, I'm . . . fine. I'm okay."

His brother pushed Latif's corpse from him and staggered to his feet. He stumbled across the floor and looped an arm around Ben's shoulders to help him rise.

The pain brought tears to Ben's eyes, but he could feel and put pressure on his leg again, the numbness subsiding.

Ben leaned back against the wall adjacent to the window he had shattered. He looked at the two men he had killed, feeling nothing, thinking instead of the third man they must have left in the car.

"Let's go," Ben said, snapping a fresh clip into his Sig.

"You can't even stand straight up," Sayeed argued. "Let me—"

"Stay back from the window," Ben ordered. "I'm going out first."

Ben eased himself forward, careful not to put too much pressure on his damaged leg. He held the gun as steady as he could, angled toward the half-open window through which he had entered the apartment just minutes before.

Ben caught a glimpse of his own reflection flickering in the glass the moment before it exploded inward, raining shards upon him as he threw himself to the floor.

CHAPTER 25

Another spray of automatic fire rocketed toward Sayeed, who went down hard, as if his legs had been yanked out from beneath him.

"Sayeed!"

"I'm all right! I'm all right!"

"The door!" Ben rasped at him from across the floor. "Move for the door! And *stay down!*"

Crawling, Sayeed reached the corridor just ahead of Ben, rising to his feet and banging into the bicycle Mohammed Latif had rested against the wall. The bike clattered to the floor of the bare hall, and Ben pushed it aside when he climbed back to his feet.

He grabbed Sayeed by the arm and drew him toward the stairwell, keeping his gun poised toward the door above as they descended. Heard the crunch of bullet-shattered window glass under heavy shoes and knew the third gunman had entered the apartment through the fire escape seconds before a fresh barrage of gunfire whizzed at them down the stairs.

He and Sayeed ran into the bakery kitchen, losing

their bearings briefly in the darkness. The scents, paradoxically, were sweet and fragrant. Supplies for tomorrow's wares mixing with today's leftovers stacked neatly on trays and long aluminum sheets.

Ben limped toward the double doors leading out of the kitchen, his injured leg board-stiff and hot with pain. Around him commercial vats and mixing machines cast giant shadows on the walls, watched over by jars and containers holding the ingredients that would eventually produce breads and pastries.

When Ben and Sayeed were halfway to the doors, the jars and containers closest to them exploded, spewing their contents in all directions and spraying the walls with baker's chocolate and white flour that left a cloud-like residue in the air. Ben hunched low, steadied his gun hand on the doorway they had burst through, and fired it blindly.

A supply door snapped open and boxes tumbled out, right into the path of a man charging into the kitchen as Ben and Sayeed darted from it. Ben saw the front door was locked even before his brother's grasp failed to budge it. He turned abruptly and lunged back through the double doors straight into the path of the third gunman.

He emptied the rest of his clip into the gunman before the man could squeeze his own trigger and watched him plummet to the floor, sending a fresh wave of flour wafting into the air.

Ben pushed back through the double doors in time to see Sayeed tossing a chair through the window, then accepted his brother's help in asing past the wedding cakes on display through the shattered glass. He still had only a single good leg to balance his weight, so Sayeed half carried him around to the alley, where Ben's rental car was parked.

"You drive," he told Sayeed when they reached the

driver's door. "The keys are in the ignition."

His brother helped Ben inside and waited for him to ease himself across the seat before climbing in behind the wheel. Ben cursed himself for not backing the car into the alleyway to assure a faster getaway, but there was nothing he could do about that now. He thought of Lewanthall from the State Department, started to reach in his pocket for his cell phone as Sayeed jammed the car into reverse.

A screech sounded behind them and Ben turned to see the dark sedan jerk to a halt at the head of the alley, blocking their way. A burst of gunfire blew out the rear window and Ben angled his pistol as best he could through the blasted glass.

A fourth man! There had been a fourth man in the car!

"Keep going!" he ordered Sayeed and opened fire.

The rental scraped against the passenger side of the alley, jostling Ben and throwing his aim off. His hip exploded anew in fiery pain, but he chewed it down and kept shooting.

"Shit!" Sayeed gasped, and twisted the wheel too much to the left, throwing the car into a fishtail that crumpled its rear quarter panel against the driver's side of the alley.

Fresh fire boomed from inside the dark sedan, and Ben reached over, clamped a hand atop his brother's head, and forced it downward. Their car spun wildly and now the windshield exploded too, glass raining out atop the hood as the car's rear end slammed broadside into the sedan and shoved it all the way across the street.

Ben rose over the seat and fired the remainder of his bullets into the darkness, watching them dig holes in the sedan's already shattered windshield.

"Go! Go! Go!" he screamed to his brother, remembering he carried only one spare clip, which was now exhausted.

Sayeed grasped the wheel and jammed the rental into drive. Ben felt it buck in protest, its tires squealing before it lurched forward. He kept his eyes locked on the sedan shrinking behind them, expecting any moment for it to burst to life and give chase.

But the sedan remained motionless, angled across the edge of the side street atop a bed of its own shattered glass.

Ben pulled his cell phone from his pocket and hit REDIAL, eyes peeled back toward the sedan until Sayeed swung round the corner and it was gone from view.

Lewanthall's number rang and rang.

Went unanswered.

CHAPTER 26

Danielle turned to the owner of the old apartment building in Umm al Fahm before fitting the key he had provided into Zanah Fahury's lock.

"Please wait for us downstairs," she instructed, and the man gratefully retreated to the stairs. An Israeli-Arab as well, he was clearly unsettled by the presence of someone from National Police. He lived off the small rents he was able to charge and spent his life doing his best to avoid trouble with the authorities.

Located fifteen miles north of Jerusalem, the village of Umm al Fahm was home to a small number of the 1.4 million Palestinians living inside Israel as citizens. In theory they were due the same rights and services as all Israeli citizens but in practice, Danielle knew, that was far from the case.

The violence of the past few years had created an atmosphere of mistrust in which Israeli government behavior vacillated between isolation and harassment. Social services had been cut back drastically. A long-planned project to replace Umm al Fahm's septic systems with sewers had been postponed indefinitely. Although this village had been spared the terrible toll taken by tanks and bulldozers in the West Bank, the streets were badly in need of repaving and huge pools of water had formed near drainage ditches the public works department had not cleared. The police and army maintained no real presence, other than an occasional patrol meant to identify any agitators. Almost everyone in Umm al Fahm, after all, had relatives in the besieged West Bank or Gaza. The resulting guilt by association adopted by the government had led to feelings of hate and mutual distrust on both sides, much to the dismay of officials like Danielle, who were powerless to do anything about it.

The door to Zanah Fahury's apartment gave after a slight thrust from Danielle, and she entered just ahead of Sergeant Ehud Cohen. Barely over the threshold, she froze. She had expected the apartment to be poorly furnished with what little a poor old woman could afford or keep patched together.

It was anything but.

The furniture was strikingly elegant, a couch and overstuffed chair covered with matching suede. The wooden end and coffee tables were big and boxy, terribly out of style and from another era, but Western in design as was everything else. The room had the look and feel of a museum and, although Danielle was no expert, she guessed much of the furniture would fit nicely in one of the more lavish of Jerusalem's antique stores. There was an old grandfather clock no longer in operation, and shelves of old books preserved in perfect condition.

The furniture had been squeezed in, too much of it for this small room, leaving barely any space between the pieces. Danielle took a few steps forward and found herself atop a plush Oriental carpet that showed not a speck of dust.

"So, Sergeant Cohen," Danielle began, putting her own thoughts together. "Our poor murder victim was apparently not so poor. Do you have any explanation for this?"

"No, Commander."

"That's right. You never spoke with the old woman's friends or neighbors?"

"By all accounts, she had no friends."

"And you never bothered to speak with the neighbors."

"Why should I? Arabs are never forthcoming in our interviews with them."

"Zanah Fahury was an Israeli citizen. She deserved better, and we're going to make sure she gets it," Danielle said, the conviction clear in her voice.

Cohen followed sheepishly as Danielle entered the dead woman's bedroom. A queen-sized bed had been jammed into the small room, leaving just enough floor space for a single large bureau. To one side was a small closet with a curtain drawn before it. Danielle eased it open and stepped back so Cohen could see.

"What do you make of these, Sergeant?"

"An extensive collection."

Danielle ran a hand gently across the fabrics. "Old, long out of style . . ." She leaned in closer and sniffed. ". . . and, judging by the slight scent of mothballs, many of them not worn for some years."

"I . . . don't know what to make of this."

"Neither do I, Sergeant. That's why we investigate murders. That's what detectives are for."

"So it could have been a robbery gone bad. The crime may not have been random at all."

"That's right. But where was Zanah Fahury going? What draws a recluse out of her apartment?"

"I don't know."

"Maybe the building owner can tell us."

"YOU'LL NOTICE that I have not brought a pad with me to take notes," Danielle told the building owner downstairs in his apartment. "I will not write your name down and I have already forgotten it, because I'm not interested in your identity, only your answers. Is that clear?"

The man nodded, looking somewhat reassured.

"Good," she continued, as Ehud Cohen looked on. "How well did you know Zanah Fahury?"

"Not well at all."

"How long has she lived here?"

"I'm not sure. I took over this building after my uncle was arrested by the Je—" The landlord cut himself off. "Er, by the Israeli authorities."

"And when was that?"

"A year ago. Zanah Fahury had already been a tenant for many, many years before that."

"Did you ever see the inside of her apartment?"

"No."

"Not even after she was murdered?"

"Her rent is paid through the year. Her apartment is not mine to enter."

Paid through the year, Danielle noted. Another anomaly for a woman who was by all indications a poor recluse.

"How often did you see her?"

"Almost never. She hardly ever went out. She had no phone. I don't know if she had a television."

"But you did see her leave the building."

"Not very often. Once in a while. Every few months, I think."

"Shopping?"

The landlord shook his head. "I saw her return a few times, never carrying anything."

"What did she do about food?"

"She paid extra to have it delivered."

"She ever have visitors?"

"Never."

"And you have no idea where she might have gone on her rare excursions?"

"None, I'm afraid."

"Don't be," Danielle said and started for the door. "We won't be bothering you again."

"I TOLD you it was a waste of time, Commander," Sergeant Cohen said when they were back outside.

"You must not have been listening to the interview I conducted, Sergeant."

"Commander?"

"The old woman goes out and comes back with nothing in hand. What does that tell you, Sergeant?"

Cohen stood there dumbly.

"It should tell you that if she wasn't bringing something back," Danielle continued, "perhaps she was taking something out with her."

Before she could continue, Danielle's cell phone rang—a staple for every Israeli, even more common, she had heard remarked once, than guns.

"Barnea."

"It's David Vordi, Commander." Danielle recognized his slightly nasal voice. "I hope I'm not disturbing you."

"Not at all, Minister."

"We need to meet."

"I can come right over."

"No, not at the ministry. Somewhere more private. Shall we say the Bistro on Mahane Yehuda?"

"I suppose."

"I'll see you there in an hour."

CHAPTER 27

The café wasn't crowded, and Danielle saw David Vordi rise from a corner booth when she entered. He beckoned her to join him, smiling as if she were an old friend.

"Would you like to order something?" he asked after she had sat down. "The pastries are the best in the city."

"I'd like to know why you wanted to see me."

"At least some coffee," he tried.

"Please, Minister," Danielle said stiffly.

Vordi frowned. "How was your dinner last night?"

Danielle felt a flutter in her stomach. Did Vordi know she had dined with Colonel al-Asi? "Is that what you wanted to see me about?" she asked, pushing the tentativeness from her voice.

"Should it be? I like to think I can trust my people, that it isn't necessary to keep tabs on them."

"Where is this going?"

Vordi looked at Danielle's hands crossed atop the table. "I'm the one who brought you back here, Danielle. I'm the one who fought on your behalf. There's a lot on the line here for both of us, a line you seem determined to keep crossing."

"I'm doing the job you called me back here to do."

Vordi's eyes narrowed. "I was hoping we could enjoy a more honest . . . relationship."

"I'm sorry if I've disappointed you."

"I went out on a limb. I'd like to feel that's appreciated."

"If you mean—"

"There has been a complaint lodged against you by the chief of the Jerusalem police. He was quite adamant about his displeasure over your interference in one of his cases."

Danielle breathed slightly easier. "Which case was he referring to?"

"The murder of an old woman named Zanah Fahury. Could you explain your involvement?"

"Zanah Fahury's murder was not being actively investigated."

"She was an Israeli-Arab, correct?"

"That's right.

"Our resources are stretched precariously thin already, Commander. You and I both know it's a question of priorities."

"No murder investigation in Jerusalem should be allowed to be lost in bureaucratic cracks."

"Others in the Ministry of Justice might not see things that way." Vordi stiffened, his expression sliding from harsh to almost sad. "I can only go so far on your behalf, Danielle, without receiving consideration in kind. Don't push me."

"I wasn't aware I had."

Vordi frowned slightly in displeasure. "No? What

about those pages you recovered from Akram Khalil's hideout yesterday?"

"Have you received the translation?"

"I was about to ask you the same question." He paused, as if choosing his next words carefully. "Last night a fax message nearly three minutes in duration was logged from your line to a number in Boston, Massachusetts, registered to the private security firm you were briefly employed by."

Danielle swallowed hard.

"I am going to assume that the message was sent to your former Palestinian associate, Ben Kamal. Yes or no?"

"What's the difference?"

"Plenty, because right now I'm the only one in the Ministry of Justice who knows about this."

Because you're the only one keeping tabs on me, Danielle almost said.

"But you can see how such a thing would look to those in the ministry who were against your return to begin with, especially coupled with your insistence on looking into an Arab's murder. I can't hold them back forever, Danielle, especially without a reason to."

"And I thought you asked me here to have coffee . . ."

Vordi scowled at her. "I'm starting to regret calling you back."

"I'm starting to regret coming."

Vordi shook his head, slightly disturbing the wavy curls that draped over his ears and hung slightly toward his brow. "You still haven't learned to choose your battles . . . or your friends."

"Is that what you want to be, Minister, my friend?"

"I already am, Danielle. But I won't be much longer."

"Is that a warning?"

"See, you prove my point for me. Everything to you

must be a confrontation. I only want what's best for the both of us."

Danielle felt heat building behind her cheeks. "Which includes having dinner together, or maybe just coffee."

"You would prefer we keep things strictly professional, then," Vordi said, his voice drooped in concession.

"Yes, I would."

Vordi rose, nearly tipping his chair over backward. "Fine. Then understand that conducting unauthorized raids and corresponding with unauthorized parties will no longer be tolerated. I know how much being named commissioner means to you . . . Commander. You would be wise to consider your actions with that in mind in the future."

Danielle kept her voice even. "Thank you for your advice, Minister."

CHAPTER 28

"What now?" Sayeed asked, parked on the street across from the Hyatt Regency-Dearborn, a perfectly manicured lawn separating them from the hotel entrance.

"As soon as I'm out of the car, drive to the Marriott Hotel, leave the car, get into the next cab that stops there, and go home. Pack up your family and hide."

"Hide *where*?"

"You have friends in Dearborn, Sayeed. More favors to call in than you could use in a lifetime from people who are good at this sort of thing, and both of us know it."

"So my contacts can do some good at last," Sayeed said ironically.

"Your contacts are what got you into this."

"You think I'll be targeted?"

"I don't know, I don't know. There's someone else involved here besides Khalil, Hamas, and the State Department. And whoever it is killed Latif."

"What was this delivery, Bayan? What was Latif talking about?"

"Let me figure that out. You just worry about getting yourself and your family to safety."

Sayeed gazed across the seat, trapped between emotions. "They're your family too, my brother."

Ben managed a smile and tried to look reassuring. "Call my cell phone number when you're settled. And if something goes wrong, if for any reason you can't reach me . . ."

"What?"

"Get to our cabin on Saginaw Bay."

"Of all places," Sayeed muttered.

"Exactly. Get to the cabin and I'll meet you there."

Ben tried to open the passenger-side door. The pounding the car had taken made it stick until he thrust his shoulder against it and climbed out, grimacing from a fresh bolt of pain in his leg.

"Let me help you inside," Sayeed offered through the open window.

"No," Ben ordered, leaving no room for doubt. "Get your wife, my niece and nephew, and our mother, and find somewhere safe to go. Tonight. *Now!* "

"Very well," Sayeed agreed. "Bayan?"

"What?"

"Nothing. We'll talk tomorrow."

Ben stood on the street until his brother drove off. Then he started toward the hotel, taking the circular route to it on the sidewalk. The Hyatt Regency was an anchor of the Fairlane Town Center, twenty-five hundred-acre complex of businesses, shops, and entertainment establishments built directly across from Ford's corporate headquarters.

The pain seemed to lessen with each stride, his leg and hip both loosening. His mind was something else again. The fact that the night's events might have put his remaining family in jeopardy made the events of ten years ago seem like they had happened only yesterday. He had lost his own wife and children then, and forgotten in the years during his self-imposed exile that he had any more family left to lose. The reality that he did struck him hard and fast now as he cursed himself for not standing up to Lewanthall's veiled threats.

Lewanthall had come at him with the mentality he had tried to leave behind in Palestine, where individuals shrank next to the awesome power of the state to do to them what it wished. Again and again only the power of Colonel Nabril al-Asi had spared Ben the wrath of his enemies. But this was the United States, where the sanctity of the individual was protected by laws, and rights remained sacrosanct. He had let Lewanthall scare and threaten him. He had let the power of the State Department manipulate him into enlisting his brother's aid in what had become a life-threatening mission.

Ben reached the elevator and pressed four. The pain in his leg and hip had been reduced to just a dull ache now, as if his anger had flushed it out. He would call the State Department first thing tomorrow morning, go over Lewanthall's head, and tell them all to go fuck themselves.

The thought of doing that actually brought a smile to

Ben's face as he inserted his key card into its slot, watched the light go green, and opened the door.

"Don't turn on the light," a voice he recognized as Alan Lewanthall's said from the corner of the room.

CHAPTER 29

"You switched off your phone," Ben said, closing the door behind him, too startled to let his rage tumble outward.

Lewanthall sat in a chair he'd moved to the corner of the room facing the door. An overcoat wrapped his body like a blanket. A cloud of smoke hung over him, drifting slowly across the room.

"I wasn't alone," Lewanthall explained, raising a cigarette to his mouth and then flicking the ashes to the carpet. "I couldn't afford to have any attention drawn to me."

"Latif is dead."

"I figured."

"You knew the men I called you about were *killers*, didn't you?"

"Never mind that."

"Answer my question!"

"I thought there was a pretty good possibility of that, yes."

"And you chose not to warn me?"

"If I had warned you how dangerous this was, would you have gone through with it?"

"No."

"Then there's your answer." Lewanthall took another

drag of his cigarette. "Now, at the apartment, did you find anything, did Latif talk?"

"He said something about a delivery."

"What kind of delivery?"

"I don't know. Now it's your turn. You knew the man who sent Latif here, Akram Khalil, was dead, didn't you?"

"Not until last night, after we met."

"But you knew Latif was in grave danger. Right or wrong?"

"It's not that simple. The possibility existed, yes, only—"

"Cut the double-talk! I know what this is about now. There's a plot against America and Latif was in the center of it."

Ben could see the shock on Lewanthall's face from across the room. "How could you *know* that?"

"Because Akram Khalil had a *fatwa* in his Gaza hideout, an edict giving him permission to bring about the Last of Days—here, in the United States."

"Oh my God . . ."

"You're talking to me now, not Him."

"You don't understand."

"I understand you knew about this plot all along and didn't mention a damn thing about it in Boston yesterday."

"Would you like to help me stop it, Mr. Kamal?" Lewanthall asked with a strange calm.

"Is that what I'm here for?"

Lewanthall dropped the cigarette to the carpet and stamped it out. "Just answer my questions, starting with this delivery Latif mentioned. Did he say anything else about it, anything at all?"

"Nothing."

"Think, for God's sake!"

Lewanthall started to come out of his chair until Ben

stormed forward into the last of the cigarette smoke wafting forward.

"Listen to me, you son of a bitch, my family's involved in this now. Our discussion's finished until you get them to someplace safe, somewhere they can be protected. You hear what I'm saying?"

Lewanthall sat back down. "Lower your voice. I hear you."

"Good."

"But there's nothing I can do."

Ben took a few steps closer, the pained grimace on his face adding to the single-mindedness of his order. "I must not be hearing *you*."

"I didn't say I wouldn't; I said I *can't*."

"Bullshit! You're the goddamn State Department! Pick up the phone and call somebody."

"There's no one to call," Lewanthall said feebly. "No backup, no help, no reinforcements."

"You're not making any sense!"

"None of this makes any sense," Lewanthall shot back and instantly lowered his voice. "It didn't in the beginning and it doesn't now. We knew that, *I* knew that, but it didn't stop me."

"What are you talking about?"

"Sit down, Mr. Kamal." Lewanthall sighed, no longer trying to sound calm. "This is going to take a while to explain. . . ."

CHAPTER 30

Layla Aziz Rahani had just sat down for dinner at Bolo in the Chelsea section of New York City, when a tall, broad-shouldered man entered from Twenty-second Street and approached her table.

"Expecting someone, *Sayyida* Rahani?" he asked, looming over her.

"Karim Amir Matah... What a pleasant surprise! Please, Major, pull up a chair."

Matah scrutinized the long, narrow restaurant, scanning those seated at tables as well as those at the bar.

"It's you I was expecting," Rahani continued. "Please, sit down."

Matah stiffly took the chair across from her but didn't pull it in under the table.

"You won't need to see a menu because, I suspect, you won't be staying long." Layla leaned forward and cupped her chin in her hands. "I'm sure the Saudi secret service will understand. Can I assume you're here for my protection, dispatched by the royal family to make sure no harm comes to me while visiting the United States?"

Karim Amir Matah wrinkled his nose, frowning. "In Riyadh, *sayyida,* wearing those clothes would be grounds for arrest and incarceration."

"Which I'm sure you and my brother would be more than happy to arrange."

"He has informed me of your father's ... condition."

Layla tried not to show any reaction. "Tell me, Major,

do you remember the last time you came to see me in the United States? I believe it was in the hospital."

Matah nodded. "Many years ago, *sayyida.*"

"It doesn't seem like that many to me. You were what, a lieutenant then?"

"I was."

"My father, I believe, was instrumental in securing your current position. He was always grateful for your help."

"As I was for his. But you are in this country illegally, *sayyida.*"

"Which my brother was kind enough to inform you of, I'm sure."

"Your actions disappoint him as well."

"Do you know my brother, Major?"

"We've spoken."

"Oldest son of my father's second wife. He would have you believe he is going to take my father's place in the line of succession." Layla Aziz Rahani leaned slightly across the table. "I'm going to let you in on a little secret, Major. My father has left detailed instructions about that line of succession and it is I who has been chosen to succeed Abdullah Aziz Rahani. You would be wise to remember that."

Matah sat across from her, unmoved. "Your brother wishes you to return to Riyadh immediately. Your plane is ready. I am to escort you to the airport."

"Perhaps you didn't hear what I just said, Major."

"I heard, *sayyida.*"

"Then . . ."

"It is not for me to say."

"What isn't for you to say, Major?" When Matah failed to respond, Layla Aziz Rahani added. "My father sent you to my side fifteen years ago because he trusted you. May I trust you as well?"

"I am here at your brother's bequest," Matah said stiffly. "I serve at his discretion."

"*His* discretion? What's happened? What's going on?"

Major Matah rose and clumsily smoothed out the folds on his suit jacket. "I will be in a car outside. Please enjoy your meal, *sayyida*. I'll be waiting."

DAY FIVE

CHAPTER 31

"*If you wanted to catch terrorists, what would you do?*"

With that question the night before, Alan Lewanthall had begun his explanation of what he had involved Ben in, the truth behind an operation that left the State Department unreachable for them. An hour later Ben left the hotel without checking out, walked five blocks, and hailed a cab, which took him to a small motel with a VACANCY sign. He checked in, paid cash for a decent room with cable television, and soaked in bathwater as hot as he could stand, glad to be rid of the smell of his own blood and sweat.

He lay awake for hours, replaying the final part of his conversation with Lewanthall over and over again.

"If you wanted to catch terrorists, what would you do?" Lewanthall had lit another cigarette, while Ben considered the answer.

"Why don't you tell me?"

"You'd form a group meant to attract the cells that live in the shadows, waiting to be activated. The radicals whose one purpose in life is to do this country harm.

"Operation Flypaper," Lewanthall resumed after a brief pause to let his words sink in. "That's what we called it. We brought Operation Flypaper to the State Department hierarchy in the wake of 9/11 on the pretext of sucking in Al-Qaeda elements, their sleeper cells, and then killing them."

"But the hierarchy didn't go for it, did they?"

"A few of them did. Not enough. The ones behind us, well, let's just say they supported our desire to bring it about without sanction."

"And without backup," Ben added, starting to seethe.

"We had backup. What State wanted was deniability if anything went wrong. You know how Washington works."

"Not really."

"It's competitive as hell, and nobody trusts anybody else. Worse, everyone's afraid to step forward and get things done because it means laying your ass, and your neck, on the line. We didn't care about that. For us the bigger picture—ferreting out and trapping the terrorists determined to destroy the country and our way of life— was more important."

Ben's eyes had begun to adjust to the darkness, enough to see the agitation in Lewanthall's eyes, not just hear it in his voice. "What went wrong?"

"Nothing," the man from the State Department said, taking a deep drag of his cigarette. "The operation went *too* well. *That* was the problem."

"Keep talking."

"We dug deep into their world, laid our own roads over theirs. Put out the word, just the way they do, using many of the same channels and conduits. It began to come together much faster than we'd ever imagined. We had them *trapped*! Hamas, Al-Qaeda, sucked in by bait they couldn't resist: the destruction of America."

"Every terrorist's dream."

"And we wanted them to think we could make it come true. We had the plan, the bait. It was risky but, Jesus Christ, the stakes called for it. You of all people should understand that."

"Why? Because I'm not a terrorist?"

If the remark stung Lewanthall, he didn't show it. "No, because the Arabs who are have made it impossible for you to fly on a plane without being searched. Have dinner in a restaurant without being watched. And they've bankrupted your people, killed your dreams. Hell, terrorists have done more damage to the people they claim to represent than anyone else."

"Wait a minute, you said you had *bait*?"

"That doesn't matter right now. What matters is we *had* them. Eight of the twenty most-wanted terrorists in the world, or their immediate representatives. We had them all. Videotapes, audiotapes, e-mail addresses, safe houses."

"Surveillance?"

Lewanthall shook his head and brushed the smoke from his face. "We didn't have the manpower."

"Because your operation wasn't authorized."

"Something would have leaked if it had been, something would have broken down. Don't you see? This way, only a few people had to know."

"And only a few people could help."

Ben could see Lewanthall squeeze his eyes closed through the darkness. "It still would have worked, *should* have worked."

"What went wrong?"

"We lost them."

"How, for God's sake?"

Lewanthall's face looked like that of a pale granite statue. "Somebody started killing the terrorists we'd sucked into our trap, each and every one."

"Like Akram Khalil," Ben realized.

"How do you know about Khalil?" Lewanthall demanded again.

"Never mind how I know. Yes or no? He was the one in charge of this cell you had trapped, wasn't he?"

"Yes," the man from the State Department confirmed. "Mohammed Latif was his ranking deputy here."

"What about this delivery Latif mentioned before he was killed?"

"It could only mean one thing." Lewanthall shifted in his chair and enough light caught his eyes for Ben to see them blinking rapidly. "We had to offer the terrorists something they wanted, something they couldn't get without us. Bring something to the table so they'd sit with us."

"What'd you bring, Mr. Lewanthall?"

The man from the State Department started to raise his cigarette back to his lips, then lowered it again. "Smallpox."

"YOU GAVE them *smallpox*?"

"No, for Christ's sake, we provided a plan to steal it. That was the bait."

"I thought all significant reserves of it were destroyed years ago."

"So did the terrorists, Mr. Kamal; that was the point. In fact, reserves, significant reserves of smallpox were maintained in the labs of USAMRIID on the grounds of Fort Detrick in Maryland."

"*Were*. You said *were*."

"Because they're gone," Lewanthall said, a quiver in his voice. "Somebody put our plan into action three days ago. The same time the terrorists started dying."

"THE LAST of Days," Ben muttered.

"Pardon me."

"Khalil had left papers behind, some sort of *fatwa*, a religious edict that gave him permission to bring on what the Koran calls the Last of Days. In the United States."

Lewanthall began fidgeting in his chair, his cigarette forgotten. "Khalil's plan would have been to have someone else release the smallpox for him, someone in this country, to deflect the blame from his group."

"That must have been the delivery Latif was talking about," Ben concluded. "Assume he masterminded the Fort Detrick theft, acting on Khalil's instructions. Only something went wrong."

The man from the State Department nodded rapidly. "Whoever's help Khalil enlisted decided to wipe out his network, any link back to the source. . . ."

"It's not that simple. Think about it, Lewanthall. Knocking off terrorists in this country is one thing, but getting Khalil at his hideout in the Gaza Strip?"

"What are you saying?"

Ben watched the cigarette burning down in Lewanthall's hand, the ashes lengthening. "Someone else is involved here. You asked me how I knew Akram Khalil was dead. An Israeli commando team found him and his guards all murdered when they arrived at his compound. Someone had beaten them to the task, someone who wanted to finish the job of covering the tracks that started here. Someone very, very good."

"We find the smallpox, stop the release, nothing else matters," the man from the State Department said weakly.

"We'll need help," Ben said pointedly.

"I'll have to bring Washington into the loop."

"That will mean your career, Mr. Lewanthall."

The man from the State Department almost smiled. "I can live with that."

CHAPTER 32

Exhausted, Ben at last fell asleep in his clothes atop the covers. He had made plans to meet Lewanthall that afternoon, long enough, he hoped, to give the man from the State Department time to brief his superiors on what the country was facing. They would rendezvous at Ford Field, where the annual Dearborn Homecoming celebration was going on. The celebration included a fairgroundslike atmosphere complete with carnival rides and crowds Ben could feel safe among, although he wondered if he'd ever feel safe again until all this was over.

His cell phone rang, the planned call from his brother awaking him at eight A.M. sharp. A car picked him up outside the motel an hour later, driven by a young man in his twenties Ben guessed was one of the Palestinian "students" Sayeed had sponsored in the States.

The young man had nothing to say, and Ben wasn't in the mood for conversation anyway. They passed dozens of restaurants on the way and Ben began to feel his stomach contracting, feel himself coming back to life with the first pangs of hunger, but resisted the temptation to stop for food.

Instead his driver wheeled onto the freeway, then took the exit for the suburb of Livonia, an area dominated by Palestinian Christians who had settled there after the initial influx that included the Kamal family. The homes were newer and slightly higher-end than those in Dearborn, testament to the sprawl of development to meet the needs of the growing Arab population of metropolitan Detroit.

The young man slowed as they approached a stately colonial revival house that could have been home to any middle-class suburban American family. Ben wondered why his brother had chosen to hide the family here, until he caught flecks of motion inside the windows along with the slight glint of gun barrels their wielders made no effort to conceal.

The guns were everywhere. The man who opened the door for Ben had one. So did the two watching the front and back windows. His brother greeted him away from the door, out of view from the street.

"Our mother is upstairs," Sayeed reported. "My wife and children too. I haven't told them very much."

Ben glanced up the stairs, the shadow of another gunman looming there. "Have you told them this is your fault?"

"No more than the nature of your involvement. But we're safe here," Sayeed assured him.

"Don't count on that. Things are worse than I thought."

"You spoke with the man from the State Department?"

"We talked."

"He couldn't help?"

"He will. I'll know more this afternoon."

Sayeed glanced up the stairs. "Our mother's been waiting to see you."

HIS MOTHER was upstairs, sitting near the door in one of the bedrooms the Kamal family had appropriated. Ben had not asked about this house, or the men guarding it, and his brother hadn't volunteered any information, because the only thing that mattered was that the closest family Ben had left in the world was safe.

His mother seemed to look older every time he saw her, after changing hardly at all over the course of the first thirty years of his life. Ben had thought returning to the States and visiting her more often would make the passage of time seem kinder. But it hadn't. She had been a young woman and then overnight she was old, the grasp on youth impossible to recover once it had slipped away. Her spine was bent slightly and inches seemed to melt from her frame with each of his visits. Her eyes and mind, though, remained as sharp as ever.

"I had more than my share of times like these with your father," she told him. "Jafir Kamal was a great man."

"You don't have to tell me that."

"No, but it helps me to say it. It's all I have left of him to convince me he didn't leave us and die back in Palestine for nothing."

"He died because he couldn't compromise his beliefs. That made him a threat."

Ben's mother stared at him pointedly. "You should learn from him, Bayan." A car raced down the street outside, tires squealing, and she tensed until the sound passed. "You and your brother never got along, you know," his mother continued. "Since you were babies, always fighting like cats and dogs. So different, no matter what your father and I did. We thought coming to America would make a difference. It didn't. Neither did your father's death. Or," she added, after swallowing a hefty breath, "the passing of your family and then Sayeed's son. Now you get along. The look on your faces, the way you talk to each other. It warms my heart."

"You don't look happy."

"Because look what it took. And because you can't

stop behaving like your father. Your brother has always accepted the fact that he is ordinary. That's why I believe the two of you never got along, because he couldn't accept that you were not. Then your father's death made him feel even more inferior to you, even though he was older. I think he has accepted that now." She sighed heavily. "Just as I accepted what I must."

"You speak in riddles."

His mother's strong yet weary eyes sought him out. "Like your father, you must always have your battles to fight. One after the other, no matter where you go, what path your life takes." She stopped and then started again just as quickly, her eyes darting with her mind. "The Israeli woman could not live with you, even here, in America?"

"Something happened."

"And if it hadn't?" his mother asked, not bothering to probe that subject further.

"She couldn't turn down the chance to run National Police. I told her she should go. To be happy."

"Implying she couldn't be with you, because, my son, she knows what I know. She figured it out a long time ago, even though she may not realize it. I understand, believe me. Listen to me and think on my words."

"I have, and it's not just who I am; it's who we both are. She lives for her battles too. It's not that we wait for them, just that we know they're coming."

"Warriors, both of you. Just like your father was."

"He couldn't help it, could he?"

"No more than you can. He was cursed by the ability to always see the bigger picture."

"The measure of a great man," he said.

"And often a lonely one. Even with his family Jafir Kamal was lonely." Her gaze turned quizzical. "Why is that, Bayan?"

"Because we were a part of his life, never all of it."

"When he left, though, he knew he had something to come back to. And that is what pains me about you, my son. You have left yourself nothing to come back to."

Ben took her wrinkled hands in his and held them tight. "But this time I'm not going anywhere."

CHAPTER 33

"It's that one right up there, Commander," Sergeant Ehud Cohen said to Danielle, directing her toward a tall, narrow building sloping up a rise in the Old City. "I'll wait outside if you want."

"You've spoken to the man inside?"

"Only to show him a picture of Zanah Fahury and ask if he recognized her."

Danielle gazed across the street, then back at the young detective. David Vordi's veiled threats aside, she had no intention of abandoning this investigation now. "I see you've had a change of heart, Sergeant."

"The fingerprints on the bus ticket to Jerusalem matched the dead woman's. And I was able to find a second bus driver who remembers picking her up at the central depot on Jaffa Street and taking her here to the Old City."

"Interesting he would remember a simple old woman."

"He said she had been taking his bus regularly for years."

"Every few months."

"Something like that. The driver remembered dropping her off always on this block. I interviewed the local

merchants and found one who recognized our victim."
Cohen's eyes drifted toward a third-floor jewelry shop.
"Up there."

"A lot of legwork to expend on the murder of an
Arab, Sergeant."

Cohen hesitated, then lowered his voice. "I didn't realize who you were. I've read about all your accomplish-
ments and the famous cases you've solved." He stopped,
but quickly started again, his mind shifting gears. "And
my grandfather knew your father."

"Your grandfather," Danielle repeated, realizing that
the young man before her came from an entirely different generation.

Cohen nodded. "They served together before your father became head of strategic planning."

"That won't matter if your superiors find out you're
cooperating with me."

"I don't really care what my superiors think anyway,"
the young detective continued obstinately.

"Then in that case, Sergeant," Danielle said to him
before crossing the street, "you should join me when I
question this shopkeeper whom you found."

They dodged the frantic, maddening traffic together
and climbed an outdoor set of stairs to a shop occupying
the topmost floor of the building, perched at an odd,
upward angle. The jewelry store had no sign advertising
its presence here, only thickly barred display windows
filled with the shop's wares. Elegant pieces that lacked
none of the glisten or glitter found in Stern's and more
prestigious jeweler's elsewhere in Jerusalem at considerably higher prices.

"Mr. Glickstein," Cohen said to a broad, bearded Has-
idim squeezed behind the counter, a jeweler's glass
pressed against his eye and a diamond in his hand, "this
is Commander Barnea of National Police."

"Nice to meet you," Glickstein greeted her, not looking up from his inspection of the diamond. "Just give me a minute."

It was at least that long before he eased the diamond into a padded case and lowered the jeweler's glass from his eye.

"We're here about Zanah Fahury," Cohen told him.

"A name that means nothing to me."

"The old woman who was murdered."

"I never knew her name. I told you that."

"We're wondering if robbery might have been a motive in her murder," Danielle said, speaking for the first time. "Something she purchased in your shop, perhaps."

"She didn't purchase anything here. She never purchased anything here."

"You saw her frequently?"

"Regularly. Sometimes every two months, sometimes every three, at most four. She seldom looked at me straight. Never smiled. Always hid her face with a head scarf." Here the man behind the counter made a motion with his hand before his cheeks. "I always recognized her from her eyes. Sad eyes. Lonely eyes."

"But she didn't buy anything from you," said Danielle, still trying to discern the murdered woman's purpose in coming here.

"Never."

"Then what—"

"She sold. She comes to me because I give a fair price. No haggling. No bickering."

Danielle exchanged a glance with Ehud Cohen before returning her gaze to the store's proprietor. "What was it she sold to you?"

The man plucked from the case the stone he'd been examining when they entered the shop. "Diamonds," he said, holding it outward. "Just like this one."

DANIELLE LOOKED at the small stone glistening in the shop's bright lighting. "Every few months, you say . . ."

Glickstein rocked his head from side to side, weighing the question. "Give or take. I could look it up."

"And the diamonds, they were always this size?"

"More or less. Decent stones, but nothing special."

"Old?"

Glickstein nodded. "I'd say so, yes, because of their cut."

"Heirlooms, then."

"But finished and set by a jeweler somewhere else." He examined the last stone the old woman had brought him again. "America, I'd say."

"Did you notice anything different the last time you saw her?"

"Nothing special. Oh, just that her leg seemed to be bothering her. I helped her down the stairs, waited a few minutes with her until the bus came. That's all." Glickstein's eyes narrowed, as if he had just remembered something else. "Well . . ."

"What, Mr. Glickstein?"

"I noticed a man watching from across the street. I thought he was watching me. But when I returned after helping the old woman onto the bus he was gone."

Danielle exchanged a glance with Ehud Cohen. "Did you get a good look at him?"

"Not particularly, Commander. He was big, though, at least a head taller than those who passed him on the street. And his eyes . . ."

"What about them?"

"He wore a patch over one."

CHAPTER 34

"How long has he been here?" Colonel Walter McClendon yelled at one of the guards manning the front gate of USAMRIID on the grounds of Fort Detrick.

"Twenty minutes, a half hour maybe, sir."

McClendon's eyes swept the grounds beyond the building, searching. "And you just let him walk on?"

"He had clearance, sir. I've never seen clearance like he had, direct from the White House. We tried to call you, several times."

"You should have kept trying." McClendon felt the sweat lifting off his flesh, creeping down his shirt, thickening with each word. "We're in a state of high alert and . . . Damn it, never mind. Just point me in the right direction. Which way did he go?"

COLONEL MCCLENDON found Professor Albert Paulsen in an open stretch of field halfway to the security fence at the tree line. He was kneeling in the grass, leaning over as if to sniff the ground. McClendon approached, and with each step his shoes seemed to sink a little deeper into the soft ground.

"What are you doing, Albert?" he called, quickening his pace the last stretch of the way.

Paulsen flapped a hand in the air as if to silence him.

He wore a white terry-cloth bathrobe over a pair of old jeans and penny loafers. The bathrobe was badly soiled around the edges from being dragged through the mud. Frayed strands dangled from the sleeves.

Paulsen lifted his face from the turf. "I'm trying to pick up their trail," he told McClendon finally. Then he rose and faced him. "It's gone cold. Sorry. Smell's the most underrated of our senses, you know. Nose can do amazing things. Not here, though, not today."

"I heard you were coming."

"Interesting, since I didn't know myself." He brushed his hands off on his bathrobe, dragging fresh streaks of brown down the white of the robe. There were patches on the knees of his jeans. The tip of his flattened nose had some dirt on it. Paulsen looked around him, sniffed the air. "I was here when this place was built. This used to be a leaching field, you know, until they built that new drainage system. Thing gave me an idea. Want to hear it?"

"Do I have a choice?"

"No. Forget traditional ordnance, bios and nukes. Daisy cutters and bunker busters. You want to fuck the enemy up? Drop a shit bomb on a city. Ultimate anti-personnel weapon. Can you picture it, people walking around covered in the stuff? Imagine the effect on morale. Think about it."

"Jesus, Albert. I told them they were wasting their time bringing you in on this."

"A Code Seventeen. That's the word for a major fuck-up these days. My opinion they should just call it a fuck-up. First class in this case. You check the garbage, by the way?"

"For what?" McClendon asked, shaking his head.

"You'd know if you found it."

Paulsen sank back to his knees and lowered his face to the ground again. McClendon observed he was using his eyes more than his nose this time, and watched the old man's spine stiffen just before he parted the grass and began smoothing the topsoil away with a hand.

"Here," he called to McClendon, "take a look."

The colonel moved close enough to peer over Paulsen's shoulder, saw something white poking out of the ground. "Is that—"

"One of the HazMat suits used by the impostors? Very observant, Walter. The others must be in this area somewhere. . . ." Paulsen shifted sideways and recommenced his inspection of the ground.

"How did you—"

"You've been busy these last couple days. The obvious was bound to slip your mind. The imposters couldn't get off the premises in their isolation suits, so they took them off."

"They obviously had something on beneath them."

"Right again, Walter. I suspect your security cameras might have picked up six naked men streaking toward the security fence." Paulsen turned and looked up at McClendon, squinting into the sun. "Try army uniforms. The impostors have them on underneath. Strip off their isolation suits and they look like soldiers securing the fields. Think about it."

It was clear from his face that this idea had never occurred to McClendon. "That still doesn't explain how they got the storage cases off the premises. You remember those, don't you, Albert?"

"The ones rigged with an explosive device that can be remote-detonated in the event of just this sort of emergency? Sure. *I* designed them."

"Then what happened to your digital coding system that's supposed to prevent the cases from being opened? A million different combinations that change every sixty seconds, you said."

'Yes, Walter, I did." The sun dipped behind a cloud,

and Paulsen stopped squinting. "Twelve years ago. Before the days of hand-held computer encoders, the hundred-gigabyte machines that used to take up a wall and now fit in your palm. Steel-belted radials that don't go flat, progressive-scan DVD players, e-mail, DHL . . . The only thing that hasn't changed are Girl Scout cookies. Think about it."

"Pardon me?"

"Come on, Walter, you get my point. But you must not have gotten the memos I wrote my first few years out, warning you to upgrade the system. I gave up when I moved to the woods."

"I asked for the upgrades, but we weren't considered a priority anymore. Our system was thought to be adequate, given the nature of reliable threats we could reasonably expect to face."

Paulsen looked around at the soldiers and vehicles dotting the perimeter of the USAMRIID complex. "What you're telling me is that the Fifth Army got here late," he said.

"The world changed in September 2001, Albert, after you moved to the woods. Before then nobody anticipated something like this. We've been slow catching up."

Paulsen climbed to his feet and brushed the dirt from his knees. "I'm off to the White House. President invited me for a sleep-over."

McClendon's face paled a bit. "You'll have to tell him about—"

"I know," Paulsen said. "More good news to brighten up his day."

CHAPTER 35

"There's something you're not telling me, Colonel," Danielle said, climbing into the backseat of a cab driven by Nabril al-Asi.

She had noticed al-Asi seated behind the wheel of the taxi as soon as she and Sergeant Ehud Cohen reached the bottom of the stairs outside Glickstein's shop. She told the confused detective she wanted to check a few other things on her own and approached the waiting cab as Cohen retraced his path up the stairs to ask the jeweler some follow-up questions.

Al-Asi flipped on his meter as soon as she closed the door behind her. "You don't have to tip me."

"You knew I was coming here."

"Actually, I followed you. Couldn't wait for you to update me on your investigation into Zanah Fahury's murder, so I thought I'd come in person. Besides, I may need a new line of work before too long." Al-Asi's bright smile flickered in the rearview mirror. "What did you find inside the jeweler's?"

"Why don't you tell me what you're holding back first?"

Al-Asi smiled devilishly. "A man in my position never tells everything he knows. Besides, if I told you everything at once, then I'd risk losing the pleasure of your company. Since Inspector Kamal left, I must say I've come to enjoy our visits."

Danielle saw no reason not to share her information. "According to the jeweler, the murdered old woman was selling diamonds. One every few months."

"You've been to her apartment, I imagine."

"As have you, I'm sure."

"Odd place, don't you think?"

"She was hiding from something."

"Interesting assumption, Chief Inspector."

"It's more than that. The jeweler noticed a man in the street outside his shop the day she was killed." Danielle paused. "A big man with an eye patch."

Al-Asi's face twisted tightly, the way it did on those rare occasions when he learned something he didn't know, or suspect, already. "Hakim's giant," he recalled. "One of the gunmen who killed Khalil and his guards."

"What does an old Arab-Israeli woman have to do with a ranking Hamas terrorist, Colonel? How could this kind of man possibly be involved in both their deaths?"

"We'd need to know a good deal more about the old woman in order to answer those questions, Chief Inspector."

"That's where I was hoping you could help out. You know something about Zanah Fahury you're not telling me, don't you?"

"I didn't before," al-Asi said, nodding slightly. "I believe I do now."

"Your turn," Danielle said. "I'm listening."

"Are you a student of history, Chief Inspector?"

"All Israelis are students of history, Colonel."

"Good." The colonel pulled out into traffic to a chorus of horns and squealing brakes protesting his sudden move. "I'll explain everything on the way."

"Where are we going?" Danielle asked him, looking about.

"You'll see when we get there." He slammed on his brakes, jostling Danielle forward in the backseat, traffic caught in a typical Jerusalem snarl. "Which should give me plenty of time to tell you a story I've managed to piece together over the years that began in the wake of the Six-Day War. . . ."

"WE'RE ALL in agreement, then," Prime Minister Golda Meir said to the two men seated in twin chairs before her desk.

Defense Minister Moshe Dayan and Foreign Minister Abba Eban were disparate thinkers, the former narrow and soldierlike, the latter inspired to much bolder, more intellectual strokes. While their methods may have been different, though, their vision was the same: the survival of Israel.

Now that survival, nearly two years after the Six-Day War of 1967, seemed precarious at best. Although Israel had masterfully beaten back a multipronged attack in swift and furious fashion, her Arab enemies would learn from their mistakes and regroup. The next war promised to end differently.

"We are agreed on the problem, yes," said Abba Eban, "but not on the means to deal with it."

"The means are obvious," Dayan disagreed. "We must attack. Not the armies that sit by our borders, but the source that continues to fund their intrusions into our land."

"Saudi Arabia," said Prime Minister Meir. "You would have us attack Saudi Arabia."

"You said you were confident of your intelligence in this matter."

"I am. The Saudis may remain passive in their actions, but not their bank accounts. Saudi money has been flowing unchecked into Syria, Jordan, and Egypt ever since we crushed them in the Six-Day War. They mean the next war to be the last."

"Precisely why we should crush them now," Dayan avowed. *"Believe me, things will get much worse before they get better."*

"Our American friends would never sanction that," said Eban.

"The solution to that is simple: We tell the Americans nothing of our plans."

"And risk losing the only ally we have in the world?" Abba Eban shook his head violently as he retrained his gaze on Golda Meir. *"That is pure madness, Madame Prime Minister."*

"What would you suggest as an alternative?" she asked him.

"We bring the Americans into this. Now. They're the ones who are in bed with the Saudis over oil. Let them deal with the situation, through back channels if necessary."

"We all agree that we have relied on the Americans too much in the past. Now you want to entrust them with our future?" Moshe Dayan shook his head just as adamantly as his counterpart had. *"I think not. I know not."*

"I agree that we need to act ourselves," argued Israel's aging prime minister, *"but I also agree that an overt military response is not an option. Do that and we risk losing America's friendship, and that, gentlemen, is something we can't afford."*

"Which puts us back where we started," said Dayan, obviously frustrated.

In that instant Golda Meir smiled ever so tightly and both men realized whatever she was about to say had been well thought out in advance of their coming. *"Not necessarily. What if there were a way we could infiltrate Saudi Arabia at the highest levels?"*

"Impossible!" roared Eban.

Golda Meir rose from behind her desk. The effort taxed her, betraying her age and infirmity. The years *had blessed her with a mind as sharp as ever but had cursed her with a body that was rapidly decaying. Her hands trembled. She rested them on the edge of the desk to support herself.*

"Not at all, gentlemen. One of our young generals has conceived a plan that is low in risk, fiendish in simplicity, and with high potential for tremendous reward. We call it Operation Blue Widow, and I have summoned him to explain it to you himself." Meir smiled and looked to a closed door that led into a conference room adjoining her office. "General," she called.

The door opened and a man in Israeli military dress entered, coming immediately to attention. He was of medium height and build, unimpressive in stature except for the rigid cast of his gaze. He looked straight ahead, not even acknowledging the presence of Dayan and Eban.

"Gentlemen," Golda Meir resumed, "I would like you to meet General Yakov Barnea. . . ."

"MY FATHER," Danielle muttered, shocked by al-Asi's tale.

"Operation Blue Widow was his plan," al-Asi continued. "One of the most daring in your country's storied history and perhaps the least known of any. Also one of the most tragic. Buried by your government for all these years for good reason."

"Except to you."

Al-Asi smiled humbly. "Based on rumors and half-truths accumulated over the years. Too many similar tales told to be easily dismissed."

Traffic started moving again and the colonel began to edge the taxi forward.

"And what, Colonel, do these rumors and half-truths have to do with a murdered old Arab-Israeli woman selling diamonds to support herself?"

Al-Asi looked across the seat at Danielle. "Why don't we go see if we can find out?"

CHAPTER 36

Layla Aziz Rahani took two Xanax before boarding her plane and a third when she still didn't feel relaxed enough to sleep. A sedative-induced sleep was usually dreamless, and dreams were something to be avoided now.

She remembered what had felt like a dream from long ago. So painful she had begged for waking to relieve her, only to realize as her thoughts cleared that the hospital around her was not the product of a dream at all. Nor was the pain that ravaged her insides. She had lain in that hospital bed remembering its origins. The boy thrusting himself into her again and again. His stale breath, reeking of beer, blowing into her face. The sheets stank with his sweat and Layla remembered almost vomiting but swallowing it back down when it flooded her throat.

Stop . . .

Had she said the word or only thought it?

Stop! Stop! Stop!

Her mind clouded, a memory of the boy handing her the soft drink she had requested at a party. Wrinkling her nose at the strange aftertaste. Finishing it anyway so as not to hurt his feelings. Keeping her hands in her pockets when he walked her back to her dorm room before everything went dark and she had awoken in the hospital with the first of the memories coming alive, accompanied by the pain.

When the haze finally passed, she had found Karim Matah of the Saudi intelligence service hovering over her bedside. Her father had dispatched him to bring her home and deal with the American authorities. It was decided best for all concerned not to pursue matters further. Hence, there was no investigation. On Matah's instructions, Layla had not cooperated with the police or campus officials. Instead she withdrew from a school she had never wanted to attend in the first place.

She had begged her father not to make her go to the world of her mother, a world that still terrified her from afar. But he had insisted, explaining that Western education would be vital to her involvement in the family business. So she had gone, closeting herself in her room between classes. Eating at odd hours so she could avoid crowds and attention.

Halfway through her second year she had settled into a routine comfortable enough to allow her to relax. She made friends with other Saudi girls, who had adopted far more of the Western social life than she and agreed to accompany them to a party without realizing the kind of party it would be. Alcohol flowed freely. Layla was shocked to see the Saudi girls swallowing glass after glass and dancing with Americans in a suite room that had been cleared of furniture.

Layla had clung to a corner until a young man brought her a soft drink. She took it and thanked him shyly, but he didn't leave. There was a mirror across from the chair where she sat, and Layla had been studying herself in it when he came over. She almost didn't recognize the figure in the mirror with the long, dark hair tumbling past her shoulders. The girls dancing in the other room didn't have hair nearly as nice or eyes as deep and piercing. At one point Layla had risen and studied the curves and lines of her body in the mirror, only to quickly return to her chair in embarrassment over her sudden selfish awareness of her own physical beauty.

I look like my mother.

The very notion of that terrified her, and she was on the verge of rushing out of the party when the boy appeared with the soft drink. Layla liked the way his eyes responded to her, liked the way he gently touched her wrist and shoulder. She thought his touch would make her stiffen, but it didn't. She watched her image and that of the boy in the mirror and at once enjoyed seeing herself this way.

He offered to walk her back to her dorm and halfway there her mind stopped working. She was dimly aware of lying in a room she had never seen before and then the smell of him was on her. She remembered thinking of her mother, that this was her world, the world she had wanted to drag Layla into fifteen years before.

A world she hated. A world of nothing but pain.

The pain was worse by the time Matah had gotten her back to the family palace outside Riyadh. Even her father was cold toward her, so much so that Layla had told no one about the pain until it grew unbearable, leaving her sweating and feverish. They brought her to the hospital, and an hour later she was in surgery.

When she awoke the pain was gone but an emptiness rose in its place. Layla had been unable to define it until in her father's presence the doctors explained they had been forced to remove her uterus. She would never be able to bear children, but for some reason Layla didn't care. It was apt punishment for what she had let happen the night of the assault. Two terrible events had now come to define her life: the rape and, fifteen years before that, the death of her mother by stoning. In that sense the West, America, had killed both of them.

For her father, Layla's rape had been the last straw. First her mother had betrayed him and now this. Hate became his passion, an unfathomable desire to see the world that had nearly destroyed both him and his daughter destroyed too.

He had come to Layla's hospital bed after the operation, knelt and grabbed her hand, pledging to her and her alone what he planned to do.

They will pay. They will all pay.

Layla remembered taking great solace in those words, that vow, never imagining it would fall upon her to complete. But she embraced the opportunity with the kind of passion that had been forever snuffed out that night long ago in the dormitory room.

Layla's trip to take her father's place at the venture-capital meeting marked her first return to the world she was now committed to destroying. And she had found it unchanged, the men and women seated at the conference table before her nothing more than grown-up versions of the young college student who had stolen her womanhood. She had looked across the room and saw them as they would soon be, having fallen victim to her plot of assuring the destruction of their society.

Her brother Saed was in for a surprise once she returned home. Their father had promised Layla her due. Once the stroke had incapacitated him months ago, she had taken over and run the company flawlessly. Keeping the truth of his condition, and prognosis, a secret even from members of the royal family. Using a computer to forge his signature on memos and checks. Picking up his work so seamlessly that the world accepted the great Abdullah Aziz Rahani had become a recluse. She knew how much he detested Saed, embarrassed to have a drunken playboy as his oldest son.

The lines of traditional succession were going to be broken. Rahani Industries was going to be hers, to remake within the new shape of the world that was coming.

CHAPTER 37

Ben sat on the bench of the fairgrounds midway, waiting for Alan Lewanthall to arrive. The pungent smells of fresh popcorn and cotton candy permeated the air. He could hear the excited, high voices of children, the occasional complaint of a boy or girl begging for another ride on the ancient merry-go-round or Ferris wheel. The music blaring from the rides as they spun and twisted provided the background to all the festivities.

The annual Homecoming celebration had been a tradition in Dearborn for over twenty years now, although it had grown considerably in size and scope since he had brought his own children to Ford Field. Ben remembered brushing the popcorn from his son's shirt and looking at the cotton candy leave sticky, pink trails down his daughter's face. The ancient rides and games had remained virtually the same, outfitted with new names and a fresh coat of paint but unchanged underneath.

They looked similarly unchanged today, but Ben now saw them for the rusted relics that they were. An insurance claim waiting to happen. He had asked Lewanthall to meet him here at Ford Field not just because of the sprawl and clamor, but also because it was a place that still made Ben feel safe and secure. He had taken a stroll about the grounds when he first arrived, which brought him face-to-face with many carny hawkers and workers he felt certain he had seen on his last visit here over a decade before. The face painting and temporary-tattoo parlors were new, the fortune-teller and guess-your-weight stations as ancient as time itself.

But Ben had other things on his mind as well. Old and foreign feelings gnawed at him, raw in their unfamiliarity. He was scared in a way he hadn't been in longer than he could remember, for he had come to realize he had something to lose. He had fled this world after the murder of his family into one of self-loathing and doubt. He had ended up in Palestine in search of purpose when all he really wanted was peace. It could have been anywhere, Ben realized now; the results would have been the same. And, in the process, distance had blurred links to the family he had left, as if they too had fallen prey a decade before.

That family was now in hiding, protected by soldiers to whom his brother had given his support and sponsorship. But how long could they stay there? How long could Sayeed's associates offer sanctuary from a shadowy force that had grown all-powerful before the witness of government watchdogs now powerless to stop it?

The idea of losing his family brought the cold grasp of fear down on him hard and fast. And, sitting there on the midway, Ben realized the only person he had felt anything for in those ten years was Danielle Barnea.

A woman he knew in his heart he could never have, rendering her safe from the same emotions that had already betrayed him. Was that why he hadn't tried harder to talk her out of returning to Israel? Through his first years in Palestine he'd had nothing to lose. Meeting Danielle had changed everything, taught him he could care again, but even that came with a price, as he learned the only thing harder than being apart from her was being together.

Ben crossed his legs, then uncrossed them, wincing as he used his hands to lower the banged-up left one to the concrete. Lewanthall was late. There had been no call to Ben's cell phone alerting him that the plan had changed, so he had to assume the man from the State Department was still coming. Finally, when his tardiness reached the half-hour mark, Ben plucked the phone from his jacket and started to dial Lewanthall's number.

"Put that in your pocket," a voice said from just behind him.

Ben turned and saw Lewanthall with his foot propped up on the section of the bench facing the opposite direction, pretending to tie his shoe.

"Stand up and walk away," the man from the State Department continued, reeking of cigarette smoke. The stench hugged his body like a wetsuit. "Don't turn around. Whatever you do, don't look at me."

"What's wrong?" Ben asked, rising.

"I was followed here. Now start moving. Walk."

Ben did. "Who are they?"

Lewanthall fell into step slightly behind him. "Whoever's behind this. Whoever wiped out the terrorists we lured together."

Ben started to turn around. "How could—"

"Face forward! Don't look at me, for Christ's sake! They make you and neither one of us gets out of here alive."

They were nearing the end of the midway, the smells of popcorn and cotton candy drifting away as they passed the ancient collection of rusted, clanking rides.

"Latif," Ben said.

"What?"

"Latif told us he'd completed his delivery."

"I couldn't confirm that."

"That must be who's here now, the group that has the smallpox, after us."

"Not us—me. Just keep walking."

"I've got a phone. Let me—"

"Call who? Don't you get it, Ben? There isn't anyone out there who can help us."

"Us."

"That's right. Now. I've got to get back to Washington. Try to convince my superiors just how badly I fucked up. You've got a car?"

"Yes."

"Bring it around to the exit we're heading toward. I'll be waiting. Maybe I can lose them."

"Don't bullshit me."

"One of us has to get out of here, Ben. We can't walk out together. Now, go."

Ben quickened his pace, widening the gap between them. He fought the urge to look back, see what Lewanthall was doing, where he was headed.

A plan to bring on the end of all things . . .

It was all laid out, fashioned by the madmen Lewanthall and others from the State Department had drawn together and then lost. All being killed now by some unknown force. Khalil, Latif—who knew how many others.

The bait had been taken, the trap set and sprung.

So what had gone wrong? Where had the plan, what Lewanthall called Operation Flypaper, broken down?

Ben's breath shortened as he cleared the grounds and hurried across the street into a grassy field that doubled as a parking lot today, trying to remember which row he had parked the car his brother had provided. Swing it around the front, throw open the door so Lewanthall could jump in. After that . . .

After that, *what?*

Ben found the car, climbed in, and slammed the door

behind him. He turned the key, thinking of a bomb in the last moment before the engine whirred to life. His heart steadied. He took a few deep breaths and backed up.

A horn blared. Tires screeched.

In the rearview mirror Ben glimpsed a woman with a minivan full of children screaming at him. He was so jumpy he had forgotten to look first. He waited for the minivan to pass, then started to reverse again.

He had parked just fifty yards from the entrance to the festival grounds, but heavy traffic, combined with cars parked on both sides of the streets beyond, made the process of getting there agonizingly slow. Finally he squeezed past a car that had stopped to drop off its load of kids and neared the main entrance set between a pair of booths offering tickets to the rides and attractions.

A crowd had gathered, murmuring among themselves. Ben edged the car closer, saw a Dearborn policeman crouched over a man who looked to be sitting down on the pavement, his back against one of the ticket booths.

Lewanthall!

Ben caught a glimpse of his face as he approached behind the line of cars, not daring to stop and knowing already there was no reason to. A trickle of blood ran from the corner of Lewanthall's mouth. One of his eyes had locked open. The cop jostled him, and he slumped over, revealing a bloodstain on the cracked wood of the old ticket booth.

A head shot, Ben figured, they had taken Lewanthall with a head shot, very likely from up close.

Ben pulled around the two cars remaining before him and accelerated. He wondered if one or more in the mingling crowd had been watching for him, seen him, even.

It didn't matter. Only escape mattered now.

Back on the road, Ben waited to make sure he wasn't being followed before collecting his thoughts, contemplating his next move. He drew the cell phone from his pocket and held it briefly before hitting the first number programmed into its memory.

"John Najarian's office."

"It's Ben Kamal, Helen," he said to Najarian's assistant. "I need to talk to John."

"He's in transit, Mr. Kamal."

"This is an emergency. Patch me through."

It took a minute before Najarian came on the line, his voice raised slightly over the blare of engine sounds. "Ben, what's wrong?"

"Lewanthall's dead."

"*Our* Lewanthall, from the State Department? How?"

"Shot. Murdered. He put us on to something much bigger than a simple fugitive hunt. He used us, John. He goddamn used us."

"Slow down, Ben. I've got to think this out."

"There's nothing to think out. You need to reach someone in the State Department. We've got to come in and turn all this over."

"You're not making sense."

"With good reason," Ben told Najarian. "Lewanthall made a mess and hired us to help him clean it up before it was too late. He went rogue and he dragged us, the company, with him."

A pause.

"Are you still in Detroit, Ben?"

"The general area, yes."

"Can you get to Washington? Is it safe for you to fly?"

"I'll get to Washington," Ben assured him. "You just get us a meeting with the highest-ranking official you can get your hands on."

"That kind of thing takes time."

"We don't have it. Tell them you know what's missing from USAMRIID."

Ben could feel the tension through the silence on the line.

"That's the army's biowarfare headquarters," Najarian said finally.

"That's all you need to know. Tell whoever you reach at State to check Lewanthall's file and look for something called Operation Flypaper. It'll all be there for someone with the clearance to read it."

"What do I tell them about you?"

"That Lewanthall told me everything before he died," Ben said. "And none of it's good."

CHAPTER 38

"What is it we're looking for exactly?" Danielle asked al-Asi as they methodically searched Zanah Fahury's apartment in Umm al Fahm, each strangely respectful of the dead woman's possessions. On the drive north from Jerusalem they had heard heavy gunfire coming from the village of Jenin and had to stop for a time to allow a convoy of Israeli tanks and armored personnel carriers to cross the road. Danielle still found it strange how the constant sights of such war machines and the sound of gunfire had so easily melted into the backdrop of Israeli life. She remembered once thinking how sad that was. Now it just was.

"Good question, Chief Inspector," al-Asi said and closed another drawer. "Let's start with what we don't see. An old woman's residence—it's fairly clear what's missing."

"Pictures," Danielle noted. "Memorabilia of any kind."

"An old woman without any family, perhaps," the colonel followed, not sounding convinced by the words. "Without family or memories."

"Or perhaps trying to hide them. But how does that explain her connection to whoever killed Akram Khalil, Colonel?"

"It doesn't. Not yet. That's the problem. Why I wanted to come back here."

Danielle stopped and gazed across the room at al-Asi. He seemed to have aged significantly in the year since she and Ben had first found themselves in the United States. More salt and less pepper in his carefully groomed hair. His blazing eyes less lively, less playful, less sure. She knew al-Asi to be in his midforties, but he looked older than that now.

She blamed it on the fact he was out of his element so much now, or, worse, had no element at all. He had worn one of his expensive Western suits two nights before at dinner in the King David Hotel's restaurant, a brief reminder of the lifestyle he had prided himself on living before the bottom fell out of the Palestinian Authority and the various security satellites it operated.

"Then tell me this," Danielle said suddenly. "What's my father's connection here? Are you saying he knew Zanah Fahury?"

"I suspect he did, Chief Inspector. But not as Zanah Fahury."

"What happened in Golda Meir's office that day? What was Operation Blue Widow?"

Al-Asi looked up from the contents of a drawer he had just opened and began to speak.

"*GENERAL BARNEA,*" Prime Minister Golda Meir continued, "*I'm sure needs no introduction. He fought with the Haganah in forty-eight, was a hero in the Fifty-six War, and led the assault on Jerusalem during the Six-Day. He developed Operation Blue Widow in consultation with Mossad, which agreed jointly with him not to distribute any memos or briefings until everything was set in place.*"

"*No disrespect was meant, sirs,*" Barnea began, seeing the derision in the looks Moshe Dayan and Abba Eban were giving him, the soldier and the diplomat equally scornful. "*But the operation was so precarious, so riddled with obstacles, that it never would have been approved based on a proposal. And even if it had been, the likelihood of success was so small as to offer nothing but futility and failure.*"

"*Get to the point, General!*" Dayan ordered.

Yakov Barnea looked at one, then the other. "*Sirs, infiltrating Saudi society had already been ruled an impossibility for a male operative, but what about a female?*"

"*In a repressive society like the Saudi's, what could a woman hope to accomplish?*"

"*That depends on her placement or, should I say, their placement: One hundred women have been chosen for Operation Blue Widow.*"

"*Chosen?*" Eban challenged, aiming his words at Golda Meir. "*You mean this plan is already operational?*"

"*For two years now,*" the prime minister said and looked back toward Yakov Barnea. "*Go on, General.*"

"*All one hundred are widows who lost their husbands to enemy fire,*" he resumed. "*Each and every one of them in their early twenties with no children or dependents. All have stellar army records and the proper psychological profile.*"

"Psychological profile to do what?" Dayan demanded.

"Infiltrate Saudi society by marrying into it."

Eban and Dayan exchanged a disbelieving glance. "You're joking," Dayan said for both of them.

"Not at all," said Barnea. "The women worked for months adapting their looks, learning the language, studying Saudi culture and society so they would know exactly what was expected of them."

"And then what?" challenged Eban. "You just drop them in Saudi society and hope a man proposes or a marriage is arranged. This is absurd!"

"Please, sir, let me finish. The women were never meant to take on the guise of Saudis, they only had to pass as Americans. American college students."

Eban and Dayan looked at each other, dumbfounded. "A hundred, you say," Dayan muttered.

"That's the number we inserted as students in America," Yakov Barnea continued, "all at elite institutions attended in impressive numbers by children of the royal family and its offshoots. They have enrolled in the same classes, attended the same social events—that much we've seen to. The rest will require an element of luck, but our hope is that three or four might end up being of service."

"Unless their luck turns bad," Abba Eban said grimly. "Tell me, General Barnea, are these women aware that success in their mission means they will likely never be able to return to Israel, at least not alive?"

"Quite, sir."

"And did they also understand the embarrassment and disgrace Israel would face if they buckled under interrogation?"

"The volunteers had only one contact," Barnea explained, not bothering to mention that contact was himself. *"And none of them knew anything about the larger scope of the plan."*

"You should know," started Golda Meir, *"that four of the original group of women are already in Saudi Arabia."*

"What about the other ninety-six?" Eban wanted to know.

"Some are still in training, others are already in the United States, more are awaiting placement. Others have been recalled."

"And do we have reason to hope any of the four in Saudi Arabia now will yield something of promise?" asked Dayan.

"One whose cover is most firmly established," Barnea replied.

"And why is that, General?"

"Because a few months ago she gave birth to her first child."

DANIELLE SWALLOWED past the lump that had formed in her throat. "Zanah Fahury?"

"I have no way of being sure yet, Chief Inspector, but I have my suspicions, yes," al-Asi said from across the room, as he removed another drawer from the dresser.

"Any idea how long she's been living here?"

"Our records, limited as they are, indicate thirty years."

"Nineteen seventy-three."

Al-Asi stuck his hand inside the dresser and began to feel about in the area behind the drawer. "Yes."

Danielle watched al-Asi's expression change as he

twisted his body to better his angle, probing deeper into the dresser.

"I think I've found something, Chief Inspector," he said.

CHAPTER 39

Darkness fell while Ben sat in his car inside a long-term-parking garage at Detroit Metropolitan Airport, waiting for John Najarian to call him back with instructions. He had contacted his brother and warned him that the risk he and his family faced was even greater now. And they wouldn't be safe so long as Lewanthall's killers remained at large.

Sitting in the car, Ben felt numb with dread. The familiar bottleneck of breath, the thickness in his muscles, the tension in his shoulders. He thought of Danielle, looked at his watch, dialed her number in Israel.

"Hello," she answered sleepily.

"What time is it over there?" he asked.

"Late."

"I'm sorry if I woke you."

"I wasn't asleep," she said, her neck and shoulders stiff from slumping over a table for hours, studying what Colonel al-Asi had uncovered in Zanah Fahury's dresser:

A photograph, tattered and warped, its fading colors giving a painting-like quality to the faces of the two young girls pictured, their ages difficult to discern. Danielle guessed three and five. Both were smiling. Same white shiny teeth, heavy-lidded eyes that looked strangely adult, dark wavy hair. Something about the faces was familiar to Danielle but she couldn't identify what exactly.

She had tried inspecting the background with a magnifying glass, but it was too faded to yield any clue as to where the photo had been taken or how many years back. Could it be that Zanah Fahury had given birth to the girls in her guise as one of the Blue Widows, as Colonel al-Asi's tale suggested? Were the children distant, pained memories of a lost life?

But why bother hiding the picture?

Then again, perhaps it had belonged to the chest of drawers' previous owner. Maybe the explanation for the photo's placement was innocent, simply the result of an overstuffed drawer being yanked out, this one picture stripped from an album and left stuck to the wood.

Danielle abandoned that possibility as quickly as she had considered it. Colonel al-Asi believed that Zanah Fahury was one of her father's Blue Widows, part of his plan to infiltrate the Saudi government thirty-six years before in the wake of the Six-Day War. The rest of her life remained a mystery Danielle was determined to solve, because she had been murdered by the same one-eyed man who had been identified as one of the executioners of terrorist leader Akram Khalil.

What was the connection?

"The end of all things is real," Ben said, shocking her back to the present. "A rogue State Department operation gone bad, a major fuck-up."

"Please tell me I'm dreaming this."

"I'd like to, believe me. But somebody's got enough smallpox to infect half the world, starting with the U.S."

"Khalil's dead, remember?" she said after a pause.

"But the operation *isn't.* Listen to me, Danielle. Khalil was killed because he was part of something the American government created and then lost control of. They were trying to trap terrorists but something went wrong."

"Someone started killing the terrorists," Danielle concluded, making it sound obvious.

"And whoever it was set this whole thing up. They've got the smallpox now. Latif delivered it to them. The plan must have been to deflect blame off Hamas or any Arab terrorist group for its release."

"A witness claims Khalil was arguing with his killers before the shooting began."

"Those killers are the ones behind this, Danielle. That's who we've got to find. Are you any closer to identifying them?"

"No," Danielle said, thinking once more about the one-eyed giant.

"Keep trying. Najarian's setting me up with someone at the State Department who can help from this end. Unless it's too late. That's what I'm worried about. That it's already too late."

BEN'S PHONE rang just seconds after he had said goodbye to Danielle.

"Are you safe, Ben?" Najarian's voice demanded as soon as he answered. "Are you all right?"

"John, I can hardly hear you."

"I'm in my car, heading toward Logan so I can meet you in Washington."

"You reached someone," Ben said, feeling his chest relax.

"They'll have further instructions for me when I get down there. Everything's fuzzy right now. I've been on the phone since I got off with you. I'm told to hang up, then somebody calls me right back, doesn't identify himself. I keep telling the story, starting over every time."

"They believe you. . . ."

"I can tell from their voices, Ben: They're scared."

"So am I."

"I'm sorry I got you into this."

"Just put it on the government's bill, under pain and suffering," Ben told him, surprised he had settled down enough even to attempt a joke.

"Well, they don't know it yet but they're paying for your plane flight too. I booked you on the nine o'clock out of Detroit Metro into Dulles. I'll be waiting at the gate," Najarian finished. "With friends."

THEY ALMOST didn't let Ben board the plane. A single man traveling without luggage on a one-way ticket.

An Arab.

Despite all the frisks and pat-downs, it took a call to an airline supervisor, who interpreted a code provided by whoever had reserved Ben's ticket, before he was waved on last and allowed to take his seat, watched intently by every passenger he passed down the aisle.

The flight seemed interminably long, Ben's tension having resulted in a splitting headache no amount of aspirin could relieve. He sat squeezed into a middle seat, acutely aware of every engine sound, every minor course change, every flight attendant call bell that went off. He drank black coffee. Used the men's room four times, stood in line for three of them, glad to be on his feet in the relative open space of the cabin. The middle seat made it seem as if the world were closing in on him, the battle for the armrests long lost, leaving his elbows jammed against his body.

He kept shifting about, trying to stretch out his legs, searching futilely for comfort. He concentrated on the second hand sweeping across the face of his watch as time crawled. Made out the low din of the Walkman the passenger next to him had on. A baby cried. Someone laughed.

Then, at last, the flight was over. The plane's taxi to the gate was equally slow, followed by another delay as the flight crew waited for their slot to open up.

Ben saw himself bolting up the aisle as soon as the plane was stopped. But the hiss of the engines idling down was accompanied by a flight attendant moving to the aisle directly before him, impeding his exit.

He held his ground with the others, took his turn in line, and filed off the plane down the jetway toward the gate at Dulles. John Najarian would be waiting along with officials from the State Department. Ben would share what he knew with them, and they would take over. Sort out the mess they had inadvertently created.

Ben walked briskly up the jetway exit and into the artificial air of the terminal, fighting the lingering pain in his hip from the beating he had taken the night before. He saw John Najarian, huge frame stuffed into a tan overcoat, standing rock-shouldered before him. He slumped that way when he was nervous. He noticed Ben and forced a slight smile, trying to look reassuring. Ben tried to pick out the operatives from the State Department amid the crowd around Najarian.

A pair of men springing out of nowhere grabbed both Ben's arms simultaneously. Ben saw the wall an instant before his face slammed into it, his lips mashed into the tile so he couldn't cry out if he wanted to. He winced in pain, tasted blood instead of stale coffee. An arm pressed against the back of his neck held him there, while someone's hands dug around his belt and pockets. His bad hip flared with fresh agony.

"Hey," he heard John Najarian say from nearby, "this wasn't part of the deal!"

"We'll have to ask you to stand back, sir," a new voice said with a modicum of politeness.

"But—"

"Stand back, sir!" An order this time.

Ben felt his hands wrenched cruelly together, something cold and tight fastened around them an instant before he heard the click of the handcuffs locking home.

CHAPTER 40

"You are not welcome here," Layla Aziz Rahani said, as soon as she saw her brother Saed admiring the artwork that adorned the foyer of the palace.

"I came to see our father," Saed said, his blue eyes blinking rapidly. He was short and awkward-looking, prematurely bald, which exaggerated the billiard-ball shape of his head. Layla could smell the alcohol on his breath. Scotch, she thought.

As always, she had slipped into the private jet's shower during the final leg of her journey. Recoiffed her hair so it could more easily be concealed by a head scarf and pulled the robe worn by all Saudi women over her Western dress and jewelry.

The car had brought her straight to the Rahani palace from the airfield. In regal majesty it was the equal of any palace in Saudi Arabia, a lavish assemblage of excess layered with pools and fountains, both inside and out. Exquisite paintings adorned a museumlike entry foyer, above which stairs encased in priceless Persian carpet wound upward toward two dozen bedrooms and as many baths.

The palace had been designed on the grand scale of those long lost to the ages, gilded lavishly in twenty-karat gold that was reflected in the twin pools bracketing a walkway of polished red granite. Abdullah Aziz Rahani himself had once tended the gardens that enclosed them, his hand so unsteady in the weeks before his stroke that the family's gardeners had to clean up after him, repairing the damage to flowers and shrubs.

As a girl, Layla had walked these grounds often with her father, listening to him speak of their vast holdings. Having borne no sons, Abdullah Aziz Rahani had already resigned himself to passing his wealth and power to his daughter and bore no regrets over that fact. But, after the death of her mother, he had taken a second wife, who bore him three sons, Saed being the oldest.

"I'm asking you to leave," Layla said to her brother. "Don't make me call the guards."

"You should watch your tongue, my sister." Saed smirked, his speech slurred slightly. "Otherwise, I will rethink my decision to let you remain here once our father has passed on."

Layla felt a surge of heat move through her and stripped off the robes that covered her Chanel suit. "You should leave, my brother. I trust you're not driving. It would be most embarrassing if a patrol found you intoxicated behind the wheel."

"No more embarrassing than that stunt you pulled with the American investor group."

"Stunt?"

"Theme parks and entertainment centers? Saudi Arabia as a center for tourism? You can't really be serious."

"Change is inevitable, my brother. It's strictly a matter of who can best see how to use it."

"This time your vision has deceived you. My first order of business upon taking over Rahani Industries will be to inform the Americans that this project has been scuttled."

"You?" Layla challenged, shaking her head. "Our father would never entrust the fruits of his labor and life's work to a playboy drunk." Layla paused, choosing her next words carefully to better enjoy them. "He has chosen me to succeed him. And *my* first order of business will be to have the paperwork on the American deal drawn up."

Saed smiled broadly, as if she had fallen into his trap. "Really? The documents he left with the council reveal a different decision."

"Then you must have read them under the usual influence," Layla said, but she felt suddenly uneasy; something was all wrong about her brother's demeanor. Crass as always, yet somehow confident and insolent. Was it possible he was telling the truth?

"Come now, my sister," Saed taunted, seeming to enjoy himself, "did you really think our father would shame himself by entrusting everything he built to a woman's hands, much less a woman who would build roller coasters and water parks? It would have made Rahani Industries pariahs in the country we helped to build."

" 'We,' my brother?"

"He kept me closer than you realize, my sister. I only wish you could hear it from him directly. Based on his condition, though, it's clear that won't be happening." Saed shook his head dramatically, the scotch exaggerating the motion. "Did you think I wouldn't figure out what you were up to?"

Layla shook her head. "I don't believe this, not any of it."

"You can see the papers for yourself. Check our father's signature."

"No. He wouldn't. He *couldn't*."

Saed advanced closer to her. "Why? Because you were his eldest, his favorite? A woman, and half American to boot, with a mother who disgraced the family? He didn't deceive you, my sister. You deceived yourself."

"I refuse to accept this," Layla said firmly.

"You have no choice," Saed sneered. "Unless you can get our father to change his mind, of course. Then again, he has no mind left, does he?"

Layla willed herself to stay strong, to hide the shock and disappointment enveloping her. "This isn't over, Saed."

"No, it won't be over until I have officially taken charge. In the meantime I have removed your signatory powers and begun the process of informing our associates of the change in procedure. Feel free to keep your office, though."

"How generous of you."

"But you will not be permitted to use it without my approval. From this point on, you will not be permitted to enter the building without that same approval and never"—here Saed cast her a disapproving stare—"as you are dressed today." A thin smile crept over his face. "Try as you may, you are not our father, my sister."

"Nor are you."

"Close enough."

"We'll see."

DAY SIX

They went at Ben for hours, stealing his sense of time, merging day and night in a windowless room kept alternately too hot and too cold. He might have been back in the People's Brigade compound in Pine Valley before Danielle had come to his rescue, minus the physical punishment.

Ben knew the drill; he'd run it on plenty of suspects himself in his detective days. But this wasn't inner-city Detroit, and these men weren't cops. It was Washington, DC, and the men in suits worked for the State Department. Beyond that, Ben had never done anything that remotely qualified him as a suspect. But the mere mention of "national security" seemed to render that meaningless.

The first group of men, his escorts, had led him out of Dulles Airport in handcuffs, evoking cheers from pedestrians and racial slurs slung Ben's way. An Arab-looking man taken limping out of an airport in custody in the company of men in dark suits and close-cropped haircuts . . . What was the public supposed to think?

They dragged him outside and shoved him into the back of a van sandwiched between a pair of sedans the color of the pavement.

"I'm telling you this isn't necessary!"

John Najarian's husky voice cut through the night before they slammed the van door. They had pushed him back at the gate when he tried to yank Ben from their collective grasp and warned Najarian not to follow them down the concourse.

"You're supposed to be here for his protection, for God's sake! I was given assurances!"

The van doors clunked closed.

"You won't get away with this! You're fucking with the wrong American!"

Najarian's final words would have been muffled by the doors and the engine cranking up, if he hadn't shouted them so loud.

"You hungry?" the leader of the original shift of interrogators asked Ben hours into the questioning. The man had taken his jacket off and rolled up his shirt-sleeves. He seemed to enjoy exhibiting the nine-millimeter he wore tucked into a shoulder holster that still smelled new.

"No," Ben said, "I'm not."

" 'Cause you look hungry. I can get you something to eat if you want."

"I'd rather you just listened to what I've been telling you."

The man rested his palms on the wood-laminate desk-top. The butt of his pistol poked a little forward. "That's the problem. You haven't done a very good job of convincing us. Let's start at the beginning."

"The Israelis are much better at this than you are," Ben told the man.

"We contacted them about you. They sent us all the files they had."

"I didn't know I rated files in the plural sense."

"You caught their interest, just like you caught ours."

"You didn't catch me," Ben reminded. "I walked off the plane to meet you. Of my own free will. Maybe nobody told you that. Maybe you just forgot." He leaned back, folded his arms, the hours and exhaustion leaving him almost giddy, not caring anymore. "Last time I checked, we were on the same side."

His latest inquisitor sat down on the desk, trying to make the motion look comfortable. "Well, that's the problem, isn't it? According to the Israelis, you're a royal pain in the ass. They believe you're dangerous." The man narrowed his gaze, glaring at Ben now, his eyes the same chocolate color as the handle of his pistol. "Is that why you left and came to this country?"

"I came home, or did your computer misplace my citizenship information somewhere?"

"You lived with an Israeli agent for two months upon your return."

"Israeli *detective*," Ben corrected. "And she has nothing to do with this."

"Really? Then you deny receiving a fax from her in your office three days ago and you deny calling her later that same night?"

"Yes—I mean, no, I don't deny that. I just deny it had anything to do with Alan Lewanthall."

"You say he hired you."

"That's right."

"To find this . . ." The man consulted a small notebook he kept tucked in his right palm, fingers curved around it to prevent Ben from peeking at the contents. ". . . Mohammed Latif."

"Right again."

"Only there's no record of Lewanthall contracting an outside vendor."

"How many times to how many people do I have explain this? It was off the books because *Lewanthall* was off the books, along with Operation Flypaper."

"That's what he called it."

"Several times."

"No record of that either."

"Because it wasn't authorized!" Ben jerked his chair

inward, and his inquisitor flinched, maybe thought about going for his gun. "It was rejected by whoever rejects those kinds of things around here. But Lewanthall and a few others activated it on their own. Set the whole thing up."

"The idea being to trap terrorists."

"With a plot they wouldn't be able to resist. Al-Qaeda, Hamas, Hezbollah—the all-star assholes of the world."

"Too bad Lewanthall can't confirm any of that."

"There are others in State who can. He wasn't working alone."

"You want us to start a witch-hunt."

"I want you to save your country while you still have a country to save."

The man looked satisfied. "My country . . ."

"What?"

"You said *my* country. Not *our.*"

"Oh, for God's sake . . ."

"Isn't it Allah?"

"I'm a Christian."

"But you still speak Arabic," said the man. "And translate it too."

"What does this have to do with—"

"I'll tell you what it has to do—"

"No! You only know about those pages because I told you about them."

"They were sent to you by Danielle Barnea."

"She found them in a raid on a Hamas leader's hideout. Wanted to know what they said."

"That standard procedure in that part of the world? To send documents halfway around the globe when Israel probably has a roomful of translators? That the way detectives over there work?"

"*Commander* Barnea had her reasons."

"And the pages predicted the end of the world."

"The Last of Days in America," Ben corrected. "And the pages weren't a prediction; they provided permission in the form of a religious edict, or *fatwa*, to bring it to pass."

The man's eyelids flickered. "Our sources in Israel inform us that you have a penchant for that. Going off on your own. Not following orders. Is that what this is about?"

"This is about saving this country before it's too late. Cleaning up the mess your man Lewanthall made. He opened up the smallpox store, served the virus right on a silver platter. Then somebody took it and now that somebody is going to use it unless you damn well do something fast!"

The man seemed unmoved by Ben's assertion. "You're sure it was Lewanthall's mess?"

"What do you mean?"

"Let's talk about your brother, Mr. Kamal."

CHAPTER 42

Professor Albert Paulsen ran his fingers along the edge of a framed portrait of Lincoln hanging on the far wall in the Oval Office.

"Nice picture," he said, turning toward the president. "Can I have it?"

Stephanie Bayliss rolled her eyes, mouthing *I told you so* toward the president.

"Help us out, Professor," the president said, "and you can take possession of the entire National Portrait Gallery."

Paulsen stooped in front of the fireplace and poked at the grate. The sleeve of his bathrobe got caught in the steel and he tore it free, shredding more of the fabric. "Got a better idea. I'll trade you for it. Looks like you could use some firewood. I got plenty stacked and dried."

The president came out from behind his desk and wedged his hands in his pockets as he drew even with Paulsen. "The fireplace doesn't work."

"What do you mean it doesn't work?"

"The chimney's been sealed for security reasons. The fireplace is just decoration now."

"That's the problem with things these days. Too much decoration. Doesn't matter if it works or not, so long as it looks good."

"Is that why you left USAMRIID?"

Paulsen's brow furrowed, as if he were considering the question for the first time. "More or less, I suppose. Mostly it was the bullshit."

"I know how you feel," said the president.

"I warned them this would happen. Even broke it down mathematically. Language you'd think they'd understand."

"Tell me what we're facing, Professor."

Paulsen moved to a Ming Dynasty–era vase displayed atop a marble pedestal.

"A gift from the premier of China," the president explained.

Paulsen lifted the vase from the pedestal and faked tossing it. "Catch," he said, gaining a flinch from the president. "Got ya!" Then he looked back at the vase. "The reserves of smallpox at USAMRIID were stored in liquid form, but would have to be converted to a gas before being released." Paulsen held the vase out before him. "This much liquid aerosolized would be enough to infect eighty million people."

"And how much was stolen from the facility?"

"Five times this amount, but even that tells only a small part of the story." Paulsen replaced the vase atop the pedestal and looped his thumbs through the belt loops of his terry-cloth bathrobe. "Smallpox spreads directly from person to person, primarily by droplet nuclei expelled from the oropharynx or respiratory mucosa of the infected person."

"In English please, Professor."

"Cough and everyone within ten square feet stands a good chance of getting infected. That means the disease spreads geometrically." Paulsen reached out to stroke the Ming vase again. "Half this much released strategically in aerosol form could infect the entire country in ten weeks. One mass release could do it, if you exposed enough people in a large enough setting."

"Does that take into account the incubation period?" Colonel Stephanie Bayliss wondered.

"That's our other problem, General."

"Colonel," Bayliss corrected.

"I'm thinking ahead," Paulsen said, then looked back at the president. "The incubation period of smallpox is unusually long, twelve to seventeen days by best estimates, and anyone infected is contagious for virtually the entire duration."

"What happens after twelve to seventeen days?" the president asked.

"Infection shows up as high fever, malaise, headache and muscle pain, sometimes severe abdominal pain and delirium as well. A masopapular rash appears next, first on the mucosa of the mouth and pharynx, face and forearms, before spreading to the trunk and legs. Within one or two days after appearing, the rash becomes vesicular and later pustular. These pustules are typically round, tense, and deeply embedded in the dermis. Crusts begin to form about the eight or ninth day. When the scabs separate, pigment-free skin remains, and eventually disfiguring, pitted scars form, if the patient is lucky enough to survive."

"The mortality rate is thirty percent," Stephanie Bayliss added.

"Very good, General. You should also mention that there is no treatment."

"But there is a vaccine," Bayliss noted to the president. "Approximately one hundred forty thousand vials are in storage at the Centers for Disease Control and Prevention, each containing fifty doses. Experiments have confirmed that the vaccine is still effective when diluted on the order of five. We're conducting further experiments to see if that order can be increased to ten or even fifteen."

"Don't bother," Paulsen advised.

"Why?"

Paulsen grasped his bathrobe's frayed lapels and looked at the Oval Office fireplace. "Because the vaccine doesn't work either."

CHAPTER 43

Danielle was seated behind her desk, expectantly waiting for Ben's call when the phone rang. She snatched the receiver from its cradle before the first ring was even complete.

"Commander Barnea," she said, hoping to hear Ben's voice on the other end of the line.

"It's Isser Raskin, Commander. I've got something on your one-eyed giant. Can you come down to the lab?"

"On my way."

For security reasons, the city of Jerusalem was outfitted with tiny video cameras on many streets, working on a constant loop to help identify terrorists, preventing some incidents and helping to unravel others. Danielle hoped that one of those cameras had been placed on Yefet Street and might have caught the tall, one-eyed man on tape outside the Old City jewelry shop on the day Zanah Fahury was murdered. Toward that end she had asked Isser Raskin of National Police's forensics division to run the tapes to see if they yielded anything.

"The cameras placed around Yefet Street yielded nothing," Raskin reported as soon as she was seated in his office on the basement level of National Police headquarters.

Danielle felt her shoulders sink, the news deflating her hopes. "Thanks for trying, Isser."

"Wait, Commander, you didn't let me finish. The cameras on Yefet Street yielded nothing, but one on Terful Street, where the old woman lived in the village of Umm al Fahm, that's something else."

"I wasn't aware we had placed surveillance cameras in the Arab villages."

"Neither are the Arabs," Raskin noted wryly, as he reached for his printer and lifted a sheet of thick paper from the tray.

"Is this your man, Commander?" he asked, and extended the picture across his desk.

Danielle inspected it, amazed at the computer-enhanced clarity. The man framed by the shadows of the street was lanky and gaunt, his scarred face almost skeletal and dominated by the black eye patch. She recognized him instantly from the Gaza refugee camp, the man who had killed Hakim.

"When was this taken, Isser?"

"The same day your Israeli-Arab woman was killed."

He gestured toward the page he had handed her. "The information's on the reverse side."

Danielle kept staring at the face. "Have you tried to identify him?"

"That's the bad news, Commander. I drew a blank. If he's on file in Israel, it's on databanks I can't access."

"Don't worry," Danielle said, more glad than ever that her first move upon being named commander of National Police was to promote Isser Raskin. "I know someone who can."

"I HOPE you know what you're doing," Harry Walls said to Danielle before she had a chance to even say hello. Harry wasn't smiling, looking even more bellicose and disapproving than at their last meeting.

"You've got a name for that man in the photo I e-mailed you, don't you?"

"A name? Oh, I've got a name for you, all right. But I'm not going to give it to you, not until you tell me what this is about."

They were meeting at Jerusalem's Holyland Hotel, a favorite haunt of Danielle's since her father had brought her there as a child. Over the years she had watched a miniature reconstruction of biblical Jerusalem being erected one building at a time. The detail, right down to the etchings over tiny buildings, was perfect, the work of a single man who had watched Danielle grow up as his creation came to life. He hadn't finished the project yet and claimed he never would. Danielle envied him that much, a world without expectation immersed in creative endeavor. No complications other than the occasional inconsiderate visitor who touched what he wasn't supposed to.

"He's the suspect in a murder," Danielle told Walls.

"Whose murder?"

"An old woman's. The picture I sent you was taken by a security camera outside her apartment the day she was killed. And he was identified by one of the last people to see her alive as well."

"His name is Sharif Ali Hassan. That mean anything to you?"

"Should it?"

Walls spoke without notes as always, although from the look on his face, Danielle guessed much of what he was about to share had been committed to memory long before today. "Native Egyptian. Served in their intelligence service, quite brutally I might add. Dismissed when links to several radical groups were uncovered. Resurfaced in Saudi Arabia soon after that and was later identified as an al-Qaeda trainer in Afghanistan at a few of Bin Laden's camps. Reputedly part of his inner circle of guards for a time. Wounded and captured in Tora Bora during that stage of the war and was eventually transferred to American custody at Guantanamo Bay."

"You're telling me he's in *Cuba*?"

"I'm telling you he was."

"None of the Guantanamo prisoners escaped. The Americans would have informed us if they had."

"Six months ago, they were being moved from their cages and relocated during a hurricane scare. The storm hit and the marines bunkered the prisoners down as best they could. When it cleared, the two prisoners Hassan had been shackled to were dead and his chains had been snapped."

"Snapped?"

"Not cut, not broken. Snapped. By hand."

Danielle considered the strength it would take for a man to do that. Not a single person she'd ever encountered could have managed it. "He still would have to get off the base."

"This is where it gets interesting," Walls reported. "The marines trailed Hassan to the ocean."

"Are you saying he tried to *swim*?"

"That's what the *Americans* are saying. That's why they never reported an escape. They searched for him for days. They believed Hassan had to be dead."

"Apparently they were wrong."

"He's a certifiable psycho, Danielle. Word out of Guantanamo was that even the other prisoners were glad to see him gone." Walls's expression tensed, hardened. "But a man like Hassan doesn't surface in Israel to kill old ladies, does he? There's something more going on here I believe you forgot to share with me."

Danielle waited until a pair of tourists snapping pictures strolled past them. "What if I told you Hassan was part of the assault team that took out Akram Khalil earlier this week?"

"I'd tell you that makes even less sense than him killing old ladies."

"You're right; it makes no sense at all."

Walls's eyes bore into hers. "What else?"

She said nothing, looked down over the miniature streets of Jerusalem, eerie in their detail, and wished she could lose herself within them. "I can't tell you. Not yet."

"Why am I not surprised? Let me give you some advice: Drop it, drop the whole thing now. Otherwise you'll be giving them the ammunition they need to ruin you forever."

" 'Them,' Harry?"

"Vordi's not running interference for you anymore. Apparently, his attraction had its limits. He's let the lions loose, and they're on your tail."

"I can't drop this now. I don't have a choice. There

was a *fatwa* recovered from Akram Khalil's hideout. It foretold the end of all things in the U.S. I gave it to Vordi."

"I know."

"*You* know?"

"Vordi's report indicated that the pages had been too badly damaged to confirm much of anything."

"You're telling me he never warned the Americans about the threat?"

"He had something more important he wanted to accomplish," Walls said, staring straight at her. "Stringing you along."

"He told me he hadn't checked on the translation yet."

"So you took it upon yourself to send the pages to Kamal?" Walls shook his head in disgust. "My God, Danielle, what did you think they'd do when they found out, especially now?"

"Why?"

"Because Ben Kamal is currently in the custody of the United States State Department, linked to the very plot you helped him uncover."

"That's ridiculous!" Danielle snapped, as much scared as angry.

Walls shook his head. "You never could play the game, Danielle. Instead you played right into their hands."

Danielle turned and started to walk away.

"Don't go back to your office, Commander."

She stopped and looked back at him.

"Vordi's waiting for you there. And not to ask you for a date this time."

"That bastard . . ."

"They're all bastards, Danielle, and you've given them everything they need to destroy you."

"Not yet."

CHAPTER 44

"What do you mean it doesn't work?" the president asked, taking a step toward the pedestal holding the Ming Dynasty vase, where Paulsen was still standing.

"The Dryvax vaccine the general mentioned has been stored since production ended in 1983. It was found to have lost its potency five years ago."

"But the reports I've been getting . . ."

Paulsen turned toward Stephanie Bayliss. "Misinformation, General, meant to deceive anyone contemplating a smallpox release."

"Was it meant to deceive me as well?" the president asked him.

"Now that you mention it, yes. They asked me what to do when they discovered the vaccine was useless. They did what I told them."

"Apparently, the decision wasn't cleared by anyone at a high level."

"I told them that too. It was the whole point."

The president took a deep breath and let it out slowly. "I can't say I disagree with you, Professor, but I'd like to know where that leaves us."

Paulsen looked toward Stephanie Bayliss. "You want to take that one, General?"

"Sir," the director of homeland security began, "our response plan never called for mass vaccination of the U.S. population in advance of a smallpox outbreak anyway. Instead we intended to inoculate rings of personal contacts—family members and coworkers of those infected, for example."

"Ring vaccination," Paulsen elaborated. "It helped wipe out smallpox in the late seventies."

"But you don't think it would help us today."

"Not at all, sir," Paulsen answered, moving to a display of crystal animals set atop a wall table. He slid the tiger and bear together, face-to-face, beneath the portrait of Abraham Lincoln. "Who do you think would win?" he asked, crouching to be eye-to-eye with them.

"Is there a point to this, Professor?" the president asked impatiently.

"Half the people you ask would say the tiger and the other half would say the bear. Same thing here, sir. Different strategies for dealing with a smallpox outbreak were bandied about for years. But none of the scenarios considered an attack of this potential magnitude."

"Then we're in agreement that a complete vaccination of the entire country is called for," Bayliss suggested.

"Called for, yes. Conceivable, you tell me."

"Mr. President, a few months after 9/11 we contracted with a British pharmaceutical firm called Immutech to produce enough smallpox vaccine for every man, woman, and child in America."

"Meaning you can expect to take delivery by 2005," pointed out Paulsen. "A little late, don't you think?"

"Sir, Immutech is prepared to begin shipping the vaccine within four days."

"Using the vaccinia virus grown in live tissue culture, General?" Paulsen wondered.

"In keeping with the standards you set, Professor."

"And this Immutech claims they can have three hundred million doses shipped within ten weeks?"

"Shortly after we contracted with them, Immutech built the most advanced production and processing facility in the world," Bayliss explained proudly. "Eliminates the need to further refine and process the vaccine. It arrives fully processed and divided into vials instead of in bulk form."

"What's the cost?"

"Just under three dollars per dose."

"Cheap."

"Economical," Bayliss agreed. Then, to the president, "Immutech's credentials are impeccable, and they're used to handling large-scale government contracts."

"Nothing like this, I'd venture to say, Director."

"No, sir. But they've got the production line to manage it, and our observers on site assure me they can meet these dates, if they go to a twenty-four-hour operating schedule."

"What happens once Immutech delivers the vaccine?"

Bayliss gazed at Paulsen before responding. "We are in the process of setting up between twenty and fifty clinics per state, which will operate eighteen hours a day. Each clinic will handle a preselected geographical grid. We are also currently selecting the ten thousand health-care workers and volunteers required to staff the clinics. The report's on your desk, sir."

"And does the report say how long it will take before the last man, woman, and child are vaccinated, Director?"

"Seventeen days, sir."

The president weighed Bayliss's words, then turned to Paulsen. "Do you concur, Professor?"

"Last time we tried something like this was the swine flu epidemic of the mid-seventies," Paulsen replied somberly. "Took four months, reached only a quarter of the population, and was administered improperly thirty percent of the time. But God created the world in a week," he continued after a pause, "so I suppose anything is possible."

CHAPTER 45

"Where can we find your brother, Mr. Kamal?" the man from the State Department resumed.

"He has nothing to do with this," Ben said, trying to sound calm.

"But you went to him to help you find . . ." Again the man consulted his notes. ". . . Mohammed Latif."

"My brother was Latif's sponsor in this country."

The man's lips flirted with a smile. "Then I guess your brother does have something do with this, doesn't he?"

"He didn't know Latif was working with Akram Khalil."

"Your brother has had dealings with Palestinian terrorist groups in the past."

"In the past he's raised money for groups loosely associated with them, yes, but not anymore."

The man leaned a little closer to Ben. "Then why won't you tell us where he is?"

"Because I don't want to get him killed."

"By us?"

"By whomever killed Lewanthall."

The man kept at it like a machine gun, his words spat out in nonstop staccato bursts. "You said earlier that your brother was safe, that he was being protected. By who, Mr. Kamal?"

"Whom."

"Excuse me?"

"Whom. I was correcting your grammar. I can do that because I was educated entirely in this country, *my* country. I have a master's degree in criminal justice, and I can recite you the Constitution and the Bill of Rights by heart, if that means anything."

The man smiled smugly. "Not anymore. Now tell me, Mr. Kamal, who is protecting your brother?"

"It's not important."

"Hamas?"

"No."

"Was your brother involved with Mohammed Latif? Is that why he had Lewanthall killed?"

The question hit Ben like a kick to the chest, the first one the man had posed he hadn't heard before. "That's what you think?" he asked, recovering his senses. "You interrogate me for all these hours and that's the best you can do?"

"Your brother has a thick file with us, Mr. Kamal. I don't know who's been pulling strings to keep us off him, but that stopped yesterday."

Ben looked past the man to the wall, where he was certain hidden cameras were perched. "Is there someone in authority here I can speak to?"

The man shrugged. "Sorry."

"How about someone with a brain, at least some common sense? You're in here, dicking around with me, instead of looking for whoever killed your man and plans to turn smallpox into the common cold."

The man's expression didn't change. "Where can we find your brother, Mr. Kamal?"

"This isn't about my brother!"

"Then why has he gone into hiding? Missed classes, appointments, students outside waiting for him during scheduled office hours yesterday and today?"

"Because I thought he might be in danger."

"Why would that be the case, if this isn't about him, Mr. Kamal?"

Ben almost laughed, couldn't believe this man from

the State Department was actually serious. "Because he was with me when Latif was killed. Because his life was in danger." He stopped, then started again almost instantly. "What about the gunmen at the bakery? Did you find anything about them?"

"You're referring to the men you killed."

"In self-defense."

"You must be a very good shot."

"Not really. I've just had a lot of practice."

"You didn't call the police."

"No."

"Were you alone?"

"What's the difference?"

"You said your brother was with you."

"He helped me find Latif," Ben said. "I told you that."

"That doesn't answer my question."

"You didn't ask one. What about the gunmen?"

"That's none of your concern."

"It is if they were part of the same group that killed Lewanthall. And it should be your concern too, but that doesn't seem to matter much to you."

Ben's inquisitor crossed his arms, hardened his expression. "Maybe we should just start at the beginning again. . . ."

"Go ahead," Ben said. "I'm not going anywhere."

CHAPTER 46

"You can go now, Marta," Layla Aziz Rahani said to the nurse hovering near the foot of her father's hospital bed.

Marta bowed slightly and left the room, her face cov-

ered by the ever-present black veil, leaving only a narrow slit for her eyes and matching her black robe, known
as an *abaiya*.

Layla Aziz Rahani watched Marta walk through the
door built in the rear of the room. This had once been
her father's office, the place where she would sit in his
lap while he did business on the speakerphone or stand
next to him while he held audience to his many business
suitors. He was most happy within these walls, surrounded by memorabilia and documents comprising the
successful pursuits of his vision. It was here, together,
that they had spawned the concept of pushing tourism
as the basis for Saudi Arabia's financial future. And the
scale models of the various projects they envisioned still
adorned tables set throughout the sprawling room. Layla
had left them in place, unchanged, knowing in her heart
this was as close as Abdullah Aziz Rahani would ever
come to seeing them completed. She turned from the
models back to the shape in the bed before her, now an
empty shell.

"How are you, my father?" It had been nearly a day
since she had returned, that much time needed to confirm
her brother's claims about Abullah Aziz Rahani's plans
for succession, destroying the dream she had so long
counted on.

How could you have done this? she wanted to ask
him. *After all I've done, after all you promised me . . .*

But she didn't, having tried to convince herself it had
all been Saed's doing, that her father wasn't to blame.
Besides, what was done was done, and her father was
all she had left. "I have much to tell you today," she
said, her stomach turning slightly from the antiseptic
smell of air freshener, pumped into the room at regular
intervals.

Her father lay before her, covered to his neck by a
sheet. Tubes ran in and out of him. Wires strung him to

the various machines enclosing the bed that had kept him alive since a stroke had killed his brain. Most of him had died that day, but a part still clung to life, and Layla remained convinced he could hear her even though he could not respond.

"Your plan, the one you first spoke of as I lay in the hospital all those years ago, goes well, my father. Soon the United States will pay for what it did to both of us. Their government has made it so easy, responded just as you predicted every step of the way." She stopped briefly to choke back tears and settle herself. "The doctors say there's no chance you'll ever awaken again. I ask only for a few moments in the coming days, a few moments when you open your eyes so I can tell you the destruction of their world is soon to begin. I have followed your plan, my father. I want for us to share our success, our triumph, together."

Sometimes the days of the plot's true beginnings drifted away from her. But when Layla was close to her father, listening to the machines pushing air into his lungs and helping his heart to beat, the memories returned as if it had all happened only yesterday. . . .

THEY HAD been on a trip to London, Layla with her mother and younger sister, Kavi. Mostly shopping, which Layla only pretended to enjoy. The truth was she missed her father horribly during these trips. Clearly he was her favorite while Kavi favored their mother.

Her parents had met while her father was finishing his studies in the United States. Abdullah Aziz Rahani had brought back a degree in business and his soon-to-be wife, who, though American, did her best to embrace all the customs and traditions of Saudi Arabia. The land *for their palace had been a wedding gift from the king himself, and the palace was finally completed just before Layla was born. Kavi followed in far less ceremonial fashion two years later. To this day Layla held the distant memory of her father stealing away to be alone. She had followed and caught him crying, not realizing until much later that his tears sprang from the fact that his wife had given birth to a second daughter instead of a son.*

As she grew older, though, he seemed increasingly unbothered by that, having taken Layla under his wing, teaching her as he would have a boy. And Layla embraced the opportunity right from the start. She found herself utterly disinterested in the Western ways of her mother, and came to loathe the trips to London on which she was forced to go.

Then late one night, on one of those trips, her mother had shaken her awake in one of the bedrooms of their hotel suite.

"We must get dressed."

Layla sleepily looked toward the window to find the blinds still drawn and darkness shining beyond. "I'm not ready to get up yet," she had said.

"You must."

"Are we going home?"

That had drawn a smile from her mother, but Layla remembered thinking it looked more sad than happy. "Yes, we're going home."

Layla was barely five years old at the time, but sensitive and acutely aware of her surroundings. Her mother helped her dress and then moved on to Kavi, who wouldn't stop sobbing from having her sleep interrupted. Layla wondered where the servants were who usually handled these menial tasks. Weren't they staying in the next few rooms down? But on this night the only one in evidence was Kavi's governess Habiba, who hurried to pack the toddler's small bag.

Kavi fell back to sleep in a chair once she was dressed. Layla watched her mother scurry around the suite, gathering things into a small suitcase Layla had never seen before.

The last thing her mother stuffed into the suitcase was her jewelry box, filled with the lavish treasures her father was fond of surprising her with. Layla had never seen her mother take the box with her on these trips, had never seen her take it out of their big house at all. Something was alarming about her motions. She seemed scared.

Layla started crying. Her mother came to her side instantly, took Layla in her arms.

"Everything's going to be all right. I promise."

Layla couldn't stop crying.

Her mother eased her gently away but kept her hands clasped about Layla's tiny shoulders. "We're just going on another trip. To a place you've never been before, a wonderful place."

"I don't want to go!" Layla sobbed. "I want to go home!"

"We are going home, to my home."

She drew Layla close to her again, but Layla stiffened and pushed her away.

"I want Daddy!" she cried. "I want my daddy!"

Her wailing awoke Kavi, who began to wail again, causing Habiba to take the toddler in her arms for comfort. Layla felt sick to her stomach and thought she might throw up. She rushed into the bathroom and closed the door behind her.

Layla leaned over the toilet and gasped for breaths between her wails. But the sickness passed as quickly as it came, and she was left there on the floor breathing hard, the tears hot and wet on her cheeks.

Then she saw the phone. It seemed strange for a bathroom to have a phone, but there it was. She picked up the receiver, heard the dial tone. She searched her memory and dialed her father's private number in Saudi Arabia, careful to make sure she stuck her hand in the right hole of the dial before turning it.

The phone made a grinding sound. She heard clicking in the receiver.

"*Front desk,*" *a voice that wasn't her father's announced.*

"*I want my daddy.*"

"*How can I help you, miss?*"

"*I want my daddy! I tried to call him. . . .*"

"*What's the number, then?*"

Layla recited it from memory. Silence followed, and she laid the receiver on the floor, crying once again until she heard her father's voice coming from the receiver. Layla fumbled it to her ear.

"*Mommy's taking me away, Daddy.*"

To this day, Layla did not know whether she spoke the words in English or Arabic.

"*I don't want to go, Daddy! I don't want to go to her home!*"

Her father had started to respond, when Layla's mother entered the bathroom to find the phone cradled in both her hands. Layla watched her draw it to her ear, listen briefly, and slam it back onto its cradle. Then she grabbed her harshly by the arm and jerked her to her feet. Layla resisted, but her mother dragged her back to the living room section of the suite.

Her mother had never hurt her before. She started crying again. She missed her father badly, terrified by what all this meant.

Her mother plopped her down in a chair and reached for a phone on the table. Dialed a number quickly. Layla could hear it ring from the chair, her mother agitated now, clearly frightened as . . .

B elow her, in his hospital bed, Abdullah Aziz Rahani had started to wheeze. A bubbly, frothy sound came in fits and starts that drew Layla out of her trance back to the present. Almost instantly, one of the machines squeezed next to his bedside began chirping a metallic warning.

At the sound of the alarm, the veiled nurse Marta reappeared.

"Go," Layla Aziz Rahani ordered. "I can handle it."

And Marta disappeared back through the door.

The tube feeding air to Abdullah Aziz Rahani's lungs, breathing for him, needed to be cleared. A simple process she had performed dozens of times since his stroke. But today the past drew uncomfortably close, and her hand fumbled the plastic and she felt the tube grate against his throat passage. Layla winced, feeling the pain he could no longer feel for himself. Not that her brother Saed cared about such things. He had never spent time with their father while he was alive. And he only bothered now that Abdullah Aziz was dying because as rightful heir, he wanted to show the proper decorum. The hypocrisy and unfairness of that left Layla seething. But she comforted herself with thoughts of the great plan she was completing on his behalf. This was how she would make herself worthy of the faith her father had once shown in her. Let him see how she had grown to be everything his true heir should be.

"Yu'sifuni hada," she apologized, as if he could hear her.

She finished clearing her father's tube and listened to him wheeze steadily again as the machines sustaining him clunked and whirred. He'd been such a handsome man in his youth, before age and the stroke had whittled away at his bones, turned his flesh pasty and left it painted thinly on his brittle bones.

They had grown inseparable once her mother and sister were gone. There were times when Layla imagined what her life would have been like if things had developed differently. But she had to admit her years growing up alone with her father were the happiest of her life. Teaching her the ways of his business. Imbuing in her a strength and power seldom known by Saudi women. She had always believed it would be her lot as his oldest child to take his position when the fates dictated. Now that her brother had shattered that dream, she turned to the other that was coming ever closer to fruition.

"You'd be proud of me, *walid*," Layla said, stroking his forehead. "I know you'd be proud."

Her cell phone rang, and for a moment she ignored the sound, passing it off as yet another made by the array of machines channeling what passed for life into her father. Finally she snapped alert, plucked the phone from her belt, and pressed it to her ear.

"Yes?"

"There's a problem," said a voice at the other end. She recognized it as that of a Saudi double agent with deep contacts in Israeli intelligence.

"Explain."

"You asked me to monitor the investigation into that old woman's murder in Jerusalem."

"And you assured me the Israeli police would simply file the case."

"According to my source, they did—at least, tried to."

"What happened?"

"A commander from National Police has reopened the investigation."

"When?" Layla Aziz Rahani asked, feeling suddenly chilled.

"Yesterday."

"And you waited until now to tell me?"

"I only just learned the details myself. Her investigation, I'm told, was not authorized."

"*Her* investigation?"

"Don't let her gender fool you. She's very tenacious. Very effective."

Layla Aziz Rahani realized all of a sudden how cold the room was. "I want her file, everything you can find about her. Use the usual electronic channel."

"Of course."

"And I'll want your Israeli contacts to monitor all of her movements."

"That's a problem," the man said, after a pause.

"Why?"

"Because she's disappeared. Even her own superiors in the Ministry of Justice can't find her."

"Use every resource you can. When she surfaces, I want to know it. Is that clear?"

Silence.

"Is that *clear*?" Layla Aziz Rahani repeated.

"All this because of an old woman's murder?"

"You have no idea," she told the man.

CHAPTER 48

Danielle found Colonel al-Asi seated on a wooden bench in the shade of an orange grove. He had half peeled an orange and extended another to her when she sat down.

"I picked them myself. Thought you might want one."

She didn't really, but took the orange the colonel offered and began to peel it anyway. The kibbutz, located in a valley southwest of Jerusalem, was heavily guarded by both army and civilian personnel, making it seem even stranger to find al-Asi here.

"My counterparts in your government have been gracious enough to provide me refuge," he explained, as if reading her mind. "In return for my services, of course."

"What else?"

Al-Asi finished peeling away the rind and pried a section free. "All the fruit I can eat," he said, and eased it into his mouth.

"Where's your family, Colonel?"

He worked another section of the orange free. "Safe."

"Resettled?"

"Isn't that what I just said?" Al-Asi stuck the second section into his mouth, trying to look nonchalant.

"Ben told me you have a wife and three children. My government got them out, didn't they? That's why you're working for us."

Al-Asi looked up from his orange, clearly stung. "You think I'm a traitor, Chief Inspector?"

"I didn't say that."

"Yes, you did. Sitting here with you right now would more than qualify me as one in the minds of some. But everything I do, I do with the greatest good of Palestine in mind. I serve my people, not yours, because my government has stopped doing so."

"I need your help."

The colonel popped another section of orange into his mouth and gulped it down. "I suppose that makes us both traitors, Chief Inspector. Ironic, isn't it? that I have only your people to rely on while you, apparently, have only me."

"Ben's in trouble," Danielle said. "He needs me."

Al-Asi tensed. "You're a world away, Chief Inspector."

"We've always been a world away, Colonel. It never stopped us before."

"I know about Pine Valley, Chief Inspector," al-Asi said softly.

"From Ben?"

"Other sources this time." The colonel stopped, apparently finished, until suddenly he continued. "In the FBI. They wanted me to keep an eye on you. Apparently, they don't trust the Israelis very much."

"They think I killed one of their men."

"They told me as much. And did you?"

Danielle looked at al-Asi briefly before speaking. "I don't know. I doubt I ever will. They were about to raid the People's Brigade compound anyway. It was just bad luck."

"And their agent who had infiltrated the group was shot and killed in the battle."

"The response team that flooded the compound videotaped the entire raid, including me running into the woods with Ben. His face was obscured. Mine wasn't. I left the country before they had the chance to identify me."

"No links back to Inspector Kamal or Security Concepts," al-Asi surmised.

"That was the idea."

"You came back to spare both him and the company the scrutiny."

"The job offer made it easier."

"How long was it on the table, Chief Inspector?"

"Longer than I led Ben to believe," Danielle said evasively, before changing the subject. "Hollis Buchert was never found. He's still out there."

"But that's not why you want to return to America."

"Ben's a prisoner again, Colonel, of the U.S. State Department this time."

Al-Asi's eyes flashed with concern. "A more difficult rescue operation, I should think."

"One requiring different tactics, that's for sure."

"What do you need from me, Chief Inspector?" al-Asi asked her.

"Just what I told you on the phone: help in getting out of Israel. They're waiting for me back at National Police. When I don't return, they'll be looking for me everywhere."

Al-Asi reached into his pocket, removed a thick, padded envelope, and placed it on the bench between them. "I had these papers made for my wife in the event I needed to get my family out of the region fast. A passport, birth certificate, even a driver's license—all American." He paused, looking suddenly sad to Danielle. "There's a diplomatic travel voucher inside as well to help book and pay for your flight."

Danielle lifted the envelope onto her lap. "Are you sure you won't need this for your family someday, Colonel?"

"Inspector Kamal is my family too, Chief Inspector. I'm going to contact a counterpart of mine in the CIA to see if he can be of some service."

"One of your famous favors?" Danielle posed, trying to smile.

Al-Asi's gaze had turned reflective. "His son, also in the agency, was captured in Afghanistan. I used my . . . influence to secure the young man's release. Helping you will relieve him of his debt to me."

"I don't know how to thank you, Colonel."

"There's someone else you should look up while you're in Washington, Chief Inspector: the chargé d'affaires at the Israeli embassy."

"Why?"

"Because he was the number-two man thirty-six years ago on Operation Blue Widow," al-Asi explained somberly.

Danielle thought of Zanah Fahury, the crinkled snapshot of two young girls found hidden inside her dresser.

"That makes him the one man alive who knows the rest of the story," the colonel finished.

DAY SEVEN

CHAPTER 49

"My name's Van Dam, Mr. Kamal," the man said, closing the door behind him.

They'd finally moved him to a different room some indeterminate number of hours before. The kind normally found in a cheap motel, except there was no television and the bed was smaller. His guards had opened the door with a key card, and when Ben tried the handle after they were gone it didn't budge. He tried to sleep and must have managed it for a time, because he was startled awake by the door clicking open. A man he recognized from yesterday carried in a cafeteria tray packed with a hearty breakfast: eggs, toast, doughnuts, juice, coffee, and a Danish. Treating him differently all of a sudden. Something obviously had changed even before Van Dam showed on the scene.

Ben sat up straight on his bed and stared at the man's somber eyes, set far back in his head, and his dark hair. "You're kidding, right?"

"Pardon me?"

"About your name being Van Dam. Because you look like James Mason in the Hitchcock film *North by Northwest*. That's the name of the character he played."

The new man from the State Department didn't look as though he was kidding at all. "There've been some new developments we need to discuss with you."

Ben wondered if this was part of the routine. Send someone different in to see him outside of the interrogation room that for nearly a day had been his home.

Somebody older, with a more authoritative air. The ID badge clipped to Van Dam's lapel was a different color from that of the other interrogator's, signifying additional access and authority. A man usually bothered only by things that mattered.

"It concerns your family, I'm afraid," Van Dam continued.

Ben had been expecting that, more standard procedure, these State Department men handling him through a textbook.

"Mr. Kamal, you should really listen to me. A local police patrol in the Detroit suburb of Livonia responded to suspicious activity at a house. They found five bodies inside."

Something cold clamped onto Ben's insides.

"Two of the dead men were carrying false identification," Van Dam continued. "Two others, sponsored by your brother, were in the country on student visas but had dropped out of sight. The final body was that of a woman the authorities were able to identify." The man's eyes sought him out somberly. "Your mother, Mr. Kamal."

BEN'S SENSES numbed, the nightmare unfolding around him. Van Dam was still speaking; at least his lips were moving, but Ben couldn't hear his words. It felt as if water were clogging his ears. The only thing he could hear was his own heart beating. Then it seemed to stop. He realized he wasn't breathing, tried to suck some air in but seemed to forget how.

"What about my brother, his wife," Ben forced out. "His two children."

Van Dam shook his head.

"They're both in high school," Ben continued. "A son and a daughter. I don't know what year." As if that were important.

"There's no sign of them, Mr. Kamal. We know there was a gunfight that took the lives of all four men—"

"My mother too?" Ben broke in.

The man nodded reluctantly. "I'm sorry, Mr. Kamal."

"I'm the one who should be sorry. It was my fault. I got them all into this."

Van Dam stepped a little closer. "All indications are that some people did get out of the house. But we don't know who exactly, or where they went from there. Your brother and his family could still be safe."

"The police haven't heard from them?"

Van Dam shook his head. "They're looking."

"Do they know how many gunmen?"

"They don't know anything for sure. Everything's changed, though. That's why I'm here." Van Dam's expression looked honestly pained. "Everything you've told us checks out to a degree," he continued, the volume of Ben's hearing rising with each word. "We've retraced as many of Alan Lewanthall's movements as we could, including his recent trip to Boston to see you. You understand nothing he did was authorized, totally below board and off the books—"

"He cost my mother her life."

"That includes his retaining your services and those of your company. There was no log or record anywhere to support your claims."

"What about the men who killed my mother?" Ben demanded.

"As I said, we don't know who they were. But we have managed to identify the bodies of those four men whose bodies we found at that bakery in Dearborn. Traced them to a radical group formerly based in Idaho. The People's Brigade, Mr. Kamal. Have you ever heard of it?"

CHAPTER 50

"How confident are we of this information, Director?" the president asked Director of Homeland Security Stephanie Bayliss.

"Absolutely positive, sir," she reported, not bothering to hide the grimness from her voice.

"Professor Paulsen, are you listening?"

Paulsen sat with legs apart on the Oval Office carpet just outside the presidential seal, his terry-cloth bathrobe splayed out to either side. He was fiddling with an ancient set of jacks he had found in the bottom drawer of the White House guest room where he had spent the previous night. The game seemed to fascinate and confound him at the same time, left him staring angrily at the pieces when the tiny ball refused to bounce on the carpet as he intended.

"Did you get my doughnuts?"

"Professor?"

"They told me I could have anything I wanted for breakfast. I said I wanted doughnuts. They told me they didn't have any, that they'd get some. Not the kind you buy in a grocery store, the fancy kind. You know."

"Let me find out for you," the president said, and hit the button on his phone for the kitchen.

"And, yes, I was listening," he added, failing miserably to master the jacks once again. "Something about a man named Kamal in State Department custody who's telling quite a tale."

"Part of it checks out," said Bayliss. "The State Department has confirmed the death of their operative. But at the same time they've been unable to confirm all of this man's story."

"This dead operative is good enough for me," said Paulsen. He stood up quickly, scattering jacks all over the rug. "I'm going out for a while, have a talk with this Ben Kamal myself."

"And ask him what, Professor?" Bayliss replied.

Paulsen straightened his bathrobe. "Well, General, maybe I'll ask him about Girl Scout cookies. Be a hell of a lot easier to poison the country with those than smallpox. That's what's bothering me here, what I haven't figured out yet."

Both Bayliss and the president looked at him quizzically.

"Why the perpetrators stole smallpox when they had their choice of a dozen other germs and viruses that could do infinitely more damage."

"You think Kamal can tell you that?"

"Right now, he might be the only person who can. Tell the kitchen I'll have my doughnuts for lunch instead."

CHAPTER 51

Danielle had waited only a few minutes when Hyram Berger, chargé d'affaires of the Israeli embassy in Washington, appeared at the large doorway to the reception room.

"I must say, this is quite a surprise," he greeted, taking her hand warmly in both of hers. "To finally meet the daughter of Yakov Barnea after all these years ... To what do I owe this pleasure? What brings you to Washington?"

"I'd like to hear about Operation Blue Widow," Danielle said, without missing a beat.

The warmth disappeared from Berger's expression. Her hand slipped out of his suddenly slack grasp. "I'm afraid I—"

"The plan was to infiltrate the Saudi hierarchy thirty-six years ago after the Six-Day War by placing Israeli war widows in the most powerful families."

Berger's face relaxed, looked almost sad. "The operation saved Israel."

"Then why don't you sound proud?"

"Because I'm not." Berger sighed. "And neither was your father."

"I'M READY," Hanna Frank told Yakov Barnea, the phone pressed tightly against her ear.

"Can you get out of the hotel?"

"Yes, I think so." She turned away to avoid her older daughter Layla's penetrating stare. Across the way, the governess Habiba continued holding Kavi. "But we must hurry."

"My men are already in position."

She didn't regret what she had done for a moment. Her husband had served under Barnea, been killed taking Jerusalem in the Six-Day War. They had met for the first time when Barnea had expressed his sympathies at the funeral, having never failed to attend those of the men who fell in his command.

She was surprised but grateful when the general had stayed in touch. Even more grateful when he made her *an offer that could fill the vast void in her life. He had come to her apartment, where they discussed his proposal over tea. Hanna had accepted without hesitation or thought. The opportunity to serve Israel, to seek a measure of revenge against those responsible for her husband's death, had been too much to pass up.*

The training had begun immediately afterward at a secret base dug out of the Negev Desert: indoctrination, language training, a bit of cosmetic work to make her appear a few years younger, young enough to pass as an American college student. A new identity that would stand up to the utmost scrutiny, constructed for her with the help of the American CIA. Hanna Frank had ceased to exist, for all intents and purposes. She became Anna Pagent, junior transfer student at Brown University in Providence, Rhode Island, whose mission was to meet and seduce the son of a powerful Saudi businessman with familial ties to the royal family named Abdullah Aziz Rahani.

Hanna Frank had come to Brown as Anna Pagent in the fall of 1967, equipped with an intimate knowledge of Rahani's habits and schedule. Where he ate, when he practiced the two sports that were his passion, sailing and fencing. They had taught her fencing in the Negev, and the first time she met Rahani was on the floor, where they exchanged a few parries. The Saudi had been impressed with her skill, not realizing she could have speared him with a lunge at any time and that it took all her willpower not to do so. She had looked at him and thought of her husband shot dead, thanks to men like this, bleeding to death in someone else's arms. She had always wondered what his final moments were like. Was he scared, resigned? Were his last thoughts of her and the family they would never share?

Their courtship had lasted until midway through the semester, when he graduated early and asked her to re-

turn with him to Saudi Arabia and become his wife. Rahani had been honest about the drastic changes this would mean in her life, but Anna Pagent, pretending to be in love, never wavered.

General Yakov Barnea had made three separate trips to see her at Brown through the duration of her courtship, and he was the man Hanna truly loved. It didn't matter that he was twenty years her senior and an Israeli legend to boot. Yakov Barnea was the only man who could measure up to her husband, and Hanna Frank, now Anna Pagent, had let him become a surrogate in her mind.

The last time he had debriefed her in Providence had been only a week before her scheduled departure for Saudi Arabia, in the winter of 1968. As always they had met at the counter of a restaurant called the Beef and Bun. Barnea accepted her reports in a manila envelope he'd casually slip into a worn leather satchel. But on this night he'd reached out and took her hand. Hanna was not then sure whether the gesture was meant to be simply reassuring or something else, something more. It had been snowing outside, and the waitress behind the counter was whining about going home early.

A week later Hanna was on her way to Saudi Arabia. Over the next five years, she had met with Barnea occasionally in London on her shopping trips. But the bulk of communication between them had been conducted through intermediaries, Israeli operatives planted in Riyadh in prearranged places, at predetermined times coinciding with her trips to the city. During her pregnancies, both of them difficult, months would go by without a single contact. Other times she would simply have nothing to report. Then, one fall day in 1973, had come the jackpot that justified the entire operation.

"YOU'RE TALKING about the Yom Kippur War of seventy-three," Danielle realized, when Berger paused in the midst of his tale. "We had advance warning, didn't we?"

He didn't bother answering her question, just resumed in a dull monotone. "Abdullah Aziz Rahani was meeting in his private office with a member of the Saudi intelligence service. Anna listened to their conversation on the transmitter she had planted, provided to her that snowy night in Providence, Rhode Island, by General Yakov Barnea, wrapped in a tampon. It had worked gloriously all those years, never uncovered but also, until that day, never yielding anything pertinent. Apparently, the Saudi intelligence officer had come with instructions on where the bulk of the funds required to finance the Yom Kippur War were to be channeled. The Bank of Rahani was to be the conduit."

Berger stopped again, staring blankly ahead. When he resumed, his voice was softer, slightly broken.

"Four days later Hanna Frank passed a note to one of our agents in Riyadh's central bazaar. That information was passed to General Barnea in Israel, just two days before the most reverent of Jewish holy days. Enough time, fortunately, to prepare a response while pretending not to be prepared at all. A preemptive strike was out of the question without more proof, as was mobilizing forces or informing the Americans. No, the Israeli government decided this would constitute the perfect rationale to utterly decimate the forces of their Arab enemies. Prevent a similar attack for years, even decades to come."

Berger's eyes sharpened. He scanned the room, as if to look for Danielle, aiming his next words directly at her.

"Operation Blue Widow saved the state of Israel, Danielle, but it nearly destroyed your father in the process. He promised himself he would get Hanna Frank, now Anna Pagent Rahani, back to Israel, no matter what it took. The wait for an opportunity proved agonizing but, finally, it came when she reached him about a shopping trip to London that December."

"What went wrong?"

"Everything."

CHAPTER 52

"*Can you get yourself and the children out of the hotel?*" *Yakov Barnea asked Hanna, his voice calm and composed.*

"*Yes, but I must bring Habiba the governess to help me.*"

"*Do you trust her?*"

"*Completely.*"

"*All right. I've got men in the lobby now. Don't worry, they're disguised as hotel workers so they won't give us away.*"

"*I'm not worried.*"

"*I'll have the cars brought round. We'll be waiting when you get downstairs. I'll be inside a black taxi just before the entrance. Hurry.*"

Hanna hung up the phone and gathered up the rest of the few belongings she would be taking with her.

Layla was still sobbing when she rose and extended a hand toward her.

"Come, we've got to leave."

"I don't want to go!" Layla fussed.

"Daddy's waiting for us. It was supposed to be a surprise."

Hanna looked at her oldest daughter and knew she'd been caught in the lie. Layla's gaze also revealed something else, something that looked like hate. Hanna turned back to the phone, wondered if she should phone Barnea and call the whole thing off. But it was too late. If her suspicions were correct, it was now or never. The stakes had grown frighteningly high.

Hanna signaled Habiba to bring Kavi, then reached down and grabbed Layla by the wrist.

"We're going."

"No!"

Layla was still crying when they rushed down the hall, the one suitcase Hanna had packed abandoned behind them. All she carried was a small shoulder bag, packed with her personal items and jewelry. She hit the elevator button with her elbow, reluctant to let go of Layla for fear the child might dash away at the slightest opportunity.

The elevator door slid open, its compartment empty at such a late hour of the night. Hanna pressed L, comforted instantly by the steady whir in her ears as the machine descended.

The elevator chimed upon reaching the lobby, and she held her breath as the door opened before her, terrified the security guards who accompanied her and the children in force on these trips would be waiting. But none of those in the lobby paid her any attention, and Hanna focused on the circular drive fronting the hotel's entrance. Her eyes sought out the black cab that meant freedom, the end of the nightmare these last five and a half years had been.

Hanna felt Layla resisting, still fighting. She was forced to drag her oldest daughter across the polished marble floor of the lobby. To survive her ordeal, Hanna had never considered at length the ramifications of this moment for her daughters. It meant, by necessity, that they would never again see their father or the only home they had ever known, and Layla was old enough to be profoundly affected by that. Hanna was forcing them into a different world, a different culture, forever prisoners of the difficult decisions she had made.

It was more than that, though. The children had proven the best cover she could have ever hoped for, preventing Abdullah Aziz Rahani from ever suspecting the truth even as the attention he lavished on his daughters, especially Layla, distracted him from her. In Saudi Arabia the girls had been objects, part of a plan that served her nation. Once in Israel, though, they would be only her daughters; sad and bitter about being uprooted, perhaps even hateful once the complete truth could no longer be hidden.

The notion of it all now terrified Hanna. The professional in her, completely devoted to the spirit of her mission, had insulated her from the truth of her predicament. But now the reality of it crashed down upon her.

Halfway to the door, a man dressed as a bellhop came straight for her, a grim expression on his face and a pistol coming up in his hand. . . .

CHAPTER 53

"I was the bellhop," Hyram Berger said, his spine rigid and his voice cracking a little. "Yakov Barnea remained outside in the cab. My job was to escort Hanna, her daughters, and this governess named Habiba Aswari out the door and into the car." The old man swallowed hard, his eyes suddenly looking frightened as if he were now back in the London Hilton again. "I was almost to Hanna when the Saudis charged down the stairs from the mezzanine. The men we had posted in the lobby opened fire and the Saudis returned it.

"We didn't, *couldn't,* know then that Layla had called her father. Abdullah Aziz Rahani's men, ten or twelve of them, had the entire lobby covered. I was hit in the leg and the shoulder, went down still shooting."

"What about Hanna?"

"She never stopped," Berger said, as if it still surprised him. "Kept right on moving for the door, dragging Layla. The governess Habiba was in front of her, still carrying Kavi. I caught a glimpse of Yakov Barnea bursting through the entrance alongside another of our men disguised as a taxi driver. They were firing too. You've been in that kind of fight, haven't you?"

"Much too often," Danielle replied, not caring to recall the specifics.

"Well, this was my first gunfight outside of a traditional battle in war. You know what struck me the most? How loud it was, the way the gunshots echoed in the confined space, burning my ears. I don't think I heard anything after I went down, or maybe I was screaming too loud myself, and Hanna's youngest daughter had awoken in the governess's arms and was wailing. To this day I don't know for sure everything that happened."

"But you said Hanna kept moving for the entrance, toward my father."

Berger nodded. "Just behind the governess and Kavi, until her oldest daughter pulled away from her. Hanna ran across the lobby into the center of the firefight after Layla, yelling her name, yelling at her to stop. I remember the shattered glass along the front wall blown outward just before our man dressed as the driver went down. The governess was hit too, and I remember seeing your father was standing there alone, firing with one hand and holding Kavi with the other.

"He backed out of the doorway, turned to the side to shield Kavi, who was still cradled in his arm. A car screeched to a halt behind him, the windows down. I saw muzzle flashes from inside. The child's head snapped backwards. Blood sprayed the glass, speckling it. Your father twisted and opened fire on the men in the car."

"They had shot the little girl," Danielle murmured, deeply saddened by Berger's account of the tragic events.

"Your father was holding her limp in his arms when I crawled out through a shattered glass wall. I ripped my hands apart on the jagged shards before I reached the cab. I remember not caring about the pain. Your father was covered in blood. Staggering, firing at men I couldn't even see as he lunged for the cab." Berger's gaze turned even more grim. "The next thing I knew he was pulling me into the backseat. I remember him piling the wounded governess into the car too, then the engine racing and the tires screeching before I passed out."

"You left without Hanna and her oldest daughter."

"We had no choice. Your father knew that. We could never have gotten past all that firepower in the lobby to her. He wanted to try, I'm sure he did—I could see it in his eyes."

"But there was the younger daughter to think about too. You heard her crying. She must still have been alive."

A sad, quizzical expression crossed Berger's face. "It wasn't the little girl I heard crying, Danielle. It was your father."

"THAT'S ALL I know," Berger finished, collapsing in exhaustion into the chair across from Danielle.

"What about Hanna and Layla?"

He massaged his eyelids, then held his palms over them. "I've said enough."

"But Kavi died in my father's arms. Yes or no?"

Berger nodded, head still in his hands.

"And Layla?"

"Grew up into quite a woman, I understand. Progressive by Saudi standards."

"Political?"

"Why do you ask?"

"I have my reasons. Just answer the question."

Danielle watched Berger's eyes flicker uncertainly, as if she had surprised him for the first time.

"No Saudi woman is political openly."

"What about you, Mr. Berger? What happened after that night in London?"

"I woke up in a London hospital, where I spent the next five months. I was treated like a prisoner, allowed no phone calls or visitors. By the time I recovered, and the Israeli government negotiated my return, the operation was officially over, and your father had been moved into the Office of Strategic Planning, which he would eventually head."

"Thanks to the Blue Widows . . ."

"I assure you the irony of that was not lost on him either. But the fact remains, the tragic ending aside, the operation had saved Israel from almost certain destruction in the Yom Kippur War. From that point on, we never faced another concentrated attack, and we never will again, God willing. Your father changed history, Danielle."

"The life of that one little girl was probably just as important to him."

"I can't say one way or the other," Berger told her. "I was transferred to the embassy here, and we never spoke again. I was never debriefed. No one from Israeli intelligence or military ever asked me a single question. Like nothing had ever happened and, for all intents and purposes, it never had. Operation Blue Widow, after all, had never been officially sanctioned. Your father had the only files, and my guess is he destroyed them after the rest of the women were recalled."

Berger looked down briefly, seeming to study the Oriental carpet at his feet before continuing.

"His status as a legend in Israel's history was solidified. He would have been given command of the IDF or a cabinet-level position if he hadn't clashed with Sharon over the Lebanon invasion ten years later. Militarily, of course, your father was proven correct, but the stand made him a liability politically."

"It runs in the family," Danielle said.

Berger's gaze grew slightly distant until it locked on Danielle. "I look at you and I see him. That wasn't true with either of your brothers."

"I'll take that as a compliment."

"Don't. Your father never learned to detach himself from the personalities he worked with. You should learn from his mistakes . . . and mine."

"You never told me what happened to Hanna Frank."

"It doesn't matter now. Believe me."

"I believe it *does* matter. I'm here because a week ago an old Israeli-Arab woman was murdered in Jerusalem. An old woman who lived as a recluse for years, even decades, and financed her life by selling diamonds to a jeweler in the Old City. An old woman who kept a picture of two young girls taped inside her dresser so it would never be found."

With that Danielle produced the tattered black-and-white snapshot and leaned over to hand it to Berger.

"Are these girls Layla and Kavi, Mr. Berger?"

He gazed up at her, the picture trembling in his hand. "I can't be sure, it's been so long. It looks like them, yes, but . . ."

"Yes?"

"What you're suggesting about this old woman in Jerusalem, it couldn't be true. She wasn't Hanna Frank."

"How can you be so sure?"

"Because Hanna Frank died in 1973," Berger managed, his voice cracking slightly. "She was stoned to death."

CHAPTER 54

"*Come, Layla,*" *her father said, crouching so he was eye to eye with her, "you must throw the first stone. . . .*"

LAYLA AZIZ Rahani thrashed in bed, the dream assaulting her, seeming like a videotape replay as her father pushed the rock into her hand, closed her fingers around it and . . .

. . . SHE TURNED back toward her mother, buried up to her neck, only her head showing ten feet away. Her father had kept her back when he had made her mother swallow one at a time the diamonds he had bought for her, a few still in their original settings as rings or earrings. But Layla had sneaked up closer, strangely unmoved by the agonizing grimaces that came when each stone was forced down her throat.

Then she watched her father fasten the black cloak over her mother's face before tightening Layla's hand around the rock he had given her.

LAYLA AWOKE in her bed, she and her bedsheets soaked in sweat, glad to be free of the nightmare. She rose and climbed into her bathrobe to check on her father. The nurse Marta was usually with him twenty-four hours a day, but somehow Layla found the process of checking on her father herself soothing. She lived in constant fear of the moment Marta would come to her with the inevitable news she dreaded: that her father was gone, that the machines had at last failed to pump life into him.

Even in his current condition, he was all she had, the memories of the happier times easier to conjure when she could visit his bedside.

How could you have done this, chosen Saed over me as your heir?

If Layla had been able to peer this far ahead into the future all those years ago, maybe she would have made a different choice. Maybe her mother had truly loved her more, which made the memories of those final moments even harder to bear. . . .

LAYLA DREW the rock overhead and held it there. Her father patted her shoulder in support. She gazed back, reassured by his strongly somber gaze. The rest of the men gathered held their distance behind them, looking silent and purposeful. Layla had to do this to renounce the part of her that was her mother. She hated that part, wished to excise it from her body. Her father had explained this was the only way to rid herself of it forever.

Her arm had begun to tremble now. The rock clutched in her hand felt incredibly heavy.

The first stone to be cast was hers, her father had explained, a great privilege he said she had earned by calling him from London weeks before. Layla's stomach fluttered. She felt herself weakening against all the insistence of her father to remain strong. She tried to remember the terrible thing her mother had intended to do, still felt tears beginning to well in her eyes.

So she focused on the world of her mother instead, the world that had spawned her and made her do these terrible things. That world was the reason why this was happening. That world was to blame. That world was why Layla held the rock in her hand, which she finally began to bring forward, angling down, feeling her fingers release their hold upon it. . . .

SHE HAD entered the hospital room she'd had built for Abdullah Aziz Rahani after the stroke to find the veiled nurse Marta by his side. Marta bowed slightly and took her leave as soon as she saw Layla.

Hovering over her father's bedside usually made Layla feel better, but not tonight. Tonight the memories were too strong, evoked by the inevitability of what she had committed herself to.

Her hatred for the West, for the United States, had only grown greater after the stoning. Layla had been attending a prestigious school where many of the students were the children of American businessmen living in Riyadh, and she began to get in fights with both the boys and the girls. She was warned repeatedly that such behavior would not be tolerated but did nothing to change her behavior. She liked pulling their hair or pinching them until they cried. They yelped like animals and yelled for their mothers, which only infuriated her more.

She wanted to do to them what she had done to her mother, do it to every last one of them. But there were so many, at the school and beyond. Eventually her behavior grew so intolerable that the school dismissed her in spite of the Rahani name. Her father hired tutors for her at home and used his influence to have the school closed down for religious reasons.

He began spending even more time with her, involving Layla increasingly in his day-to-day world she came to love. She welcomed the opportunity to incorporate herself into his businesses as she grew into her teens, taking vast pleasure that he showed no such attention to the children his other wife had given him, including his oldest son, Saed.

The terrible incident during her brief college tenure in the United States could have driven a stake between them, but instead it served only to draw them closer. From that moment on, Abdullah Aziz Rahani stopped visiting the palaces of his second wife and family. It was as if Layla was all that mattered to him in this darkest of times, and that, more than anything, was what gave her the strength to survive.

Today she was every bit as beautiful as she had been then, her features virtually unchanged. But her eyes had lost their spark, their life. She saw it herself in the mirror, knew the sheen returned only when she was immersed in the completion of her father's plan to make sure the decadent world of the United States would soon ruin no more lives.

American civilization had to die. If only that could be as easy as killing a person, as easy as letting the rock go and watching it . . .

. . . *SOAR FORWARD, climbing briefly before it came down and smacked her mother's hooded cheek with a dull thwack.*

Layla stepped back and listened to her mother groan. Then her father took her hand in his as he raised a rock in the other. He hurled it downward and it caught her mother's skull, snapping her head back a little.

She cried out this time, as the solemn men dressed in robes came forward, feet crunching the sand, hands clutching rocks and stones of varying sizes. They stopped even with Layla and her father, looking to him

*for a signal. He muttered a quiet prayer under his breath
and then Layla watched him nod ever so slightly. . . .*

"WE DID what we had to do," she said, holding her father's frail hand. "I never loved you more than in that
moment, until the day you knelt by my bedside in the
hospital and vowed vengeance. You read me the passage
of the last of days from the Koran, and I never forgot a
word of it."

Her father had known the answer lay not in bullets,
or atoms, or tiny microbes, all of which would leave the
United States free to emerge stronger to seek revenge.
That was where the terrorists had erred so badly in their
calculations. Misjudging America's resolve, her capacity
and willingness to strike back.

So the answer was not to kill, not to strike overtly.
The answer lay in subtlety, striking America in a way
so that the realization of the attack would come too late
to matter. By that time the great power of the West
would be dying, powerless to help itself. A slow, lingering death that would leave the United States no one
to lash back at.

*Smallpox was just a tiny beginning, utilized to bring
about a much more definitive end.*

Because the smallpox would merely provide the cat-
alyst. And once it was released the true substance of her
father's plan would be set in motion, unstoppable, its
ultimate success inevitable.

Fate smiled. Fortune grinned.

Then, suddenly, fate's expression had changed a
month ago when she made a trip to a London jewelry
store and saw a diamond ring featured in the display
case. A ring she knew very well because her mother had

often let her wear it on her thumb as a child. Once she thought she'd lost it and spent the entire day in terror searching, only to learn her mother had slipped the ring from her hand as she slept. Layla had stared through the glass of the London jewelry store's display case at the ring in utter disbelief, trying to make sense of the sight, find some explanation for it other than the incredible possibility that her mother was still alive.

Suddenly the culmination of her father's plan of vengeance against America no longer seemed as important. Another task awaited her, equally dire and pressing. She had traced the ring's origins from the London jewelry store to a much smaller one in the Old City of Jerusalem. Then she dispatched Hassan to Umm al Fahm in Israel, which should have been the end of it and would have been if an Israeli detective hadn't doggedly pursued the investigation.

Why would the murder of an old Israeli-Arab woman matter to Danielle Barnea? Why would it matter to anyone?

Layla Aziz Rahani's thoughts were interrupted by the chirp of her cell phone.

"Barnea's in Washington," said the voice of the Saudi Arabian double agent with a pipeline into Israeli intelligence. "She's been to the Israeli embassy."

"I'm still waiting for you to send me everything you have on her."

"Everything?"

"Is that a problem?"

"Not if you have a lot of time to read."

"I intend to have plenty soon," said Layla Aziz Rahani.

CHAPTER 55

"They're led by a man named Hollis Buchert," Van Dam resumed when Ben said nothing. "Formerly based in Idaho but with satellite groups in a dozen locations all over the country and still dedicated to overthrowing the government."

"Formerly," Ben repeated.

"The brigade's base compound was raided ten months ago, almost two dozen killed and at least that many captured by the FBI, after one of their agents died in the shootout. The details remain sketchy. A private group was suspected of doing some of the killing. There are stories about a woman infiltrating the base on her own. You haven't heard any of this before?"

"No," Ben said, even number.

"You know nothing of this woman."

Ben shook his head demonstratively.

"And you've never had any previous contact with the People's Brigade?"

"None."

Ben tried to make sense of what Van Dam was saying, pictured the People's Brigade wiping out the rest of the terrorists Operation Flypaper had lured together and ending up with the smallpox. But this wasn't Buchert's plan; Akram Khalil's assassination proved that. Khalil had set up Buchert, just as someone else had set up Khalil.

"We should talk more about your brother, Mr. Kamal," said Van Dam.

"This isn't about my brother," Ben told him, forcing the words out. "It never was."

"But he's been involved, knowingly or not, through sponsorship and support, with terrorists. He's helped a few of them melt into our society and disappear, including two of the men who were found dead in that house. It's not a good time to keep the wrong friends in this country, Mr. Kamal. I shouldn't need to tell you that."

Ben rose to his feet so he could look Van Dam in the eye. "You've got to let me out of here."

"We can help you find your brother. Tell us where to look."

"And I'm supposed to trust you. . . ."

"I'm all you've got."

"The State Department was all Lewanthall had, Mr. Van Dam, and look where that got him."

CHAPTER 56

"What now, Mr. Jenkins?" Danielle asked the CIA man, when they pulled up across the street from the State Department.

She had rendezvoused with the man near the Korean War Memorial on the Mall, not sure if Jenkins was his real name or not. She had expected the CIA man to be standoffish and bitter over being forced into this favor. Surprisingly, he was simply relieved, it seemed, to finally be rid of the debt he had owed Colonel al-Asi, who had saved the life of his son.

For her part, Danielle fought against the distraction caused by Hyram Berger's final words to her: *If Hanna*

Frank had been stoned to death, who was Zanah Fahury? Danielle thought she had begun to figure everything out. Now she had to reconsider her information, especially the connection between the old Israeli-Arab woman's murder and the killing of Akram Khalil. That had been the link she had followed to the source of the end of all things. Without it, she had nothing.

Soon, though, she would have Ben.

"How do we handle this?" Danielle continued, when Jenkins remained silent.

"I have something for you," the man from the CIA said, reaching into his pocket.

"Transfer documents so you can take Ben Kamal into your custody," she said hopefully.

His eyes scoffed at her. "Hardly."

"I thought—"

"You thought we could simply walk into the State Department and take custody of their prisoner? This isn't Israel, Ms. Barnea." Jenkins finally produced a single, thin envelope. "You'll find a State Department identification and badge inside the envelope, complete with your picture."

"*My* picture?"

"There are tunnels running under the State Department connecting it to the White House, Capitol, every major building in Washington. Updated in the wake of September 11, 2001, for use in an emergency or to access the underground bunkers reserved for high-level personnel."

Jenkins stopped and gazed across the street at the State Department's imposing structure.

"There are no detention facilities inside the State Department," he continued. "Your friend Mr. Kamal is being held in an area of rooms for personnel stranded in the city, or too busy to go home."

"The access to these tunnels . . ."

"I'll get you that far and point you in the right direction. The tunnels rely on an electronic surveillance system that includes video cameras that will be conveniently down for the next two hours until . . ." Jenkins checked his watch. ". . . six o'clock. But if you're caught in the tunnels or the building, I won't be able to help you."

Danielle opened the envelope and inspected the ID card and badge. "You mean, if these don't hold up."

"I did the best I could on short notice, Ms. Barnea. You can tell your friend the colonel this makes us even."

CHAPTER 57

Ben sat on the edge of the bed, face buried in his palms. He felt helpless again, his mother lost to him just as his wife and children were years before. The feeling too painful, too familiar, too much to bear.

We'll be safe, his brother Sayeed had assured him, confident in the protection provided in his own world by men beholden to him. But those men had not been enough. Two had died, taking two of the enemy with them. The others had fled.

Ben started picturing it in his head, battling his brain to stop and failing.

The house stormed in an all-out assault by Hollis Buchert's men deep in the night. Sayeed's guards caught by surprise but still able to fight back, mount enough of a response for Sayeed to gather up the family. His mother killed, sacrificing herself so Sayeed and his family could get out. This final part was cloudy and vague but Ben somehow knew it was true. Or maybe that was merely his way of lending some value to his mother's death and helping to absolve himself of the guilt that racked him.

Ben imagined what it would have been like if Van Dam had delivered the news that Sayeed, his wife, Irsi, and their two children were dead too. He shuddered, wrapped his arms about himself, and drummed his feet on the tile floor.

If you get in trouble, if you can't reach me, go to the cabin on Saginaw Bay and I'll meet you there. . . .

Those had been Ben's instructions to Sayeed, and now everything rested in the hope that he had complied. The cabin, pride and joy of Ben's father during his brief time in the States and a place few were aware existed. Ben's mother had stubbornly refused to sell the cabin, even though no one in the family had used it since his father had left and never returned. She'd never even had the deed changed from the fake name Jafir Kamal had given the seller after the real estate agent had warned he didn't like Arabs. So anyone trying to follow Sayeed's movements would be hard-pressed to trace him to the cabin, nestled hundreds of miles from Dearborn.

Ben hadn't told Van Dam about his instructions to Sayeed and had no intention of doing so. That would lead only to more men being dispatched and the very real possibility that the wrong ones would reach the cabin first.

Hollis Buchert . . .

If only he and Danielle had killed him when they'd had the chance. Because they hadn't, Buchert had gone underground and had ended up taking delivery of the smallpox from Mohammed Latif after it was stolen from USAMRIID.

Ben rose from the side of the bed and felt his knees

crack from the sudden movement. He tried to stretch some blood and life back into his arms, then lowered himself to the floor, slid under the bed, and began to feel along the mattress for a bedspring, something steel and sharp he could turn into a pick to unlock the door to his room. It took only a few minutes for his probing fingers to find a strand of thick steel wire looped through a slot that allowed the bed to be adjusted.

He shimmied farther under the bed and worked his hand about the wire, trying to loosen and stretch it. The final twist came quicker than he expected and the wire hit the floor with a clink. He pawed the floor for the wire, closed on its still-curled shape, and pushed himself back out from under the bed.

CHAPTER 58

The tunnels underneath the buildings of the State Department were well lit and surprisingly clean. Not what Danielle had expected at all. Then again, they were seldom used, and few knew of their expansive extent.

The tunnels were constructed of ten-foot-wide channels that curved their way beneath the center of Washington, twisting in corkscrew fashion to avoid the adjacent Metro tunnels. Jenkins had guided Danielle to an entrance disguised as a Metro stop under construction.

"How many of these are there in the city?" she had asked Jenkins.

"Enough," the CIA man had said evasively. "Not all

of them disguised the same way this one is."

"And not just for emergency escape either."

Jenkins hadn't bothered trying to deny her assertion. "No. They also provide essential personnel a wide number of access points to use in the event of that same emergency. These are people who have to get to their desks no matter what. The world ends, that's where you'll find them, so long as they can get there," he'd said. "Thanks to these tunnels, they should be able to."

Jenkins had led Danielle down the stairs to a steel slab door marked CONSTRUCTION PERSONNEL ONLY. He'd used a strangely shaped key to unlock it and then shoved the door open. Its bottom had scratched against the rough asphalt, screeching metallically.

"Don't I need that?" Danielle had asked, as he repocketed the key.

"The doors open from the inside, not the out," Jenkins had explained. "This is the closest one to the State Department annex, but there are others located close by to the west and south. Follow the tunnels with the red lines along the walls to station forty-two. The door there leads directly up into the section of the State Department equipped with the overnight rooms." Jenkins had reached into his pocket and emerged with a key card, which he handed to Danielle "You'll find Ben Kamal in the room marked *R* on the fourth floor of the building."

BEN HAD managed to straighten the bedspring wire but was having no luck at all deciphering the door's delicate lock mechanism. He had never tried to pick a door from the inside, much less one that was activated electronically. For all he knew, it might not even be possible.

Still Ben continued to try, easing the wire into the

mechanism, searching for tumblers that continued to elude him. At least he was doing something, although it was hardly enough to take his mind off his mother.

He had thought his return to America would reinvigorate the relationship with her as well as with his brother. But his work for Security Concepts had conspired against his plans, both in terms of time and logistics. He could do nothing about the relocation of the company's headquarters from Detroit to Boston and very little about the long hours and travel the job required. Ben had never really quizzed John Najarian on his exact responsibilities, assuming they would be mundane if not boring.

But 9/11 changed all that. Suddenly private security companies were being asked to take on jobs previously entrusted to professional law enforcement personnel, now severely strapped for time, or never entrusted to anyone at all. Ben's police experience, coupled with his expertise in languages, had made him a valuable asset to a company that grew tenfold in a single year. There were background interviews to be conducted, allegations of corporate espionage to be investigated, security procedures to be designed and taught to dozens of Fortune 500 companies who woke up one morning and found themselves in a different world.

Danielle's departure in the wake of Pine Valley had led him to plunge even deeper into his work. Security Concepts became all-consuming, as if he had come home to a business instead of a country. But the money was good and allowed his mother to keep the family cabin when an overdue tax bill climbed well into five figures.

Just sell the damn place, Ben had chided. He remembered the look on his mother's face when he had said that, his brother across the room shaking his head, glad the words hadn't been his.

His hand cramped, and he yanked it back from the door. The bedspring wire dropped to the floor. He leaned over to retrieve it and had just reinserted it into the door when a hollow click sounded and the door popped open.

Ben figured, incredibly, he must have hit the spot, springing upright from a crouch when the door swung open before him.

"I hope I'm not interrupting anything," greeted Danielle Barnea.

CHAPTER 59

B en lost himself in Danielle's arms, not believing it was really her until he smelled her hair, her skin. Missing for so long but never forgotten and always familiar.

"God, this feels good," he said softly as he held her.

A moment later he felt Danielle ease him away. "We've got to get out of here right now."

Ben fought the urge to take her back in his grasp. "Yes," he agreed, thinking of his brother and the cabin on Saginaw Bay, "we do."

WITH BEN at her side, Danielle retraced her steps down through the stairwell, checking her watch when they reached the tunnels.

"We only have a few more minutes before the security cameras go active again."

"How'd you manage that? No, don't tell me: It must have been al-Asi."

Danielle nodded.

"Is that how you found me too, how you learned I was here?"

"No, I found that out from a Mossad agent," Danielle replied, setting a brisk pace down the sprawling expanse of the tunnels.

"I never mentioned a thing about you. Your name barely even came up."

"They traced our communications, knew about the fax I sent you. Apparently our intelligence services exchanged notes. Has anything changed since we spoke two days ago?"

"My mother's dead." Ben was surprised the words emerged so plainly, so flatly, especially when the news was still so raw, like a sucking wound.

"Oh, my God . . . I'm so sorry." Danielle stopped in the tunnel and took his hands in hers again. "How?"

"I told you about my brother's involvement. He went into hiding, assured me he was safe."

"Someone got to him."

"The People's Brigade."

Danielle shook her head, eyes wide with shock. *"They're* involved?"

"I killed four of the Brigade's soldiers in a bakery in Dearborn. They're the ones Latif delivered stores of the smallpox virus to."

"Hollis Buchert?"

"Undoubtedly. You heard him talk, Danielle. He'd like nothing better than to bring this country down. Now he's got the means to do just that."

She turned and brushed some more hair from her face. The thin light shining down from the hole above framed her face in shadows that made her features seem unusually vibrant and vital. "Unless we stop him."

ALBERT PAULSEN sat on the small bed in the room occupied until ninety minutes earlier by Ben Kamal,
bouncing slightly as Van Dam looked on.

"What'd you feed him?" Paulsen asked suddenly.

"I really couldn't—"

"Wasn't Girl Scout cookies, was it? Because that
would be enough reason to explain why he escaped."

"We've put the word out. We'll have him back soon."

"No, you won't," Paulsen said, and looked around the
room again. "I'll want to listen to the tapes of your interviews with him."

"There's nothing on them that can possibly help you."

"We'll see."

DAY EIGHT

CHAPTER 60

"A great pleasure to have you here, Ms. Rahani." The plant manager, Hazeltine, clasped Layla Aziz Rahani's right hand between his own almost reverently.

Rahani slid it from his grasp uneasily. "I trust my coming here has been kept strictly between us."

"Of course, as per your instructions. We British are quite adept at exercising discretion, unlike our American brethren, if you don't mind me saying."

Rahani forced herself to share a smile with the man. "I quite agree. Rahani Industries' continued interest in Immutech remains contingent on the preservation of secrecy. I'm sure you understand."

"Quite," Hazeltine nodded, even though it was clear he didn't, couldn't, understand.

"Very well, then," Layla said. "I trust things are going well."

"Splendidly, madam, splendidly! As my daily memos have indicated, we are operating twenty-four hours a day to meet the timetable of our American friends. Since the line was already set up to meet the vaccine's specifications, expanding the process proved to be of only minor inconvenience. Just a matter of jobbing out other production contracts to additional facilities. I anticipate we won't miss a single delivery."

"That is excellent," Rahani complimented him. "I noticed a few Americans on my way through the complex a few minutes ago."

"Very perceptive of you, madam. Just observers sent by the U.S. government to oversee the process."

"But not supervise."

"Of course not."

"And none of them have raised any questions about the Rahani family interest in Immutech."

"That is business, madam," Hazeltine reminded her. "And, as such, is none of their concern. Your interests, in this regard, are what concern me."

"It occurs to me, Mr. Hazeltine, that your vested shares will be worth nearly seventy million dollars once this deal is complete. They're your interests too."

The contract for the vaccine had been awarded to Immutech only after the company built an ultramodern, state-of-the-art facility on the outskirts of a business park developed by British financier John Madjeski. Located just beyond a turnoff for the primary M-4 freeway and only twenty minutes from Heathrow Airport, Immutech occupied the development's largest tract of land within clear view of a similarly new soccer stadium Madjeski had built for Reading's professional team. The plant had set a new standard for the pharmaceutical industry and helped Immutech achieve domination in a fairly specialized niche. The company produced bulk quantities of antimalaria drugs, tetanus boosters, dysentery pills, and hepatitis vaccines—the assortment of drugs the American government required travelers to take as a condition for obtaining a visa to any number of countries.

Including, ironically, Saudi Arabia.

Months before, as part of his grand plan, Abdullah Aziz Rahani had financed the massive construction effort meant to place production, research, design, and storage all in the same facility. Normally vaccines were produced in bulk, only to be finished or refined at a second facility in the U.S. Immutech's new automated assembly line had rendered that procedure obsolete, meaning distribution could be achieved much faster. The stroke had disabled Abdullah Aziz before the new facility was completed, but Layla had shown him the pictures of its finished form as he lay in his hospital bed on the fourth floor of their palace.

"We're on schedule, I trust," Layla Aziz Rahani said to Hazeltine.

"Ahead of it, actually." The plant manager beamed. "We are scheduled to begin shipments in just three days' time. You'll return for that, of course."

"I wouldn't miss it for the world."

Hazeltine rose from behind his desk. "Then let's begin our tour, shall we?"

YOU'RE *WHERE?* Stephanie Bayliss asked Albert Paulsen.

"Ethiopia. Just landed in the jet you were kind enough to lend me. Hot as hell over here and they've got very big bugs."

"I thought you were going to—"

"That's because I lied. No, say I changed my mind. That will look better on the report. The bugs bite, by the way. You swat them for a while, then give up. Some insect repellent would be nice. I had plenty at my cabin but I didn't think it would chase away the kind of pests that breed in Washington, so I didn't bother bringing it with me."

"What are you looking for in Africa, Professor?"

"Ethiopia," Paulsen corrected. "You've read the transcripts of the State Department's interviews with this Ben Kamal?"

"Of course I have."

"Recall his mention of a man named Mohammed Latif?"

"Well, I—"

"Doesn't matter. What matters is I had the State Department run the man's passport. Seems the late Mr. Latif made three visits to Ethiopia. His visa listed his destination as a town called Kokobi. That's where I'm headed."

"For what possible reason, Professor?"

"Let you know when I get there, General."

CHAPTER 61

Ben squeezed his armrests tightly as the 767 broke through the clouds, revealing the city of Detroit below. His grief had come in long, dark patches over the past twenty-four hours, usually activated by a sight or smell, and the view of the Detroit skyline made the strongest impression of all.

It brought him back to the first time he had seen the city, flying in after a plane change at New York's Kennedy Airport on a day much like this in early 1967. He'd been seated next to his mother then instead of Danielle Barnea. His father had been sitting across the aisle next to his brother, Sayeed.

Ben made sure his seat belt was fastened, then turned from the window toward Danielle. But for a moment he saw his mother instead, as she had been in 1967, her hair black instead of gray, her eyes bursting with life, expectation, and trepidation too. She had taken his hand and forced herself to smile. He knew in that moment, even at the age of six, that she was as frightened as he was about the drastic change in their lives. Her stories of the wonderful world they were coming to did little to relax or placate him. They were leaving the only world they had ever known, and the necessity of that move did not make it any easier for them to bear.

Ben could never remember a moment when he had felt closer to his mother, when their bond had been stronger.

"I'm scared too," she had whispered to him, so his father wouldn't hear across the aisle. No reason to burden him with any more worries than he had already.

Ben looked down at the armrest and saw his mother holding his hand, then realized it was Danielle who had taken it, suddenly. She gazed straight ahead, leaving him alone with his thoughts, just letting him know she was there, the gesture as important as the memories that left his insides tight and his throat heavy.

UPON EXITING the tunnels beneath Washington the day before, they had gone straight to Union Station, where Danielle had bought a pair of tickets on an Acela Express train to Philadelphia. Her thinking was that all three area airports, Baltimore included, would be watched in search of Ben once his escape was detected. But Union Station was far more difficult to make secure and a far less likely avenue for him to use.

The problem remained that he had no identification with him of any kind, meaning it would be impossible for him to board a plane. But he recalled that it had always been easy to obtain false identification, especially driver's licenses, in Detroit at various shady downtown establishments. He assumed the same would be the case in Philadelphia, and it took only a single cab ride and a cooperative driver to find him what he was looking for.

The tattoo parlor did not advertise that service among the others it offered in the window. But a simple query from Ben inside led to a trip down a dark staircase into a basement humming with high-tech computers and printers. Various screens had been set up in the back of the single open room to simulate colored backgrounds consistent with the driver's license design of every state in the country.

Ben chose Michigan, giving the address at which he had lived with his wife and children in the Detroit neighborhood of Copper Canyon. The entire process took barely half an hour. Danielle paid the clerk two hundred dollars in cash and they were on their way.

They reached the airport only to find the last flight of the evening for Detroit had already left, leaving Ben still more hours to mix the grief he felt over his mother's death with worry over the fate of his brother. He had tried his brother's cell phone number repeatedly to no avail and no surprise; the cabin had been built just before new zoning regulations on the waters of Saginaw Bay outlawed all construction. So it was doubtful any cell phone provider would have found it necessary to have a tower anywhere near the area.

Throughout the trip, Danielle had said little. But her mere presence soothed him, reminding him how much he had missed her. They had barely spoken at all until last night in the airport hotel, Ben seated in a chair by the window, unable to sleep.

"Do you remember the first time we stayed in the same room?" Danielle had asked from the bed.

"That house in the West Bank," Ben had answered, glad she had spoken. "We were hiding from someone."

"We were *always* hiding from someone. . . . I miss hoping it could work."

"Between us?"

Danielle had sighed. "Our peoples. We were so close, so damn close. . . ."

"You knew all along," Ben had reminded her. "You told me as much."

"Because I realized there were too many on both sides who could never accept what peace meant."

"I guess I was more of an optimist."

"You weren't dealing with the people I'm talking about." Danielle had sat up in bed. "Do you miss being there?"

"The last few days it felt like I never left."

"You know what I mean."

"I miss *you*, that's all."

"I had to go back; you know that as well as I."

Ben had moved from the chair and sat down on the edge of the bed. "Would you have gone back if Pine Valley had never happened?"

"It *did* happen."

"The offer to take over National Police was on the table before then."

Danielle had looked away, toward the window he had just been gazing out of. "That doesn't mean I would have taken it."

"Yes, you would. A job like that had always been your dream."

Danielle had almost laughed.

"What's so funny?" Ben had asked her.

"Nothing, really. Just the fact that the only reason I was offered the job was because a deputy minister thought he could get more out of me than status reports. And when I spurned his advances, he fed me to the wolves who've been waiting to destroy me for years."

"You know how these men are."

"That's the problem: I *do* know, and I still let it happen. I played right into their hands."

"Maybe you should have just slept with this deputy minister," Ben had suggested, trying for humor.

Danielle had looked at him closely. "He's not my type." She leaned back and took a deep breath. "I shouldn't have left you, even after Pine Valley."

"You didn't do it for yourself, Danielle. You did it for your father, his legacy, your family name. Your brothers are gone. You wanted to leave something behind."

"Instead of children, you mean."

'No, I don't. This is different. It's about living up to something. Having children doesn't do that. Becoming the first woman to ever head National Police does."

She had tried not to look annoyed. "And you know this . . ."

"You forget that I went back once too: to live up to the legacy left by my father. I always knew that, but I never realized how empty failing left me until I learned my mother was gone too. For the first time I realized how you felt, why that damn job was so important to accept."

Ben had drawn back the covers and slipped into the bed beside her. "You think you failed?" she'd asked him.

"Don't you?"

"Based on what you were up against, no. You succeeded in spite of that."

"And accomplished nothing, *left* nothing."

"Do I have to review our case files?" Danielle had asked him.

"That's the problem," Ben had told her. "They're *our* case files. Everything I accomplished over there was with you, *because* of you."

"You're wrong."

"Am I?"

"I think you were afraid of success. I think you were

afraid it would do to you what it did to your father."

"It destroyed him. Turned him into a victim."

"Exactly. And you think by denying credit for what *we* accomplished, you can avoid the same fate." She paused and held his gaze through the darkness. "You can't, because other people know what you've done, what you're capable of. Like John Najarian and this man from the State Department."

"The man from the State Department used me."

"You think it was any different when that man hired us to prove the People's Brigade was holding his son? He knew the boy was dead; the FBI agent planted inside would have passed on the information. But he sent us after the People's Brigade anyway, because he knew exactly what he was getting. And when the Ministry of Justice offered me the job of commander, they knew what they were getting."

"You're blaming yourself for what happened over there."

"Because I let myself be manipulated by them, just like you let yourself be manipulated by this man Lewanthall. We're too predictable, Ben. And we have our pasts to blame for it."

"I thought if we stayed here, in America, that maybe . . . Well, things could be different. I knew I could never go back, but you always had a choice, Danielle."

"I'm sorry."

"For what?"

"Turning your own people against you."

"They were turned against me long before I met you. You were the best thing that happened to me over there. But, at the same time, you made me realize I didn't belong. That's what I meant. I belong here; I always did." Ben paused and held her gaze somberly. "You don't. You never did."

Danielle had shrugged, laid her head on his shoulder.

"You'll go back when this is over," Ben had continued, wrapping his arm around her "I know you will."

"Not this time. There's nothing to go back to."

She'd hugged him tight, and they finally drifted off to sleep, together.

THE LANDING jarred Ben alert again. He looked from the outskirts of the airport speeding by beyond the window back to the armrest where Danielle was still squeezing his hand. He squeezed back.

"We're going to save your brother, Ben," she assured him. "Whatever it takes."

CHAPTER 62

"THIS is your first visit to the production facility since it's been online, isn't it?" Hazeltine said to Layla Aziz Rahani, as they began their tour of the processing plant.

"It is," Rahani acknowledged, amazed by the sheer scope of what lay beyond her through the observation windows. She only wished her father could have been here with her to see it too.

"We continue to fine-tune the process," Hazeltine explained. "In pharmaceutical production, being even the slightest bit off can destroy an entire lot. So we test, and we continue to test under the exact specifications until we're sure we get it right."

The sight below through the glass was amazing, awe-inspiring. An assembly line stretching the width and length of two football fields side by side. One hundred-percent automated, controlled by the most sophisticated robotic technology in the history of manufacturing. No human walked the floor, all monitoring conducted and changes made from behind the same glass control room Layla Aziz Rahani stood watching from now. Nothing could be allowed to contaminate the production area, since contamination was one of the top causes of waste and spoiled runs in the industry.

Layla stood behind the glass alongside Hazeltine, marveling at what she saw.

"We're producing three million doses per day," Hazeltine narrated, "which means—"

"You'll be finished in just over ten weeks," Layla Aziz Rahani completed.

"Enough for every man, woman, and child in America." Hazeltine turned from the production process below to look at her. "Your faith and your investment has been justified. You should be quite proud."

"I am, Mr. Hazeltine. More than you can possibly realize."

CHAPTER 63

"You're kidding, right?" the UN doctor assigned to the village of Kokobi said to Professor Albert Paulsen. He had a thick British accent that emerged through a set of dry, cracked lips.

Paulsen mopped his brow with a rag he kept in the

pocket of the sleeveless khaki vest he'd received from his driver in exchange for his bathrobe. He missed the robe already, couldn't wait to buy a new one. "A hundred and ten degrees, flies the size of Volkswagens—no, Dr. Chastity—"

"That's Chastain."

"—I'm not kidding."

Chastain shook his head, clearly perturbed. "You really don't know what happened here."

"Do I look like I came on vacation?"

Chastain sighed, trying to ignore the splotches of sweat that had soaked through his white exam coat. "This village holds the remains of a major fuck-up."

"People looked fine to me."

"Oh, they're fine, all right. That's not the problem. What do you think of when you think of Africa, Professor?"

"Heat and flies."

"Medically."

"AIDS and overpopulation."

Chastain leaned forward on his stool, as if his point had been made. "And if you could do something about the latter?"

"No form of birth control has ever worked."

"The Ethiopian government tried a new one a few years back. Major breakthrough. Simple pill. They even made it chewable. They tested it here in Kokobi. Totally against protocol, I know, but this is Africa, so who would ever know?" Chastain leaned back again. "Apparently no one. It's why I'm still here, why they haven't let me leave. So no one ever will find out."

"Except me."

"You really want to hear this?"

"Can't wait."

"You can, Professor. Believe me, you can."

CHAPTER 64

"It's called Twenty Mile Point," Ben told the clerk behind the Hertz counter, after Danielle had finished signing the agreement for their car.

The clerk tapped the location into her computer and smiled politely. "Nothing under that name in our database. I'm sorry, sir."

"Try Port Hope. Or Saginaw Bay. That's it, try Saginaw Bay."

The clerk tried again, nodding this time at the results. "That did it. Here we go."

Ben leaned closer to Danielle. "We always used to stop at Port Hope on the way to the cabin. If we can find Port Hope, I can get us the rest of the way there."

But Danielle was looking back at the clerk, as their directions rolled out of her laser printer. "We're supposed to meet someone there," she said. "I wonder if they've been through the airport already."

The clerk smiled obligingly. "If you have their name . . ."

"Sorry." Danielle shrugged. "I don't know whose name the reservation would be under. But they would have asked for the same directions we did. Could you check, see if anyone else has?"

"Port Hope again? Saginaw Bay?" The clerk started typing without waiting for a response. "As a matter of fact, a party requested directions to Saginaw Bay at another Hertz terminal just ninety minutes ago. Sorry, I don't have their name. . . ."

"No problem," Danielle said, backing away from the counter. "That's all we need to know."

"SHIT!" BEN yelled when they caught a third consecutive red light after pulling out of the rental lot.

"Stay calm, Ben. We've got time," Danielle said, watching him pound the wheel in frustration.

"They've got a ninety-minute head start on us, for God's sake."

"That doesn't mean they know the exact location of the cabin, like you do. Besides . . ."

"Besides *what*?"

"You said this cabin was isolated. Nothing around for miles."

"Yes."

"Then they won't come until nighttime."

"How can you be so sure?"

Danielle held Ben's gaze. "Because that's the way I would do it."

"Could be it's not People's Brigade soldiers anyway. Could be it's State Department personnel on my brother's trail."

"It's the People's Brigade, Ben."

"How can you be so sure?"

"Because the name on the rental agreement was Heydan," Danielle told him. "The name of the lake where their Idaho compound was located."

THEY MADE good time, hugging the Michigan coast for a long stretch along Lake Huron before moving inland onto a less traveled freeway. To save time, Ben elected not to head back east toward Port Hope, believing he could recapture the route to Twenty Mile Point on Saginaw Bay once the freeway spilled back onto a coastal road farther north.

"We don't have any weapons," Ben said, stating the obvious.

"We've got something better: ourselves."

"Meaning?"

"Whoever Buchert's sending won't be expecting us to be there. He figures he's tracking a college professor, his wife, and two kids. That means they'll come at the cabin the same way they came after that house outside Dearborn: fast and hard."

"And how do we stop them without guns?"

"Leave that to me," Danielle said confidently.

THE ROUTE to Twenty Mile Point came back with surprising ease. Ben found that strange, since the family had only gone there three times prior to his father's return to Palestine. He remembered, as a first grader, counting the days until school was out in June because his father had promised they would return to the cabin the final afternoon. Pick up Ben and Sayeed at school and drive straight from there.

He also remembered the night in June his father sat transfixed in front of the television watching the coverage of the Arab attack on Israel that would later become known as the Six-Day War. Not realizing then that Jafir Kamal had been expecting this and knew what it meant for him.

Ben couldn't have known at that point he'd never see the cabin again until today, so many years later. How often he had thought of it at night after Jafir Kamal had left, recalling how his father had taught him and his brother to fish from the skiff they kept moored against a tiny dock nestled up against the rear of their property.

It was all as clear to him now as it was then. The clean scent of wood that permeated the cabin, especially strong every time they first stepped through the door. The old, heavy furniture that was uncomfortable to sit in. The water that was always cold, fresh, and much better tasting than the water in Dearborn. At night the surrounding woods had been alive with the sound of insects, replaced at dawn by birds and the quiet lapping of the bay currents against the shore.

A few times when Ben woke early, he'd spied his father standing alone on the edge of the dock looking out over the morning mist lifting off the bay. Jafir Kamal relaxed and at peace. Thinking back, that was probably what Ben had loved about the cabin more than anything. Now he tried to remember if his father had kept a gun in the cabin.

"Stop at that store!" Danielle said suddenly, pointing to a combination general store, gas station, and snack bar with a huge OPEN sign twisting in the wind.

"We're almost to the cabin," Ben told her. "Just another ten miles, I think."

"A few things we need to pick up before we get there," she explained evasively.

Ben jerked the steering wheel to the right and the car veered into the sparsely filled parking lot, causing bells to ring when it rolled over the signal wire laid before the gas pumps. He killed the engine and looked across the seat at Danielle.

"Like what?"

"You'll see," she said, and threw open her door.

BEN FOLLOWED her up and down the narrow aisles, pushing one of the store's three wagons. It had a stuck wheel, which made it a challenge to keep headed straight, a fact lost on Danielle, who continued to scan the rows, piling items in as they went.

"I think I get the idea," Ben realized, starting to catalogue them for himself.

She barely seemed to be paying attention to him. "In the Sayaret you never know what weapons will be available to you for a mission," she explained finally. "The idea is to be able to create them from whatever you have available."

Ben checked the contents of the cart again. "Very industrious."

She turned and faced him, putting her hands on his shoulders. "I liked your mother very much."

Ben looked down at her hands, the way they were touching him. "She liked you too."

"Did she approve? Of us, I mean."

"She wanted me to be happy. After you left to go back to Israel, she called me *ahmaq* for letting you go."

Danielle lowered her hands back to her sides. *"Ahmaq?"*

"Stupid," Ben translated.

"You didn't explain."

"About Pine Valley? I couldn't."

"I understand."

"No, you don't. I couldn't tell her what happened there because I didn't know how to tell her what you did. I was afraid."

"That she wouldn't approve of me, of us, anymore? That she'd know me for what I was, what I am?"

Ben could only look at her.

"I told you I understood," Danielle said.

CHAPTER 65

In the end it was the smells that told Ben they were close. He couldn't say what they were exactly—something piney and sweet—but they drew his mind back to a past he had thought was long gone.

The road wound round a rough protrusion of land called Twenty Mile Point, the bay coming alive briefly in glimpses captured through the woods, just regaining their springtime fullness. The road felt the same, lined with ruts and dips the midsize rental took no better than the Ford station wagon Jafir Kamal had bought used from a fellow employee at the Ford plant in the early months of 1967. It was narrow, with barely enough room for two cars to pass side by side, although in his previous trips here as a young boy Ben could never remember seeing another car once Twenty Mile Point was behind them.

Danielle asked him to pull over. She got out and crouched over the road, smoothing the dirt with her hand.

"I don't think any other cars have been by here in the last few hours."

"But you're not sure."

"The road's dry. The signs aren't clear enough to be sure."

"We're only a few minutes from the cabin now," Ben offered. "I'm pretty sure of that."

She looked at her watch, then glanced into the backseat crammed with brown shopping bags. "Three hours before dark. We'll have to work fast."

Ben had never felt closer to Danielle than he did in that moment. The two of them standing alone in the middle of a desolate road, the scene a microcosm of their relationship. He saw Danielle in her element, a soldier doing a soldier's work. Capable of losing herself in it while never losing track of the greater picture.

Ben's hopes that her skills would be put to good use rose when he found the entrance to the private road, long lost to overgrowth. The rental clawed past it, stubborn branches scraping against the windows on both sides. Then his heart sank when the cabin came into view.

It was nothing like he remembered. Smaller, lighter in shade, and not nearly as sturdy in appearance. Not much more than a shack, really. Hardly worthy of a place where so many boyhood dreams had been born.

Worse, it looked utterly abandoned, surrendering to the woods that had encroached on its very being. The front steps were lost to weeds, the roof barely discernible amid the overhang of trees growing out toward the bay waters beyond. The cabin had always been well shaded, Ben recalled. Today darkness enveloped it. No car was in view either, no evidence of anyone having come or gone, making him fret that his brother, for some reason, had disregarded his plan.

Ben pulled the rental to a halt and climbed out. His heart pounded, the fear that Sayeed and his family, Ben's only true remaining living relatives, were lying dead somewhere else far away from here very real now.

Suddenly the door opened with a long creak, freezing both him and Danielle. Then Sayeed Kamal emerged, his face drawn and pale, his expression utterly blank.

Ben met his brother halfway down the steps and hugged him for the first time since they'd been boys. He felt himself crying, letting the tears come now, Sayeed stiff in his arms but not pushing him away. He could feel his brother's eyes drift to Danielle and remembered they had met only once before in the wake of the murder of Sayeed's oldest son, Dawud. The reception then, understandably, had not been warm.

"Our mother, Bayan . . ." Sayeed started when they finally eased apart.

"I know, my brother."

"We barely got out alive. I wanted to go back inside the house for her but I had, well . . ."

"You did the right thing. Your wife, my niece and nephew?" Ben managed, fearing the worst.

"Safe inside."

Ben took a deep breath and let it out slowly. "The men who killed our mother will be here soon." He looked toward Danielle, then back at his brother. "After dark."

"Then we must leave. I'll tell my—"

"It's too late for that, my brother."

"What choice do we have? Even with weapons—"

"You have guns?"

Sayeed shook his head. "Not a single one."

"Then we make our stand without them."

"How, in God's name?"

"First tell me where your car is."

"Why?"

"So we can hide mine too." He looked toward Danielle again and this time he didn't turn back. "After we unload it."

"Unload what?"

Ben continued to hold Danielle's resolute stare. "What we need to make our stand."

CHAPTER 66

Sayeed's wife and teenage children emerged from the house, moving tentatively onto the porch as if waiting for someone to tell them what to do.

Danielle waved a greeting but never said a word, just opened the back door and hoisted out the first two brown paper bags. She glided past Ben and Sayeed on the steps and carried the bags through the open front door. Ben followed suit, as did Sayeed, his wife, and finally his children. It took two trips before all the bags were unloaded and laid inside the cabin, which smelled of age and disuse. Something spoiled and rotten permeated the air, as if it were dying, having surrendered to loneliness and neglect.

The cabin had smelled so differently years before, fresh and clean. Its current condition trumped the memory, invalidating it. Ben walked about past the dingy furnishings, all warped and discolored by age. The heavy wood tables and chairs had survived intact, while the upholstered furniture had not held up well at all. Cracks and tears showed in the upholstery. Bleached-out swatches gave testament to the unrelenting harshness of the sun blazing through the windows. Sleeping bags lay strewn across the floor. The remnants of a fire smoldered in the fireplace. Ben saw kerosene lanterns scattered about to provide light once night fell.

Ben turned and found Danielle standing just behind him, a final shopping bag in her arms. Her eyes swept the cabin's interior, taking everything in as she analyzed their surroundings, the base from which she would lay their defense.

"Make sure the fire's completely out," she instructed. "Close the chimney." She turned her gaze to a nearby garbage bag stuffed with trash. "You shopped on your way up here," she said to Sayeed.

"At a gas station that had a convenience store attached. They didn't have much but—"

"How far away?" Danielle interrupted.

"Ten, twelve miles maybe."

"When did you stop there?"

"Yesterday afternoon."

"There's a window broken in the front here."

"I didn't have a key to the door." Sayeed looked toward Ben. "They came so fast two nights ago, took us totally by surprise. The gunshots seemed to be coming from everywhere. The men guarding us tried to hold them back. Our mother herded my children down the stairs, making sure they stayed low."

"She had plenty of practice in Palestine," Ben said softly.

"She collapsed when she got to the bottom. From exhaustion, I thought, until I saw the blood. It was over so quickly. I had no time to say anything, no time to do anything but get my family out."

Danielle slid between Sayeed's two somber children into the kitchen area of the cabin and began the task of unpacking the bags.

"We need to get started," she told them all.

DANIELLE HAD not found everything she'd hoped for at the general store, but she'd found enough, and now she divided the items into different sections atop the counter and tables. Having inventoried these, she busied herself briefly with a check of the cabin's interior to see what else she had available. The kitchen sink was porcelain, outfitted with a rubber stopper to plug the drain. There was a second sink in the bathroom, not far from an old-fashioned cast-iron tub and shower. The water didn't work and plastic containers of bottled water covered most of the counter. The floor was badly discolored and rotting in several sections, evidence of a leaky roof. It must have been left in similar condition thirty-odd years ago, because a trio of rusty pails rested in three of the corners, their handles long frozen into place.

"All right," Danielle said, "let's get to work."

CHAPTER 67

The cleaning products came first. Danielle instructed Sayeed's wife, Irsi, and the two children as to the proper mixtures to prepare in the rusted pails. The powerful scents of ammonia and bleach filled the room instantly, burning her eyes. Ben started coughing and Danielle opened all the windows, letting the cold air blow through the cabin.

Outside the sky was starting to darken, the sun sinking rapidly beneath the tree line.

In the bathroom, Ben and Sayeed were busy dumping the fertilizer bags into the cast-iron bathtub, then adding gallon-sized containers of kerosene and stirring the mixture with a shovel handle until it matted into a paste.

Danielle, meanwhile, was glad to find a pair of ancient, old-fashioned fire extinguishers tucked away in the back of a small closet. She dragged them out, unscrewed their tops, and dumped out whatever water there was inside that had not evaporated with the years.

Then she drove the rental car down a slight hill at the edge of the forest to join Sayeed's SUV, camouflaged by brush and trees. Even the minor grade would make backing the car out a challenge, but there would be plenty of room for all of them in the SUV, and Danielle had other plans for the rental car anyway.

She returned to the house, lugging its battery with her, almost new and plenty powerful for the task required.

"Show me the generator," she said to Sayeed, while Ben continued to stir the compound in the bathtub into a smooth paste.

"It's broken."

"Show me."

DANIELLE GOT the generator working in twenty minutes. It clanked, clattered, and spewed gas fumes into the air from its slot in a furrow dug out from the underside of the cabin. Then she located the conduits running out of it into the house and sliced open some of the rubber shielding, exposing the wires. She strung yard after yard of wire toward her like fishing line, careful to leave untouched the lines running to the front of the cabin.

By the time she brought the wires into the house with her, the others had completed their tasks. Danielle poured the contents of the three pails into the old-fashioned fire extinguishers and screwed their tops back on tight. Then she washed the pails out thoroughly in the waters of the bay, returning inside to fill them half-way with gasoline, which was then mixed with moth flakes.

"Molotov cocktails," Ben said, having come up against the homemade weapon often enough in the West Bank.

"Not exactly," Danielle told him, "but close."

Dusk was falling when she carried two of the pails down the steps and began pouring their contents atop the ground. Sayeed dumped the contents of the third pail while his wife and children used a combination of shovels and rakes to make sure they were spread evenly. Outside in the crisp air, the harsh smell quickly faded, lingering no more than the stench left by a flooded car.

AROUND BACK, Ben eased the wheelbarrow down the rickety dock toward the spot where his father had kept their skiff moored. He had been amazed to find it still tucked under the cabin, covered in canvas, where they'd stowed it upon last leaving the cabin over thirty years before, even more amazed to find it still whole.

It made no sense until Ben considered the obvious, which had escaped him until this very moment: His mother not only had refused to sell the cabin, she also must have been returning periodically to tend to it. A few times a year, unbeknownst to Ben and, probably, Sayeed. Coming back here to relive those first happy months in America her own way.

She wouldn't even have stayed overnight. Probably just came early in the morning and left before dark, getting a cousin or friend to drive her here from Dearborn. Cleaning the skiff out before replacing the canvas atop it. Switching on the generator to keep it lubricated and giving the cabin a quick once-over. It could only have been she who set the pails on the floor to catch the rain where it fell through the leaky roof. But she must not have come recently, not in the past few years anyway, as evidenced by the damage to the floor.

Ben wondered if she had finally tired of the process or been too worn down by her worsening arthritis to attempt it anymore. He wished he had known about this, yet respected that it was his mother's way of dealing with the past. His had been to return to Palestine as his father had, Sayeed's to help other Palestinians find a new life in America.

Each in their own way, Ben realized, had been living a lie. They had clung to something that could not bring them what they wanted and had been betrayed in the process: Ben by the people he thought were his own, his brother by the terrorists who used him for the student visas he could provide. Even his mother, by the rotting wood and shingles that defied her attempts to keep at least something from the past unchanged.

Leaving the wheelbarrow at the end of the dock, Ben returned to the skiff and dragged it down into the water. He climbed back onto the dock and hauled it with him to its mooring. He tied it down there and slid the wheelbarrow to the very edge. Inside was the smooth paste he had shoveled from the bathtub, and now he tilted the tip downward and watched the paste began to pour slowly down into the skiff.

He was only following Danielle's instructions, unsure exactly of how she planned to use it. He was in her world now, a foreign place he had touched only on the fringes. He hated the whole process for how dependent it made him feel, loved it because it brought the only time their relationship was unconditional. All else rendered meaningless by the demands of the moment. Nothing to separate them.

But today was different. Today the lives of the last close relatives he had in the world were at stake. Watching even Sayeed yield to Danielle's counsel made Ben appreciate her power and presence even more. The very things that had intimidated him when they first met eight years before now attracted him to her. He knew he shouldn't confuse love with need, but it was just another complication in a relationship that had seen more than its share.

When he came back inside, Ben found Danielle stringing wire through a hole she had drilled in one of the cabin's front walls. She twirled the wires together and twisted them into place inside the guts of a battery-operated lantern. Then she fit the bottom of the lantern back into place and flicked it on.

"I strung the wire from the top of the private road leading down here," she explained. "A car drives over it, the connection breaks, causing the bulb to flicker."

"Ingenious."

"If it works," Danielle said.

Ben then watched her take another section of wire and loop it around the positive connection of the car battery she had placed near one of the rear windows.

"What's that for?" he asked her.

"You'll see," Danielle replied, taking the wire with her out the back door toward the dock.

CHAPTER 68

Night fell. They waited in darkness and silence. Ben's niece and nephew were huddled with their mother in the back bedroom, the bed's heavy wood frame upturned between them and the window to provide protection from flying glass. Sayeed sat

poised in the rear of the cabin before the window overlooking the inlet of the bay circling round Twenty Mile
Point. Ben and Danielle hovered near windows on either
side of the cabin's front door, their eyes never far from
the lantern, which glowed softly in the fireplace so the
light couldn't be seen from the outside.

Ben heard a shuffling sound and turned to find Sayeed
crawling up alongside him. "We should tell my wife and
children to run, get away as soon as it starts, Bayan,"
he whispered.

"That might be what the attackers' plan is designed
to accomplish," Danielle said softly from the other side
of the door. "Flush us out."

"They didn't do that in Dearborn."

"This is different."

Sayeed shrugged and slipped back to the other side
of the cabin. He'd been nothing but disapproving of her
the only other time they had met. Tonight everything
had changed.

Danielle slid over to join Ben. "If I had killed Buchert
in Pine Valley . . ."

"Latif and Khalil would have found someone else to
release the smallpox for them," Ben said softly after her
voice had drifted off.

"Why not just do it themselves?"

"Because they knew they'd be destroyed, once the
plot was linked back to them. Buchert wouldn't have
cared. He had nothing to lose anymore; he hasn't for
almost a year now, thanks to us."

"Khalil used that to get Buchert to do his bidding,"
Danielle told him. "Wipe out the other terrorists trapped
by Operation Flypaper."

"But whoever killed Khalil has been behind this from
the start. Everyone else were just pawns."

Ben's comment brought Danielle back to the tale told
by Colonel al-Asi's informant, Hakim. "It's the woman

I told you about, the one who was at Khalil's compound the day he was shot. I'm sure of it. She planned everything."

"Including an old Arab woman's murder?"

"Yes."

"You know who she is, don't you?"

"I have my suspicions," Danielle told him, thinking of Layla Aziz Rahani, daughter of Blue Widow Hanna Frank. "But Colonel al-Asi knows something he didn't tell me. Hyram Berger at the Israeli embassy too."

"What?"

Before Danielle could answer him, the lantern in the fireplace flickered.

CHAPTER 69

"It's time," Danielle said to Ben, sliding over to the door. "Move closer to the window. Keep your head just high enough to peer out and don't move it. In the dark, movement's the only thing that can give you away."

She pulled an emergency road flare from her belt and held it in her hand, pressed tight to the door just to the side of the open mail slot. Ben had felt the wind coming through it all evening, never asking Danielle why she had removed the outside flap. Now he understood.

Across the floor Sayeed held his position alongside the window overlooking the cabin's rear. He turned toward Danielle and shook his head.

"I see something," Ben said softly. "Shapes moving into the clearing."

"How many?"

"I can't tell. They're gone. . . . Wait, I see them again. Three, no, four, advancing toward the house, stopping to cover each other."

"Tell me when the lead one draws within ten feet of the front porch," she instructed, second hand joined to the emergency flare now, ready to pop its fuse.

Ben fought against the temptation to check on Sayeed in the cabin's rear, keeping his focus out the window instead. The moonless darkness gave up little, just an occasional shapeless blur that could just as easily have been a swaying tree as a man.

"There's a man a dozen feet from the porch!" he reported, catching the slight glimmer of an assault rifle's barrel.

She signaled him quiet, mouthed, *Any others?*

Ben held up three fingers, then pulled his hand back a yard to indicate how far they were behind the lead gunmen.

Danielle nodded toward Ben before tripping the flare's fuse. Instantly, it burst into a glowing orange flame, which she pushed through the mail slot and tossed forward.

From his perch, Ben watched the flare bounce once on the porch and begin rolling down the stairs. A fan of flames erupted as soon as the flare touched the ground, soaked with homemade napalm. Three of the men who had approached the cabin so stealthily were transformed into fiery specters in the night, screaming in agony as the flames devoured them.

The fire's backdraft of air hammered the front door, pushing Ben and Danielle away from the wall across the floor. The sound drew Sayeed's attention away from the rear window just before a barrage of bullets shattered the glass near him and poured into the cabin.

Sayeed went down, covering his head with his hands.

Ben dove behind a chair, while Danielle moved to the car battery and touched a wire to the negative connection.

Outside, at the cabin's rear, the fertilizer bomb packed into the old skiff exploded, sending jagged shards of wood, acting as shrapnel, in all directions. In the dazzling burst of light, Danielle saw a pair of dark figures caught in the deadly rain of wood, struck down where they stood halfway between the thin shoreline and the cabin. The brightness of the initial blast receded, but stubborn flames clung to the remnants of the dock, yielding the only light.

Ben moved for Sayeed, afraid he'd been hit by the initial barrage that had shattered the rear window. His own ears ached from the percussion of the blasts, his head full of what felt like heavy air pushing itself through his ear canals. He reached Sayeed to find him unharmed, though frozen in terror. Ben dragged his brother away from the center of the room just before fresh bursts of automatic fire tore into the front of the cabin on both sides of the door.

More glass burst inward, and the shadow of one of the gunmen flashed by the window as he moved for the door. Danielle saw the big iron knob rattle, the gunman's hand closing upon it. He never saw the puddle of water at his feet, or the wire extending under the door into it. Never heard the sizzle of electricity when Danielle jammed the cord into the socket.

The gunman lurched up to his toes, unable to release the doorknob, as he shook and spasmed. His hair caught fire in seconds, and the stench of it filled the small cabin, overpowering even that of the homemade napalm still flaming on the front grounds. A moment later sparks flew from the outlet, and the breaker feeding from the generator tripped. The man's body hit the porch still writhing, his spasms continuing even after he was dead.

Danielle did a quick count in her head. Three in the initial fire, two more when she blew the skiff, another at the front door. How many men had they come with? How many more could there be?

At least two, she thought, in the moment before fresh staccato bursts of gunfire tore into the walls and the remnants of the window glass. Danielle crawled across the floor over the shards to her former perch by the window, where one of the two fire extinguishers she'd drained and refilled with her homemade acid compound lay.

She had just taken the extinguisher in hand when a figure leaped through the window, tearing the frame away as he plunged inward, opening fire wildly while he was still in the air. Danielle held fast to her senses, grabbed the extinguisher hose, and in one motion aimed it and squeezed the handle on the extinguisher's top.

The gunman hit the floor on his feet but stumbled on impact, one of his legs sliding out from under him. Danielle hit him with a burst of her homemade acid before he could resteady his gun. Instantly he began to scream. His rifle dropped from his hands, which flailed for his face, tearing at the flesh that hissed and burned beneath his touch.

The screams pierced Ben's still-throbbing eardrums, the worst sound he had ever heard. But the smell was worse, an acrid stench as the man's face literally melted away.

His wails turned to dying rasps when another gunman hurled himself through the window on the other side of the cabin. Danielle rolled across the floor, going for the dying man's assault rifle. But his fall had pinned it beneath him and she couldn't free it before the second gunman sprayed the cabin with fire.

Ben focused on the fire extinguisher Danielle had laid aside for him, realizing it was too far away to make a try for. One of the kerosene-filled glass lanterns, though, lay directly before him and he snatched it up.

Fifteen feet away, Danielle had finally managed to yank the assault rifle from beneath the faceless man's corpse when the final gunman twisted his rifle on her.

Ben hoisted the lantern overhead and heaved it, watching it soar, watching the gunman's hand close on the trigger an instant before the glass shattered over the back and side of his head. He keeled over to the right, a burst from his rifle blasting into the ceiling to dig fresh leaks in the roof.

Danielle leaped to her feet, sweeping the cabin with the M-16 she'd salvaged as if unsure whether any more gunmen were about. She heard a car engine rev, followed by tires screeching through mud and dirt.

She charged through the front door, leaped off the porch, and charged through the flames starting to burn out and the cabin's front yard. Once on the dirt road, she steadied her barrel on the shape of a van struggling through the woods. She saw sparks erupt as her bullets pockmarked its side, the M-16 clicking empty by the time she finally steadied her aim on the cab.

That made the final count nine. Seven dead, one gone, and one still alive to tell them about Hollis Buchert.

CHAPTER 70

"I can't see!" the man shrieked, his hands bound behind him to a chair.

"Would you like to know why?" Danielle asked him quite calmly.

"*I can't see!*" he repeated, instead of answering.

"Your eyes hurt, don't they?"

"Please, please, don't do this. . . ."

"Do what?"

"I don't know anything! I can't tell you anything!"

"That's a shame. Would you like to know why?"

"I—I—I . . ."

Ben stood by the window, standing guard, all too familiar with the interrogation technique Danielle was using. He'd heard of Israeli soldiers using the very same one on the worst Palestinian prisoners they captured, the ones who refused to break. He had sent Sayeed to the back bedroom to join his family, told them not to come out no matter what they heard, in order to spare them at least the sight.

Minutes before Ben and Danielle had finished a sweep of the surrounding area to make sure no more of Buchert's People's Brigade soldiers had been left behind. His post by the window was an added precaution.

"Where can I find Hollis Buchert?" Danielle asked the man tied to the chair.

"I don't know! I swear, *I don't know!*"

"How do your eyes feel?"

"They hurt."

"That's because I've tied a compress soaked in a mixture I cooked up myself. Little battery acid, some lye, and just a touch of chlorine thrown in for good measure. The pain's probably getting worse, isn't it?"

Ben listened, chilled by the matter-of-fact tone to Danielle's voice. All business, as if she had done this before.

"Yes," their hostage said meekly.

"There's a reason for that," Danielle told him. "See, my mixture is starting to soak through the compress now. Any moment it'll start to seep into your eyelids. The pain's nothing compared to what it's going to be like in ten minutes, and ten minutes after that your cor-

neas will be memories and you'll be blind for life. So
we don't have a lot of time here to wrap up our discussion. I'll ask you again: Where is Hollis Buchert?"

"If I tell you—"

"Try to imagine him doing something worse to you
than this. Just try."

"—he'll kill me." The man bit his lip, a grimace starting to stretch across his face.

"Not if I kill him first. He's going to release the smallpox, isn't he?"

"Yes, yes! That's the plan. That's why we had to track
down the Arab who fled here," the man said, obviously
referring to Sayeed. "Make sure he couldn't tell anyone
anything."

Ben felt a realization strike him, everything at once
falling into place. "You thought Sayeed was a part of
this. . . ."

The man turned his head unseeingly toward Ben.
"Who *are* you?"

"Don't you remember? You held me hostage too. At
Pine Valley."

"*You?* No, it can't be!" The man twisted back toward
the front and Danielle's general position, as if he were
trying to spy her through the compress. "It's all true, the
things I heard. A single woman killing our soldiers. A
ghost. *You!*" he finished in a raspy, terror-filled voice
aimed toward Danielle.

"All the more reason for you to tell me where I can
find Hollis Buchert."

"My eyes," the man moaned, his face starting to curl
in agony.

"I know. It will get much worse, believe me, unless
I take the compress off."

"Minnesota!"

"Minnesota?"

"The Mall of America," the man said, then shrieked

in pain. "That's where Buchert's going to release his smallpox."

BEN AND Danielle locked stares, the truth they had suspected now confirmed. Before Danielle could speak, Ben lurched in front of her. She reached out to stop him, but it was too late. He had grabbed the People's Brigade survivor by the lapels.

"Where else?" Ben demanded, shaking him.

"My eyes . . . Please, the pain . . . Make it stop!"

"Where else are you going to release the smallpox?"

The man shrank away from Ben as much as the chair allowed him. "I don't know what you're—"

"The rest of the smallpox that was delivered to you— where else are you going to release it?"

"Delivered?" The man twisted his head, trying to recall Danielle's position. "Get him away from me. I don't know what he's talking about."

Ben grabbed the arms of the chair and leaned over him. "Do you know who I am?"

The man shook his head.

"You killed my mother. And I want to kill you. Don't make it so easy."

Danielle picked up a glass of water and tossed it into the face of the People's Brigade soldier, soaking the bandage covering his eyes. "That feels better, doesn't it?"

The man's shaking stilled. "Yes."

"It won't last. The pain will be back soon unless you tell us the truth."

"I have! I swear I have!"

"I'm talking about the smallpox. How did you get it?"

"A boat!" the man screamed. "I was with Buchert

when we picked it up. A boat in the middle of a lake five days ago."

"How much?"

"A canister, a small tank . . . I'm not sure. It looked like a can of hair spray."

Ben and Danielle looked at each other, struck by the anomaly. If only one canister had been delivered to the People's Brigade, what had happened to the remainder of the supply stolen from USAMRIID?

"What about the rest?" Ben shot at him.

"The *rest?* What rest? There was just the one canister."

"You know nothing of Fort Detrick?" Danielle probed.

"Fort *what?*" The man's head flopped about, trying to pin down Ben's location. "I don't know anything about your mother. Buchert's got the smallpox. The Mall of America—that's where you'll find him. That's all I know. Please, one of you, my eyes, they're starting to hurt again."

"When?" Danielle demanded and dropped some more water on the compress wrapped around the man's eyes. "When is Buchert coming?"

"I don't know," the man said, starting to shake again. "I swear, I don't know!"

"You're lying. Buchert wants to bring down the goverment, not kill a bunch of shoppers. It doesn't make sense."

"It makes plenty," Ben said, his voice quivering slightly, remembering an item that had crossed his desk a few weeks before. "The National Governors Conference is taking place in Minneapolis this week, and the governors are scheduled to visit the Mall of America. Tomorrow."

CHAPTER 71

Layla Aziz Rahani sat on the veranda of her hotel suite in Madain Salah, overlooking the shoreline where tourists, even women in bathing suits, frolicked on the beach. She had spread the information obtained from Israel on a wrought-iron table before her, all of it concerning the official doggedly investigating the murder of an Arab-Israeli woman named Zanah Fahury.

Danielle Barnea, currently commander and acting head of Israel's National Police.

Layla had been scrutinizing the material since her arrival here from London, allowing herself barely a glance at the world beyond, a world Rahani Industries had helped to create. Located in northwest Saudi Arabia, Madain Salah's sole claim to fame until recent years had been the ancient tombs carved into surrounding hillsides by the Nabateans, who were also responsible for building the city of Petra in Jordan.

That is until hundreds of millions of dollars raised by Rahani Industries had been pumped into new hotels, cafés, hotels, shopping malls, even amusement parks and cable cars built to ferry guests up through tree-covered mountains to the palatial resorts in Abha. There, even in summer the breezes stayed cool. Guests could step out onto their balconies and watch falcons swoop through the nearby ravines or wild monkeys playing in the valleys.

There was so much about this country the world

didn't know and never would, unless efforts were focused toward changing the stodgy image of Saudi Arabia as a vast desert wasteland dotted with steel and glass skyscrapers. Layla wanted her country to open itself more to the world, even while assuring the influx of tourists would not disturb the delicate balance set by Muslim order. As such, all female tourists were supplied with *abaiyas*, black gowns, and head scarves, and requested to don them where tradition required.

But at the Madain Salah's beachfront resort little attention was paid to such formalities. Here Western tourists could feel they were at Club Med when a half-day's drive could take them to a crumbling Ottoman fort that stood over one of the world's largest oases. Where else was it possible to swim at a resort in the morning and have Bedouin guides escort you to pristine desert encampments by night?

Most important for Layla Aziz Rahani, Madain Salah offered sanctuary. None of those Saudis she commonly did business with would ever be seen here, making it the safest spot to hold meetings and accept delivery of sensitive material like Danielle Barnea's file. Equally important, it was a place where she was safe from scrutiny by her brother Saed.

The breeze off the sea ruffled some of the pages, and Layla added a few more stones to the veranda table to hold them in place. Those pages detailed various parts of Danielle Barnea's life, an entire biography culled from a collection of file folders. But it was the simplest part of the dossier that interested Layla Aziz Rahani the most.

The Israeli's father was the late General Yakov Barnea, a hero from the establishment of the Jewish state until his death six years before. A man who had served the Israeli Defense Forces in virtually every capacity, including director of strategic planning.

The various pictures of Yakov Barnea included in the files were of him accompanied by his daughter, Danielle, at various ages. Layla Aziz Rahani flipped through the photos and stopped when she came to one picturing Yakov Barnea holding a very young Danielle in his lap, a pair of older boys, her brothers, standing on either side of him. Layla focused on Yakov Barnea's face, the flatly placid expression.

She knew that face, had seen it once before, years and years ago.

At the London Hilton. The night her mother had intended to escape back to the West with her daughters in tow until Layla had called her father from the phone in the bathroom.

Yakov Barnea was the man who had climbed out of the cab and rushed to the front of the hotel!

Layla remembered seeing his face through the glass, grim and intense. Remembered watching him take Kavi from the arms of the wounded governess Habiba after Layla had broken free of her mother's grasp and rushed across the lobby.

She remembered how much the gunshots had hurt her ears. Glass everywhere. Her sister crying. Blood spraying against windows and walls. Then her own screaming.

Everything else from that night was a blur, a bundle of memories without reason or order.

Her sister was dead. Her mother had as much as killed her.

And now the man who had haunted her dreams and thoughts for so long was more than just a face on the other side of a door. He was Yakov Barnea, Israeli war legend.

But Layla's mother was American. What could her connection possibly be to Yakov Barnea? Why had he been the one who had come to aid her escape to the West?

Questions Layla never had to consider before. And if there were answers in the life of Yakov Barnea, Layla couldn't find them.

So she turned her attention once more to the files of his daughter, Danielle. She studied her pictures. Something about her was familiar. Layla was struck by the certainty they had met before, but where and how?

She turned the photos over so as not to be distracted by them and focused instead on the files detailing Barnea's exploits. By all accounts she was an incredibly impressive and formidable woman. One who could have gone a long way, if she'd learned to keep her mouth shut. Judging by recent events, that was a lesson still lost on Danielle Barnea and that was what concerned Layla more than anything else.

By this time tomorrow, her father's plan would be in motion. The spread of smallpox would begin in the United States, just enough released to force the country to respond the only way it could. And it was that response that Layla Aziz Rahani was counting upon. It was that response that would assure the ultimate destruction of their society and people.

But Danielle Barnea's involvement continued to nag at her. Barnea had apparently left Israel without warning or notice. Disappeared, only to resurface at the Israeli embassy in Washington.

Barnea knew about the end of all things, knew about Akram Khalil. About a woman who called herself Zanah Fahury and the assassin Hassan's connection to both executions.

But all of that didn't matter. Even Danielle Barnea couldn't stop Hollis Buchert from releasing smallpox at the Mall of America, leaving the Americans no choice but to play the card she had left them.

"Ms. Rahani?"

The voice startled her, and Layla swung fast around in her chair.

"I knocked," the small man before her said, "but there was no answer."

"You are satisfied with your reinstatement at Immutech, Dr. Keefe?"

"I am most grateful, Ms. Rahani."

"I should expect so, given your less than glorious record."

Keefe swallowed hard. "I was hoping we could discuss my family."

"They're doing quite well, Doctor, thriving in a much better climate, in fact. You've been receiving their letters?"

"Yes. But I was wondering . . ."

"When you'll be able to see them?"

Keefe nodded rapidly.

"When I'm certain you've fulfilled your part of the bargain," Layla Rahani told him.

"I did everything you asked, to your exact specifications."

"A pity what happened in Kokobi, Ethiopia, Doctor."

Keefe swallowed hard once again. "I just want my family back."

"I've seen the production facility in England," Layla Rahani said. "Most impressive."

"My work is complete. The end result is inevitable."

"You're certain of that?"

"Yes!"

"Just as you were certain about the success of RU-18 in Kotobi?"

"My family. I'm begging you. Please."

"When I'm sure, Doctor," Layla told him. "When I'm sure."

DAY NINE

CHAPTER 72

B en drove slowly into the main parking lot of the Mall of America in Minneapolis. He and Danielle had driven through the night in his brother's SUV, after dropping Sayeed, Irsi, and their children at a no-frills, budget hotel.

"It's the size of a small town," Danielle said from the passenger seat.

That wasn't far from the truth, Ben realized, recalling what he knew about the 4.2-million-square-foot complex. The structure consisted of a rectangle of four interconnected buildings, separate, nearly mile-long concourses enclosing a central atrium complete with a fully functioning amusement park and featuring an offset roof of girders and glass. Two huge, seven-story concrete parking garages stretched across the entire width of the mall, connected to it by a series of asphalt and glass walkways running at multiple spots from every level.

"When are the governors scheduled to arrive?" Danielle asked.

"The morning paper says noontime," Ben replied, trying to picture the leaders of every state in the country casually ambling through the mall. Breathing the air and taking much more than souvenirs back home with them. "How's Buchert going to do it?"

"His first option would be the air exchangers," Danielle expounded. "Smallpox being an airborne virus, you spread it through the vents, you infect the largest possible number of people."

"But that's not the only possibility."

"Far from it. A single infected person could do tremendous damage by simply walking the mall, coughing, sneezing, spreading his germs."

"The disease is that contagious?"

"Incredibly so."

"I had the vaccine when I was a child."

"That provides immunity for ten years at most," Danielle told him. "Boosters were suspended after the disease was eradicated. There hasn't been a recorded case of smallpox in this country for thirty years."

"So no one's immune."

She shook her head."

"We should call in a bomb threat," Ben said, groping for a strategy. "Get the place evacuated."

"That means we lose Buchert and he just shows up somewhere else. Disney World maybe, or how about the Capitol building in Washington? This is our best chance, Ben."

"Then let's get going," he said and threw open his door.

CHAPTER 73

The walkie-talkies were good enough for their needs—tiny, palm-sized devices they'd found at Radio Shack, capable of transmitting across the mall and thereby allowing them to split up, if necessary. Inside, the Mall of America was like any other mall, multiplied three or four times. The shopper traffic was already beginning to clutter the escalators and pack the concourses. Ben and Danielle grabbed guide maps to better familiarize themselves with the mall. Each carried a single pistol salvaged from Buchert's attacking force at the cabin and were relieved to find no metal detectors awaited them upon entering the mall.

They started by memorizing all of the concourses names: West Market, East Broadway, North Garden, and South Avenue. Each ended at the entrance to a major retail anchor on all three levels, the fourth reserved for food, entertainment, restaurants, bars, and a multiplex cinema. There was an aquarium and a complete amusement park called Camp Snoopy on the ground floor. The latter featured a towering Ferris wheel, log-chute ride, and indoor roller coaster that swirled beneath them as Ben and Danielle watched it dip and dart across the atrium's entire circumference from the second-floor landing.

"How's Buchert going to get the smallpox in here?" Ben said suddenly.

Danielle started to turn toward him and watched a golf ball, straying from the Golf Mountain miniature golf course just behind them, roll toward the railing. "That depends on how he intends to release it. A gaseous state would make the most sense because that would maximize the infection. You bring a vial of the germ in its concentrated form, you could pour it on the floor and even someone who gets his shoe wet wouldn't necessarily get infected. Unless . . ."

"What?"

"How many fountains are there in this place?"

"I don't know. Several, I think."

Danielle was scanning her guide map furiously. "Damnit, this doesn't list them! We've got to check."

"Why?"

"Because the virus could be treated to become active in water. Remember that spray coming off the fountain we saw on the way in? The mist particles were too small to even notice, but they touched your skin and you're certain to have breathed at least a few of them in. The governors walk by and they board planes bound for their home states infected with the smallpox virus." Danielle shrugged and looked around her. "On a brighter note, security's much better than I was expecting. The doors to all secure areas of the mall require key cards or access codes punched into a keypad. And there are security cameras everywhere, undoubtedly even more placed where I can't see them."

"Meaning?"

"Let's say we can rule out Buchert infiltrating any unauthorized area. Assume he wouldn't take the risk. What does that leave him?"

Ben had no time to respond before Danielle grasped his arm.

"Down there, in the center of the amusement park. Look."

"What?"

"Those four men standing near each other."

Ben followed Danielle's gaze to four casually dressed men standing board stiff. Their faces were sharply angular, their close-cropped haircuts virtually identical. One of them had a beard that hung so low it obscured most of his neck.

"I recognize the one with the beard from Pine Valley," she said finally. "They're waiting for Buchert."

"To provide protection. Watch his back."

"They'll probably stay in view of him the whole time, but from a distance."

"Which means he hasn't arrived yet."

"Neither have the attendees of the governors conference."

Ben turned to look at the four People's Brigade soldiers again. It looked as if they hadn't moved an inch. "They're sure to recognize us. We move on Buchert, they move on us."

The prospects didn't seem to bother her. "Once they split up," she said, "you start looking for Buchert. You see him, hit the transmit button on your walkie-talkie twice."

"Where will you be?"

Danielle focused on the People's Brigade soldiers in the amusement park below.

"There are four of them, Danielle."

"Only for now."

DANIELLE WAITED with Ben until the four People's Brigade soldiers moved off in separate directions. She used the time to memorize their faces, assuring herself she could recognize any of them from even a moderate distance.

She followed one as he reached the second floor, figuring he was headed to a predetermined position to await the arrival of Hollis Buchert. Just after ten-thirty A.M. now. They probably had another hour or so before Buchert appeared.

She gazed down the long stretch of the Mall of America's West Market concourse, barely able to see the end, the stores stacked one after the other. Another floor below, two more above. Hollis Buchert could enter the complex anywhere, could release the smallpox anywhere. Danielle's best chance of finding him lay in letting his four guards do it for her. Watch their mannerisms, where they placed themselves. Look for a sudden change of motion or behavior indicating Buchert was here.

Danielle spent the next half hour moving about the concourses on the top three levels, charting the positions of the People's Brigade soldiers. One seated on a bench on the second floor. Another leaning over a railing directly over the spraying fountain that doubled as a wishing well on the third. The third lounging at a table in the fourth-floor food court. A final man strolling amid kiosks clustered flea-market style on the North Garden concourse at ground level. Danielle divided her attention between them, on the move at all times, afraid she might lose track of one.

BEN WALKED about the ground floor of the mall, concentrating on the center and focusing most of his efforts on the many entrances, hoping to spot Hollis Buchert. It was maddening work, so many faces to check, so many possibilities.

He framed a picture of Buchert in his mind, recalled the pale man with straw-colored hair pasted to his scalp looming over him in the barn, smelling of sweat and hair oil, secure in the certainty he was invincible. Ben kept his eyes moving, trying to focus on men with Buchert's stocky build. He could have dyed his hair but the deep canyons and valleys that pitted his face, giving it the look of old shoe leather, couldn't be disguised.

Feeling thirsty, Ben searched for the nearest beverage stand or shop. He settled on an Auntie Annie's pushcart, featuring lemonade, and pretzels, ordered a large lemonade, and started sipping it through a straw. Stopped when he caught a glimpse from the rear of a man riding an escalator up to the second floor.

Stocky, lugging a shopping bag in either hand. The hair gray, not wheat-colored, but the overall look was right, especially the neck, which looked as wide as his shoulders. Wearing corduroys and work boots.

Two shopping bags, each of them looking heavy . . .

Ben veered toward the escalator, slicing through the congestion of pedestrian traffic. Someone clipped him and his lemonade went flying, landing on the tile floor with a *splat* that scattered ice in all directions. He continued on, shouldering forward, reaching for the transmit button on the walkie-talkie wedged in his pocket.

CHAPTER 74

Hovering about the center of the third floor, Danielle heard the quick beeps and spun round.

Ben must have spotted Buchert!

She looked down and saw the People's Brigade soldier with the beard perched by the second-floor railing stiffen and slide sideways to better his view angle. He must have seen Buchert as well, and Danielle followed his line of sight downward to a man pushing his way through the crowd, hurrying to reach the escalator. Only it wasn't Buchert the brigade soldier had seen at all.

It was Ben.

The man by the railing held his ground briefly, frozen in surprise, unsure of how to react, as he watched Ben trying to weave his way through shoppers packed in on the escalator before him. The bearded man looked around to get his bearings, plotting a course to the spot where the escalator spilled out onto the second floor near a rotunda that spiraled upward through all four levels of the mall.

Danielle retrained her gaze on Ben and started moving, trying to keep pace with him from one floor above. The nearest escalator was too far away to do her any good. She made sure she had Ben in clear view, then focused on the milling crowd clustered to his rear.

The bearded man was gone. She'd lost him.

Still in motion, Danielle raised the walkie-talkie to her lips. "Ben, can you hear me?"

"I've got Buchert," his voice came back. "I'm following him right now."

"You're sure?"

"Yes. Almost."

"Listen to me. One of his guards, the bearded one, is on your tail."

"Shit! Where?"

"I lost him. I'm directly above you. Just keep moving, stay with Buchert until I figure out what to do."

THE BEARDED People's Brigade soldier could be anywhere. Ben's hand slid inside his jacket to the butt of the nine-millimeter pistol.

Danielle's warning had so rattled him he had lost sight briefly of Hollis Buchert. Twenty yards ahead, though, the crowd parted long enough for Ben to catch a glimpse of the corduroy-clad man with the pair of shopping bags, weighted heavily enough to be dragging near the floor.

Ben picked up his pace slightly, chancing a glance behind him into a sea of faces that all looked the same.

DANIELLE TUCKED the walkie-talkie back into her pocket and hurried along the third-floor concourse. She watched Ben sifting his way forward, but she could still find no sign of the bearded man on his tail. Nor could she see Buchert anywhere ahead of him.

She had run operations like this before but with a dozen or more operatives to help her. Handling it with only two was as exasperating as it was foolish.

There, maybe fifty or sixty feet back! A man jostled a pair of elderly women harshly from his path.

"The bearded man's on your tail, Ben," she said softly into her walkie-talkie. "Fifty feet behind you." She could see Ben's shoulders start to twist so he could look behind him. "No! Don't give yourself away. Use the crowd to cover you."

"Just tell me when I can get a clear shot at him."

"No! No guns!"

"Where is he? Is he any closer?"

"Leave him to me."

Even as she said that, Danielle knew she could never reach the concourse below and catch the bearded man before he caught Ben. She was considering an alternate plan, when she saw a Minneapolis policeman heading straight for her.

BEN HAD Hollis Buchert in view. Was the virus escaping from inside his shopping bag even now, infecting all who passed?

Ben fought against panic, willed himself to continue closing the gap between him and the leader of the People's Brigade, clinging to the hope it wasn't already too late.

"THERE'S A man down there with a gun!" Danielle told the cop in feigned desperation.

"Where?" the cop asked, leaning against the railing.

"The big man with the beard just passing below us, wearing the dark jacket," Danielle pointed out, indicating the man on Ben's tail. "He had a gun stuck into his belt, I'm sure of it!"

The cop drew a walkie-talkie to his lips and began whispering into it. Then he moved for the nearest escalator, hand starting to go for his pistol.

LOPING PAST an Eddie Bauer clothing store, Ben found himself with a clear path toward Buchert. Beyond them lay the glass-door entrance to the east parking garage, people streaming through it in both directions. Buchert slowed, laying one of his shopping bags on the floor to check his watch.

Ben picked up his pace, readied his shoulder. Slam into the man from behind, take him down to the floor, and pin him there so he couldn't reach the contents of his shopping bags. There'd be time enough to explain his actions to the authorities later.

Ben started forward, picking up speed.

DANIELLE HAD watched the uniformed security force converge on Buchert's soldier, had just started to breathe easier when she saw he already had a pistol in his hand. He held it low by his side and shoved a pair of teenagers ahead of him aside to clear his shot at Ben, who was closing in on a figure in corduroys and work boots.

Buchert! It had to be!

She whipped out her own pistol and angled it over the railing in both hands, sighting in on the bearded man as the mall patrons around her shrieked in fear.

THE SCREAMS rattled Ben, made him hesitate in the midst of his final lunge. Instead of barreling into Buchert, he reached out and grabbed him by the back of the coat, starting to spin the leader of the People's Brigade around when a gunshot exploded behind him.

DANIELLE HAD been an instant from firing when one of the teenagers the bearded man had pushed from his path moments before cracked into him from behind, full of strut and bravado. The impact forced his pistol upward as he fired, the bullet flying harmlessly toward the mall's roof.

She heard the echo of the glass shattering, saw flecks of it raining down like hail atop the uniformed security force that had converged on the bearded man from all angles.

BEN HEARD the commotion, as he spun the leader of the People's Brigade toward him. His other hand rose into the air and balled into a fist. He wanted to hit Buchert, wanted to feel the satisfying crack of bone and teeth beneath the strike.

The man who had killed his mother, tortured him.

Buchert lost hold of his remaining bag when Ben twisted him around. It hit the floor and its contents slid across the polished tile. Ben vaguely recorded the boxes of varying sizes, wrapped neatly in bows and birthday paper, and got his first good look at the man's face.

It wasn't Hollis Buchert.

GUN TUCKED back under her sweater, Danielle watched Ben slide away from the man who wasn't Hollis Buchert at all. She backed away from the rail and started moving again as he stood there stiffly, frozen between actions. Ben had focused on the source of the commotion behind him, the bearded man being handcuffed now with four men holding him down, and had smartly veered away. He glanced up as if to look for her, then leaned back against a trash receptacle, a cluster of passersby tightening around him to view the apparent arrest.

At the exit doors behind him, no one was leaving. Frozen in near silence, spectators watched a pair of policemen jerk the bearded man to his feet. A few of them clapped. The man's nose and mouth were bleeding. He looked angry, resentful, still twisting to fight the police a little as they led him off. Danielle watched his gaze drift briefly upward to the fourth floor and followed it.

A second of the People's Brigade soldiers leaned over the railing, looking directly at her. She saw him raise something to his mouth. His lips moved. Warning the other two that she and Ben were present in the mall, no doubt alerting them to what had just happened.

Danielle reached to her belt where the Radio Shack walkie-talkie was clipped.

It was gone.

She remembered brushing it as she went for her gun, realized she must have knocked it loose when the pistol came free. Danielle glanced back toward where she'd been standing, nothing visible on the floor amid the sea of churning feet. Then she glanced up again toward the fourth-floor railing and the second of Hollis Buchert's soldiers.

He was gone too.

BEN HAD moved away from the crowd, standing alone in a corner not far from the glass walkway leading into the parking garage. His heart hammered against his chest. He couldn't stop shaking.

Before him, the man he'd mistaken for Buchert had collected his birthday gifts, risen to his feet, and exited through the door. Ben had tried to mumble an apology to the man but couldn't be sure he'd heard. He stood still, trying to collect his thoughts, regroup.

A hundred feet away the cops were leading the bearded People's Brigade soldier away in handcuffs, the mall already getting back to normal, filling now with the lunchtime crowd. Ben gazed ahead at the quartet of cops hauling their prisoner through a service door, nearly colliding with an older man wheeling an oxygen tank alongside him. Thin plastic tubing ran out from it, clipped to his nose.

The bearded man turned back one last time before the service door closed behind him, seemed to be looking straight at the man wheeling the oxygen tank. The older man veered away, his face visible from the side.

Ben felt a chill freeze his spine. His legs wobbled.

Hollis Buchert.

CHAPTER 75

Danielle knew she'd become a target, the remaining three People's Brigade soldiers in the mall perhaps watching her even now. It was impossible to tell; the concourses were too crowded to discern anyone clearly. All the man on the fourth floor above had to do was keep her in his sights, direct the others to her, and stop her from moving on Buchert in the process. She had lost sight of Ben, couldn't warn him.

Danielle kept to the center of the third-level concourse, considering her next move. The options didn't please her, until she saw a store diagonally across the floor. The window display gave her an idea, something she had done often before but never in these conditions.

Hesitating no further, she swung to her left and moved toward the entrance to a store called the Fun Shop.

BEN FOLLOWED Buchert down the escalator to the first floor. He kept the oxygen tank in sight the whole time, wondering if its true contents were spilling out even now, contaminating the air, infecting everyone he passed.

Ben felt about his belt for the walkie-talkie clipped there and hit the transmit button twice. Then he moved his hand to the butt of his pistol.

THE COSTUME Danielle bought was a nun's dress and habit. The Fun Shop clerk seemed to have no problem with her leaving the store wearing it. Danielle had had her choice of dozens of costumes, ultimately settling on that of a nun because it was the one most likely to keep the eyes of the remaining People's Brigade soldiers off her.

While she went after them.

"DANIELLE, COME in," Ben said into his walkie-talkie. "Can you hear me?"

Ben squeezed the device in his fist, as the escalator deposited him back on the Mall of America's first floor. Danielle must have a reason for not responding. All he could do was keep Buchert in sight until she made contact.

The fake oxygen tank made Buchert an easy target to follow. Buchert undoubtedly intended to infect the thousands present in the mall right now, including the governors, but he'd do it in a way that would ensure his own survival. Be off the premises by the time the canister began to spew its contents into the air.

But how?

The roller coaster from Camp Snoopy zipped overhead, drumming in his ears. Ahead of Ben, Buchert glanced at it briefly, then joined the flow of families through the west entrance to the amusement park.

DANIELLE FOUND the first of the three remaining People's Brigade soldiers standing above the center of the mall, searching for her through the crowds below. As expected, he turned away from her as she approached, paying her no regard at all. The man raised a foot up to a bench, leaning against a railing set directly over the mall amusement park.

Danielle kept her eyes low and felt for the gun concealed inside her costume as she closed on the brigade soldier, timing her approach to coincide with the roar of the next passenger car to stream by on the nearby section of roller-coaster track below. Danielle drew the pistol when the car banked into a rise, jammed it against the brigade soldier's back just as the car dropped into a screeching descent. Fired when it passed both of them.

The man started to fall and Danielle guided him down onto the bench, leaving him slumped there. She turned away and noticed a few bystanders looking at her. She smiled serenely at them, then moved on.

INSIDE THE amusement park, Ben passed a giant inflated Snoopy that doubled as a bouncer, currently packed with kids tumbling about. Costumed figures of Lucy and Linus slid by him, and Ben ducked behind a nesting of indoor trees to keep his eye on Buchert. The People's Brigade leader walked past a collection of souvenir stands, a small food court, and Paul Bunyan's Log

Chute, then circled back around toward the Ripsaw Roller Coaster.

Ben cut across Camp Snoopy, hoping to take Buchert by surprise. Get close enough and use his pistol before any of the People's Brigade soldiers, or some hapless good Samaritan, for that matter, could intercede.

But a life-sized Snoopy figure posing for a picture with a pair of twins got in his way and slowed him up. By the time he reached the roller coaster, Buchert was already standing in line some ten places ahead. Ben watched him switch the oxygen tank to his left hand while he yanked a few dollars from his pocket with his right and exchanged them for a ticket. Ben kept his eyes on Buchert until he came to the front of the window, purchased his own ticket for the Ripsaw, and fell back into line to await one of the two cars.

Buchert's intentions here baffled him. Might his riding the roller coaster be some sort of unspoken signal? Was he stalling, waiting for his soldiers to join him down here?

No. Buchert's motions seemed composed, thought out to the point of being rehearsed. He was here because he meant to be here, in this very spot. No other explanation sufficed.

Before Ben, the Ripsaw cut a neat circle across the entire central-atrium section of the mall, visible from all floors as it sliced through the air. He watched one of its two cars come to a halt. Patrons whose ride had just been completed climbed out, and the line jostled forward with those eager to climb in. A young attendant stopped the line and refastened a chain across it to keep the next grouping behind the safety stripe. Ben counted sixteen slots in the car. That meant he and Buchert would soon be taking their places in the next car that pulled in.

Suddenly Ben heard a commotion at the entrance to

the mall. He was too far away to clearly discern what was happening, but the eruption of flashes and sight of news cameras could mean only one thing.

The nation's governors had arrived.

CHAPTER 76

Danielle saw the governors enter the mall, posing for pictures and chatting among themselves as they gawked at the sprawling expanse of the Mall of America. She resumed her stroll down the concourse, eyes searching for the third People's Brigade soldier she had glimpsed earlier. He would surely be looking for her as well, making him all the easier to spot. She avoided the gazes of passersby, keeping her eyes aimed discreetly down. A little farther on, she pretended to adjust her habit and trained her gaze upward.

On the level above, she caught sight of a man pressed tight to the rail, gazing intently down the center of the mall into the amusement park instead of toward the mall entrance, where the governors were still gathered.

It was another of Buchert's men, she was sure of it!

Danielle followed his line of sight, trying to see what had grabbed his attention. One of the two roller-coaster cars rolled off down the tracks, heading for the first climb. Another car came out of the final loop and sped back to the starting point.

So what was the man looking at?

She watched him move off, then stepped onto the escalator, riding it up. At the top she found the People's Brigade soldier in motion again, heading for the escalator nearest him along Nordstrom's Court, in which the wishing-well fountain was located. He stopped before reaching it and pressed up against the rail directly over the fountain, his body angled toward the amusement park.

Danielle saw that he had maneuvered himself to have a clear view of a line waiting to board the next roller-coaster car as it came to a stop. She recognized Ben Kamal standing there, stiff with tension, his vision alternating between the approaching car and someone ahead of him in line. She could see him toying with the pistol hidden under his jacket, as if unsure what to do with it. Another car swooped by beneath her and she suddenly realized why the People's Brigade soldier had chosen this spot.

It offered a close, clear shot at anyone riding the Ripsaw. She saw the gun tucked into the brigade soldier's belt and picked up her pace as, below, Ben Kamal climbed into the roller-coaster car.

IT WAS a nine-seat car. Ben rode alone in the sixth seat back. Buchert sat by himself in the front car. He could have used the gun on him here, but the chance of hitting a bystander made him reject the notion. Besides, he didn't dare launch his attack until he was certain the smallpox was reasonably secure.

An attendant went up and down the car's length, making sure the safety rail was locked into place over every rider. Ben slid into the center of his seat, focused five ahead on Buchert maneuvering the oxygen tank between his legs for safety.

Then the car crawled into motion and the first rise appeared directly ahead.

DANIELLE WATCHED the Ripsaw come out of the first drop fast and settle into a lower speed as it climbed for the second. Beyond that was a loop that would spill the car out directly in the gunman's line of sight. At that point, Ben would be only forty feet from him, an easily manageable shot even with a pistol.

The roller coaster exploded out of its second drop and streamed toward the loop, just seconds away from entering it. Danielle fought the urge to run, knowing that it would give her away, and walked as quickly as she dared down the concourse and veered left onto a connecting bridge directly for the People's Brigade soldier. She heard the happy shrieks of the riders as the Ripsaw passed beneath her, but focused on the brigade soldier starting to bring his pistol up, measuring off his shot, gun still concealed by his jacket.

Too many people walked past him on both sides for Danielle to chance a shot of her own. No, she had to do this with her hands, get to the gunman before he could fire.

BEN FELT his stomach lurch as the Ripsaw slung into the loop. The blood rushed from his head, and the air seemed briefly sucked out of him until the car slowed into a straightaway. Coming out of the loop he could see Buchert had removed the tubing from his nose. He seemed to be hunched over, working on his tank.

Ben imagined him loosening the valve, then tucking it under the seat and leaving it to rattle around after he exited. Buchert would have made his way out of the mall by the time it popped free, spewing its contents of the smallpox virus into the air. Low-tech but effective. All Ben had to do was wait for him to climb out, then retrieve the tank and find a way to reseal it as best as possible. No harsh action required, which meant the gun could stay in his belt where it belonged.

Then what sounded like a gunshot echoed from somewhere above them. Buchert jerked his frame around in search of its source, but his eyes fell on Ben instead.

THE PEOPLE'S Brigade soldier noticed Danielle approaching in her nun's costume but paid no attention. She slammed into the man the very instant he fired. Grabbed him by both shoulders from the rear before he could respond, and shoved him forward.

Over the rail.

He seemed to teeter there briefly, eyes terrified and furious, before he pitched downward and landed with a huge splash in the fountain below.

BEN HEARD the splash and the screams that followed, saw Buchert's eyes narrow in surprise and then recognition, the moment suspended in time as the roller coaster banked into the next rise. Then the head of the People's Brigade was reaching down for his tank again, fiddling with it.

Twisting the valve off manually, trying to release the smallpox while still on board.

Ben's stomach heaved again as the roller coaster

flashed into the drop, then settled into a straightaway that gave him the opportunity to jerk his safety rail upward and lunge forward one seat at a time.

Buchert didn't look back until Ben's final leap brought him into the front seat. By then, Ben had the pistol out and was struggling to steady it when the thrust of the Ripsaw slinging into the next loop cracked his head against Buchert's. The pistol fell from his grasp and dropped through the tracks below. But Ben maintained the presence of mind to twist one arm around Buchert's safety rail, while the other fastened tight to the tank's control valve to hold it in place.

Buchert pounded at Ben's fingers, tried to wrench them off. Ben saw the loop coming and closed his eyes. The G-forces kicked his legs out wildly, akimbo in the air. They came down hard against the seat and he found himself straddling it, half in and half out. Buchert smashed a fist into his face, and Ben felt something give in his nose. Buchert wheeled for him again, but this time Ben snapped his head forward and butted him between the eyes. Ben could see them glaze over, then sharpen again. Buchert fastened both hands on the tank as the Ripsaw climbed for its final dip.

DANIELLE TOOK the stairs, flying down them with her nun's habit billowing behind her. Mall personnel scurried from all directions toward the fountain where the People's Brigade soldier had ended up. She ignored them, focusing instead on whatever glimpses she could get of the fight between Ben and Hollis Buchert on the roller coaster. Everywhere around her people had stopped to gawk, some of them smiling, even applauding, as if this were some staged event.

Ben seemed to be battling Buchert from half in, half out of the car. Buchert had released his safety bar and had managed to raise a tank of some kind overhead, about to smash it down over Ben's face, when the car banked into its final drop, pitching him forward and separating the tank from his grasp.

BEN LUNGED and caught the tank before it hit the tracks, held it with both hands while Buchert started pounding him from behind, trying to drive his face against the rails speeding by below the car's nose. He bared his yellow teeth in a snarl, his straw-mat hair a wild tangle atop his head. Ben didn't dare let go of the tank from this high up. He needed both his hands to hold fast to it, leaving him no means to fight back.

Suddenly he felt the car begin to slow, the emergency brakes activated by attendants finally responding to the commotion on board. Ben saw Buchert rock forward, off balance, hands groping for something to hold on to. Failing to find anything, he was jerked forward again.

Ben twisted onto his side and drove the bottom of the tank upward as Buchert's furrowed face came down. Impact came with a thud that snapped Buchert's head back violently. His eyes bulged, hands still flailing for something to grab when the second car, its brakes either malfunctioning or never having been switched on, shot out of the final drop and tore forward.

Ben felt the track rumble before he saw it, braced himself as best he could before the second car rammed into the back of his. The jolt pitched Buchert into the air and over the car's nose. He landed on the track and had just enough time to glance back before the car plowed into him.

Ben thought he heard the start of a scream, then nothing as the car finally came to a complete halt thirty feet from the station. Still clutching the tank, Ben dropped down onto the track and ran toward the loading platform.

DANIELLE SAW the horde of security personnel streaming into Camp Snoopy, guns drawn. Beyond them, still clustered near the main entrance, the attendees of the governors conference and their entourages were being escorted out of the mall by a combination of uniformed and plainclothes officers.

That evacuation gave Danielle an idea, and she spotted a fire alarm covered in a clear plastic housing on the wall to her right. She lunged for it and cracked the plastic with her elbow, then jerked the handle downward.

An ear-numbing metallic chirp began to sound, leading the thousands of mall patrons to flood the exits, catching the bulk of the security guards in the chaos. Danielle fought through the mounting crowd to find Ben. She shoved people aside, forgetting about her disguise until she saw their shocked expressions.

She caught up with Ben in the center of the amusement park amid mothers holding crying children and teenagers snatching miniature Peanuts characters from the arcade games shelves. He was halfway past her when she reached out and grabbed his shoulder.

"Ben."

He swung, twisting free of her grasp, then did a double take when he finally recognized her in the nun's habit. "We've got to get this out of here," he said, holding the small tank before him.

"Is that—"

Ben's face was bloodied from a nasty wound down

the center of his forehead. "Yes," he said, and mopped the blood away with his sleeve.

"Then why are you holding it like that?"

"Because I think it's leaking."

CHAPTER 77

Danielle shielded him as they moved through the crowd. Ben kept his thumb pressed against the part of the valve stem he had felt snap when he smashed the tank against the chin of the late Hollis Buchert, whose body still lay on the Ripsaw tracks beneath one of the cars.

"I feel like I should be praying to you or something," he said.

"I'll settle for a confession later."

They were just exiting Camp Snoopy when he heard a woman scream and looked up to see the last of Buchert's soldiers shoving bystanders aside, trying to clear a path for a clean shot from his pistol.

"Go!" Danielle ordered, whipping out her own pistol and stepping in front of Ben.

The gunman fired before she could, catching a nearby woman in the back. She collapsed into Danielle, taking both of them down.

Ben tore back into Camp Snoopy, fighting his way through the clutter of families, careful to keep pressure against the valve. But his thumb was starting to throb now, already stiffening, the pain rapidly progressing from a dull ache to full-out agony. He wouldn't have long before it cramped up on him and curled away from the valve on its own.

He winced from the pain, biting his lip to distract himself. Sweat poured into his eyes. Bodies jostled into him from both sides. The tank seemed to get heavier and heavier, soon to release Buchert's promised death unless Ben could find a way to—

There, up ahead!

A sign on the wall gave Ben an idea, and he veered toward the cavelike entrance to UnderWater World, the Mall of America's aquarium.

BEN PASSED patrons streaming out, having retraced their steps and now handing the personal stereos with which they'd been provided back to a harried attendant. He surged farther down the ramp and instantly had the feeling he was trapped in a sprawling tunnel, surrounded on both sides by glass walls.

UnderWater World began with a walk through a brilliant re-creation of a Minnesota forest that spilled onto a moving walkway. Ben sprinted down the rubberized track past more patrons hurrying out, quickly surrounded by glass everywhere, including the ceiling. Around him, all manner of marine wildlife swam about, giving him the uneasy, claustrophobic feeling of being trapped underwater.

The walkway seemed to spiral slightly downward, while through the acrylic walls Ben could now see sharks of various sizes and types swimming directly overhead. The fire alarm hummed shrilly here as well, chasing out the last of those who'd been inside the aquarium when the alarm was triggered.

For a brief moment, Ben thought he might be in the

clear. Then he heard rapid footsteps pounding toward him and twisted round to see Hollis Buchert's final gunman giving chase. The gunman opened fire wildly, his bullets pocking the acrylic walls without breaking them and scattering the fish swimming nearby.

Ben neared the end of the aquarium tunnel and found himself facing a scaled-down reproduction of a pirate ship in an exhibit called Starfish Beach. He rushed to a pool-sized tank featuring stingrays swimming about when the gunman lunged over the threshold and steadied his pistol forward.

Before Buchert's soldier could shoot, gunfire erupted from behind him. The gunman's spine arched backward, his finger jerking the trigger of his semiautomatic reflexively. The bullets dug wooden shards from the pirate ship as the man dropped to his knees and then keeled over.

Ben watched Danielle enter Starfish Beach holding her still-smoking pistol. Then, hesitating no further, he dropped Buchert's tank inside the stingray pool. Air bubbles flitted to the surface as it dropped toward the bottom, drawing the attention of a curious ray, which flapped over to inspect it.

Ben turned from the pool toward Danielle, her nun's costume billowing about her.

"Very becoming," he said.

"Don't laugh. I could get used to this."

BEN CALLED John Najarian's secure cell line from a pay phone outside a gas station halfway to the airport. The pay phone was located in an old-fashioned booth, the first time he had seen one like it in years.

"Ben, where the hell are you?" he demanded.

"Watch the news; you'll know when you see it."

"I've had federal agents crawling up my ass for two days now! What were you *thinking*? The whole damn government's looking for you!"

"Danielle's here," he said, looking at her body squeezed halfway into the booth.

"*What?* I should have known, for God's sake."

"Did they tell you about my mother?"

"Tell me what?" Najarian asked.

"She's dead."

"Oh Christ, I'm sorry. How? *When?*"

"A few days ago. She's dead because of me, John. Because I let them sucker me into this."

"I wish I could—"

"Listen, John. It was the People's Brigade that killed her. They're involved in this, and they know about Danielle and me." Ben paused. "That means you could be a target too."

"I can take care of myself. Just tell me what can I do to help?"

"There's nothing."

"Screw that. Let me bring you in. We can meet these people on your terms."

"Like last time, John?"

"I can get the fucking secretary of state himself on the phone and I damn well will this time!"

"It wasn't your fault. They were just covering their asses. Nothing new there. The problem is Lewanthall buried his rogue operation so deep nobody can find it. They didn't believe what I had to tell them then, and they won't believe what I've got to tell them now."

"Which is . . ."

"Can you really get the secretary of state on the phone, John?" Ben asked, turning the receiver so Danielle could hear the response as well.

"You're damn right I can."

"Then keep this line open. We just might need him."

"Where are you going?"

Ben looked at Danielle as he replied. "To find the person who's really behind all this."

CHAPTER 78

"London?" Director of Homeland Security Stephanie Bayliss repeated, pressing the receiver tight to her ear.

"You know," said Professor Albert Paulsen, "land of lousy weather, smiling people, and not a single Girl Scout cookie to be found. Got these rock-hard things called scones instead, though. I've had three already. I press my stomach hard enough I can feel them sitting there."

"What's in London?"

"Reading, actually."

"What's in Reading?" Stephanie Bayliss asked.

"The Immutech Pharmaceuticals plant. Sound familiar?"

"The company producing our smallpox vaccine."

"That's not the only thing they produced, General. Ever heard of RU-18?"

"No."

"Nobody has, and there's a reason for that."

"You learned this in Ethiopia?"

"The village of Kokobi, where it was tested, where

Mohammed Latif visited. RU-18 was supposed to control population growth."

"I remember something about that now," Bayliss said. "It didn't work."

"Oh, it worked all right, General. It worked too well."

CHAPTER 79

Hyram Berger closed the door to his apartment in the Watergate complex and fumbled on the wall for the light switch. A lamp sprang to life, illuminating a pair of figures seated in the center of his living room.

"I hope you don't mind us making ourselves at home," Danielle Barnea greeted him.

"I thought our business was finished," Berger said, eyeing Ben Kamal, who was seated across from her.

"And it would have been, if you hadn't lied to me about my father. You did lie to me, didn't you, Mr. Berger?"

"What do you want?"

"Two business visas for Saudi Arabia."

Berger looked at Ben again briefly. "For what possible reason?"

"So I can arrest Layla Aziz Rahani for the murder of an Israeli-Arab woman named Zanah Fahury."

Berger snorted. "You really think that's what this is about?"

"Not at all. That's the point."

"Leave this alone, Danielle, for your own sake."

"Why should I?"

"Because you can't touch Layla Aziz Rahani. It's a well known fact she manages all of her family's holdings now. Billions of dollars." Berger shook his head. "You should leave now, while you still can."

"Are you threatening me?"

"It's the truth that threatens you, Danielle. Listen to me and spare yourself that truth."

She rose from the couch. "I don't have a choice in the matter anymore."

Berger frowned. "Your father didn't believe he had a choice either."

"Go back to Hanna Frank, the woman who married Abdullah Aziz Rahani as part of Operation Blue Widow. The woman you told me was stoned to death after her eldest daughter, Layla, foiled my father's plan to rescue her in London."

"I've told you everything."

"Not quite."

"How can you be so sure?"

"Because my father would never have left one of his people behind to die that way. He'd rather have died himself."

"Well, this almost killed him."

"I only want the truth," Danielle insisted.

"Lies, truth—it doesn't matter anymore."

"Let me be the judge of that."

Berger's eyes fell on Ben once again. "You don't want him to hear this."

She swallowed hard. "I keep no secrets from Ben."

"So I've heard," Berger said, not bothering to disguise the disapproval in his voice. "But in this case you'll want to, Danielle; you just don't know it."

BERGER HAD moved to the window, the ice in the drink he had made jangling from the trembling of his hand.

"You and my father stayed close," Danielle said, prodding him. "You saw him again after London."

Berger nodded, his reflection sad and drawn in the glass.

"My guess is, no matter what your records indicate, you spent little or no time in a London hospital. You went back to Israel. You remained involved."

Berger turned from the window. "Keep going. You seem to be telling this story quite well yourself."

Danielle took a step closer to him, and Ben watched their reflections framed in the darkness of the night. "Hanna Frank somehow survived the stoning, yes or no?"

Berger didn't answer her.

"You owe me this much, Mr. Berger. I need the truth."

"I owed your father more, more than I can ever repay."

"This has nothing to do with my father anymore."

"And what does it have to do with Hanna Frank?"

"I believe she somehow got back to Israel, where she lived her life as an Israeli-Arab. Hanna Frank became Zanah Fahury, who was murdered last week by a man working for Layla Aziz Rahani, Hanna's oldest daughter, who had somehow discovered who she was. Just tell me if I'm right or wrong."

Berger sighed. "Both."

"This is a bad time for riddles, Mr. Berger. The same man who killed Zanah Fahury also killed a terrorist named Akram Khalil. That links Layla Aziz Rahani to a plot that's going to take millions and millions of lives. I'm not sure exactly how yet, but you're going to help me figure it out."

"Nothing I know can help you there."

"You know what really happened all those years ago. That's where it started."

Berger shrugged. "Very well, Danielle, very well . . ."

CHAPTER 80

After the stoning ceased, Yakov Barnea watched Abdullah Aziz Rahani walk to a nearby car, still clutching his daughter Layla's hand. He refocused his binoculars on the shape buried up to her neck in the ground. Barnea saw the black cloth covering her face was still moving faintly, evidence that she was still breathing, though shallowly. Rahani had left only two men behind, their task clearly to wait for her to die and then bury the body in disgrace in an unmarked grave.

"Get ready," Barnea said to Hyram Berger.

Berger checked his pistol, making sure no sand had jammed in its slide.

"You won't be needing that."

"I thought we—"

"Kill those men and Rahani will know his wife was saved. Leave them alive and they know telling the truth will cost them their lives in much worse fashion."

The two Israelis approached out of the sun, dressed in the robes of Arab royalty. The glare and their appearance would make the two men left to dispose of Hanna Frank hesitate, provide just enough time for Berger and Barnea to draw near.

As it turned out, the Saudis were unarmed and unable to muster much resistance to the fierce attack launched at them. Berger bound their unconscious frames, while Yakov Barnea moved to Hanna Frank, knelt on the gravelly sand, and removed the black shroud fastened around her head.

Berger was too far away to see her face clearly, but he saw enough to turn his insides to mush. He nearly gagged, had to look away from the sight of a face broken and bleeding, blistered with lumps and swollen to twice its normal size.

But Yakov Barnea didn't look away. Instead he smoothed out the patches of her matted hair, whispered words of comfort, and began to dig Hanna Frank out of the ground with his hands.

Berger located two of the shovels Rahani had used to bury her under a tree and brought them over. He avoided looking at the woman the whole time he and Barnea dug her out.

"Yakov," he said, but it took a few moments before Barnea looked at him. "We should be merciful."

"She's alive, Hyram."

Barnea resumed his digging at a fever pitch. He barely stopped to breathe. Before long they had freed enough dirt to pull Hanna Frank from the living tomb in which she had been buried. She was unconscious now, and they eased her out tenderly, afraid some of her limbs might have been crushed or broken from the pressure.

Their truck, stocked with fresh produce as a cover, was parked a mile away and Yakov Barnea carried her as easily as if she were a child. Hyram Berger had left the ropes of the two Saudis loose enough so they'd be able to untie them with a minimum of effort. To save their own skin, they would return to Abdullah Aziz Rahani and report their job finished, confident he would never have an opportunity to learn the truth.

Riyadh was the nearest city, but Barnea's only contact was a much farther drive away in Abha. Berger drove while his general sat in the back of the truck with Hanna Frank, the sole success among all the Blue Widows, hidden amid the produce in case they were stopped on the road. He had called in all of the favors owed to him, and many of those owed to others, to get this far. But after Abha they were on their own.

A doctor was waiting for them in his home when they reached Abha well after sunset. Berger saw him turn away at first sight of Hanna Frank's ruined face. He forced himself to examine her, professing there was nothing he could do. Yakov Barnea had taken out a pistol and laid it on a nearby table, telling the doctor he must try.

They had no access to an X-ray machine, but the doctor was able to quickly discern that both Hanna's jaws and cheeks were broken as well as one of her eye sockets. He suspected a number of skull fractures as well, completing his examination with the grim pronouncement that she would be dead by morning even if they could get her to a hospital. The doctor left the room and came back with a large vial of morphine, asked Yakov Barnea how much to give her.

"Enough to relieve her pain," the general ordered.

"But—"

"She's going to live, Doctor," Barnea said, still tenderly holding Hanna's head in his hands. "She's going to live."

CHAPTER 81

"And she did," Danielle said to Berger thirty years later, "didn't she?"

Berger nodded slightly.

"The woman survived and my father got her back to Israel, where she lived her life out in hiding as Zanah Fahury. The diamonds Abdullah Aziz Rahani made her swallow before she was stoned gave her all the money she needed to support herself."

To Danielle it all made sense, everything coming together.

"Then her older daughter, Layla, uncovered the truth," she continued, "and sent an assassin named Hassan to finish the job her father had started. Hassan made sure Zanah Fahury's face was bashed in to prevent the medical examiner from uncovering evidence of her past wounds. That's it, isn't it?"

But much to Danielle's surprise Hyram Berger shook his head. "No."

"No?"

"Are you saying that Hanna Frank *died*, after all?"

"You didn't let me finish my story, Danielle: Hanna Frank survived. But she never left Saudi Arabia."

"WHAT DO you mean?" Danielle demanded, the walls seeming to close in around her.

"Just what I said. Anna Pagent, Hanna Frank, that is, survived her wounds, but refused to return to Israel."

"Refused?"

"That's what your father told me."

"Then you can't be sure!"

Berger nodded. "I'm sure. I could hear his voice cracking when he told me, see the tears in his eyes. Your father was never much of an actor, Danielle."

"He let her stay. . . ."

"I gather she didn't give him any choice."

"What happened to her?"

"I don't know."

"You must!"

"I don't, and that *is* the truth. The trip he and I made to Saudi Arabia wasn't sanctioned. Your father was reprimanded for his actions, and I was banished, to Washington. We never saw each other again once I was assigned here; that's the truth too."

"Then Hanna Frank could still be alive."

Berger shrugged. "It's possible, I suppose, but . . ."

"But *what*?"

Berger's expression softened, suddenly compassionate. "For all intents and purposes, she died when your father did. You should leave it at that, Danielle."

"You make it sound like a warning."

"Because that's what I meant it to be."

"Why?"

Berger turned and walked away from her toward the bar. "We're finished here."

"No, we're not. Layla Aziz Rahani killed someone she thought was her mother in Jerusalem." She followed Berger across the room as he poured himself another scotch. "There's something else going on here. There must be."

Berger finished the drink in one gulp. "You loved your father, Danielle."

"What? Of course I did."

"You trusted him."

"Yes. Yes."

Berger filled the glass higher this time. "This was something he never, never wanted you to know. That's why he didn't tell you himself."

"Tell me what?" Danielle grabbed Berger's hand before he could raise the glass again.

Berger let go of the glass. "Take this. You're going to need it."

"What's this about?"

"Kavi, Layla Aziz Rahani's younger sister."

"You told me she was shot and killed in London."

"That's what you assumed from my story, what I led you to believe, but it's not the truth." Berger's eyes bore into Danielle's. "Kavi wasn't even wounded. Your father brought her back to Israel and paid Hanna Frank back the best way he possibly could: by raising her as his own daughter. As you, Danielle."

CHAPTER 82

Danielle felt as if the air had been sucked out of her. She stood there, having to remind herself to breathe. She looked to Ben for support, reassurance, but he could only gaze back at her, shaking his head slowly, his eyes glazed with shock.

Hyram Berger moved to a desk in the corner of his living room. From the top drawer he removed a single photograph, walked back toward Danielle, and placed it on the counter atop a moist ring made by his glass.

"See for yourself," he said.

Danielle took the picture of Layla Aziz Rahani in a trembling hand and studied it beneath the room's dim recessed lighting. She saw immediately how Colonel al-Asi's contact in the refugee camp, Hakim, had confused her with Layla; the resemblance was that striking. Danielle returned the picture to the counter and thought of the snapshot al-Asi had found hidden in Zanah Fahury's chest of drawers.

Two young girls. Two sisters. Herself and Layla Aziz Rahani, a woman she was now certain was behind the plan to destroy the United States.

"Yakov Barnea was still your father," Hyram Berger said, trying to sound comforting. "I knew him better than any man alive. Believe me when I say that."

Danielle stared at him blankly.

"He was already married to your mother when he first met Hanna in 1967. You know how your father was; he wanted to help, to save, everyone."

"Stop! I've heard enough."

"No, the story's not done yet. You see, it was different with the woman who became Anna Pagent. Her husband had died under Yakov Barnea's command, which gave him an extra sense of responsibility."

"My father fell in love with her," Danielle said, still resisting Berger's tale. "That's what you're saying, isn't it?"

Berger nodded. "He told me as much when we reviewed the recruits for the mission."

"The botched raid wasn't the first time he met Hanna in London, was it?" Danielle asked, starting to realize.

"No. That was their rendezvous point once or twice a year. I remember when he came from a trip there around the time Layla was two. He broke down and told me what had happened. How sad Hanna had become, how desperately she wanted to come back to Israel."

"One thing led to another," Danielle nodded, unsure how to feel, her emotions scrambled. It hurt to picture her father with another woman, actually hurt.

"It wasn't like that. I don't think your father realized that Hanna loved him as much as he loved her. They shared that one night and one night only." Berger sighed deeply. "A month later she included in her report that she was pregnant with her second child. His child. You, Danielle."

Danielle shuddered. "And he still left her in place?"

"On the contrary, he informed Hanna she was being recalled immediately. But she refused, saying she would never be able to forgive herself if she returned under those circumstances. Her job wasn't finished. So she stayed, had her second child, and established her cover even more firmly."

Danielle plopped into the nearest chair and put her hand to her forehead. "I have no memory of those years. Nothing."

"Your father was always concerned that you would. He had prepared himself for the day you'd come to him with questions he prayed he wouldn't have to answer. But you never did."

"And my mother?"

"He told her everything. She cried a lot, then insisted that they raise you even before your father suggested it. He had made a promise to Hanna Frank, after all. And he wasn't a man to renege on his obligations, any more than your mother was."

"I miss both of them so much," Danielle said, feeling warm tears start to pour down her cheeks.

"He never wanted you to know. He was afraid you'd think differently of him. Less."

"I don't. Not at all. How could I?"

Berger's eyebrows flickered. "Imagine for a moment if Hanna Frank had been recalled once she became pregnant with you. We would've received no advance warning about the surprise attack planned for Yom Kippur seventy-three. Israel, possibly, might not even exist today."

"What are you saying?"

"That both your mothers were heroes, Danielle, each in her own way."

"They were victims too, both of them, of Operation Blue Widow."

"But one of the Blue Widows saved Israel, Danielle. There's no escaping that."

Danielle desperately tried to remember the gunfight in the Hilton lobby, being hustled into the backseat of a waiting taxi while bullets thundered everywhere. She wondered if the seeds of what she had grown into herself had been sewn that bloody night.

"Wait," she said suddenly, her mind veering in a different direction. "What about the governess Habiba? You said she plunged into the backseat of the taxi with . . . Kavi in her arms."

Berger looked confused. "I don't know. I forgot all about her."

"Say my father brought her back to Israel. Say she could never return to Saudi Arabia."

"Zanah Fahury," Berger realized. "You think Zanah Fahury was this governess?"

"It makes sense, doesn't it?"

"Then why did Layla Aziz Rahani have her killed? Why would she think this woman was her mother?"

"Because of the diamonds the old woman was living off of, that could only have been supplied by the real Hanna Frank! Layla Aziz Rahani must have found out, learned about the diamonds somehow. Killed Fahury because of the obvious conclusion she would have drawn from that. You know what this means, don't you?"

"I'm sorry, no."

"Hanna Frank may still be alive!" Danielle insisted, thinking again of the picture of two little girls taped inside a chest of drawers. Hidden there by a loving governess instead of an equally loving mother. "Otherwise, Habiba would have stopped receiving the diamonds long ago."

"No," Ben said suddenly, rising to his feet. "Why would this governess need to sell her diamonds so frequently?"

Danielle shrugged, wondered where Ben was going.

"Because," he resumed, "you must have it backwards. Hanna Frank wasn't sending Habiba diamonds; Habiba was selling them in part to send funds to Hanna Frank!"

Danielle's mouth dropped. She should have seen that before. This was the missing piece, proof Hanna Frank must still be alive. . . .

"Even if your Palestinian friend is right," Berger said disdainfully, "this woman is not your mother, Danielle. Your mother was the woman who raised you."

"You don't need to tell me that."

Berger hesitated, started to raise the glass he'd refilled with scotch, then stopped. "You asked for a business visa for Saudi Arabia."

Danielle looked at Ben. "Two."

"Layla Aziz Rahani is beyond your reach, Commander. Whatever happened all those years ago—"

"This isn't about that, Mr. Berger."

"I was a soldier too. And when things become personal . . ."

"That's the problem," Danielle told him. "They've been personal for Layla Aziz Rahani ever since she turned in her mother, *my* mother, thirty years ago. And now it's personal for me too."

DAY TEN

CHAPTER 83

Ben left Danielle to herself through the long flight aboard Saudi Arabian Airlines, wishing he could find the words to comfort her.

They had both lost their mothers, at the same time, ironically. His to a bullet, hers to a shattering, long-hidden truth. Berger had given her a photograph of Hanna Frank as a young woman, one that had been part of her file during the selection process for Operation Blue Widow, and Danielle had spent much of the flight staring at it, transfixed.

The resemblance between them was striking. They shared the same dark, wavy hair and full, piercing eyes. But the picture also showed the kind of dreamy sadness and detachment Danielle had come to know all too well from the mirror, as if Hanna Frank too had accepted a fate she was powerless to change.

"How do you deal with it?" she asked Ben finally, breaking the uncomfortable silence that had settled between them.

He looked up from the magazine one of the business-class flight attendants had given him. "With what?"

"The confusion, the lies. People not being what you expected they were."

Ben took her hand and gripped it tightly. He thought of his father, the life of secrets he led that endured well beyond his death. "You realize all that was just their facades, the appearances they put on. Inside they're no different. The way they feel about you is no different."

"Layla Aziz Rahani is my sister."

"Half-sister, but there are things more important than blood."

"But that's the irony of it all. Neither of my brothers lived long enough to marry. I have no nieces or nephews, not even any uncles or aunts left. She's my last living relative. I thought I had no one. Now I find out the person I have . . . Never mind, I'm not making any sense."

Ben looked across the seat at her, suddenly fearing again for the safety of Sayeed and his family. "Yes, you are, more than you realize. You asked me how I dealt with the lies, the confusion. The answer is I don't get surprised anymore. People are always after something; I learned that a long time ago. I thought it would be different when I came back to the West Bank, and it was worse. I thought it would be different when I stayed in America to work for Security Concepts, and it was just as bad." He twisted in his seat and looked at her tenderly. "The thing is, Danielle, you've been dealing with the lies a lot longer than you realize. They just never hit home before."

She squeezed his hand back and turned toward the window. "I guess that's where I'm going, Ben: home."

CHAPTER 84

Major Karim Amir Matah of the Saudi intelligence service felt the desert winds batter him as he stepped from the stairwell of the Nahran Mediterranean Restaurant on the rooftop of the Abha

Palace Hotel. The stiff winds had forced all the diners inside today, and Matah made his way past the empty tables overlooking Lake Saad and the city of Abha. A waiter held the door open for him, and another man Matah guessed was the maître d' escorted him to a booth in the rear where a single man sat with his back to him.

"Sit down, Major," Saed Aziz Rahani said without turning.

Matah bowed slightly. "Your Highness," he greeted him, and slid into the booth across from the man dressed in an elegant Western business suit.

"Please don't call me that here," Saed Aziz Rahani said, speaking softly as he dipped another shrimp into some cocktail sauce. "We're supposed to be inconspicuous."

"I understand."

"What do you think of the hotel?"

"Not very much, *sidi*. It reminds me of America."

"With good reason. My father negotiated the deal with Rosewood Hotels and Resorts. He spent weeks in Dallas, Texas, finalizing the plans."

"I apologize for my rudeness."

"Don't bother, Major," said Saed Aziz Rahani, his voice slightly slurred. "I quite agree. We all must make compromises. They asked for an outdoor swimming pool; my father granted them an indoor one. They insisted on a bar; my father allowed them to serve alcohol in the two restaurants. Things are changing in Saudi Arabia, too quickly for some, too slowly for others. We do not have to embrace that, but we must accept it. Change is inevitable. It's strictly a matter of who can best see how to use it." Rahani gobbled up his last shrimp, dabbed the cocktail sauce from his mouth with a napkin, and guzzled the rest of a drink until the ice cubes jangled together and smacked across his lips. He signaled the waiter for another. "Then there is my sister, Major, who threatens to disrupt all the good my family wishes to do for our country."

"I understand, *sidi*."

"No, Major, I don't think you do. If you did, you would have made sure she did not return from the United States alive, as I instructed."

"Out of respect for your father."

"My father is dying."

"But he isn't dead yet."

Saed Aziz Rahahi poked around his plate with a fork. "He always appreciated your loyalty to him."

"As I appreciated his support."

"But I wonder how the Saudi intelligence service would react if they learned that fifteen years ago you arranged the rape of his daughter on his behalf."

"*His* behalf?" Matah challenged, staring Rahani in the eye.

"He's in no position to deny it, is he?" Saed said and dabbed the corners of his mouth with his napkin once again.

"I was only doing *your* bidding. A personal favor, you called it."

"But whose version of events do you think will be accepted, yours or mine? You should have made sure my sister died back then, Major, as I suggested. Now, because you didn't, she threatens the success of everything we are trying to accomplish with developments like this and others that are being finalized even as we speak. My sister would seek to poison our work in full view of the world. Keep the world from seeing Saudi Arabia through a lens colored with something different from oil. It is a fine line we walk, Major, is it not?"

"It is, *sidi*."

"Between tradition and progress. My sister threatens both, along with your career."

Matah's eyes locked on the knife lying on the edge

of Saed Aziz Rahani's plate. Rahani moved the blade
subtly out of his reach.

"You wish to keep your name in good standing, of
course, Major?"

"What is it you wish done?"

"The next time she leaves the country, Major," Saed
Aziz Rahani told him, "my sister must not return."

"*Mafhum,*" said Matah. "I understand."

CHAPTER 85

The American business visas Hyram Berger had
provided made negotiating Saudi customs and
immigration a surprisingly smooth process at
King Khaled International Airport outside Riyadh. Tourists with no defined reason for being in the country faced
a much tougher task and endured far more rigorous
questioning. The Saudis understood business; they still
did not understand tourism and only grudgingly accepted
it as a necessary evil in the face of their shrinking oil-
based economy.

In the past two decades, the country's population had
grown from 7 million to 19 million while the per-capita
income had shrunk by more than half. Menial jobs held
by foreigners for generations were now taken by Saudis
facing economic hardship for the first time in memory.
And still millions remained unemployed and often un-
employable.

The prospects for the future were no better. Not with
40 percent of the Saudi population now under the age
of fourteen. What would these children do for work

when they came of age? How would the government support them? The vast majority would be well-educated, unsuited to the low-level jobs most available.

After clearing customs, Ben waited outside one of several changing rooms into which Danielle had ducked to don Muslim robes and a head scarf in place of her Western attire. For those women who had forgotten to bring a change, or had packed it away in their yet-to-be-retrieved suitcase, a small shop had been conveniently situated to deal with the oversight.

Once Danielle reemerged, she and Ben exited the arrivals area at the airport and entered the main terminal, where a score of drivers held up cards imprinted with names in Arabic, English, and even, surprisingly, Hebrew. Ben saw his name written in Arabic a moment before he recognized the man holding it. He headed straight for him, neither he nor his driver able to contain the smiles that reflected the deep friendship they had shared for a decade.

"How was your trip, Inspector?" beamed Colonel Nabril al-Asi.

AL-ASI MADE a show of leading them subserviently to the limousine parked outside King Khaled International Airport amid a sea of others squeezed into two rows with little room to maneuver between them.

"Our lack of luggage makes us conspicuous," Danielle noted, watching many of the other cars being loaded.

"Not to worry, Chief Inspector," the colonel soothed. He wore a tuxedo accessorized by a matching *keffiyah*, in keeping with Saudi custom. "Many guests prefer to have their bags taken directly to their hotels for them."

Al-Asi opened the limousine's rear door and helped

them enter, then climbed behind the wheel himself. A pair of matching limos had boxed theirs in on the right, the three of them glad for the time it would provide to catch up.

"Good news or bad, Colonel?" Danielle asked.

"Good, if that's what you call a meeting with Layla Aziz Rahani that can come to no good end," he answered grimly. "The real representatives of a Palestinian business consortium she's scheduled to meet with this afternoon were unavoidably detained. You will be taking their places at the family palace, where she takes all her meetings; you'll find few women doing business from high-rise offices here, Chief Inspector. I'll brief you on the way."

It was already afternoon. The length of time it had taken to make the trip here, coupled with the time difference, had conspired to make Ben and Danielle feel as if they had lost a day. Even Hyram Berger's influence could not change flight schedules, and they were lucky to have made a late-night Saudi Arabian Airlines flight out of New York's Kennedy Airport.

"How much did you really know about Zanah Fahury when you asked me to look into her murder, Colonel?"

Al-Asi turned in the front seat to look at Danielle. "About your father's secret operation, you mean."

"Apparently not so secret."

"The rumors have been around for years, dismissed by most."

"But not you," said Ben.

"Not after I met Chief Inspector Barnea. If her father was anything like her, I would put nothing past him."

"Why Zanah Fahury, though?" Danielle persisted. "She was just an old woman. You thought she was my mother, didn't you, not just a governess who could never return to her homeland of Saudi Arabia?"

Al-Asi shrugged. "Before his death, your father visited her on a regular basis."

"And you knew this because . . ."

"Files kept by far less scrupulous individuals than I with an eye toward blackmailing high-ranking Israeli officials."

"He must have been picking up funds to send to Hanna Frank in Saudi Arabia," Danielle said to Ben, recalling his theory of the reason behind Zanah Fahury's frequent diamond sales. "And then she outlived him," she added, somewhat sadly.

"I can't help you find Hanna Frank, Chief Inspector," al-Asi told her. "And you'd be well advised not to consider searching for her."

"I'm here to deal with Layla Aziz Rahani and nothing else," Danielle said, not too convincingly.

"And that too promises to be a none-too-easy task. It's a thinly kept secret among the Saudi elite that Layla now controls all of the Rahani family's vast holdings. You'll find the information already downloaded onto this car's built-in computer. Hit the return key to bring it up on the screen. I've highlighted the holding I think you'll find most pertinent."

Ben's seat was closest to the keyboard and monitor, so he hit the return key. Danielle slid closer to him as the screen brightened to life, revealing an elaborate Web site.

"Immutech?" she raised.

"The ninth-largest pharmaceuticals manufacturer in the world. Rahani Industries purchased it a year ago from a British conglomerate. The deal hasn't even been formally announced yet, a codicil of the agreement, I understand."

"A year ago," Danielle echoed.

"Dating back to the beginning of Operation Flypaper," Ben added.

Danielle reached across Ben and began to scroll down the screen. "Meaning the Rahanis bought Immutech with something already in mind."

"Clearly. But what?"

"This," Danielle said, the screen frozen before her and Ben. "Production of the vaccine for smallpox."

CHAPTER 86

"Then she never intended to infect the country with the disease," Ben theorized, thinking of Hollis Buchert in the Mall of America.

"Not all of it. Just enough to force a mass inoculation of a vaccine she now controls."

"Contaminated?" Ben posed. "Poisoned?"

Danielle shook her head. "She could have achieved that effect equally well by releasing all her smallpox, or something else from Fort Detrick. No, this is something quite different. Why else would she go through all the trouble of stealing reserves of a virus she never intended to release?"

"I pray you're wrong, Chief Inspector," al-Asi said grimly.

"I'm not. I know how Layla Aziz Rahani thinks, Colonel. The only thing she couldn't anticipate was Zanah Fahury. If she hadn't sent Hassan to kill the old woman, we'd never have made the connection and uncovered her involvement."

"Even she has her weaknesses, apparently."

"You're missing the point, both of you," Ben interjected. "What could Layla Aziz Rahani possibly be planning to do that's worse than infecting all of America with smallpox?"

THE CITY of Riyadh, some forty miles from the airport, looked like a steel-and-glass oasis in the middle of the desert. The pristine four-lane highways, their concrete colored near white instead of gray or black to better reflect the sun, stretched in a ribbon around its outskirts. The regal palace belonging to Abdullah Aziz Rahani was located north of the older sections of the city in the Sulaimaniya District.

Colonel al-Asi drove past numerous palaces as they wound through Sulaimaniya. More like walled fortresses, the palaces were all adorned with such a profusion of lush flowers, greenery, and landscaping that it was easy to forget the desert even existed.

Ben and Danielle didn't get their first glimpse of the Rahani palace until their papers had been checked and rechecked by the guards at a closed entry gate, and the limousine was thoroughly searched. An armed guard also passed a hand wand about them politely, making a show of paying respect even as he checked for weapons. Once cleared to enter the grounds, the limousine followed another armed guard on a motorcycle up the finely paved drive toward the palace.

The palace had a smooth, white-stone finish that looked like polished granite. The windows were small and unobtrusive, in keeping with more ancient designs in which windows were as much a protective addition as a decorative one.

More guards were posted at the front entry, where the limousine deposited Ben and Danielle at the foot of a multilevel entry stairway adorned with beautifully crafted statues and a fully operational marble fountain. A waiting guard opened the rear door of the limousine and then escorted Ben and Danielle up the stairs, passing them on to a tall, gaunt man in a business suit standing just inside the huge double doors of the entry.

"Sayyida Rahani will be with you momentarily," he greeted. "If you will just follow me . . ."

The entry foyer was palatial in all respects, the marble floor adorned with lavish Persian silk carpets and elegant busts placed on pedestals fashioned from alabaster, porphyry, and other precious stones. These, along with the brilliant portraits and landscapes covering the walls, provided testament to the Saudi elite's unceasing penchant for collecting priceless art treasures.

Danielle had expected their civilian escort to lead them up the stairs that branched off in two different directions on all three floors above. Instead, though, he led them down a darker hall to a private staircase covered with a scarlet Oriental runner. Ben and Danielle followed him up three flights and through a pair of double doors onto a corridor the size of one usually found in a midsize hotel.

Ben caught the pungent scent of alcohol and antiseptic in the air. *Not a hotel,* he thought, *more like a hospital.*

Their escort brought him and Danielle to a door at the near end of the hall. He opened it, bowed subserviently, and invited them to enter. The scent of alcohol was stronger now, joined by a faint beeping sound and a mechanical whir.

Ben and Danielle stepped inside, finding themselves not in an office but in a hospital room, very large and capped by a cathedral ceiling that came to a perfect point in the center. They stopped directly beneath it, uncertain how to proceed. Tables covered the room on three sides, atop which lay scale models of what Ben and Danielle recognized as hotels, resorts, and water and theme parks.

The one remaining wall contained a hospital bed surrounded by multiple whirring machines and occupied by a pale, emaciated figure with wires running from his fingers and under his shirt, a tube wedged through the corner of his mouth that snaked down his throat. The angle of the tube kept his face locked in a perpetually ghastly snarl. But the built-in shelves and elegant wood paneling told them this room had once served an entirely different function, as an office, probably.

A woman, a nurse or an attendant, hovered over the man's bedside. Dressed in black robes with a veil wrapped adroitly to cover all but her eyes, she placed a plastic catheter pouch into a disposal bag and then gently tucked in the sheet that covered the man up to the throat. The nurse never so much as looked at Ben and Danielle, going about her business as they stiffly held their ground.

"Leave us, Marta," a voice came from behind them.

Ben and Danielle turned to find a tall, stunning woman standing in the doorway, dressed in a perfectly tailored suit.

Layla Aziz Rahani. Danielle felt her heart begin to beat faster. For his part, Ben fought to show no reaction at all, though the resemblance between the two women was even more striking in person.

Layla closed the double doors behind her and came forward as the nurse named Marta exited the room through a doorway neatly tucked into a recessed wall.

"My father's nurse," she explained, drawing even with Ben and Danielle. "She's been here ever since the stroke incapacitated him. I don't know what I would do without her." She looked toward Danielle, gesturing toward her head scarf. "You can take that off now, Commander Barnea. *Yus iduni t-ta arruf ilayaka.*"

CHAPTER 87

"I can't say it's a pleasure to meet you," Danielle retorted.

"*Masa a l'hayr,* Inspector Kamal," Layla said to Ben.

"Good evening," Ben offered lamely in English. He glanced once again at Layla, then back to Danielle.

But for a few changes in features, they could be the same person. . . .

They both looked like their mother. Layla Rahani was shorter than Danielle but had a similar build. Her hair was cut shorter to make it easier to conceal beneath a head scarf, but the color and waves were the same. The only major difference between them was their eyes, Danielle's being darker and fuller—her father's eyes.

"Do you like what you see, Inspector?" Layla Aziz Rahani asked him.

Ben hadn't realized he was staring at her. "Only up to a point," he told her.

Layla turned her attention back to Danielle. "An interesting ruse you tried to pull off," she resumed. "It might have worked, if I hadn't been expecting you. I know you're unarmed. Tell me, did you expect to come in here and kill me with your bare hands?"

"Only if I have to."

"Not a wise idea," Layla said, continuing toward the bed that the servant Marta had just been tending. "I have guards posted outside the door. I thought I'd introduce myself before I turn you over to them."

"You don't want to do that," Danielle told her.

"Really? Why wouldn't I?"

"Because of the woman you had killed in Jerusalem."

Layla Aziz Rahani nodded, clearly surprised by how much Danielle had been able to surmise. "Your reputation is apparently well earned. Please, proceed."

"You thought you were finishing the job you started as a little girl, convinced yourself that woman, Zanah Fahury, was your mother."

"With good reason."

"After all these years . . ."

"That seems to be of particular concern to you, this woman's murder."

"How did you find her?" Danielle asked.

"I came across a diamond ring at a jeweler's during a business trip to London just over a month ago." Layla Rahani Aziz stopped and for a moment her expression saddened. "My mother's wedding ring, among the few possessions she had with her when she tried to take me out of London." Her gaze drifted to her father's hospital bed. "My father made her swallow many of her diamonds."

Danielle suppressed a shudder, recalling the many trips the woman who called herself Zanah Fahury had made to Glickstein's jewelry store in Jerusalem.

"I managed to remain calm long enough to inquire about the stone's origins. The store's proprietor proved most cooperative when I offered to pay double what the ring was worth." Layla Aziz Rahani reached a hand into her pocket and emerged with the ring, holding it out for Danielle to see. "Money well spent, as it turned out."

"Not really; you made a mistake."

"I think not."

"Zanah Fahury wasn't your mother. She was the governess Habiba who fled that night thirty years ago in London. She must have had your mother's jewelry case with her. *That* was where the wedding ring came from."

Layla Aziz Rahani's eyelids flickered as she weighed Danielle's assertion. She started to speak, then stopped, thinking some more.

"Habiba left London with your sister too," Danielle continued. "Kavi."

"No," Layla Aziz Rahani insisted. "Kavi's dead."

Danielle moved closer to the hospital bed, Ben trailing slightly behind her. "That's right, she is. She died in London that night thirty years ago. Only she wasn't shot or stabbed. Her life just started over again. In Israel, where she was raised as a Jew by Yakov Barnea."

In spite of herself, Layla Aziz Rahani drew in her breath sharply, fighting to remain in control.

"I'm surprised you never figured it out for yourself," Danielle continued. "My sister."

"You lie!"

"You know it's the truth," Danielle said forcefully, watching uncertainty bloom in Layla's eyes.

Layla Aziz Rahani shook her head slowly. "I share no blood with you!"

"Only half, because Yakov Barnea was my *real* father. That's why he was so willing to raise me as his own, because that's what I was." Danielle paused to let her words sink in. "So how does it feel, having an *Israeli* for a sister?"

"*I'm not your—*" Layla Aziz Rahani started to raise her voice, then broke her words off altogether, remembering some of her father's final words to her mother, accusing her of having an affair. Could it be, was it possible that affair had been with *Yakov Barnea*?

"Yes, you are, and you know it. You can feel it just as I can. Look in the mirror and tell me who you see looking back."

Layla shook with rage. "It was your father who saved the whore's life, wasn't it?"

"If you want to call whatever she had afterwards a life, yes." Danielle stopped, gaining confidence. "So what's the plan, you going to stone me now, maybe Inspector Kamal too?"

Layla twisted toward Ben derisively. "A Palestinian who sleeps with a Jew. You deserve a worse fate than that."

"I'm also American," Ben told her.

"Which is more than our mother was," Danielle followed. She waited for fresh surprise to display itself on Layla Aziz Rahani's features before resuming. "She was Israeli. Her real name was Hanna Frank. Part of my father's operation to save the state of Israel, and Abdullah Aziz Rahani fell right into her hands. So, my sister, your father was a traitor, and you never even knew it." Danielle looked down at Abdullah Aziz Rahani's inert figure once more. "Our mother never loved him. My father was her true love."

Layla Aziz Rahani, trembling with new rage, steadied herself with a few deep breaths. "Your father didn't save his world, my sister, he only postponed its destruction. Just as he didn't save our mother's life; he only prolonged her death." Layla's face flushed red. "I, on the other hand, should kill you now."

"Go ahead," Danielle dared. "It won't change why we're here, the fact that we know what you're up to, what you've got planned."

"You couldn't possibly."

"Close enough. You tried to kill your mother . . . *my* mother," Danielle added, having trouble forming those words. "You blamed the West because you couldn't bear to blame yourself. Is that the reason why you're so determined to destroy the United States?"

"So you figured that much out. Congratulations."

"Why don't you explain the rest to me?"

Rahani nodded tightly. "I suppose I can. You, after all, have been through much the same thing."

"I think you're confused."

"Am I? The plan it's fallen on me to finish is the work of my father, conceived after I was raped at an American college. First my mother's terrible betrayal, then that. He saw what he had to do, what needed to be done. I merely picked up where he left off."

"As a mass murderer."

"Is calling me that supposed to unnerve me? It doesn't, you know. I threw the first rock when my mother was stoned, and I didn't feel anything then either. I don't think I've felt anything since, except to believe in my father's vision. I've dedicated my life to seeing his work completed."

"So it was he who purchased Immutech Pharmaceuticals. Because of the smallpox vaccine."

Layla Aziz Rahani raised her eyebrows. "Very impressive, my sister. We must have the same blood in our veins, after all. Tell me, what else have you managed to figure out?"

But it was Ben who replied. "You controlled Akram Khalil and his people, bankrolled them. His operatives in the United States stole the smallpox from the USAMRIID facility at Fort Detrick for you, then made sure some of it ended up in the hands of Hollis Buchert."

"Call it a sample," Rahani acknowledged, "enough to show your country what could be coming."

"And trigger a mass inoculation. Then you killed Khalil for his efforts," Danielle picked up.

"A pity, since I set up the Israelis to do the job for me. But Khalil realized I had used him before your government responded to the information I made sure reached them. He threatened to expose me to the rest of his leadership, threatened my entire plan."

"To fulfill the prophecy of the Last of Days," Ben said softly.

"But only for America. That was the beauty of my father's plan, hatched in the wake of my mother's treachery and my own—" Layla stopped suddenly. "It doesn't matter now. What's done is done."

"How? What is it you're going to do?"

"No more than what was done to me. The decadence of that country, the animals who inhabit it, stole my womanhood, condemned me to a life alone. I bless my father for acting on his rage and I thank God for the strength to finish his work when the stroke struck him down. Surely it was fate, because I must have been meant to be the one to see the plot to its conclusion all along."

Layla Aziz Rahani stopped, as if expecting Danielle to respond, then started again when she didn't.

"I could have released the smallpox we stole, yes, to poison their world, but that wouldn't have destroyed their society, their way of life. They would endure, rise to fight another day as they have done before. War unfolds in an instant. Fate can take a lifetime, several lifetimes. I couldn't destroy their world, my sister, but I could end it."

"How?"

Layla smiled slightly. "You disappoint me, my sister. I'm surprised you haven't figured that out too. Then again," she added bitingly, "it wouldn't have affected you."

"Affected *me*? What are you talking about?"

"No," Ben muttered, shuddering as he realized.

"So the Palestinian has figured it out. Tell her what I meant. Tell her why my plans for America wouldn't have touched her."

Danielle looked at Ben, then back at Layla Aziz Rahani before he could speak.

"Why don't you tell her yourself?" Ben told Rahani

"Very well." Layla nodded and turned again to Danielle. "I said you'd been through the same thing yourself, my sister, because you've lost two children to miscarriages. The last one, I understand, was thanks to a bullet that left you unable to conceive another."

Danielle swallowed hard, stung by the strike at her own personal misery as a larger picture of Layla Aziz Rahani's terrifying vision took shape before her. "Conceive," she repeated.

Layla Aziz Rahani smiled ever so slightly. "RU-18, a birth control drug designed by Immutech Pharmaceuticals to quell rampant population growth in the African continent. And it did, my sister . . . by rendering the women of an entire town irreversibly sterile. The same thing it is going to do to America."

CHAPTER 88

"White House operator."

Professor Albert Paulsen shifted the telephone from his right hand to his left. "I'd like to speak to the president, please."

"We only take messages, sir."

"See, I lost the private number I had for him and the general."

"The general?"

"General Bayliss, head of homestead security. If you could just put me through to the Oval Office."

"As I said, sir, we only take messages."

Paulsen squeezed the receiver between his shoulder

and ear, so he could take out his notepad. "Okay, tell them the village of Kokobi was the key."

"Kokobi?"

"In Africa," Paulsen said, and spelled the letters out. "An experiment was conducted on the villagers to test a new birth control drug, something called RU-18. The drug introduced an antigen into the women's bloodstream that kept them from ovulating by forming a protein shield around the egg, effectively killing it. Are you getting all this down?"

"Yes, sir."

Paulsen heard the sound of computer keys clicking on the other end. "Ever been a member of the Girl Scouts?"

"No, sir."

"Good. Now, this antigen was only supposed to work for thirty days or so. Perfect for African countries where the birth rate was out of control. Think about it. As things turned out, though, the antigen's effects were permanent. Underline that." Paulsen waited briefly, then continued. "The antigen, once introduced, renders the eggs permanently dormant. Turned out the damn thing is self-replicating. Chokes off every egg produced forever. *Forever.* You know what that means?"

"No, I don't, sir."

"No babies ever again. The end of procreation and Girl Scout cookies forever. And here's the kicker: RU-18 was produced by Immutech, the same pharmaceutical company that's manufacturing the smallpox vaccine. Get it?"

"Er—"

"Doesn't matter. General Bayliss will. Tell her to put two and two together and then call me."

"What's your number, sir?"

"That's right," Paulsen remembered, "I don't have one right now. No problem. Just tell the general to leave a message."

CHAPTER 89

"You've contaminated the smallpox vaccine with RU-18."

"A version of the drug, yes," Rahani said, smiling broadly. "A secret shared until now by only my father, myself, and a few select others. It feels good to speak of it, to be able to celebrate the work of my father with others who can appreciate it. Imagine, my sister, just imagine a society no longer able to procreate."

Danielle felt suddenly light-headed. She teetered briefly, feeling faint, until Ben grasped her arm and held her steady.

"The vaccine will spare no one, my sister," Layla Aziz Rahani continued. "The disease would have spared far too many."

"Then the effects . . ."

"Won't be known for years, decades, generations. America won't die quickly but she will die completely. I won't be here to witness that final end; I don't have to be. The satisfaction of knowing its inevitability is enough for me."

Layla Aziz Rahani saw Danielle's eyes darting about, searching the area of her father's bedside. "Go ahead, my sister. Search for a syringe, some sharp object, a weapon of any kind your deadly skills can make use of. His work is finished now."

The entry doors opened again, allowing five men to enter, one standing head and shoulders above the others: Hassan.

"Shipment of the vaccine starts tomorrow," Layla told them, sliding away. "There's nothing you can do to stop its distribution. America is desperate now to save itself from smallpox. Your little adventure in Minneapolis actually helped my cause more than hurt it: Now the whole country believes the smallpox is in the hands of a group, this People's Brigade, that has every intention of using it. Lines at hospitals were around the block this morning, demanding a vaccine that waits in the Immutech warehouses. The two of you have done me a great service. I'm sorry you won't live to see the results, as I will."

"And what of Saudi Arabia?" Danielle challenged. "Without U.S. dollars to buy your oil, how long will it be before poverty destroys everything men like your father built here? You seem willing to destroy your own world too."

"Let Saudi Arabia be destroyed so it can be remade in a different image," Layla Aziz Rahani insisted, thinking hatefully of her brother Saed. "An image in which I could take my rightful place as my father's heir. If only he could know I have done this for him, completed the work that consumed him for years, all that would change. I know it would." Layla Aziz Rahani's gaze tightened into a mixture of sadness and rage, her mouth puckered outward, her eyes blazing as she looked down at the inert body upon the bed. "His heart was broken long before his body followed. He honestly loved our mother, was never genuinely happy again after that night in London. One of his children stolen from him, a wife who had betrayed him in the worst way imaginable, and finally my . . . violation. What choice did he have?"

Layla Aziz Rahani backed away from the bed as four of the gunmen who had entered the room edged forward, all but Hassan, who held his ground by the door. "Now, you'll have to excuse me. I'm needed elsewhere."

Danielle lunged to the head of Abdullah Aziz Rahani's bed, her fingers locked on his throat, guns steadying upon her. "Tell them to back off, my sister."

But the look on Layla's face told her she had badly miscalculated, even before Ben spoke.

"That's what she wants, Danielle," he said with his eyes on Layla. "For you to do what she can't. Don't give her the satisfaction."

Danielle eased her fingers away slowly, backed off.

"You're smart for a Palestinian," Layla Aziz Rahani said to Ben. "Smart enough to realize that Israel won't last long once America falls. I'm doing your people a favor. With America gone, Israel will be overrun once and for all, as it should have been in 1973." She backpedaled toward the double doors, stopping briefly in Hassan's huge shadow. "Enjoy your eternities, both of you. Come, Hassan, there is somewhere we must be."

The huge, one-eyed man stepped from the room with her and closed the door behind them, leaving the four gunmen alone with Ben and Danielle. The look in their eyes told her it was going to end here and now, with Abdullah Aziz Rahani, what was left of him anyway, bearing silent witness. Two of the gunmen started to turn their guns on Ben, while the other pair kept theirs fixed on Danielle.

The door through which the nurse had disappeared minutes earlier opened inward, and Marta reemerged wheeling a cart containing a large bowl and sponges. She headed straight for Abdullah Aziz Rahani, ignoring the men holding guns on Ben and Danielle.

"Get out of here, you wretch!" one of them spat at her in Arabic.

But Marta kept right on wheeling the cart, stopping only when she reached the far side of the bed.

"I said—"

A hail of silenced gunfire swallowed his words, muzzle flashes bursting from a weapon hidden inside Marta's cart. Ben and Danielle instinctively threw themselves to the floor, the soft spits echoing in their ears. Spent shells rattled against the tile, the four gunmen stitched by bullets.

Ben and Danielle watched them fall, then turned toward Marta as she yanked a submachine gun from beneath the cloth covering the cart. Gun smoke wafted through the air, its acrid, sulfur smell overpowering that of the blood that had just begun to rise. The nurse kept one hand coiled around the submachine gun while the other slowly stripped off her veil.

Danielle gasped at the sight of the horribly scarred face revealed beneath it.

Marta was Hanna Frank.

CHAPTER 90

Little resemblance to Hanna Frank remained from the photo of her Berger had given Danielle, except for the eyes. Still bright and strong, piercing in their intensity.

The woman's face was grotesquely misshapen, pocked by scar tissue that had formed over jagged shards of bone that had never healed properly. It was a face bathed in the shadows formed by the ridges and fissures that appeared upon and beneath a horribly misshapen forehead. Her cheeks were crusted with marble-sized lumps. Her mouth was cracked perpetually open on one side and bent to the left, her jaws hanging low and loose as though permanently unhinged.

Danielle found herself back on her feet, unable to tear

her eyes away, yet she didn't find the sight of Hanna ugly or revolting at all. Ben stood just to her side, his arm gripped tightly around both her shoulders.

"Come, you must leave," Hanna Frank said, her voice a lispy, crackling garble.

Danielle couldn't move, felt as if she were floating.

"I know a secret route," the woman continued, stowing her submachine gun atop the cart. "But we must hurry, before they check the room."

Danielle's gaze locked with hers, and for that moment she saw Hanna Frank as the beautiful woman with whom both Abdullah Aziz Rahani and Yakov Barnea had fallen in love. She felt tears brimming in her eyes. She wanted to embrace Hanna Frank, found the desire but not the will. Her emotions clashed. She didn't know what to feel for this stranger who was her real mother and had lived a life of pain, isolation, and sacrifice that had begun with Operation Blue Widow. She had given so much, lost so much, and gained nothing in return from the night Danielle had been stuffed into the back of a cab and driven off to begin a new life. Danielle imagined Hanna Frank waiting in Saudi Arabia for all these years after Yakov Barnea had rescued her, living off funds channeled somehow from Zanah Fahury, just for the opportunity to complete her mission, which at last had come. She had returned to the Rahani palace in the guise of a nurse, tending to her husband in the very room where she'd overhead mention of the plot to invade Israel in 1973.

"Danielle," Ben said softly, whispering in her ear. "Danielle."

It occurred to her then, suddenly, all that her father had accomplished. The terrible truths he'd been forced to keep along the way, the sacrifices that dominated his life too. But thanks to Hanna Frank he had saved Israel.

Just as it was left to Danielle today to save much, much more.

She found her feet, her tongue, was about to speak, when the woman her father had turned into Anna Pagent pulled the veil back over her face and moved for the door at the head of Abdullah Aziz Rahani's bed. She stopped when she reached it and lifted the veil from her twisted mouth once more.

"You must leave now, my daughter," she said from the doorway, her voice cracking and raw, as if she were unused to speaking. "There's a car waiting for you."

Ben could see the pain in Danielle's eyes, the shock that had turned her perpetually even expression into a mask of hesitance and uncertainty. He tucked into his belt a pistol lifted from a dead gunman and started to ease Danielle toward the stairway beyond the frail figure of Hanna Frank.

"I should have killed Layla," her real mother told her, as they drew closer. "A hundred times I had the chance, and I could never do it." Her eyes turned downward, embarrassed. "Any more than I could let them kill you."

"I understand." Danielle nodded. She wanted so much to take Hanna Frank into her arms and lose herself in the hope that the embrace might somehow compensate for all the lost years. Before she could, though, someone began pounding on the entrance to Abdullah Aziz Rahani's domain.

"Go. Go and stop her," Hanna Frank said, her eyes regaining their intensity. "Otherwise, all this was for nothing."

Once again, Hanna Frank pulled the veil back over her face and for a brief, fleeting moment Danielle again saw her as the beautiful woman with whom her father had fallen in love. She stepped back and let Ben and Danielle pass her, holding Danielle's gaze until she closed the door behind them.

THE STAIRS wound downward, spilling out at a service entrance to the palace where a Mercedes was warmed and ready. Ben moved around to the driver's side, while Danielle took a last look at the windows above, thought she briefly glimpsed the figure of Hanna Frank looking down at them.

"Danielle," Ben called softly. "Danielle, get in. We've got to go."

He hurried back around the car and eased her toward the passenger door. He opened it for her and guided her in.

"Come on," Ben said, sliding behind the wheel, "let's finish your mother's work."

A set of windows four stories above blew out in a deafening blast, flames chasing the glass into the air. A secondary explosion coughed more flames outward, dragging black smoke with them.

An alarm began to wail. Men were shouting and screaming.

The acrid stench of smoke reached Danielle in the passenger seat of the Mercedes, where she suddenly found herself. She saw the tinted window beside her roll electronically upward and placed her hands against it, reaching for the woman who had once been her mother, as Ben turned the key and gave the big car gas.

But he waited until the guards at the front gate had charged up the drive toward the palace before screeching forward. He felt the Mercedes buck slightly when he floored the accelerator and crashed through the gate. The windshield shattered, and he turned away from the wheel, regaining control just before the big car pitched off the road.

HE DROVE straight to the airport, Danielle silent and transfixed next to him.

"What about al-Asi?" she said finally.

"Don't worry. He'll probably beat us out of the country."

"We've got to call Najarian."

"I know."

"He's got to get to somebody in Washington. Get production at that pharmaceutical plant suspended. Get the whole place shut down."

"He will."

Danielle stared through the windshield. "My father and Hanna Frank loved each other, Ben. I could see it in her eyes."

"Your father loved your mother too."

"This was different. Hanna Frank refused to come back to Israel because she knew it would destroy everything he was, everything he had built. She didn't want him responsible for her too; she'd already given him me. So she did the only thing she could: waited for the opportunity to complete her mission. Find her way back into the Rahani palace, even though there was no one left to report to."

"Both our fathers were good at keeping secrets," Ben told her.

"And now both our mothers are dead."

"Yours died in Israel ten years ago, Danielle."

DANIELLE FOUND a phone built into the console, dialed John Najarian's secure cell number, and put him on the speaker.

"Ben, where the hell are you?" came Najarian's gruff greeting.

"Saudi Arabia, on our way to England."

"England?"

"Call the secretary of state, John, and tell him to have his people meet us at the Immutech Pharmaceuticals plant in Reading tomorrow morning."

"Can I tell him why?" Najarian asked.

"To save the country."

DAY ELEVEN

CHAPTER 91

The first of the trucks arrived at Immutech Pharmaceuticals' production plant at nine A.M. sharp. A line of them stretched back as far as the eye could see along the access road leading to the complex, and a steady stream was visible exiting the nearby M-4.

The whole process should have started days ago, lamented Layla Aziz Rahani as she viewed the trucks from inside the gate. But rearranging flights out of Heathrow Airport to accommodate the fleet of C-130 transports onto which the vaccine would be loaded had proven more difficult and time-consuming than anticipated.

Layla Aziz Rahani reveled in the reports coming from America of the widespread panic that had risen in the aftermath of smallpox being found at the Mall of America. Terrified citizens were demanding a response, leaving Washington with no choice but to assure them mass inoculations of the vaccine would begin in as little as ten days' time. The American public didn't want to hear about side effects, two-week incubation period, or the greatest public health crisis in U.S. history. They just wanted their shots.

And Layla Aziz Rahani would make sure there was a dose for each and every one of them.

BEN AND Danielle stood near the cluster of press personnel just outside the entrance to the Immutech Pharmaceuticals complex. They had flown into London's Heathrow Airport the night before. From there they had rented a car and driven the short distance to Reading, finding a room well past midnight at a small bed-and-breakfast not far from the famed Reading School.

The vaccine conceived to destroy the United States could never be permitted to leave Immutech. At any moment, whomever John Najarian had arranged to have dispatched from the State Department would arrive to begin the process of shutting down the production process and sealing off the facility.

Ben checked his watch nervously again. "They should have been here by now."

"They could be inside the facility already, laying the groundwork."

"Without knowing the specifics?"

"Najarian's a persuasive man, Ben. I'm sure he knew what to say."

Her words didn't satisfy him. "I'm going back to the car, give John another call."

"I'll wait here," Danielle said, and watched Ben walk down the road to where they had parked their rental car.

Her thoughts returned to Hanna Frank, Marta, as she watched him go. She had blown up the room back at the palace to cover up the truth of what had transpired, a final sacrifice by a woman who had already given up everything. Danielle stood in awe of what her real mother had managed to accomplish heroically and humbly, never receiving any credit for her tragic mission. It made Danielle reflect on her own life, the risks she had taken and danger she accepted to fight for the State of Israel. She, too, had made sacrifices, although nothing like those made by Hanna Frank. The similarities between them added to the sadness Danielle had felt since her eyes locked with her mother's that last time on the stairwell. She hadn't wanted to leave her alone; it didn't seem fair. Hanna Frank had no one. Danielle, at least, had Ben.

She wished she could find some memory of this woman hidden in the deepest recesses of her mind. But the woman who became Anna Pagent, American college student, remained a specter, a shadow, purged from her mind long ago. Maybe the terror of that final night in London had triggered the block. It was as though she had never been Kavi. As though Kavi had never existed.

"Ms. Barnea?" The voice shook her from her daze, and she found herself facing a tall man with an Immutech security badge dangling from his neck. Four other broad-shouldered men, virtual clones of each other, stood subserviently behind him.

"Yes."

"We've been asked to escort you inside. Representatives of the U.S. State Department are waiting for you."

Danielle cast her gaze down the road. "We should wait for Mr. Kamal to return. He's gone to the car to—"

"I have my orders, ma'am," the man interrupted. "Time is of the essence, as I'm sure you'll understand. I'll leave one of my men behind to wait for Mr. Kamal."

Something in his tone was slightly off, but his eyes proved the giveaway, more intense than they should have been. Danielle felt her senses sharpen. If she could take this man and the others by surprise . . .

Then she saw the gun in his hand.

"If you'll just come with me, Ms. Barnea."

"MR. NAJARIAN'S line," a voice answered.

"Where's John?" Ben asked.

"Who is this, please?"

"Just put Mr. Najarian on the line."

"If you'll just tell me—"

"Shut up and get Najarian for me. This is an emergency!"

"I'll say it is," the man replied, his tone sharpening slightly. "John Najarian was found dead in his office six hours ago."

CHAPTER 92

"W e've got her."

Hassan lowered the small walkie-talkie the Immutech people had provided from his ear and nodded toward Layla Aziz Rahani. Word of what had transpired back at the palace had not reached her until she had landed the night before. She had cried for her father, cursing herself for not having Danielle Barnea and the Palestinian killed by Hassan in her presence.

Why hadn't she done it?

Because she couldn't while her father lay in the room, no matter how incapacitated he was. What if he maintained some flicker of awareness? She had always been a little girl to him; he had proven that much by failing to name her his heir. If only he could have seen her now, if only he could have seen his plan brought to fruition, thanks to her. How proud he would have been.

He had lived so many of his years in misery and now, perhaps, in death, he would be able to see his final success. Layla's mother hadn't just betrayed Abdullah Aziz Rahani; she had betrayed his people and his country, humiliating him in the process. Layla remembered his utter blankness as he bore witness to the stoning of her mother, all the emotion sucked out of him. She had not seen it in his face again until that night in the hospital years later when he pledged the vengeance she was now on the verge of completing in his stead.

Layla stood behind the glass of the production plant's second level, watching the vaccine being proportioned into individual-dose vials below. At the end of the automated assembly line, those vials were being loaded into cushioned cartons built especially to their specifications. The cartons would then be taken underground via conveyor belt and ferried to the warehouse for a brief stay before being loaded onto trucks destined for the airport. Ten days from now, the first American would receive the vaccine.

And the end of all things would have begun.

But not before she had a chance to deal with her half-sister. Ben Kamal's conversation with an associate in the United States had been recorded, as all calls made from Rahani business telephones were. So Layla had learned not only that Kamal and Barnea were headed here to Immutech, but also that they were expecting help from the United States State Department. Eliminating that help was as simple as eliminating the man making the arrangements. With John Najarian out of the way, Layla would be free to rid herself of Kamal and Barnea once and for all.

"Is something wrong?" Hazeltine, the plant manager, asked from the monitoring station for the controls.

"No," Layla told him. "Everything's going just as planned."

BEN RETURNED to the front gate of Immutech to find Danielle nowhere in sight. He veered to the right and took cover behind the long line of trucks waiting to enter the complex. Peering out from behind a pair of them, he honed in on a pair of burly Immutech security guards joining a third in scanning the area. He longed for a gun. Earlier that morning he'd been able to obtain no more than a razor-sharp armed forces knife at a local store. The clerk insisted on showing Ben how the knife's handle unscrewed, revealing matches, a tiny compass, razor wire, and a thick knot of twine inside.

Ben cursed under his breath. Layla Aziz Rahani had somehow gotten to Najarian and must have known they were coming. He tried not to think of Danielle's fate right now, focusing instead on finding a means to infiltrate the facility.

The cackle of voices and sound of shoe soles scraping asphalt made him look to his right. He saw that an entourage of media personnel were being led past him onto the grounds. Ben slipped into their midst and melted in among the cameras and microphones, finding himself heading toward a tented area reserved for news personnel.

THE GUARDS brought Danielle through a private entrance into Immutech's processing plant, bypassing the clutter of reporters intent on turning the initial shipments of the smallpox vaccine into a major media event. She considered trying to escape her armed escorts on several occasions. But they had clearly been warned of her prowess and kept a discreet distance, making it impossible for her to strike at all of them before one shot her.

She knew she was being taken to Layla Aziz Rahani.

Layla's murderous life that had begun with a stoning and continued with her own rape had turned her into a monster. She could say she was merely completing the work of her father, but Danielle knew that to be only part of it. Layla was carrying out the plot as much for herself as for her father. Turning her hate on others so self-loathing wouldn't consume her.

That phone call Layla Aziz Rahani had placed to her father from a London hotel all those years ago was both the ultimate betrayal and the defining moment of her life. Danielle thought of that, thought of Hanna Frank dying yesterday as she had lived. Alone, alone because of what her eldest daughter had done in 1973.

In that instant, Danielle knew she had to kill Layla Aziz Rahani. As soon as an opportunity availed itself, she wouldn't hesitate, sacrificing herself just as her mother had.

Inside the building, Danielle's escorts led her up three flights of stairs and down a narrow service corridor to a heavy steel door. One of the security guards knocked, and the hulking killer Hassan thrust the door open.

"Good morning, my sister," greeted Layla Aziz Rahani from inside the control center. "How nice of you to join us."

ONCE INSIDE the grounds, Ben got his first clear glimpse of what was obviously the plant's storage facility. The building was flat-roofed and rectangular, outfitted with six loading bays. Trucks had already backed into position in front of all of the bays, others waiting to replace them as soon as they pulled out. Ben pictured the entire warehouse filled with containers holding the smallpox vaccine. The reserves accumulated thus far had to be destroyed, but how could he manage that task, given the circumstances and with only a knife for a weapon?

Unless . . .

The idea struck him hard and fast.

It might work. He would make it work. . . .

Ben slid away from the cluster of media personnel and headed toward the line of trucks waiting for their turn at the storage depot's loading docks.

"I SEE your lover isn't with you," Layla Aziz Rahani continued, her voice biting. She turned to Hassan. "Find him. But don't bother bringing him here."

The giant nodded his understanding and slid past Danielle through the still-open door.

"Ms. Rahani," said Hazeltine. "Who are these men, this woman? No one without clearance is permitted in the—"

Hazeltine stopped when he saw the gun in the hand of one of the fake security guards. He started to back up, and a silenced bullet took him in the chest, slamming him against a wall of monitors and gauges. He slumped down slowly, eyes already glazing.

"You shouldn't have killed him," Layla Aziz Rahani said to Danielle calmly.

"Is that the best you can do for a story?"

"I'm not as skilled as you in such matters, my sister, but I'm learning."

"Then you should realize your plan can't possibly succeed."

"So you say, my sister. We'll see." She beckoned Danielle toward her. "Come and join me, my sister. Come and watch the death of America begin."

THE SAUDI assassins who had come on Karim Matah's orders to Immutech in the guise of cameramen looked up toward the control room's view window and saw Layla Aziz Rahani standing sideways to the glass now. One of them raised a cell phone to his ear.

"Major Matah," he said softly. "We await your order."

CHAPTER 93

The loading process for the first line of trucks was almost completed when Ben slid beneath the chassis of the truck at the far edge of the bays. At each bay, prepackaged crates containing the vaccine rolled down a conveyor belt directly into the truck's cargo hold, where they were stacked by a trio of men. Ben knew none of these men could see him, but that still left him with the patrolling guards to contend with by pretending to move for the cab of the last truck down. Once there, he had dropped to the concrete and shimmied into position.

Ben quickly located the truck's gas tank and poked at it with the tip of the knife. Feeling the metal slice with surprising ease, he jabbed the knife harder into the tank, puncturing it in three places.

The stench of diesel fumes assaulted him instantly. Some of the gas splashed back onto his shirt. Ben stifled a cough and slid out from under the truck, rolling immediately beneath the next one in line.

Less than five minutes later, he finished slicing the gas tanks of all the trucks backed into the six warehouse loading bays and ducked behind one of the trucks that would be loaded as soon as the first grouping pulled away. There, he unscrewed the cap on the knife's handle, just as the clerk in the shop had shown him that morning, and removed one of the thick wooden matches.

The spent fuel would ignite once he lit and tossed it, destroying the containers of vaccine already loaded and, hopefully, spreading into the warehouse to ruin the remaining stores. Beyond him, Ben noticed a few drivers emerging from their cabs, having finally noticed the fuel spreading across the pavement. He ducked around the rear of the truck and struck his match. The flame sizzled, settled, and Ben flung it into the pool of diesel fuel.

"I SHOULD have known you wouldn't die so easily, my sister," Layla Aziz Rahani continued, much of her bravado undoubtedly coming from the three guards who still had their pistols trained on Danielle. "But you will die today. Rest assured of that."

"Are you going to kill me?"

"I might."

Danielle shook her head, feeling surprisingly calm, judging her chances. Could she take Rahani now, pounce and snap her neck before the guards opened fire?

"No," she told Layla Aziz Rahani confidently, "you're not good enough. You weren't good enough to kill our mother either. She got the last laugh on you, and you still don't realize it."

Layla Aziz Rahani turned from the production process

continuing beyond the glass and faced Danielle.

"Our mother returned to your home after all these years. She's been living right under your nose." Rahani looked at her dismissively until Danielle added a single word. "Marta."

Layla Aziz Rahani's expression wavered. "You lie."

"It's no lie. It was she who covered up our escape . . . and ended your father's life in the process."

"That changes nothing!"

"Doesn't it? She rescued Ben and me, and now we've come to stop you."

At that, the control room seemed to tremble, quake, the distant sound of an alarm penetrating the walls of the production facility. Below, the reporters had become agitated, searching for an exit and for the source of the blast.

"Where is the Palestinian?" Layla Aziz Rahani demanded. "Where is he?"

She grabbed Danielle by the jacket and jerked her backward. Danielle turned easily into the move and spun Layla into the gunman at her side, jarring him.

Now!

Danielle went for the man's gun and twisted him into the path of Layla's other two guards, who converged on her, almost there when the huge glass window before them exploded behind a fusillade of bullets.

THE EFFECTS were even greater than Ben had hoped for. The flames had caught instantly, spreading fast across the pavement and ensnaring the six trucks lodged against the loading bays. Men had already begun running in all directions when the first truck exploded, its back end lifted off the ground a moment before its cab disappeared in a fiery blast that came when the flames ignited the fumes in its engine.

An alarm began to wail, quickly drowned out when the second truck went up in similar fashion, bashing into another waiting for that bay slot and catching it on fire as well. Ben's nose was stung by the stench of fumes and burning steel, and he peered around the truck behind which he had taken cover. He felt the superheated air sear his skin, leaving it feeling sunburned, and squinted through the smoke and flames toward the warehouse.

The bay doors were closing, sliding electronically downward, no doubt triggered by the fire alarm.

Ben threw himself into motion. He held his breath as he skirted the edge of the flames and leaped atop the loading bay. The nearest bay door was two-thirds of the way down when Ben dashed straight for it. He hit the concrete surface beneath a backdraft of flames that left his back steaming and his hair crackling, but managed to stay on the move. Rolling now toward the closing door, shutting his eyes when it seemed he wouldn't make it.

Ben dared to open his eyes only when he heard the *thwack* of the bay door sealing closed. He found himself safe on the other side, inside the warehouse, and pulled himself to his feet just in time to avoid a crate rolling off a conveyor belt. He hadn't realized the warehouse was fully automated as well. Though the warehouse was sealed now, the automated process had not stopped, and as a result crates began clanging against all six of the bay doors, already bunching up.

The timing of the machines had been thrown out of whack by the explosions. Across the warehouse floor, some of the loader apparatus's pincer extensions wheeled madly from the incoming conveyor that ran from a belowground tunnel to the outside with nothing in their grasp. Everywhere automated loaders continued to spin and spin, repeatedly banging into each other in what looked like a robotic war.

Ben started forward, careful to avoid their flailing arms. Automated forklifts rolled forward, toting massive containers toward nowhere. One drove straight into a wall, filling the warehouse with the sound of glass shattering. He coughed, realizing the warehouse had begun to fill with smoke.

Ben gazed about, studying the controls for the bay doors, each of them equipped with a manual override safety pull, similar to the standard garage variety, to prevent anyone from being trapped inside in an emergency. Open those doors, let the flames in, and the remaining reserves of the vaccine would be destroyed either by flames, heat, or water once the sprinkler system activated.

He moved to the first of the bay doors and reached up for the emergency pull, had his hand on it when a bullet sizzled by his ear. Ben heard, actually *heard* it, before he dropped to the floor beneath the cover of the conveyor belt. Looking back, he saw the huge shape of Sharif Ali Hassan surging toward him, gun roaring.

CHAPTER 94

Danielle felt the bullets pound the body of the guard she had spun before her. The barrage caught the other two as well, spinning both men around violently before dropping them.

Danielle dove to the floor and felt a fresh spray of bullets surge over her, smashing into the control console and sending a shower of sparks into the air. Assassins in disguise, she surmised, sent to kill Layla Aziz Rahani.

A few yards away Layla, covered in glass, stirred, moaning softly. Danielle crawled carefully across the floor, feeling shards of glass prick her palms and elbows. The gunfire had stopped, the assassins no longer a threat. Danielle climbed back to her feet before the smoking control panel, lined with video monitors showing the automated production process at varying stages still proceeding.

This was the chance she'd been seeking.

Danielle studied the digital readouts and nearby controls that set the specifications for the line. Different medicines meant different procedures, according to container specs. She began twisting the knobs randomly, changing those specifications to confuse the mindless machines in the processing facility below.

The monitors showed her the results instantly. Clear fluid, the vaccine itself formed of superheated and extracted compounds, began spilling everywhere as machines poured too much of it into vials. And with it perished the deadly ingredient formed from RU-18, the horribly failed birth control drug that held the means to destroy a society.

Farther up the line, the vials containing the smallpox vaccine were smashed to bits by the automated sealers now programmed to cap much bigger vials. And those vials that had already proceeded through this station were obliterated by the packagers, now trying to squeeze sixty-four dispensers into thirty-two slots.

Fresh alarms wailed. Red lights flashed. Someone was banging on the locked control room door.

Layla Aziz Rahani lay on the floor. "My brother," she managed to mutter hatefully. "Saed . . ."

Danielle looked down at her and sucked in her breath sharply.

Layla Aziz Rahani's beautiful face was . . . gone, lost to blood and shards of glass still sticking out of it. One of her eyes was closed. Her mouth was swollen open, her tongue swabbing futilely at her quivering lips.

Layla tried feebly to reach for a pistol pinned under the body of one of her dead guards. But Danielle jammed her foot over the gun before she could grasp it. Layla looked up at her scornfully, tried to speak, then passed out a moment before the control room door burst open and armed security men stormed inside.

MORE OF Hassan's bullets ricocheted off the conveyor belt as Ben rolled to the other side. He gazed up to find the huge killer looming over him, smiling as he steadied his pistol.

A rampaging loader smashed into Hassan from the rear, spoiling his aim as he fired and pitching him onto the conveyor next to Ben. The errant bullet struck a heat sensor and activated the warehouse's sprinklers, the heavy spray of water drenching both of them.

Suddenly the conveyor belt began to churn in the opposite direction, heading back through the warehouse. Hassan reached out and grabbed Ben by the throat, squeezing, the man's strength incredible. Ben felt his cartilage beginning to crush and flailed outward with his hands, managing to jam a thumb deep into the killer's good eye.

Hassan screamed in pain and released his hold of Ben's throat, rocketing a fist downward instead. Something that felt like iron slammed into Ben's face, his nose erupting in a spray of blood. Another blow rattled his jaw, the next two deflected into glancing blows that stung nevertheless.

Then Hassan closed both his hands over Ben's throat again, leaving no room for doubt this time. Ben tried to pry the hands off, then groped for something to grasp, to lash out at, but the killer's arms were so long, fully extended, that Ben could reach nothing. The conveyor belt carrying them rolled deeper into the warehouse, approaching a loading station manned by automated pincers spinning wildly toward the conveyor and then away with nothing to lay upon it.

Ben focused on those pincers, knew his timing would have to be perfect. He readied his legs along with his arms as the breath bottlenecked in his constricted throat and air bubbled in his brain.

The pincer apparatus swung left, then right. Left, then right . . . Left, then—

He jerked Hassan upward with all his strength. Not very far, barely even budging the death grip on his throat. Just enough to push him into the pincers' reach. Ben heard something crunch, watched Hassan's eye bulge as he thrashed wildly before the pincers spun him away from the conveyor belt, digging deeper into his spine.

Back and forth, they twisted him, back and forth . . .

"SHE TRIED to kill me!" Danielle screamed from the floor when the security force charged in, Layla Aziz Rahani's blood smeared over her face. "Please, a doctor! I'm hurt! I need a doctor!"

The head of the security force surveyed the scene quickly, his gaze holding for a moment on the body of the plant manager Hazeltine, before he reached down to help Danielle up.

"It's all right, Ms. Rahani," he said to Danielle, Layla

Aziz Rahani's inert body lying just beneath her. "We've captured the gunmen who did this. Help is already on the way."

BEN LEANED against a support beam, streams of water from the sprinklers continuing to cascade over him.

"You must be Kamal," a voice said.

Ben swung to his right to find a disheveled man wearing a white terry-cloth bathrobe approaching him.

"Recognized you from your picture," the man said. "Nice work. I'll take things from here."

"Who . . ."

"Am I? Roger Ramjet, president of the Girl Scouts of America."

Ben continued to stare at him.

The man took off his bathrobe, rung out the water, and offered it to Ben. "Here, put this on. It'll help you get out of here. Don't worry, it's brand-new. I stole it from the hotel." Then he removed a security pass that was looped around his neck. "This too. Look down, act a little crazy, and they'll think you're me."

Ben took the bathrobe and pass, eyeing the neatly stacked crates everywhere around him. "The vaccine . . ."

"I know all about it. Leave the rest to me."

Ben had turned and started to walk off when the man's voice caught him.

"Oh, I almost forgot." The man pulled something from his pants pocket and tossed it to Ben. "It's a scone. In case you get hungry on the way to wherever you're going."

EPILOGUE

Danielle stood in the shade of the grove of olive trees, gazing down at the freshly dug grave and the coffin that had been lowered into it. Around her the air smelled sweet, and a breeze blew the hair onto her face. She let go of Ben's hand, knelt, and picked up a handful of dirt. Then she tossed the dirt down atop the coffin, watching it spread and slide down the sides.

The slight hill above held the graves of her parents and brothers. It had taken some arm twisting to make this spot in the Jerusalem cemetery available, several favors called in. It took still more for Colonel al-Asi to obtain what few remains of Hanna Frank Saudi officials had salvaged from the fire that had ultimately gutted a good portion of the Rahani palace's fourth floor, so there would be something to bury.

Ben came forward and took Danielle's hand as she stood over the open grave. He turned briefly to meet the gaze of Colonel Nabril al-Asi, who stood ten feet back, the only other person in attendance besides the rabbi who had presided over the simple ceremony.

"I've only been here once since my father died," Danielle said suddenly. "We used to come here together to visit my mother's grave. And my brothers'."

"It doesn't usually help much," Ben said to her softly. "Memories."

"You don't find those in graves," he said, waiting for her to look at him before continuing as he tapped his head with his free hand. "You find them in here."

Danielle turned again to the grave. "I wish I remembered something about Hanna Frank. A smile, a laugh, a look—something to hold on to."

Ben felt her squeeze his hand tighter.

"I wonder how I would've felt about my father, if I had known the truth."

"No differently."

"How can you know that?"

"Because I know you."

Colonel al-Asi drew up even with them. "The two of you need to leave. The car is waiting."

"That's right," Danielle said ironically. "We're fugitives."

"Give me some time to sort things out," al-Asi told her.

"Take all the time you want. I'm done trying to go back." She turned to Ben, smiling slightly. "What about you, Inspector?"

He shrugged. "I think I've finally run out of places to go back to."

"The car," Colonel al-Asi said, easing them both away by the shoulders. "Please."

"Then I guess we'll just have to find someplace new, won't we?" Danielle asked, leaning her head against Ben. "Do you have a preference?"

Ben looped an arm around Danielle's shoulder. "I'll let you know when we get there."